Ladies in Black
Volume 1

Ladies in Black
Volume 1

15 Tales of Ghosts and Terror by the Mistresses of
Supernatural Fiction
Including 'The Old Nurse's Story', 'Satan's Circus',
'The Yellow Wallpaper', 'The Vengeance of a Tree'
and 'Where Their Fire is Not Quenched '

Compiled by

Eunice Hetherington

LEONAUR

Ladies in Black
Volume 1
15 Tales of Ghosts and Terror by the Mistresses of Supernatural Fiction
Including 'The Old Nurse's Story', 'Satan's Circus', 'The Yellow Wallpaper',
'The Vengeance of a Tree' and 'Where Their Fire is Not Quenched'
Compiled by Eunice Hetherington

FIRST EDITION

Leonaur is an imprint of Oakpast Ltd

Copyright in this form © 2024 Oakpast Ltd

ISBN: 978-1-916535-80-0 (hardcover)
ISBN: 978-1-916535-81-7 (softcover)

http://www.leonaur.com

Publisher's Notes

Contents

The Old Nurse's Story   7
By Elizabeth Gaskell

The Ghost of Charlotte Cray   27
By Florence Marryat

Green Branches   43
By Fiona Macleod

Satan's Circus   57
By Eleanor Smith

Let Loose   73
By Mary Cholmondeley

Luella Miller   89
By Mary Wilkins Freeman

Man-Size in Marble   103
By Edith Nesbit

The Yellow Wallpaper   117
Charlotte Perkins Gilman

Reality or Delusion?   133
By Mrs Henry Wood

The Open Door   149
By Mrs Oliphant

The Vengeance of a Tree   189
By Eleanor F. Lewis

The Devil's Motor   193
By Marie Corelli

The Hidden Door   199
By Vernon Lee

Where Their Fire is Not Quenched   223
By May Sinclair

The Affair at Grover Station   243
By Willa Cather

The Old Nurse's Story

Elizabeth Gaskell

You know, my dears, that your mother was an orphan, and an only child; and I daresay you have heard that your grandfather was a clergyman up in Westmoreland, where I come from. I was just a girl in the village school, when, one day, your grandmother came in to ask the mistress if there was any scholar there who would do for a nursemaid; and mighty proud I was, I can tell ye, when the mistress called me up, and spoke of me being a good girl at my needle, and a steady, honest girl, and one whose parents were very respectable, though they might be poor. I thought I should like nothing better than to serve the pretty young lady, who was blushing as deep as I was, as she spoke of the coming baby, and what I should have to do with it.

However, I see you don't care so much for this part of my story, as for what you think is to come, so I'll tell you at once. I was engaged and settled at the parsonage before Miss Rosamond (that was the baby, who is now your mother) was born. To be sure, I had little enough to do with her when she came, for she was never out of her mother's arms, and slept by her all night long; and proud enough was I sometimes when missis trusted her to me. There never was such a baby before or since, though you've all of you been fine enough in your turns; but for sweet, winning ways, you've none of you come up to your mother. She took after her mother, who was a real lady born; a Miss Furnivall, a grand-daughter of Lord Furnivall's, in Northumberland.

I believe she had neither brother nor sister, and had been brought up in my lord's family till she had married your grandfather, who was just a curate, son to a shopkeeper in Carlisle—but a clever, fine gentleman as ever was—and one who was a right-down hard worker in his parish, which was very wide, and scattered all abroad over the Westmoreland Fells.

When your mother, little Miss Rosamond, was about four or five years old, both her parents died in a fortnight—one after the other. Ah! that was a sad time. My pretty young mistress and me was looking for another baby, when my master came home from one of his long rides, wet and tired, and took the fever he died of; and then she never held up her head again, but just lived to see her dead baby, and have it laid on her breast, before she sighed away her life. My mistress had asked me, on her death-bed, never to leave Miss Rosamond; but if she had never spoken a word, I would have gone with the little child to the end of the world.

The next thing, and before we had well stilled our sobs, the executors and guardians came to settle the affairs. They were my poor young mistress's own cousin, Lord Furnivall, and Mr. Esthwaite, my master's brother, a shopkeeper in Manchester; not so well to do then as he was afterwards, and with a large family rising about him. Well! I don't know if it were their settling, or because of a letter my mistress wrote on her death-bed to her cousin, my lord; but somehow it was settled that Miss Rosamond and me were to go to Furnivall Manor House, in Northumberland, and my lord spoke as if it had been her mother's wish that she should live with his family, and as if he had no objections, for that one or two more or less could make no difference in so grand a household.

So, though that was not the way in which I should have wished the coming of my bright and pretty pet to have been looked at—who was like a sunbeam in any family, be it never so grand—I was well pleased that all the folks in the Dale should stare and admire, when they heard I was going to be young lady's maid at my Lord Furnivall's at Furnivall Manor.

But I made a mistake in thinking we were to go and live where my lord did. It turned out that the family had left Furnivall Manor House fifty years or more. I could not hear that my poor young mistress had never been there, though she had been brought up in the family; and I was sorry for that, for I should have liked Miss Rosamond's youth to have passed where her mother's had been.

My lord's gentleman, from whom I asked as many questions as I durst, said that the Manor House was at the foot of the Cumberland Fells, and a very grand place; that an old Miss Furnivall, a great-aunt of my lord's, lived there, with only a few servants; but that it was a very healthy place, and my lord had thought that it would suit Miss Rosamond very well for a few years, and that her being there might perhaps amuse his old aunt.

I was bidden by my lord to have Miss Rosamond's things ready by a certain day. He was a stern, proud man, as they say all the Lords Furnivall were; and he never spoke a word more than was necessary. Folk did say he had loved my young mistress; but that, because she knew that his father would object, she would never listen to him, and married Mr. Esthwaite; but I don't know. He never married, at any rate. But he never took much notice of Miss Rosamond; which I thought he might have done if he had cared for her dead mother. He sent his gentleman with us to the Manor House, telling him to join him at Newcastle that same evening; so there was no great length of time for him to make us known to all the strangers before he, too, shook us off; and we were left, two lonely young things (I was not eighteen) in the great old Manor House.

It seems like yesterday that we drove there. We had left our own dear parsonage very early, and we had both cried as if our hearts would break, though we were travelling in my lord's carriage, which I thought so much of once.

And now it was long past noon on a September day, and we stopped to change horses for the last time at a little smoky town, all full of colliers and miners. Miss Rosamond had fallen asleep, but Mr. Henry told me to waken her, that she might see the park and the Manor House as we drove up. I thought it rather a pity; but I did what he bade me, for fear he should complain of me to my lord. We had left all signs of a town, or even a village, and were then inside the gates of a large wild park—not like the parks here in the south, but with rocks, and the noise of running water, and gnarled thorn-trees, and old oaks, all white and peeled with age.

The road went up about two miles, and then we saw a great and stately house, with many trees close around it, so close that in some places their branches dragged against the walls when the wind blew; and some hung broken down; for no one seemed to take much charge of the place;—to lop the wood, or to keep the moss-covered carriage-way in order. Only in front of the house all was clear. The great oval drive was without a weed; and neither tree nor creeper was allowed to grow over the long, many-windowed front; at both sides of which a wing protected, which were each the ends of other side fronts; for the house, although it was so desolate, was even grander than I expected.

Behind it rose the Fells; which seemed unenclosed and bare enough; and on the left hand of the house, as you stood facing it, was a little, old-fashioned flower-garden, as I found out afterwards. A door opened out upon it from the west front; it had been scooped out of the thick, dark wood for some old Lady Furnivall; but the branches of the great forest-trees had grown and overshadowed it again, and there were very few flowers that would live there at that time.

When we drove up to the great front entrance, and went into the hall, I thought we would be lost—it was so large, and vast and grand. There was a chandelier all of bronze, hung down from the middle of the ceiling; and I had never seen one before, and looked at it all in amaze. Then, at one end of the hall, was a great fire-place, as large as the sides of the houses in my country, with massy andirons and dogs to hold the wood; and by it were heavy, old-fashioned sofas. At the opposite end of the hall, to the left as you went in—on the western side—was an organ built into the wall, and so large that it filled up the best part of that end. Beyond it, on the same side, was a door; and opposite, on each side of the fire-place, were also doors leading to the east front; but those I never went through as long as I stayed in the house, so I can't tell you what lay beyond.

The afternoon was closing in, and the hall, which had no fire lighted in it, looked dark and gloomy, but we did not stay there a moment. The old servant, who had opened the door for us, bowed to Mr. Henry, and took us in through the door at the further side of the great organ, and led us through several smaller halls and passages into the west drawing-room, where he said that Miss Furnivall was sitting. Poor little Miss Rosamond held very tight to me, as if she were scared and lost in that great place; and as for myself, I was not much better.

The west drawing-room was very cheerful-looking, with a warm fire in it, and plenty of good, comfortable furniture about. Miss Furnivall was an old lady not far from eighty, I should think, but I do not know. She was thin and tall, and had a face as full of fine wrinkles as if they had been drawn all over it with a needle's point. Her eyes were very watchful, to make up, I suppose, for her being so deaf as to be obliged to use a trumpet.

Sitting with her, working at the same great piece of tapestry, was Mrs. Stark, her maid and companion, and almost as old as she was. She had lived with Miss Furnivall ever since they both were young, and now she seemed more like a friend than a servant; she looked so cold, and grey, and stony, as if she had never loved or cared for anyone; and I don't suppose she did care for anyone, except her mistress; and, owing to the great deafness of the latter, Mrs. Stark treated her very much as if she were a child. Mr. Henry gave some message from my lord, and then he bowed goodbye to us all,—taking no notice of my sweet little Miss Rosamond's outstretched hand—and left us standing there, being looked at by the two old ladies through their spectacles.

I was right glad when they rung for the old footman who had shown us in at first, and told him to take us to our rooms. So we went out of that great drawing-room and into another sitting-room, and out of that, and then up a great flight of stairs, and along a broad gallery—which was something like a library, having books all down one side, and windows and writing-tables all down the other—till we came to our rooms, which I was not sorry to hear were just over the kitchens; for I began to think I should be lost in that wilderness of a house.

There was an old nursery, that had been used for all the little lords and ladies long ago, with a pleasant fire burning in the grate, and the kettle boiling on the hob, and tea-things spread out on the table; and out of that room was the night-nursery, with a little crib for Miss Rosamond close to my bed. And old James called up Dorothy, his wife, to bid us welcome; and both he and she were so hospitable and kind, that by-and-by Miss Rosamond and me felt quite at home; and by the time tea was over, she was sitting on Dorothy's knee, and chattering away as fast as her little tongue could go.

I soon found out that Dorothy was from Westmoreland, and that bound her and me together, as it were; and I would never wish to meet with kinder people than were old James and his wife. James had lived pretty nearly all his life in my lord's family, and thought there was no one so grand as they. He even looked down a little on his wife; because, till he had married her, she had never lived in any but a farmer's household. But he was very fond of her, as well he might be.

They had one servant under them, to do all the rough work. Agnes they called her; and she and me, and James and Dorothy, with Miss Furnivall and Mrs. Stark, made up the family; always remembering my sweet little Miss Rosamond! I used to wonder what they had done before she came, they thought so much of her now. Kitchen and drawing-room, it was all the same. The hard, sad Miss Furnivall, and the cold Mrs. Stark, looked pleased when she came fluttering in like a bird, playing and pranking hither and thither, with a continual murmur, and pretty prattle of gladness.

I am sure, they were sorry many a time when she flitted away into the kitchen, though they were too proud to ask her to stay with them, and were a little surprised at her taste; though to be sure, as Mrs. Stark said, it was not to be wondered at, remembering what stock her father had come of. The great, old rambling house was a famous place for little Miss Rosamond. She made expeditions all over it, with me at her heels; all, except the east wing, which was never opened, and whither we never thought of going. But in the western and northern part was many a pleasant room; full of things that were curiosities to us, though they might not have been to people who had seen more. The windows were darkened by the sweeping boughs of the trees, and the ivy which had overgrown them; but, in the green gloom, we could manage to see old china jars and carved ivory boxes, and great heavy books, and, above all, the old pictures!

Once, I remember, my darling would have Dorothy go with us to tell us who they all were; for they were all portraits of some of my lord's family, though Dorothy could not tell us the names of every one. We had gone through most of the rooms, when we came to the old state drawing-room over the hall, and there was a picture of Miss Furnivall; or, as she was called in those days, Miss Grace, for she was the younger sister. Such a beauty she must have been! but with such a set, proud look, and such scorn looking out of her handsome eyes, with her eyebrows just a little raised, as if she wondered how anyone could have the impertinence to look at her, and her lip curled at us, as we stood there gazing. She had a dress on, the like of which I had never seen before, but it was all the fashion when she was young; a hat of some soft white stuff like beaver, pulled a little over her brows, and a beautiful plume of feathers sweeping round it on one side; and her gown of blue satin was open in front to a quilted white stomacher.

'Well, to be sure!' said I, when I had gazed my fill. 'Flesh is grass, they do say; but who would have thought that Miss Furnivall had been such an out-and-out beauty, to see her now.'

'Yes,' said Dorothy. 'Folks change sadly. But if what my master's father used to say was true, Miss Furnivall, the elder sister, was handsomer than Miss Grace. Her picture is here somewhere; but, if I show it you, you must never let on, even to James, that you have seen it. Can the little lady hold her tongue, think you?' asked she.

I was not so sure, for she was such a little sweet, bold, open-spoken child, so I set her to hide herself; and then I helped Dorothy to turn a great picture, that leaned with its face towards the wall, and was not hung up as the others were. To be sure, it beat Miss Grace for beauty; and, I think, for scornful pride, too, though in that matter it might be hard to choose. I could have looked at it an hour, but Dorothy seemed half frightened at having shown it to me, and hurried it back again, and bade me run and find Miss Rosamond, for that there were some ugly places about the house, where she should like ill for the child to go. I was a brave, high-spirited girl, and thought little of what the old woman said, for I liked hide-and-seek as well as any child in the parish; so off I ran to find my little one.

As winter drew on, and the days grew shorter, I was sometimes almost certain that I heard a noise as if someone was playing on the great organ in the hall. I did not hear it every evening; but, certainly, I did very often, usually when I was sitting with Miss Rosamond, after I had put her to bed, and keeping quite still and silent in the bedroom. Then I used to hear it booming and swelling away in the distance. The first night, when I went down to my supper, I asked Dorothy who had been playing music, and James said very shortly that I was a gowk to take the wind soughing among the trees for music; but I saw Dorothy look at him very fearfully, and Bessy, the kitchen-maid, said something beneath her breath, and went quite white. I saw they did not like my question, so I held my peace till I was with Dorothy alone, when I knew I could get a good deal out of her. So, the next day, I watched my time, and I coaxed and asked her who it was that played the organ; for I knew that it was the organ and not the wind well enough, for all I had kept silence before James.

But Dorothy had had her lesson, I'll warrant, and never a word could I get from her. So then I tried Bessy, though I had always held my head rather above her, as I was evened to James and Dorothy, and she was little better than their servant. So she said I must never, never tell; and if ever I told, I was never to say *she* had told me; but it was a very strange noise, and she had heard it many a time, but most of all on winter nights, and before storms; and folks did say it was the old lord playing on the great organ in the hall, just as he used to do when he was alive; but who the old lord was, or why he played, and why he played on stormy winter evenings in particular, she either could not or would not tell me. Well! I told you I had a brave heart; and I thought it was rather pleasant to have that grand music rolling about the house, let who would be the player; for now it rose above the great gusts of wind, and wailed and triumphed just like a living creature, and then it fell to a softness most complete, only it was always music, and tunes, so it was nonsense to call it the wind.

I thought at first, that it might be Miss Furnivall who played, unknown to Bessy; but one day, when I was in the hall by myself, I opened the organ and peeped all about it and around it, as I had done to the organ in Crosthwaite church once before, and I saw it was all broken and destroyed inside, though it looked so brave and fine; and then, though it was noon-day, my flesh began to creep a little, and I shut it up, and run away pretty quickly to my own bright nursery; and I did not like hearing the music for some time after that, any more than James and Dorothy did. All this time Miss Rosamond was making herself more and more beloved. The old ladies liked her to dine with them at their early dinner.

James stood behind Miss Furnivall's chair, and I behind Miss Rosamond's all in state; and after dinner, she would play about in a corner of the great drawing-room as still as any mouse, while Miss Furnivall slept, and I had my dinner in the kitchen. But she was glad enough to come to me in the nursery afterwards; for, as she said, Miss Furnivall was so sad, and Mrs. Stark so dull; but she and I were merry enough; and by-and-by, I got not to care for that weird rolling music, which did one no harm, if we did not know where it came from.

That winter was very cold. In the middle of October the frosts began, and lasted many, many weeks. I remember one day, at dinner, Miss Furnivall lifted up her sad, heavy eyes, and said to Mrs. Stark, 'I am afraid we shall have a terrible winter,' in a strange kind of meaning way. But Mrs. Stark pretended not to hear, and talked very loud of something else. My little lady and I did not care for the frost; not we! As long as it was dry, we climbed up the steep brows behind the house, and went up on the Fells, which were bleak and bare enough, and there we ran races in the fresh, sharp air; and once we came down by a new path, that took us past the two old gnarled holly-trees, which grew about half-way down by the east side of the house. But the days grew shorter and shorter, and the old lord, if it was he, played away, more and more stormily and sadly, on the great organ.

One Sunday afternoon—it must have been towards the end of November—I asked Dorothy to take charge of little missy when she came out of the drawing-room, after Miss Furnivall had had her nap; for it was too cold to take her with me to church, and yet I wanted to go. And Dorothy was glad enough to promise, and was so fond of the child, that all seemed well; and Bessy and I set off very briskly, though the sky hung heavy and black over the white earth, as if the night had never fully gone away, and the air, though still, was very biting and keen.

14

'We shall have a fall of snow,' said Bessy to me. And sure enough, even while we were in church, it came down thick, in great large flakes,—so thick, it almost darkened the windows. It had stopped snowing before we came out, but it lay soft, thick and deep beneath our feet, as we tramped home. Before we got to the hall, the moon rose, and I think it was lighter then—what with the moon, and what with the white dazzling snow—than it had been when we went to church, between two and three o'clock. I have not told you that Miss Furnivall and Mrs. Stark never went to church; they used to read the prayers together, in their quiet, gloomy way; they seemed to feel the Sunday very long without their tapestry-work to be busy at.

So when I went to Dorothy in the kitchen, to fetch Miss Rosamond and take her upstairs with me, I did not much wonder when the old woman told me that the ladies had kept the child with them, and that she had never come to the kitchen, as I had bidden her, when she was tired of behaving pretty in the drawing-room. So I took off my things and went to find her, and bring her to her supper in the nursery.

But when I went into the best drawing-room, there sat the two old ladies, very still and quiet, dropping out a word now and then, but looking as if nothing so bright and merry as Miss Rosamond had ever been near them. Still I thought she might be hiding from me; it was one of her pretty ways,—and that she had persuaded them to look as if they knew nothing about her; so I went softly peeping under this sofa, and behind that chair, making believe I was sadly frightened at not finding her.

'What's the matter, Hester?' said Mrs. Stark, sharply. I don't know if Miss Furnivall had seen me, for, as I told you, she was very deaf, and she sat quite still, idly staring into the fire, with her hopeless face.

'I'm only looking for my little Rosy Posy,' replied I, still thinking that the child was there, and near me, though I could not see her.

'Miss Rosamond is not here,' said Mrs. Stark. 'She went away, more than an hour ago, to find Dorothy.' And she, too, turned and went on looking into the fire.

My heart sank at this, and I began to wish I had never left my darling. I went back to Dorothy and told her. James was gone out for the day, but she, and me, and Bessy took lights, and went up into the nursery first; and then we roamed over the great, large house, calling and entreating Miss Rosamond to come out of her hiding-place, and not frighten us to death in that way. But there was no answer; no sound.

'Oh!' said I, at last, 'can she have got into the east wing and hidden there?'

But Dorothy said it was not possible, for that she herself had never been in there; that the doors were always locked, and my lord's steward had the keys, she believed; at any rate, neither she nor James had ever seen them: so I said I would go back, and see if, after all, she was not hidden in the drawing-room, unknown to the old ladies; and if I found her there, I said, I would whip her well for the fright she had given me; but I never meant to do it. Well, I went back to the west drawing-room, and I told Mrs. Stark we could not find her anywhere, and asked for leave to look all about the furniture there, for I thought now that she might have fallen asleep in some warm, hidden corner; but no! we looked—Miss Furnivall got up and looked, trembling all over—and she was nowhere there; then we set off again, everyone in the house, and looked in all the places we had searched before, but we could not find her.

Miss Furnivall shivered and shook so much, that Mrs. Stark took her back into the warm drawing-room; but not before they had made me promise to bring her to them when she was found. Well-a-day! I began to think she never would be found, when I bethought me to look into the great front court, all covered with snow. I was upstairs when I looked out; but, it was such clear moonlight, I could see, quite plain, two little footprints, which might be traced from the hall-door and round the corner of the east wing. I don't know how I got down, but I tugged open the great stiff hall-door, and, throwing the skirt of my gown over my head for a cloak, I ran out. I turned the east corner, and there a black shadow fell on the snow; but when I came again into the moonlight, there were the little foot-marks going up—up to the Fells. It was bitter cold; so cold, that the air almost took the skin off my face as I ran; but I ran on crying to think how my poor little darling must be perished and frightened.

I was within sight of the holly-trees, when I saw a shepherd coming down the hill, bearing something in his arms wrapped in his maud. He shouted to me, and asked me if I had lost a bairn; and, when I could not speak for crying, he bore towards me, and I saw my wee bairnie, lying still, and white, and stiff in his arms, as if she had been dead. He told me he had been up the Fells to gather in his sheep, before the deep cold of night came on, and that under the holly-trees (black marks on the hill-side, where no other bush was for miles around) he had found my little lady—my lamb—my queen—my darling—stiff and cold in the terrible sleep which is frost-begotten. Oh! the joy and the tears of having her in my arms once again! for I would not let him carry her; but took her, maud and all, into my own arms, and held her near my own warm neck and heart, and felt the life stealing slowly back again into her little gentle limbs. But she was still insensible when we reached the hall, and I had no breath for speech. We went in by the kitchen-door.

'Bring me the warming-pan,' said I; and I carried her upstairs and began undressing her by the nursery fire, which Bessy had kept up. I called my little lammie all the sweet and playful names I could think of,—even while my eyes were blinded by my tears; and at last, oh! at length she opened her large blue eyes. Then I put her into her warm bed, and sent Dorothy down to tell Miss Furnivall that all was well; and I made up my mind to sit by my darling's bedside the live-long night. She fell away into a soft sleep as soon as her pretty head had touched the pillow, and I watched by her till morning light; when she wakened up bright and clear—or so I thought at first—and, my dears, so I think now.

She said, that she had fancied that she should like to go to Dorothy, for that both the old ladies were asleep, and it was very dull in the drawing-room; and that, as she was going through the west lobby, she saw the snow through the high window falling—falling—soft and steady; but she wanted to see it lying pretty and white on the ground; so she made her way into the great hall; and then, going to the window, she saw it bright and soft upon the drive; but while she stood there, she saw a little girl, not so old as she was, 'but so pretty,' said my darling, 'and this little girl beckoned to me to come out; and oh, she was so pretty and so sweet, I could not choose but go.' And then this other little girl had taken her by the hand, and side by side the two had gone round the east corner.

'Now you are a naughty little girl, and telling stories,' said I. 'What would your good mamma, that is in heaven, and never told a story in her life, say to her little Rosamond, if she heard her—and I daresay she does—telling stories!'

'Indeed, Hester,' sobbed out my child, 'I'm telling you true. Indeed I am.'

'Don't tell me!' said I, very stern. 'I tracked you by your foot-marks through the snow; there were only yours to be seen: and if you had had a little girl to go hand-in-hand with you up the hill, don't you think the footprints would have gone along with yours?'

'I can't help it, dear, dear Hester,' said she, crying, 'if they did not; I never looked at her feet, but she held my hand fast and tight in her little one, and it was very, very cold. She took me up the Fell-path, up to the holly-trees; and there I saw a lady weeping and crying; but when she saw me, she hushed her weeping, and smiled very proud and grand, and took me on her knee, and began to lull me to sleep; and that's all, Hester—but that is true; and my dear mamma knows it is,' said she, crying. So I thought the child was in a fever, and pretended to believe her, as she went over her story—over and over again, and always the same. At last Dorothy knocked at the door with Miss Rosamond's breakfast; and she told me the old ladies were down in the eating parlour, and that they wanted to speak to me. They had both been into the night-nursery the evening before, but it was after Miss Rosamond was asleep; so they had only looked at her—not asked me any questions.

'I shall catch it,' thought I to myself, as I went along the north gallery. 'And yet,' I thought, taking courage, 'it was in their charge I left her; and it's they that's to blame for letting her steal away unknown and unwatched.' So I went in boldly, and told my story. I told it all to Miss Furnivall, shouting it close to her ear; but when I came to the mention of the other little girl out in the snow, coaxing and tempting her out, and willing her up to the grand and beautiful lady by the holly-tree, she threw her arms up—her old and withered arms—and cried aloud, 'Oh! Heaven forgive! Have mercy!'

Mrs. Stark took hold of her; roughly enough, I thought; but she was past Mrs. Stark's management, and spoke to me, in a kind of wild warning and authority.

'Hester! keep her from that child! It will lure her to her death! That evil child! Tell her it is a wicked, naughty child.' Then, Mrs. Stark hurried me out of the room; where, indeed, I was glad enough to go; but Miss Furnivall kept shrieking out, 'Oh, have mercy! Wilt Thou never forgive! It is many a long year ago———'

I was very uneasy in my mind after that. I durst never leave Miss Rosamond, night or day, for fear lest she might slip off again, after some fancy or other; and all the more, because I thought I could make out that Miss Furnivall was crazy, from their odd ways about her; and I was afraid lest something of the same kind (which might be in the family, you know) hung over my darling. And the great frost never ceased all this time; and, whenever it was a more stormy night than usual, between the gusts, and through the wind, we heard the old lord playing on the great organ.

But, old lord, or not, wherever Miss Rosamond went, there I followed; for my love for her, pretty, helpless orphan, was stronger than my fear for the grand and terrible sound. Besides, it rested with me to keep her cheerful and merry, as beseemed her age. So we played together, and wandered together, here and there, and everywhere; for I never dared to lose sight of her again in that large and rambling house. And so it happened, that one afternoon, not long before Christmas-day, we were playing together on the billiard-table in the great hall (not that we knew the right way of playing, but she liked to roll the smooth ivory balls with her pretty hands, and I liked to do whatever she did); and, by-and-by, without our noticing it, it grew dusk indoors, though it was still light in the open air, and I was thinking of taking her back into the nursery, when, all of a sudden, she cried out,

'Look, Hester! look! there is my poor little girl out in the snow!'

I turned towards the long narrow windows, and there, sure enough, I saw a little girl, less than my Miss Rosamond—dressed all unfit to be out-of-doors such a bitter night—crying, and beating against the window-panes, as if she wanted to be let in. She seemed to sob and wail, till Miss Rosamond could bear it no longer, and was flying to the door to open it, when, all of a sudden, and close upon us, the great organ pealed out so loud and thundering, it fairly made me tremble; and all the more, when I remembered me that, even in the stillness of that dead-cold weather, I had heard no sound of little battering hands upon the window-glass, although the phantom child had seemed to put forth all its force; and, although I had seen it wail and cry, no faintest touch of sound had fallen upon my ears.

Whether I remembered all this at the very moment, I do not know; the great organ sound had so stunned me into terror; but this I know, I caught up Miss Rosamond before she got the hall-door opened, and clutched her, and carried her away, kicking and screaming, into the large, bright kitchen, where Dorothy and Agnes were busy with their mince-pies.

'What is the matter with my sweet one?' cried Dorothy, as I bore in Miss Rosamond, who was sobbing as if her heart would break.

'She won't let me open the door for my little girl to come in; and she'll die if she is out on the Fells all night. Cruel, naughty Hester,' she said, slapping me; but she might have struck harder, for I had seen a look of ghastly terror on Dorothy's face, which made my very blood run cold.

'Shut the back-kitchen door fast, and bolt it well,' said she to Agnes. She said no more; she gave me raisins and almonds to quiet Miss Rosamond; but she sobbed about the little girl in the snow, and would not touch any of the good things. I was thankful when she cried herself to sleep in bed. Then I stole down to the kitchen, and told Dorothy I had made up my mind. I would carry my darling back to my father's house in Applethwaite; where, if we lived humbly, we lived at peace. I said I had been frightened enough with the old lord's organ-playing; but now that I had seen for myself this little moaning child, all decked out as no child in the neighbourhood could be, beating and battering to get in, yet always without any sound or noise—with the dark wound on its right shoulder; and that Miss Rosamond had known it again for the phantom that had nearly lured her to her death (which Dorothy knew was true); I would stand it no longer.

I saw Dorothy change colour once or twice. When I had done, she told me she did not think I could take Miss Rosamond with me, for that she was my lord's ward, and I had no right over her; and she asked me would I leave the child that I was so fond of just for sounds and sights that could do me no harm; and that they had all had to get used to in their turns? I was all in a hot, trembling passion; and I said it was very well for her to talk; that knew what these sights and noises betokened, and that had, perhaps, had something to do with the spectre child while it was alive. And I taunted her so, that she told me all she knew at last; and then I wished I had never been told, for it only made me more afraid than ever.

She said she had heard the tale from old neighbours that were alive when she was first married; when folks used to come to the hall sometimes, before it had got such a bad name on the country side: it might not be true, or it might, what she had been told.

The old lord was Miss Furnivall's father—Miss Grace, as Dorothy called her, for Miss Maude was the elder, and Miss Furnivall by rights. The old lord was eaten up with pride. Such a proud man was never seen or heard of; and his daughters were like him. No one was good enough to wed them, although they had choice enough; for they were the great beauties of their day, as I had seen by their portraits, where they hung in the state drawing-room. But, as the old saying is, 'Pride will have a fall;' and these two haughty beauties fell in love with the same man, and he no better than a foreign musician, whom their father had down from London to play music with him at the Manor House. For, above all things, next to his pride, the old lord loved music.

He could play on nearly every instrument that ever was heard of, and it was a strange thing it did not soften him; but he was a fierce dour old man, and had broken his poor wife's heart with his cruelty, they said.

He was mad after music, and would pay any money for it. So he got this foreigner to come; who made such beautiful music, that they said the very birds on the trees stopped their singing to listen. And, by degrees, this foreign gentleman got such a hold over the old lord, that nothing would serve him but that he must come every year; and it was he that had the great organ brought from Holland, and built up in the hall, where it stood now. He taught the old lord to play on it; but many and many a time, when Lord Furnivall was thinking of nothing but his fine organ, and his finer music, the dark foreigner was walking abroad in the woods with one of the young ladies; now Miss Maude, and then Miss Grace.

Miss Maude won the day and carried off the prize, such as it was; and he and she were married, all unknown to anyone; and before he made his next yearly visit, she had been confined of a little girl at a farmhouse on the Moors, while her father and Miss Grace thought she was away at Doncaster Races. But though she was a wife and a mother, she was not a bit softened, but as haughty and as passionate as ever; and perhaps more so, for she was jealous of Miss Grace, to whom her foreign husband paid a deal of court—by way of blinding her—as he told his wife.

But Miss Grace triumphed over Miss Maude, and Miss Maude grew fiercer and fiercer, both with her husband and with her sister; and the former—who could easily shake off what was disagreeable, and hide himself in foreign countries—went away a month before his usual time that summer, and half-threatened that he would never come back again. Meanwhile, the little girl was left at the farm-house, and her mother used to have her horse saddled and gallop wildly over the hills to see her once every week, at the very least; for where she loved she loved, and where she hated she hated.

And the old lord went on playing—playing on his organ; and the servants thought the sweet music he made had soothed down his awful temper, of which (Dorothy said) some terrible tales could be told. He grew infirm too, and had to walk with a crutch; and his son—that was the present Lord Furnivall's father—was with the army in America, and the other son at sea; so Miss Maude had it pretty much her own way, and she and Miss Grace grew colder and bitterer to each other every day; till at last they hardly ever spoke, except when the old lord was by.

The foreign musician came again the next summer, but it was for the last time; for they led him such a life with their jealousy and their passions, that he grew weary, and went away, and never was heard of again. And Miss Maude, who had always meant to have her marriage acknowledged when her father should be dead, was left now a deserted wife, whom nobody knew to have been married, with a child that she dared not own, although she loved it to distraction; living with a father whom she feared, and a sister whom she hated.

When the next summer passed over, and the dark foreigner never came, both Miss Maude and Miss Grace grew gloomy and sad; they had a haggard look about them, though they looked handsome as ever. But, by-and-by, Maude brightened; for her father grew more and more infirm, and more than ever carried away by his music; and she and Miss Grace lived almost entirely apart, having separate rooms, the one on the west side, Miss Maude on the east—those very rooms which were now shut up. So she thought she might have her little girl with her, and no one need ever know except those who dared not speak about it, and were bound to believe that it was, as she said, a cottager's child she had taken a fancy to.

All this, Dorothy said, was pretty well known; but what came afterwards no one knew, except Miss Grace and Mrs. Stark, who was even then her maid, and much more of a friend to her than ever her sister had been. But the servants supposed, from words that were dropped, that Miss Maude had triumphed over Miss Grace, and told her that all the time the dark foreigner had been mocking her with pretended love—he was her own husband. The colour left Miss Grace's cheek and lips that very day for ever, and she was heard to say many a time that sooner or later she would have her revenge; and Mrs. Stark was forever spying about the east rooms.

One fearful night, just after the New Year had come in, when the snow was lying thick and deep; and the flakes were still falling—fast enough to blind anyone who might be out and abroad—there was a great and violent noise heard, and the old lord's voice above all, cursing and swearing awfully, and the cries of a little child, and the proud defiance of a fierce woman, and the sound of a blow, and a dead stillness, and moans and wailings dying away on the hillside!

Then the old lord summoned all his servants, and told them, with terrible oaths, and words more terrible, that his daughter had dis-

22

graced herself, and that he had turned her out of doors—her, and her child—and that if ever they gave her help, or food, or shelter, he prayed that they might never enter heaven. And, all the while, Miss Grace stood by him, white and still as any stone; and, when he had ended, she heaved a great sigh, as much as to say her work was done, and her end was accomplished.

But the old lord never touched his organ again, and died within the year; and no wonder! for, on the morrow of that wild and fearful night, the shepherds, coming down the Fell side, found Miss Maude sitting, all crazy and smiling, under the holly-trees, nursing a dead child, with a terrible mark on its right shoulder. 'But that was not what killed it,' said Dorothy: 'it was the frost and the cold. Every wild creature was in its hole, and every beast in its fold, while the child and its mother were turned out to wander on the Fells! And now you know all! and I wonder if you are less frightened now?'

I was more frightened than ever; but I said I was not. I wished Miss Rosamond and myself well out of that dreadful house for ever; but I would not leave her, and I dared not take her away. But oh, how I watched her, and guarded her! We bolted the doors, and shut the window-shutters fast, an hour or more before dark, rather than leave them open five minutes too late. But my little lady still heard the weird child crying and mourning; and not all we could do or say could keep her from wanting to go to her, and let her in from the cruel wind and the snow. All this time I kept away from Miss Furnivall and Mrs. Stark, as much as ever I could; for I feared them—I knew no good could be about them, with their grey, hard faces, and their dreamy eyes, looking back into the ghastly years that were gone.

But, even in my fear, I had a kind of pity for Miss Furnivall, at least. Those gone down to the pit can hardly have a more hopeless look than that which was ever on her face. At last I even got so sorry for her—who never said a word but what was quite forced from her—that I prayed for her; and I taught Miss Rosamond to pray for one who had done a deadly sin; but often when she came to those words, she would listen, and start up from her knees, and say, 'I hear my little girl plaining and crying very sad—oh, let her in, or she will die!'

One night—just after New Year's Day had come at last, and the long winter had taken a turn, as I hoped—I heard the west drawing-room bell ring three times, which was the signal for me. I would not leave Miss Rosamond alone, for all she was asleep—for the old lord had been playing wilder than ever—and I feared lest my darling should waken to hear the spectre child; see her, I knew she could not. I had fastened the windows too well for that. So I took her out of her bed, and wrapped her up in such outer clothes as were most handy, and carried her down to the drawing-room, where the old ladies sat at their tapestry-work as usual. They looked up when I came in, and Mrs. Stark asked, quite astounded, 'Why did I bring Miss Rosamond there, out of her warm bed?'

I had begun to whisper, 'Because I was afraid of her being tempted out while I was away, by the wild child in the snow,' when she stopped me short (with a glance at Miss Furnivall), and said Miss Furnivall wanted me to undo some work she had done wrong, and which neither of them could see to unpick. So I laid my pretty dear on the sofa, and sat down on a stool by them, and hardened my heart against them, as I heard the wind rising and howling.

Miss Rosamond slept on sound, for all the wind blew so Miss Furnivall said never a word, nor looked round when the gusts shook the windows. All at once she started up to her full height, and put up one hand, as if to bid us to listen.

'I hear voices!' said she. 'I hear terrible screams—I hear my father's voice!'

Just at that moment my darling wakened with a sudden start: 'My little girl is crying, oh, how she is crying!' and she tried to get up and go to her, but she got her feet entangled in the blanket, and I caught her up; for my flesh had begun to creep at these noises, which they heard while we could catch no sound. In a minute or two the noises came, and gathered fast, and filled our ears; we, too, heard voices and screams, and no longer heard the winter's wind that raged abroad. Mrs. Stark looked at me, and I at her, but we dared not speak. Suddenly Miss Furnivall went towards the door, out into the ante-room, through the west lobby, and opened the door into the great hall.

Mrs. Stark followed, and I durst not be left, though my heart almost stopped beating for fear. I wrapped my darling tight in my arms, and went out with them. In the hall the screams were louder than ever; they seemed to come from the east wing—nearer and nearer—close on the other side of the locked-up doors—close behind them. Then I noticed that the great bronze chandelier seemed all alight, though the hall was dim, and that a fire was blazing in the vast hearth-place, though it gave no heat; and I shuddered up with terror, and folded my darling closer to me. But as I did so the east door shook, and she, suddenly struggling to get free from me, cried, 'Hester! I must go. My little girl is there! I hear her; she is coming! Hester, I must go!'

I held her tight with all my strength; with a set will, I held her. If I had died, my hands would have grasped her still, I was so resolved in my mind. Miss Furnivall stood listening, and paid no regard to my darling, who had got down to the ground, and whom I, upon my knees now, was holding with both my arms clasped round her neck; she still striving and crying to get free.

All at once, the east door gave way with a thundering crash, as if torn open in a violent passion, and there came into that broad and mysterious light, the figure of a tall old man, with grey hair and gleaming eyes. He drove before him, with many a relentless gesture of abhorrence, a stern and beautiful woman, with a little child clinging to her dress.

'Oh, Hester! Hester!' cried Miss Rosamond; 'it's the lady! the lady below the holly-trees; and my little girl is with her. Hester! Hester! let me go to her; they are drawing me to them. I feel them—I feel them. I must go!'

Again she was almost convulsed by her efforts to get away; but I held her tighter and tighter, till I feared I should do her a hurt; but rather that than let her go towards those terrible phantoms. They passed along towards the great hall-door, where the winds howled and ravened for their prey; but before they reached that, the lady turned; and I could see that she defied the old man with a fierce and proud defiance; but then she quailed—and then she threw up her arms wildly and piteously to save her child—her little child—from a blow from his uplifted crutch.

And Miss Rosamond was torn as by a power stronger than mine and writhed in my arms, and sobbed (for by this time the poor darling was growing faint).

'They want me to go with them on to the Fells—they are drawing me to them. Oh, my little girl! I would come, but cruel, wicked Hester holds me very tight.' But when she saw the uplifted crutch, she swooned away, and I thanked God for it. Just at this moment— when the tall old man, his hair streaming as in the blast of a furnace, was going to strike the little shrinking child—Miss Furnivall, the old woman by my side, cried out, 'Oh father! father! spare the little innocent child!'

But just then I saw—we all saw—another phantom shape itself, and grow clear out of the blue and misty light that filled the hall; we had not seen her till now, for it was another lady who stood by the old man, with a look of relentless hate and triumphant scorn. That figure was very beautiful to look upon, with a soft, white hat drawn down over the proud brows, and a red and curling lip. It was dressed in an open robe of blue satin. I had seen that figure before. It was the likeness of Miss Furnivall in her youth; and the terrible phantoms moved on, regardless of old Miss Furnivall's wild entreaty,—and the uplifted crutch fell on the right shoulder of the little child, and the younger sister looked on, stony, and deadly serene. But at that moment, the dim lights, and the fire that gave no heat, went out of themselves, and Miss Furnivall lay at our feet stricken down by the palsy—death-stricken.

Yes! she was carried to her bed that night never to rise again. She lay with her face to the wall, muttering low, but muttering always: 'Alas! alas! what is done in youth can never be undone in age! What is done in youth can never be undone in age!'

The Ghost of Charlotte Cray

Florence Marryat

Mr Sigismund Braggett was sitting in the little room he called his study, wrapped in a profound—not to say a mournful—reverie. Now, there was nothing in the present life nor surroundings of Mr Braggett to account for such a demonstration. He was a publisher and bookseller; a man well to do, with a thriving business in the city, and the prettiest of all pretty villas at Streatham. And he was only just turned forty; had not a grey hair in his head nor a false tooth in his mouth; and had been married but three short months to one of the fairest and most affectionate specimens of English womanhood that ever transformed a bachelor's quarters into Paradise.

What more could Mr Sigismund Braggett possibly want? Nothing! His trouble lay in the fact that he had got rather more than he wanted. Most of us have our little *peccadilloes* in this world—awkward reminiscences that we would like to bury five fathoms deep, and never hear mentioned again, but that have an uncomfortable habit of cropping up at the most inconvenient moments; and no mortal is more likely to be troubled with them than a middle-aged bachelor who has taken to matrimony.

Mr Sigismund Braggett had no idea what he was going in for when he led the blushing Emily Primrose up to the altar, and swore to be hers, and hers only, until death should them part. He had no conception a woman's curiosity could be so keen, her tongue so long, and her inventive faculties so correct. He had spent whole days before the fatal moment of marriage in burning letters, erasing initials, destroying locks of hair, and making offerings of affection look as if he had purchased them with his own money. But it had been of little avail. Mrs Braggett had swooped down upon him like a beautiful bird of prey, and wheedled, coaxed, or kissed him out of half his secrets before he

27

knew what he was about. But he had never told her about Charlotte Cray. And now he almost wished that he had done so, for Charlotte Cray was the cause of his present dejected mood.

Now, there are ladies *and* ladies in this world. Some are very shy, and will only permit themselves to be wooed by stealth. Others, again, are the pursuers rather than the pursued, and chase the wounded or the flying even to the very doors of their stronghold, or lie in wait for them like an octopus, stretching out their tentacles on every side in search of victims.

And to the latter class Miss Charlotte Cray decidedly belonged. Not a person worth mourning over, you will naturally say. But, then. Mr Sigismund Braggett had not behaved well to her. She was one of the '*peccadilloes*,' She was an authoress—not an author, mind you, which term smacks more of the profession than the sex—but an 'authoress,' with lots of the 'ladylike' about the plots of her stories and the metre of her rhymes. They had come together in the sweet connection of publisher and writer—had met first in a dingy, dusty little office at the back of his house of business, and laid the foundation of their friendship with the average amount of chaffering and prevarication that usually attend such proceedings.

Mr Braggett ran a risk in publishing Miss Cray's tales or verses, but he found her useful in so many other ways that he used occasionally to hold forth a sop to Cerberus in the shape of publicity for the sake of keeping her in his employ. For Miss Charlotte Cray—who was as old as himself, and had arrived at the period of life when women are said to pray 'Any, good Lord, any!'—was really a clever woman, and could turn her hand to most things required of her, or upon which she had set her mind; and she had most decidedly set her mind upon marrying Mr Braggett, and he—to serve his own purposes—had permitted her to cherish the idea, and this was the Nemesis that was weighing him down in the study at the present moment. He had complimented Miss Cray, and given her presents, and taken her out a-pleasuring, all because she was useful to him, and did odd jobs that no one else would undertake, and for less than anyone else would have accepted; and he had known the while that she was in love with him, and that she believed he was in love with her.

He had not thought much of it at the time. He had not then made up his mind to marry Emily Primrose, and considered that what pleased Miss Cray, and harmed no one else, was fair play for all sides. But he had come to see things differently now. He had been married

28

three months, and the first two weeks had been very bitter ones to him. Miss Cray had written him torrents of reproaches during that unhappy period, besides calling day after day at his office to deliver them in person. This and her threats had frightened him out of his life. He had lived in hourly terror lest the clerks should overhear what passed at their interviews, or that his wife should be made acquainted with them.

He had implored Miss Cray, both by word of mouth and letter, to cease her persecution of him; but all the reply he received was that he was a base and perjured man, and that she should continue to call at his office, and write to him through the penny post, until he had introduced her to his wife. For therein lay the height and depth of his offending. He had been afraid to bring Emily and Miss Cray together, and the latter resented the omission as an insult. It was bad enough to find that Sigismund Braggett, whose hair she wore next her heart, and whose photograph stood as in a shrine upon her bedroom mantelpiece, had married another woman, without giving her even the chance of a refusal, but it was worse still to come to the conclusion that he did not intend her to have a glimpse into the garden of Eden he had created for himself.

Miss Cray was a lady of vivid imagination and strong aspirations. All was not lost in her ideas, although Mr Braggett *had* proved false to the hopes he had raised. Wives did not live for ever; and the chances and changes of this life were so numerous, that stranger things had happened than that Mr Braggett might think fit to make better use of the second opportunity afforded him than he had done of the first. But if she were not to continue even his friend, it was too hard. But the perjured publisher had continued resolute, notwithstanding all Miss Cray's persecution, and now he had neither seen nor heard from her for a month; and, manlike, he was beginning to wonder what had become of her, and whether she had found anybody to console her for his untruth. Mr Braggett did not wish to comfort Miss Cray himself; but he did not quite like the notion of her being comforted.

After all—so he soliloquised—he had been very cruel to her; for the poor thing was devoted to him. How her eyes used to sparkle and her cheek to flush when she entered his office, and how eagerly she would undertake any work for him, however disagreeable to perform! He knew well that she had expected to be Mrs Braggett, and it must have been a terrible disappointment to her when he married Emily Primrose.

Why had he not asked her out to Violet Villa since? What harm could she do as a visitor there? particularly if he cautioned her first as to the peculiarity of Mrs Braggett's disposition, and the quickness with which her jealousy was excited. It was close upon Christmas-time, the period when all old friends meet together and patch up, if they cannot entirely forget, everything that has annoyed them in the past, Mr Braggett pictured to himself the poor old maid sitting solitary in, her small rooms at Hammersmith, no longer able to live in the expectation of seeing his manly form at the wicket-gate, about to enter and cheer her solitude. The thought smote him as a two-edged sword, and he sat down at once and penned Miss Charlotte s note, in which he inquired after her health, and hoped that they should soon see her at Violet Villa.

He felt much better after this note was written and despatched. He came out of the little study and entered the cheerful drawing-room, and sat with his pretty wife by the light of the fire, telling her of the lonely lady to whom he had just proposed to introduce her.

'An old friend of mine, Emily. A clever, agreeable woman, though rather eccentric. You will be polite to her, I know, for my sake.'

'An *old* woman, is she?' said Mrs Braggett, elevating her eyebrows. 'And what do you call "old," Siggy, I should like to know?'

'Twice as old as yourself, my dear—five-and-forty at the very least, and not personable-looking, even for that age. Yet I think you will find her a pleasant companion, and I am sure she will be enchanted with you.'

'I don't know that: clever women don't like me, as a rule, though I don't know why.'

'They are jealous of your beauty, my darling; but Miss Cray is above such meanness, and will value you for your own sake.'

'She'd better not let me catch her valuing me for *yours*,' responded Mrs Braggett, with a flash of the eye that made her husband ready to regret the dangerous experiment he was about to make of bringing together two women who had each, in her own way, a claim upon him, and each the will to maintain it.

So he dropped the subject of Miss Charlotte Cray, and took to admiring his wife's complexion instead, so that the evening passed harmoniously, and both parties were satisfied.

For two days Mr Braggett received no answer from Miss Cray, which rather surprised him. He had quite expected that on the reception of his invitation she would rush down to his office and into his arms, behind the shelter of the ground-glass door that enclosed his chair of authority. For Miss Charlotte had been used on occasions to indulge in rapturous demonstrations of the sort, and the remembrance of Mrs Braggett located in Violet Villa would have been no obstacle whatever to her. She believed she had a prior claim to Mr Braggett. However, nothing of the kind happened, and the perjured publisher was becoming strongly imbued with the idea that he must go out to Hammersmith and see if he could not make his peace with her in person, particularly as he had several odd jobs for Christmas-tide, which no one could undertake so well as herself, when a letter with a black-edged border was put into his hand. He opened it mechanically, not knowing the writing; but its contents shocked him beyond measure.

> Honoured Sir,—I am sorry to tell you that Miss Cray died at my house a week ago, and was buried yesterday. She spoke of you several times during her last illness, and if you would like to hear any further particulars, and will call on me at the old address, I shall be most happy to furnish you with them.—
> Yours respectfully,
> Mary Thompson.

When Mr Braggett read this news, you might have knocked him over with a feather. It is not always true that a living dog is better than a dead lion. Some people gain considerably in the estimation of their friends by leaving this world, and Miss Charlotte Cray was one of them. Her persecution had ceased for ever, and her amiable weaknesses were alone held in remembrance. Mr Braggett felt a positive relief in the knowledge that his dead friend and his wife would never now be brought in contact with each other; but at the same time he blamed himself more than was needful, perhaps, for not having seen nor communicated with Miss Cray for so long before her death. He came down to breakfast with a portentously grave face that morning, and imparted the sad intelligence to Mrs Braggett with the air of an undertaker.

Emily wondered, pitied, and sympathised, but the dead lady was no more to her than any other stranger; and she was surprised her husband looked so solemn over it all. Mr Braggett, however, could not dismiss the subject easily from his mind. It haunted him during the business hours of the morning, and as soon as he could conveniently leave his office, he posted away to Hammersmith. The little house in which Miss Cray used to live looked just the same, both inside and

31

outside: how strange it seemed that *she* should have flown away from it forever! And here was her landlady, Mrs Thompson, bobbing and curtseying to him in the same old black net cap with artificial flowers in it, and the same stuff gown she had worn since he first saw her, with her apron in her hand, it is true, ready to go to her eyes as soon as a reasonable opportunity occurred, but otherwise the same Mrs Thompson as before. And yet she would never wait upon *her* again.

'It was all so sudden, sir,' she said, in answer to Mr Braggett's inquiries, 'that there was no time to send for nobody.'

'But Miss Cray had my address.'

'Ah! perhaps so; but she was off her head, poor dear, and couldn't think of nothing. But she remembered you, sir, to the last; for the very morning she died, she sprung up in bed and called out, "Sigismund! Sigismund!" as loud as ever she could, and she never spoke to anybody afterwards, not one word.'

'She left no message for me?'

'None, sir. I asked her the day before she went if I was to say nothing to you for her (knowing you was such friends), and all her answer was, "I wrote to him. He's got my letter." So I thought, perhaps, you had heard, sir.'

'Not for some time past. It seems terribly sudden to me, not having heard even of her illness. Where is she buried?'

'Close by in the churchyard, sir. My little girl will go with you and show you the place, if you'd like to see it.'

Mr Braggett accepted her offer and left.

When he was standing by a heap of clods they called a grave, and had dismissed the child, he drew out Miss Cray's last letter, which he carried in his pocket, and read it over.

> You tell me that I am not to call at your office again, except on business, nor to send letters to your private address, lest it should come to the knowledge of your wife, and create unpleasantness between you; but I *shall* call, and I *shall* write, until I have seen Mrs Braggett, and, if you don't take care, I will introduce myself to her and tell her the reason you have been afraid to do so.'

This letter had made Mr Braggett terribly angry at the time of reception. He had puffed and fumed, and cursed Miss Charlotte by all his gods for daring to threaten him. But he read it with different feelings now Miss Charlotte was down there, six feet beneath the ground he stood on, and he could feel only compassion for her frenzy, and resentment against himself for having excited it. As he travelled home from Hammersmith to Streatham, he was a very dejected publisher indeed.

He did not tell Mrs Braggett the reason of his melancholy, but it affected him to that degree that he could not go to office on the following day, but stayed at home instead, to be petted and waited upon by his pretty wife, which treatment resulted in a complete cure. The next morning, therefore, he started for London as briskly as ever, and arrived at office before his usual time. A clerk, deputed to receive all messages for his master, followed him behind the ground-glass doors, with a packet of letters.

'Mr Van Ower was here yesterday, sir. He will let you have the copy before the end of the week, and Messrs Hanleys' foreman called on particular business, and will look in today at eleven. And Mr Ellis came to ask if there was any answer to his letter yet; and Miss Cray called, sir; and that's all'

'*Who* did you say?' cried Braggett.

'Miss Cray, sir. She waited for you above an hour, but I told her I thought you couldn't mean to come into town at all, so she went.'

'Do you know what you're talking about, Hewetson? You said *Miss Cray!*'

'And I meant it, sir—Miss Charlotte Cray. Burns spoke to her as well as I.'

'Good heavens!' exclaimed Mr Braggett, turning as white as a sheet. 'Go at once and send Burns to me.' Burns came.

'Burns, who was the lady that called to see me yesterday?'

'Miss Cray, sir. She had a very thick veil on, and she looked so pale that I asked her if she had been ill, and she said "Yes." She sat in the office for over an hour, hoping you'd come in, but as you didn't, she went away again.'

'Did she lift her veil?'

'Not whilst I spoke to her, sir.'

'How do you know it was Miss Cray, then?'

The clerk stared. 'Well, sir, we all know her pretty well by this time.'

'Did you ask her name?'

'No, sir; there was no need to do it.'

'You're mistaken, that's all, both you and Hewetson. It couldn't have been Miss Cray! I know for certain that she is—is—is—not in London at present. It must have been a stranger.'

'It was not, indeed, sir, begging your pardon. I could tell Miss Cray anywhere, by her figure and her voice, without seeing her face. But I *did* see her face, and remarked how awfully pale she was—just like death, sir!'

'There! there! that will do! It's of no consequence, and you can go back to your work.'

But anyone who had seen Mr Braggett, when left alone in his office, would not have said he thought the matter of no consequence. The perspiration broke out upon his forehead, although it was December, and he rocked himself backward and forward in his chair with agitation.

At last he rose hurriedly, upset his throne, and dashed through the outer premises in the face of twenty people waiting to speak to him. As soon as he could find his voice, he hailed a hansom, and drove to Hammersmith. Good Mrs Thompson opening the door to him, thought he looked as if he had just come out of a fever.

'Lor' bless me, sir! whatever's the matter?'

'Mrs Thompson, have you told me the truth about Miss Cray? Is she really dead?'

'*Really dead,* sir! Why, I closed her eyes, and put her in the coffin with my own hands! If she ain't dead, I don't know who is! But if you doubt my word, you'd better ask the doctor that gave the certificate for her.'

'What is the doctor's name?'

'Dodson; he lives opposite.'

'You must forgive my strange questions, Mrs Thompson, but I have had a terrible dream about my poor friend, and I think I should like to talk to the doctor about her.'

'Oh, very good, sir,' cried the landlady, much offended. 'I'm not afraid of what the doctor will tell you. She had excellent nursing and everything as she could desire, and there's nothing on my conscience on that score, so I'll wish you good morning.' And with that Mrs Thompson slammed the door in Mr Braggett's face.

He found Dr Dodson at home.

'If I understand you rightly,' said the practitioner, looking rather steadfastly in the scared face of his visitor, 'you wish, as a friend of the late Miss Cray's, to see a copy of the certificate of her death? Very good, sir; here it is. She died, as you will perceive, on the twenty-fifth of November, of peritonitis. She had, I can assure you, every attention and care, but nothing could have saved her.'

'You are quite sure, then, she is dead?' demanded Mr Braggett, in a vague manner.

The doctor looked at him as if he were not quite sure if he were sane.

'If seeing a patient die, and her corpse coffined and buried, is being sure she is dead, *I* am in no doubt whatever about Miss Cray.'

'It is very strange—most strange and unaccountable,' murmured poor Mr Braggett, in reply, as he shuffled out of the doctor's passage, and took his way back to the office.

Here, however, after an interval of rest and a strong brandy and soda, he managed to pull himself together, and to come to the conclusion that the. doctor and Mrs Thompson *could* not be mistaken, and that, consequently, the clerks *must*. He did not mention the subject again to them however; and as the days went on, and nothing more was heard of the mysterious stranger's visit, Mr Braggett put it altogether out of his mind.

At the end of a fortnight, however, when he was thinking of something totally different, young Hewetson remarked to him, carelessly,—

'Miss Cray was here again yesterday, sir. She walked in just as your cab had left the door.'

All the horror of his first suspicions returned with double force upon the unhappy man's mind.

'Don't talk nonsense!' he gasped, angrily, as soon as he could speak. 'Don't attempt to play any of your tricks on me, young man, or it will be the worse for you, I can tell you.'

'Tricks, sir!' stammered the clerk. 'I don't know what you are alluding to. I am only telling you the truth. You have always desired me to be most particular in letting you know the names of the people who call in your absence, and I thought I was only doing my duty in making a point of ascertaining them—'

'Yes, yes! Hewetson, of course,' replied Mr Braggett, passing his handkerchief over his brow, 'and you are quite right in following my directions as closely as possible; only—in this case you are completely mistaken, and it is the second time you have committed the error.'

'Mistaken!'

'Yes!—as mistaken as it is possible for a man to be! Miss Cray *could* not have called at this office yesterday.'

'But she did, sir.'

'Am I labouring under some horrible nightmare?' exclaimed the publisher, 'or are we playing at cross purposes? Can you mean the Miss Cray I mean?'

'I am speaking of Miss Charlotte Cray, sir, the author of *Sweet Gwendoline*,—the lady who has undertaken so much of our compilation the last two years, and who has a long nose, and wears her hair in curls. I never knew there was another Miss Cray; but if there are two, that is the one I mean.'

'Still I *cannot* believe it, Hewetson, for the Miss Cray who has been associated with our firm died on the twenty-fifth of last month.'

'*Died*, sir! Is Miss Cray dead? Oh, it can't be! It's some humbugging trick that's been played upon you, for I'd swear she was in this room yesterday afternoon, as full of life as she's ever been since I knew her. She didn't talk much, it's true, for she seemed in a hurry to be off again, but she had got on the same dress and bonnet she was in here last, and she made herself as much at home in the office as she ever did. Besides,' continued Hewetson, as though suddenly remembering something, 'she left a note for you, sir.'

'A note! Why did you not say so before?'

'It slipped my memory when you began to doubt my word in that way, sir. But you'll find it in the bronze vase. She told me to tell you she had placed it there.'

Mr Braggett made a dash at the vase, and found the three-cornered note as he had been told. Yes! it was Charlotte's handwriting, or the facsimile of it, there was no doubt of that; and his hands shook so he could hardly open the paper. It contained these words:

'You tell me that I am not to call at your office again, except on business, nor to send letters to your private address, lest it should come to the knowledge of your wife, and create unpleasantness between you; but I *shall* call, and I *shall* write until I have seen Mrs Braggett, and if you don't take care I will introduce myself to her, and tell her the reason you have been afraid to do so.'

Precisely the same words, in the same writing of the letter he still carried in his breast-pocket, and which no mortal eyes but his and hers had ever seen. As the unhappy man sat gazing at the opened note, his whole body shook as if he were attacked by ague.

'It is Miss Cray's handwriting, isn't it, sir?'

'It looks like it, Hewetson, but it cannot be. I tell you it is an impossibility! Miss Cray died last month, and I have seen not only her grave, but the doctor and nurse who attended her in her last illness. It is folly, then, to suppose either that she called here or wrote that letter.'

'Then *who could it have been* sir?' said Hewetson, attacked with a sudden terror in his turn.

'That is impossible for me to say; but should the lady call again, you had better ask her boldly for her name and address.'

'I'd rather you'd depute the office to anybody but me, sir,' replied the clerk, as he hastily backed out of the room.

Mr Braggett, dying with suspense and conjecture, went through his business as best he could, and hurried home to Violet Villa.

There he found that his wife had been spending the day with a friend, and only entered the house a few minutes before himself.

'Siggy, dear!' she commenced, as soon as he joined her in the drawing-room after dinner; ' I really think we should have the fastenings and bolts of this house looked to. Such a funny thing happened whilst; I was out this afternoon. Ellen has just been telling me about it.'

'What sort of a thing, dear?'

'Well, I left home as early as twelve, you know, and told the servants I shouldn't be back until dinner-time; so they were all enjoying themselves in the kitchen, I suppose, when cook told Ellen she heard a footstep in the drawing-room. Ellen thought at first it must be cook's fancy, because she was sure the front door was fastened; but when they listened, they all heard the noise together, so she ran upstairs, and what on earth do you think she saw?'

'How can I guess, my dear?'

'Why, a lady, seated in this very room, as if she was waiting for somebody. She was oldish, Ellen says, and had a very white face, with long curls hanging down each side of it; and she wore a blue bonnet with white feathers, and a long black cloak, and—'

'Emily, Emily! Stop! You don't know what you're talking about. That girl is a fool: you must send her away. That is, how could the lady have got in if the door was closed? Good heavens! you'll all drive me mad between you with your folly!' exclaimed Mr Braggett, as he threw himself back in his chair, with an exclamation that sounded very like a groan.

Pretty Mrs Braggett was offended. What had she said or done that her husband should doubt her word? She tossed her head in indignation, and remained silent If Mr Braggett wanted any further information, he would have to apologise.

'Forgive me, darling,' he said, after a long pause. 'I don't think I'm very well this evening, but your story seemed to upset me.'

'I don't see why it should upset you,' returned Mrs Braggett. 'If strangers are allowed to come prowling about the house in this way, we shall be robbed some day, and then you'll say I should have told you of it.'

'Wouldn't she—this person—give her name?'

'Oh! I'd rather say no more about it. You had better ask Ellen.'

'No, Emily! I'd rather hear it from you.'

'Well, don't interrupt me again, then. When Ellen saw the woman seated here, she asked her her name and business at once, but she gave no answer, and only sat and stared at her. And so Ellen, feeling very uncomfortable, had just turned round to call up cook, when the woman got up, and dashed past her like a flash of lightning, and they saw nothing more of her!'

'Which way did she leave the house?'

'Nobody knows any more than how she came in. The servants declare the hall-door was neither opened nor shut—but, of course, it must have been. She was a tall gaunt woman, Ellen says, about fifty, and she's sure her hair was dyed. She must have come to steal something, and that's why I say we ought to have the house made more secure. Why, Siggy! Siggy! what's the matter? Here, Ellen! Jane! come, quick, some of you! Your master's fainted!'

And, sure enough, the repeated shocks and horrors of the day had had such an effect upon poor Mr Braggett, that for a moment he did lose all consciousness of what surrounded him. He was thankful to take advantage of the Christmas holidays, to run over to Paris with his wife, and try to forget, in the many marvels of that city, the awful fear that fastened upon him at the mention of anything connected with home. He might be enjoying himself to the top of his bent; but directly the remembrance of Charlotte Cray crossed his mind, all sense of enjoyment vanished, and he trembled at the mere thought of returning to his business, as a child does when sent to bed in the dark.

He tried to hide the state of his feelings from Mrs Braggett, but she was too sharp for him. The simple, blushing Emily Primrose had developed, under the influence of the matrimonial forcing-frame, into a good watch-dog, and nothing escaped her notice.

Left to her own conjecture, she attributed his frequent moods of dejection to the existence of some other woman, and became jealous accordingly. If Siggy did not love her, why had he married her? She felt certain there was some other horrid creature who had engaged his affections and would not leave him alone, even now that he was her own lawful property. And to find out who the 'horrid creature' was became Mrs Emily's constant idea. When she had found out, she meant to give her a piece of her mind, never fear! Meanwhile

Mr Braggett's evident distaste to returning to business only served to increase his wife's suspicions. A clear conscience, she argued, would know no fear. So they were not a happy couple, as they set their faces once more towards England. Mr Braggett's dread of re-entering his office amounted almost to terror, and Mrs Braggett, putting this and that together, resolved that she would fathom the mystery, if it lay in feminine *finesse* to do so. She did not whisper a word of her intentions to dear Siggy, you may be sure of that! She worked after the manner of her amiable sex, like a cat in the dark, or a worm boring through the earth, and appearing on the surface when least expected.

So poor Mr Braggett brought her home again, heavy at heart indeed, but quite ignorant that any designs were being made against him. I think he would have given a thousand pounds to be spared the duty of attending office the day after his arrival. But it was necessary, and he went, like a publisher and a Briton. But Mrs Emily had noted his trepidation and his fears, and laid her plans accordingly. She had never been asked to enter those mysterious precincts, the house of business. Mr Braggett had not thought it necessary that her blooming loveliness should be made acquainted with its dingy, dusty accessories, but she meant to see them for herself today. So she waited till he had left Violet Villa ten minutes, and then she dressed and followed him by the next train to London.

Mr Sigismund Braggett meanwhile had gone on his way, as people go to a dentist, determined to do what was right, but with an indefinite sort of idea that he might never come out of it alive. He dreaded to hear what might have happened in his absence, and he delayed his arrival at the office for half-an-hour, by walking there instead of taking a cab as usual, in order to put off the evil moment. As he entered the place, however, he saw at a glance that his efforts were vain, and that something had occurred. The customary formality and precision of the office were upset, and the clerks, instead of bending over their ledgers, or attending to the demands of business, were all huddled together at one end whispering and gesticulating to each other. But as soon as the publisher appeared, a dead silence fell upon the group, and they only stared at him with an air of horrid mystery.

'What is the matter now?' he demanded, angrily, for like most men when in a fright which they are ashamed to exhibit, Mr Sigismund Braggett tried to cover his want of courage by bounce.

The young man called Hewetson advanced towards him, with a face the colour of ashes, and pointed towards the ground-glass doors dumbly.

'What do you mean? Can't you speak? What's come to the lot of you, that you are neglecting my business in this fashion to make fools of yourselves?'

'If you please, sir, she's in there.'

Mr Braggett started back as if he'd been shot. But still he tried to have it out.

'*She!* Who's *she?*'

'Miss Cray, sir.'

'Haven't I told you already that's a lie.'

'Will you judge for yourself, Mr Braggett?' said a grey-haired man, stepping forward. 'I was on the stairs myself just now when Miss Cray passed me, and I have no doubt whatever but that you will find her in your private room, however much the reports that have lately reached you may seem against the probability of such a thing.'

Mr Braggett's teeth chattered in his head as he advanced to the ground-glass doors, through the panes of one of which there was a little peephole to ascertain if the room were occupied or not. He stooped and looked in. At the table, with her back towards him, was seated the well-known figure of Charlotte Cray. He recognised at once the long black mantle in which she was wont to drape her gaunt figure—the blue bonnet, with its dejected-looking, uncurled feather—the lank curls which rested on her shoulders— and the black-leather bag, with a steel clasp, which she always carried in her hand. It was the embodiment of Charlotte Cray, he had no doubt of that; but how could he reconcile the fact of her being there with the damp clods he had seen piled upon her grave, with the certificate of death, and the doctor's and landlady's assertion that they had watched her last moments?

At last he prepared, with desperate energy, to turn the handle of the door. At that moment the attention of the more frivolous of the clerks was directed from his actions by the entrance of an uncommonly pretty woman at the other end of the outer office. Such a lovely creature as this seldom brightened the gloom of their dusty abiding-place. Lilies, roses, and carnations vied with each other in her complexion, whilst the sunniest of locks, and the brightest of blue eyes, lent her face a girlish charm not easily described. What could this fashionably-attired Venus want in their house of business?

'Is Mr Braggett here? I am Mrs Braggett. Please show me in to him immediately.'

They glanced at the ground-glass doors of the inner office. They had already closed behind the manly form of their employer.

'This way, madam,' one said, deferentially, as he escorted her to the presence of Mr Braggett.

Meanwhile, Sigismund had opened the portals of the Temple of Mystery, and with trembling knees entered it. The figure in the chair did not stir at his approach. He stood at the door irresolute. What should he do or say?

'Charlotte,' he whispered.

Still she did not move.

At that moment his wife entered.

'Oh, Sigismund!' cried Mrs Emily, reproachfully, 'I knew you were keeping something from me, and now I've caught you in the very act. Who is this lady, and what is her name? I shall refuse to leave the room until I know it'

At the sound of her rival's voice, the woman in the chair rose quickly to her feet and confronted them. Yes! there was Charlotte Cray, precisely similar to what she had appeared in life, only with an uncertainty and vagueness about the lines of the familiar features that made them ghastly.

She stood there, looking Mrs Emily full in the face, but only for a moment, for, even as she gazed, the lineaments grew less and less distinct, with the shape of the figure that supported them, until, with a crash, the apparition seemed to fall in and disappear, and the place that had known her was filled with empty air.

'Where is she gone?' exclaimed Mrs Braggett, in a tone of utter amazement.

'Where is who gone?' repeated Mr Braggett, hardly able to articulate from fear.

'The lady in the chair!'

'There was no one there except in your own imagination. It was my great-coat that you mistook for a figure,' returned her husband hastily, as he threw the article in question over the back of the armchair.

'But how could that have been?' said his pretty wife, rubbing her eyes. 'How could I think a coat had eyes, and hair, and features? I am sure I saw a woman seated there, and that she rose and stared at me. Siggy! tell me it was true. It seems so incomprehensible that I should have been mistaken.'

'You must question your own sense. You see that the room is empty now, except for ourselves, and you know that no one has left it. If you like to search under the table, you can.'

'Ah! now, Siggy, you are laughing at me, because you know that would be folly. But there was certainly someone here—only, where can she have disappeared to?'

'Suppose we discuss the matter at a more convenient season,' replied Mr Braggett, as he drew his wife's arm through his arm. 'Hewetson! you will be able to tell Mr Hume that he was mistaken. Say, also, that I shall not be back in the office today. I am not so strong as I thought I was, and feel quite unequal to business. Tell him to come out to Streatham this evening with my letters, and I will talk with him there.'

What passed at that interview was never disclosed; but pretty Mrs Braggett was much rejoiced, a short time afterwards, by her husband telling her that he had resolved to resign his active share of the business, and devote the rest of his life to her and Violet Villa. He would have no more occasion, therefore, to visit the office, and be exposed to the temptation of spending four or five hours out of every twelve away from her side. For, though Mrs Emily had arrived at the conclusion that the momentary glimpse she caught of a lady in Siggy's office must have been a delusion, she was not quite satisfied by his assertions that she would never have found a more tangible cause for her jealousy.

But Sigismund Braggett knew more than he chose to tell Mrs Emily. He knew that what she had witnessed was no delusion, but a reality; and that Charlotte Cray had carried out her dying determination, to call at his office and his private residence, until she had seen his wife!

Green Branches

Fiona Macleod

In the year that followed the death of Mànus MacCodrum, James Achanna saw nothing of his brother Gloom. He might have thought himself alone in the world, of all his people, but for a letter that came to him out of the west. True, he had never accepted the common opinion that his brothers had both been drowned on that night when Anne Gillespie left Eilanmore with Mànus. In the first place, he had nothing of that inner conviction concerning the fate of Gloom which he had concerning that of Marcus; in the next, had he not heard the sound of the *feadan*, which no one that he knew played, except Gloom; and, for further token, was not the tune that which he hated above all others—the Dance of the Dead—for who but Gloom would be playing that, he hating it so, and the hour being late, and no one else on Eilanmore? It was no sure thing that the dead had not come back; but the more he thought of it the more Achanna believed that his sixth brother was still alive. Of this, however, he said nothing to anyone.

It was as a man set free that, at last, after long waiting and patient trouble with the disposal of all that was left of the Achanna heritage, he left the island. It was a grey memory for him. The bleak moorland of it, the blight that had lain so long and so often upon the crops, the rains that had swept the isle for grey days and grey weeks and grey months, the sobbing of the sea by day and its dark moan by night, its dim relinquishing sigh in the calm of dreary ebbs, its hollow baffling roar when the storm-shadow swept up out of the sea, one and all oppressed him, even in memory. He had never loved the island, even when it lay green and fragrant in the green and white seas under white and blue skies, fresh and sweet as an Eden of the sea.

He had ever been lonely and weary, tired of the mysterious shadow that lay upon his folk, caring little for any of his brothers except the eldest—long since mysteriously gone out of the ken of man—and almost hating Gloom, who had ever borne him a grudge because of his beauty, and because of his likeness to and reverent heed for Alison. Moreover, ever since he had come to love Katreen Macarthur, the daughter of Donald Macarthur who lived in Sleat of Skye, he had been eager to live near her; the more eager as he knew that Gloom loved the girl also, and wished for success not only for his own sake, but so as to put a slight upon his younger brother.

So, when at last he left the island, he sailed southward gladly. He was leaving Eilanmore; he was bound to a new home in Skye, and perhaps he was going to his long-delayed, long dreamed-of happiness. True, Katreen was not pledged to him; he did not even know for sure if she loved him. He thought, hoped, dreamed, almost believed that she did; but then there was her cousin Ian, who had long wooed her, and to whom old Donald Macarthur had given his blessing. Nevertheless, his heart would have been lighter than it had been for long, but for two things. First, there was the letter. Some weeks earlier he had received it, not recognising the writing, because of the few letters he had ever seen, and, moreover, as it was in a feigned hand. With difficulty he had deciphered the Manuscript, plain printed though it was. It ran thus:—

"Well, Sheumais, my brother, it is wondering if I am dead, you will be. Maybe ay and maybe no. But I send you this writing to let you see that I know all you do and think of. So, you are going to leave Eilanmore without an Achanna upon it? And you will be going to Sleat in Skye? Well, let me be telling you this thing. *Do not go.* I see blood there. And there is this, too: neither you nor any man shall take Katreen away from me. You know that; and Ian Macarthur knows it; and Katreen knows it: and that holds whether I am alive or dead. I say to you: do not go. It will be better for you and for all. Ian Macarthur is away in the north-sea with the whaler-captain who came to us at Eilanmore, and will not be back for three months yet. It will be better for him not to come back.

"But if he comes back, he will have to reckon with the man who says that Katreen Macarthur is his. I would rather not have two men to speak to, and one my brother. It does not matter to you where I am. I want no money just now. But put aside my portion for me. Have it ready for me against the day I call for it. I will not be patient that day: so, have it ready for me. In the place that I am I am content. You will be saying: why is my brother away in a remote place (I will say this to you: that it is not farther north than St Kilda nor farther south than the Mull of Cantyre!), and for what reason? That is between me and silence. But perhaps you think of Anne sometimes. Do you know that she lies under the green grass?

"And of Mànus MacCodrum? They say that he swam out into the sea and was drowned; and they whisper of the seal-blood, though the minister is wroth with them for that. He calls it a madness. Well, I was there at that madness, and I played to it on my *feadan*. And now, Sheumais, can you be thinking of what the tune was that I played?

"Your brother, who waits his own day,

"Gloom."

"Do not be forgetting this thing: *I would rather not be playing the 'Damhsa-na-mairbh!'* It was an ill hour for Mànus when he heard the Dàn-nan-Ròn; it was the song of his soul, that; and yours is the Davsa-na-Mairv."

This letter was ever in his mind: this, and what happened in the gloaming when he sailed away for Skye in the herring-smack of two men who lived at Armadale in Sleat. For, as the boat moved slowly out of the haven, one of the men asked him if he was sure that no one was left upon the island; for he thought he had seen a figure on the rocks, waving a black scarf. Achanna shook his head, but just then his companion cried that at that moment he had seen the same thing. So, the smack was put about, and when she was moving slow through the haven again, Achanna sculled ashore in the little coggly punt.

In vain he searched here and there, calling loudly again and again. Both men could hardly have been mistaken, he thought. If there were no human creature on the island, and if their eyes had not played them false, who could it be? The wraith of Marcus, mayhap; or might it be the old man himself (his father), risen to bid farewell to his youngest son, or to warn him?

It was no use to wait longer; so, looking often behind him, he made his way to the boat again, and rowed slowly out towards the smack.

Jerk—jerk—jerk across the water came, low but only too loud for him, the opening bars of the Damhsa-na-Mairbh. A horror came upon him, and he drove the boat through the water so that the sea splashed over the bows. When he came on deck, he cried in a hoarse voice to the man next him to put up the helm, and let the smack swing to the wind.

"There is no one there, Callum Campbell," he whispered.

"And who is it that will be making that strange music?"

"What music?"

"Sure, it has stopped now, but I heard it clear, and so did Anndra MacEwan. It was like the sound of a reed-pipe, and the tune was an eerie one at that."

"It was the Dance of the Dead."

"And who will be playing that?" asked the man, with fear in his eyes.

"No living man."

"No living man?"

"No. I'm thinking it will be one of my brothers who was drowned here, and by the same token that it is Gloom, for he played upon the *feadan*; but if not, then . . . then . . ."

The two men waited in breathless silence, each trembling with superstitious fear; but at last, the elder made a sign to Achanna to finish.

"Then . . . it will be the *Kelpie*."

"Is there . . . is there one of the . . . the cavewomen here?"

"It is said; and you know of old that the *Kelpie* sings or plays a strange tune to wile seamen to their death."

At that moment, the fantastic jerking music came loud and clear across the bay. There was a horrible suggestion in it, as if dead bodies were moving along the ground with long jerks, and crying and laughing wild. It was enough; the men, Campbell and MacEwan, would not now have waited longer if Achanna had offered them all he had in the world. Nor were they, or he, out of their panic haste till the smack stood well out at sea, and not a sound could be heard from Eilanmore.

They stood watching, silent. Out of the dusky mass that lay in the seaward way to the north came a red gleam. It was like an eye staring after them with blood-red glances.

"What is that, Achanna?" asked one of the men at last.

"It looks as though a fire had been lit in the house up in the island. The door and the window must be open. The fire must be fed with wood, for no peats would give that flame; and there were none lit when I left. To my knowing, there was no wood for burning except the wood of the shelves and the bed."

"And who would be doing that?"

"I know of that no more than you do, Callum Campbell."

No more was said, and it was a relief to all when the last glimmer of the light was absorbed in the darkness.

At the end of the voyage Campbell and MacEwan were well pleased to be quit of their companion; not so much because he was moody and distraught, as because they feared that a spell was upon him—a fate in the working of which they might become involved. It needed no vow of the one to the other for them to come to the conclusion that they would never land on Eilanmore, or, if need be, only in broad daylight, and never alone.

The days went well for James Achanna, where he made his home at Ranza-beag, on Ranza Water in the Sleat of Skye. The farm was small but good, and he hoped that with help and care he would soon have the place as good a farm as there was in all Skye.

Donald Macarthur did not let him see much of Katreen, but the old man was no longer opposed to him. Sheumais must wait till Ian Macarthur came back again, which might be any day now. For sure, James Achanna of Ranza-beag was a very different person from the youngest of the Achanna-folk who held by on lonely Eilanmore; moreover, the old man could not but think with pleasure that it would be well to see Katreen able to walk over the whole land of Ranza, from the cairn at the north of his own Ranza-Mòr to the burn at the south of Ranza-beag, and know it for her own.

But Achanna was ready to wait. Even before he had the secret word of Katreen he knew from her beautiful dark eyes that she loved him. As the weeks went by, they managed to meet often, and at last Katreen told him that she loved him too, and would have none but him; but that they must wait till Ian came back, because of the pledge given to him by her father. They were days of joy for him. Through many a hot noontide hour, through many a gloaming, he went as one in a dream. Whenever he saw a birch swaying in the wind, or a wave leaping upon Loch Liath, that was near his home, or passed a bush covered with wild roses, or saw the moonbeams lying white on the boles of the pines, he thought of Katreen: his fawn for grace, and so lithe and tall, with sun-brown face and wavy dark mass of hair and shadowy eyes and rowan-red lips.

It is said that there is a god clothed in shadow who goes to and fro among the human kind, putting silence between lovers with his waving hands, and breathing a chill out of his cold breath, and leaving a gulf of deep water flowing between them because of the passing of his feet. That shadow never came their way. Their love grew as a flower fed by rains and warmed by sunlight.

When midsummer came, and there was no sign of Ian Macarthur, it was already too late. Katreen had been won.

During the summer months, it was the custom for Katreen and two of the farm girls to go up Maol Ranza, to reside at the shealing of Cnoc-an-Fhraoch: and this because of the hill-pasture for the sheep. Cnoc-an-Fhraoch is a round, boulder studded hill covered with heather, which has a precipitous corrie on each side, and in front slopes down to Lochan Fraoch, a lochlet surrounded by dark woods. Behind the hill, or great hillock rather, lay the shealing. At each week-end Katreen went down to Ranza-Mor, and on every Monday morning at sunrise returned to her heather-girt eyrie. It was on one of these visits that she endured a cruel shock. Her father told her that she must marry someone else than Sheumais Achanna. He had heard words about him which made a union impossible, and, indeed, he hoped that the man would leave Ranza-beag.

In the end, he admitted that what he had heard was to the effect that Achanna was under a doom of some kind; that he was involved in a blood feud; and, moreover, that he was fey. The old man would not be explicit as to the person from whom his information came, but hinted that he was a stranger of rank, probably a laird of the isles. Besides this, there was word of Ian Macarthur. He was at Thurso, in the far north, and would be in Skye before long, and he—her father—had written to him that he might wed Katreen as soon as was practicable.

"Do you see that lintie yonder, father?" was her response to this.

"Ay, lass; and what about the birdeen?"

"Well, when she mates with a hawk, so will I be mating with Ian Macarthur, but not till then."

With that she turned, and left the house, and went back to Cnoc-an-Fhraoch. On the way she met Achanna.

It was that night that, for the first time, he swam across Lochan Fraoch to meet Katreen.

The quickest way to reach the shealing was to row across the lochlet, and then ascend by a sheep-path that wound through the hazel copses at the base of the hill. Fully half-an-hour was thus saved, because of the steepness of the precipitous corries to right and left. A boat was kept for this purpose, but it was fastened to a shore-boulder by a padlocked iron chain, the key of which was kept by Donald Macarthur. Latterly he had refused to let this key out of his possession. For one thing, no doubt, he believed he could thus restrain Achanna from visiting his daughter. The young man could not approach the shealing from either side without being seen.

But that night, soon after the moon was whitening slow in the dark, Katreen stole down to the hazel copse and awaited the coming of her lover. The lochan was visible from almost any point on Cnoc-an-Fhraoch, as well as from the south side. To cross it in a boat unseen, if any watcher were near, would be impossible, nor could even a swimmer hope to escape notice unless in the gloom of night, or, mayhap, in the dusk. When, however, she saw, half way across the water, a spray of green branches slowly moving athwart the surface, she knew that Sheumais was keeping his tryst. If, perchance, anyone else saw, he or she would never guess that those derelict rowan-branches shrouded Sheumais Achanna.

It was not till the estray had drifted close to the ledge, where, hid among the bracken and the hazel undergrowth, she awaited him, that Katreen descried the face of her lover, as with one hand he parted the green sprays and stared longingly and lovingly at the figure he could just discern in the dim fragrant obscurity.

And as it was this night, so was it on many of the nights that followed. Katreen spent the days as in a dream. Not even the news of her cousin Ian's return disturbed her much.

One day the inevitable meeting came. She was at Ranza-Mòr, and when a shadow came into the dairy where she was standing, she looked up, and saw Ian before her. She thought he appeared taller and stronger than ever, though still not so tall as Sheumais, who would appear slim beside the Herculean Skye man. But as she looked at his close curling black hair, and thick bull neck, and the sullen eyes in his dark wind-red face, she wondered that she had ever tolerated him at all.

He broke the ice at once.

"Tell me, Katreen, are you glad to see me back again?"

"I am glad that you are home once more safe and sound."

"And will you make it my home for me by coming to live with me, as I've asked you again and again."

"No, as I've told you again and again."

He gloomed at her angrily for a few moments before he resumed.

"I will be asking you this one thing, Katreen, daughter of my father's brother: do you love that man Achanna who lives at Ranza-beag?"

"You may ask the wind why it is from the east or the west, but it won't tell you. You're not the wind's master."

"If you think I will let this man take you away from me, you are thinking a foolish thing."

"And you saying a foolisher."

"Ay?"

"Ay, sure. What could you do, Ian-mhic-Ian? At the worst, you could do no more than kill James Achanna. What then? I too would die. You cannot separate us. I would not marry you, now, though you were the last man on the world and I the last woman."

"You're a fool, Katreen Macarthur. Your father has promised you to me, and I tell you this: if you love Achanna you'll save his life only by letting him go away from here. I promise you he will not be here long."

"Ay, you promise *me*; but you will not say that thing to James Achanna's face. You are a coward."

With a muttered oath the man turned on his heel.

"Let him beware o' me, and you, too, Katreen-mo-nighean-donn. I swear it by my mother's grave and by St Martin's Cross that you will be mine by hook or by crook."

The girl smiled scornfully. Slowly she lifted a milk-pail.

"It would be a pity to waste the good milk, *Ian-gorach*; but if you don't go, it is I that will be emptying the pail on you, and then you'll be as white without as your heart is within."

"So, you call me witless, do you? Ian-gorach! Well, we shall be seeing as to that; and as for the milk, there will be more than milk spilt because of *you*, Katreen-donn."

From that day, though neither Sheumais nor Katreen knew of it, a watch was set upon Achanna.

It could not be long before their secret was discovered; and it was with a savage joy overmastering his sullen rage that Ian Macarthur knew himself the discoverer, and conceived his double vengeance. He dreamed, gloatingly, on both the black thoughts that roamed like ravenous beasts through the solitudes of his heart. But he did not dream that another man was filled with hate because of Katreen's lover—another man who had sworn to make her his own; the man who, disguised, was known in Armadale as Donald McLean, and in the north isles would have been hailed as Gloom Achanna.

There had been steady rain for three days, with a cold raw wind. On the fourth the sun shone, and set in peace. An evening of quiet beauty followed, warm, fragrant, dusky from the absence of moon or star, though the thin veils of mist promised to disperse as the night grew.

There were two men that eve in the undergrowth on the south side of the lochlet. Sheumais had come earlier than his wont. Impatient for the dusk, he could scarce await the waning of the afterglow. Surely, he thought, he might venture. Suddenly his ears caught the sound of cautious footsteps. Could it be old Donald, perhaps, with some inkling of the way in which his daughter saw her lover, in despite of all; or, mayhap, might it be Ian Macarthur tracking him, as a hunter stalking a stag by the water-pools? He crouched, and waited. In a few minutes he saw Ian carefully picking his way. The man stooped as he descried the green branches; smiled as, with a low rustling, he raised them from the ground.

Meanwhile, yet another man watched and waited, though on the farther side of the lochan, where the hazel copses were. Gloom Achanna half hoped, half feared the approach of Katreen. It would be sweet to see her again, sweet to slay her lover before her eyes, brother to him though he was. But there was the chance that she might descry him, and, whether recognisingly or not, warn the swimmer. So it was that he had come there before sundown, and now lay crouched among the bracken underneath a projecting mossy ledge close upon the water, where it could scarce be that she or any should see him.

As the gloaming deepened, a great stillness reigned. There was no breath of wind. A scarce audible sigh prevailed among the spires of the heather. The churring of a nightjar throbbed through the darkness. Somewhere a corncrake called its monotonous *crék-craik*—the dull harsh sound emphasising the utter stillness. The pinging of the gnats hovering over and among the sedges made an incessant rumour through the warm sultry air.

There was a splash once as of a fish; then silence. Then a lower but more continuous splash, or rather wash of water. A slow susurrus rustled through the dark.

Where he lay among the fern Gloom Achanna slowly raised his head, stared through the shadows, and listened intently. If Katreen were waiting there she was not near.

Noiselessly he slid into the water. When he rose, it was under a clump of green branches. These he had cut and secured three hours before. With his left hand he swam slowly, or kept his equipoise in the water; with his right he guided the heavy rowan bough. In his mouth were two objects, one long and thin and dark, the other with an occasional glitter as of a dead fish.

His motion was scarce perceptible. None the less he was nigh the middle of the loch almost as soon the other clump of green branches. Doubtless the swimmer beneath it was confident that he was now safe from observation.

The two clumps of green branches drew nearer. The smaller

seemed a mere estray—a spray blown down by the recent gale. But all at once the larger clump jerked awkwardly and stopped. Simultaneously a strange low strain of music came from the other.

The strain ceased. The two clumps of green branches remained motionless. Slowly at last the larger moved forward. It was too dark for the swimmer to see if any one lay hid behind the smaller. When he reached it he thrust aside the leaves.

It was as though a great salmon leaped. There was a splash, and a narrow dark body shot through the gloom. At the end of it something gleamed. Then suddenly there was a savage struggle. The inanimate green branches tore this way and that, and surged and swirled. Gasping cries came from the leaves. Again, and again the gleaming thing leaped. At the third leap an awful scream shrilled through the silence. The echo of it wailed thrice with horrible distinctness in the corrie beyond Cnoc-an-Fhraoch. Then, after a faint splashing, there was silence once more. One clump of green branches drifted loosely up the lochlet. The other moved steadily towards the place whence, a brief while before, it had stirred.

Only one thing lived in the heart of Gloom Achanna—the joy of his exultation. He had killed his brother Sheumais. He had always hated him because of his beauty; of late he had hated him because he had stood between him, Gloom, and Katreen Macarthur, because he had become her lover. They were all dead now except himself—all the Achannas. He was "Achanna." When the day came that he would go back to Galloway there would be a magpie on the first birk, and a screaming jay on the first rowan, and a croaking raven on the first fir. Ay, he would be their suffering, though they knew nothing of him meanwhile! He would be Achanna of Achanna again. Let those who would stand in his way beware. As for Katreen: perhaps he would take her there, perhaps not. He smiled.

These thoughts were the wandering fires in his brain while he slowly swam shoreward under the floating green branches, and as he disengaged himself from them, and crawled upward through the bracken. It was at this moment that a third man entered the water from the farther shore.

Prepared as he was to come suddenly upon Katreen, Gloom was startled when, in a place of dense shadow, a hand touched his shoulder, and her voice whispered, "*Sheumais, Sheumais!*"

The next moment she was in his arms. He could feel her heart beating against his side.

"What was it, Sheumais? What was that awful cry?" she whispered.
For answer he put his lips to hers, and kissed her again and again.
The girl drew back. Some vague instinct warned her.

"What is it, Sheumais? Why don't you speak? "

He drew her close again.

"Pulse of my heart, it is I who love you—I who love you best of all. It is I, Gloom Achanna!"

With a cry, she struck him full in the face. He staggered, and in that moment, she freed herself.

"You *coward!*"

"Katreen, I . . . ."

"Come no nearer. If you do, it will be the death of you!"

"The death o' me! Ah, bonnie fool that you are, and is it you that will be the death o' me? "

"Ay, Gloom Achanna, for I have but to scream and Sheumais will be here, an' he would kill you like a dog if he knew you did me harm."

"Ah, but if there were no James, or any man, to come between me an' my will!"

"Then there would be a woman! Ay, if you overbore me, I would strangle you with my hair, or fix my teeth in your false throat!"

"I was not for knowing you were such a wild-cat! But I'll tame you yet, my lass! Aha, wild-cat!" and, as he spoke, he laughed low.

"It is a true word, Gloom of the black heart. I *am* a wild-cat, and like a wild-cat I am not to be seized by a fox, and that you will be finding to your cost, by the holy St Bridget! But now, off with you, brother of my man!"

"Your man . . . ha! ha! . . . ."

"Why do you laugh?"

"Sure, I am laughing at a warm white lass like yourself having a dead man as your lover!"

"A . . . dead . . . man?"

No answer came. The girl shook with a new fear. Slowly she drew closer till her breath fell warm against the face of the other. He spoke at last.

"Ay, a dead man."

"It is a lie."

"Where would you be that you were not hearing his goodbye? I'm thinking it was loud enough!"

"It is a lie . . . it is a lie!"

"No, it is no lie. Sheumais is cold enough now. He's low among the weeds by now. Ay, by now; down there in the lochan."

"*What* . . . you, *you devil!* Is it for killing your own brother you would be!"

"I killed no one. He died his own way. Maybe the cramp took him. Maybe . . . maybe a *kelpie* gripped him. I watched. I saw him beneath the green branches. He was dead before he died. I saw it in the white face o' him. Then he sank. He's dead—James is dead. Look here, girl, I've always loved you. I swore the oath upon you—you're mine. Sure, you're mine now, Katreen! It is loving you I am! It will be a south wind for you from this day, *muir-nean mochree!* See here, I'll show you how I . . . ."

"Back . . . back . . . *murderer!*"

"Be stopping that foolishness now, Katreen Macarthur! By the Book, I am tired of it! I am loving you, and it's having you for mine I am! And if you won't come to me like the dove to its mate, I'll come to you like the hawk to the dove!"

With a spring he was upon her. In vain she strove to beat him back. His arms held her as a stoat grips a rabbit.

He pulled her head back, and kissed her throat till the strangulating breath sobbed against his ear. With a last despairing effort she screamed the name of the dead man—"*Sheumais! Sheumais! Sheumais!*" The man who struggled with her laughed.

"Ay, call away! The herrin' will be coming through the bracken as soon as Sheumais comes to your call! Ah, it is mine you are now, Katreen! He's dead an' cold, . . . an' you'd best have a living man . . . an' . . . ."

She fell back, her balance lost in the sudden releasing. What did it mean? Gloom still stood there, but as one frozen. Through the darkness she saw at last that a hand gripped his shoulder—behind him a black mass vaguely obtruded.

For some moments there was absolute silence. Then a hoarse voice came out of the dark.

"You will be knowing now who it is, Gloom Achanna!"

The voice was that of Sheumais, who lay dead in the lochan. The murderer shook as in a palsy. With a great effort, slowly he turned his head. He saw a white splatch—the face of the corpse. In this white splatch flamed two burning eyes, the eyes of the soul of the brother whom he had slain.

He reeled, staggered as a blind man, and, free now of that awful clasp, swayed to and fro as one drunken.

Slowly Sheumais raised an arm, and pointed downward through

54

the wood towards the lochan. Still pointing, he moved swiftly forward. With a cry like a beast, Gloom Achanna swung to one side, stumbled, rose, and leaped into the darkness.

For some minutes Sheumais and Katreen stood, silent, apart, listening to the crashing sound of his flight—the race of the murderer against the pursuing shadow of the Grave.

Satan's Circus

Eleanor Smith

A grim, tragic tale of the strange horror that surrounded the wife of the circus-owner

1

Once asked a circus artist, whom I knew to have worked at one time with the Circus Brandt, whether or not he had enjoyed traveling with this well-known show. His reply was a curious one. Swiftly distorting his features into a hideous grimace, he spat violently upon the floor. Not another word would he say. My curiosity was, however, aroused, and I went next to an old Continental clown, now retired, who had the reputation of knowing every European circus as well as he knew his own pocket.

"The Circus Brandt?" he said thoughtfully. "Well, you know, the Brandts are queer people, and have an odd reputation. They are Austrian, and their own country-people call them gipsies, by which they mean nomads, for the Brandts never pitch in their own land but wander the whole world over as though the devil himself were at their heels. In fact, some call them Satan's Circus."

"I thought," I said, "that the Circus Brandt was supposed to be a remarkably fine show?"

"It is," he said, and lit his pipe; "it's expensive, ambitious, showy, well run. In their way these people are artists, and deserve more success than they have had. It's hard to say why they're so unpopular, but the fact remains that no one will stay with them more than a few months, and, what's more, wherever they go, India, Australia, Rumania, Spain, or Africa, they leave behind them a nasty, unpleasant sort of reputation as regards unpaid bills, which," he added, blowing smoke into the air, "is odd, for the Brandts are rich."

"How many Brandts are there?" I inquired, for I wished to know more about Europe's most elusive circus.

"You ask too many questions," said he, "but, this being my last reply to them, I don't mind telling you that there are two, and that they
are man and wife. Carl and Lya. The lady is a bit of a mystery, but if
you ask my opinion, I would say that she is of Mexican blood, that she
was at some time or other a charmer of snakes, and that of the two,
she is on the whole the worse, although that is saying a good deal.
However, all this is pure guess-work on my part, although, having seen
her, I can tell you that she's a handsome piece, still a year or two on
the right side of forty. And now," he said firmly, "I will speak no more
of the Circus Brandt."

And we talked instead of Sarrasani, of Krone, of Carmo, and of
Hagenbeck.

A year passed, and I forgot the Circus Brandt, which no doubt
during this period of time wandered from Tokio to San Francisco and
Belgrade up to Stockholm and back again as though the devil himself
were at its heels.

And then I met an old friend, a famous juggler, whom I had not
seen for many months. I offered him a drink and asked him where he
had been since our last meeting. He laughed and said that he had been
in hell. I told him I was not much of a hand at riddles. He laughed
again.

"Oh, hell," he said, "perhaps that's an exaggeration. But anyhow
I've been as near to it as ever I want to. I've been touring with the
Circus Brandt."

"The Circus Brandt?"

"Exactly. The Balkan states, Spain, North Africa. Then Holland and
Belgium, and finally France. I cleared out in France. If they'd doubled
my salary, I'd not have stayed with them."

"Is the Circus Brandt, then," I asked, "as rough as all that?"

"Rough?" he said. "No, it's not rough. I can stick roughness. What I
can't stand, however, is working with people who give me the creeps.
Now you're laughing, and I'm not surprised, but I can assure you that
I've lain awake at night in my wagon sweating with fear, and I'm by
no means a fanciful chap."

By this time, I was keenly interested.

"Please tell me," I asked, "what it was that frightened you so much."

"That I can't do," he replied, and ordered another drink, "for the
fact is that I, personally, was not treated badly during the tour. The
Brandts were very civil to me—too civil, in fact, for they'd ask me

into their wagon sometimes for a chat between shows, and I hated going—it gave me goose-flesh down my back. Somehow—and you'll laugh again, I know—it was like sitting there talking to two big cats that were just waiting to pounce after they'd finished playing with you. I swear I believed, at the time, that Carl and Lya could see in the dark. Now, of course, that's ridiculous, and I know it, but I still get the creeps when I think about them. I must have been nervy, over-tired, you know, at the time."

I asked whether anyone else at the circus had been similarly affected by the Brandts, and he wrinkled his brows, trying to remember, with obvious distaste, any further details of his tour.

"There's one thing that happened so that all could see," he remarked after a pause, "and that was in a wild part of Rumania, somewhere near the Carpathian Mountains. We were passing through a little village, on our way to a town a few miles distant, and the peasants came flocking out to watch us pass, which was, of course, only natural, for the show is a very fine one. Then, in the village street, a van stuck, and the Brandts came out of their big living-wagon to see what had happened."

"Well?" I asked, for he paused again.

"Well, it was funny, that's all. They scattered like rabbits — rushed into their cottages and banged the doors. The wagon was shoved out of the rut and we went on, but in the next village there was no sign of life, for everything was deserted and the doors were barred. But on each door was nailed a wreath of garlic-flowers."

"Anything else?" I asked, for he had relapsed into silence.

"Oh, one little thing I remembered noticing. The menagerie. The Brandts seldom bother to inspect that part of the show. They're too busy about the ring and the ticket-office. But one day she—Madam Brandt—had to go through the horse-tent and the menagerie to find some agent who was talking to the boys there. It really was a bit odd— the noise was blood-curdling. It was as though the lions and tigers were frightened; not angry, you know, or roaring for their food, but quite a different sort of row. And, when she had gone, the horses were sweating. I felt 'em myself, and it was a chilly day."

"Really," I said, "it's time you came back."

"Oh," he replied, "I don't expect you to believe me. Why should you? I wouldn't have talked if you hadn't asked me about the Circus Brandt. I'd just have said I was glad to be home. But as you asked me . . . oh, well, one day I'll tell you why I left them in France. It's not a pretty story. But I won't tell it tonight. I avoid the Brandts as a bedtime topic — I've been dreaming about them lately."

2

It took me some time to coax the juggler's tale from him. One morning, however, as we were walking along Unter den Linden in pale but radiant spring sunshine he consented to tell it. Translated into English, this is the story:

While the Circus Brandt was touring Northern Africa, when it was in fact only a few days from Tangier, a man arrived asking for work. He was, he said, an Alsatian, and had been a stoker, but his ship had abandoned him at Tangier and he had been seeking a job ever since. This man was interviewed by Carl Brandt himself, who had been accosted by him on the lot. They were a curiously contrasted pair as they stood talking together outside the steps of the Brandt's palatial living-wagon. The Alsatian was fair, a big, handsome young man with thick blond hair, a tanned skin, and honest, rather stupid, blue eyes.

Carl Brandt was tall, too, but emaciated, wasted, and swarthy dark; he had a smooth darting black head like a snake's head; his long face was haggard, and yellow as old ivory; he wore a tiny dark Imperial beard; his black eyes were feverishly alive in heavy purple hollows and his teeth were sharp and broken and rotten. He was said to drug, and indeed he had very much the appearance of an addict. While the two men were talking, the door of the wagon opened and Madam Brandt appeared on the threshold asking her husband what the stranger wanted of him.

She herself was incidentally a remarkably handsome woman, although no longer young. She was powerfully but gracefully made, with quantities of shining blue-black hair, delicate features, oblique, heavy-lidded eyes, and one of those opaque white skins that always look like milk. She had no colour, but was all black and white. Even her lips were pale, not being painted, and her face was heart-shaped against the shadow of her dark hair. She wore white in hot countries and black in the North, but somehow one never noticed that she was not dressed in colours. She seldom looked at the person to whom she was talking, so that when she did it was rather a shock. Her voice was low, and she never showed her teeth, making one imagine that they must be bad, like her husband's.

Both Brandts stayed talking to the Alsatian for about ten minutes in the hot sunshine. It was impossible to eavesdrop, but once the Alsatian was heard reiterating rather warmly that he was a stoker by profession. Finally, however, Carl Brandt took the man off to the head keeper of the menagerie and said that he was to be given work. The Alsatian, for his part, said that his name was Anatole and that he was used to rough jobs. Soon afterward the circus went on toward Tunis.

The new hand, Anatole, was a good-natured, genial, simple fellow who soon became popular not only with the tent-men and grooms but also with the more democratic of the performers, who amused themselves, during the tedium of long "jumps," by making him sing to them, for he had a rich and beautiful voice. Generally, he sang German *lieder* or long-forgotten French music-hall songs, but sometimes he favoured them with snatches of roaring, racy, impudent ballads couched in an argot with which they were every one unfamiliar. On one occasion, before the evening show, when Anatole was shouting one of these coarsely cheerful songs inside the Big Top the flap was suddenly opened to reveal Madam Brandt's pale watchful face in the aperture.

Instantly, although some of the small audience had not seen her, a curious subtle discomfort fell upon the gay party. Anatole, whose back was turned toward the entrance, immediately became aware of some strain or tension among his listeners, and wheeling round, stopped abruptly in the middle of a bar. The little group scrambled awkwardly to its feet.

Madam Brandt murmured in her low voice:

"Don't let me interfere with your concert, my friends. Go on, you"—to Anatole—"that's a lively song you were singing. Where did you pick it up?"

Anatole, standing respectfully before her, was silent. Madam Brandt did not look at him or seem to concern herself with him in any way, but sent her oblique eyes roving over the empty seats of the great tent, yet somehow, in some curious way, it became obvious to her listeners that she was stubbornly determined to drag from him an answer.

Anatole at length muttered:

"I learned the song, Madam, on board a Portuguese fruit-trader many years ago."

Madam Brandt made no sign of having heard him speak.

After this incident, however, she began to employ the odd hand on various jobs about her own living-wagon with the result that he had less time to sing and not much time even for his work in the menagerie. Anatole, good-humoured and jovial as he was, soon conceived a violent dislike of the proprietress which he took no pains to hide from his friends, who were incidentally in hearty agreement with him on this point. Everyone hated the Brandts—many feared them.

The circus crossed to Spain and began to tour Andalusia. Several performers left, new acts were promptly engaged. Carl Brandt had always found it easy to rid himself of artists. Ten minutes before the show was due to open, he would send for some unlucky trapezist and pointing to the man's apparatus, complicated and heavy, slung up to one of the big poles, he would say casually:

"I want you to move that to the other side of the tent before the show."

The artist would perhaps laugh, thinking the director was making some obscure joke.

Brandt would then continue, gently: "You had better hurry, don't you think?"

The artist would protest indignantly. "It's impossible, sir; how can I move my apparatus in ten minutes?"

Brandt would watch him, sneeringly, for a few seconds. Then he would turn away, saying suavely:

"Discharged for insubordination," and walk off to telegraph to his agent for a new act.

Madam Brandt took a curious perverse pleasure in teasing Anatole. She knew that he feared her, and it amused her to send for him, to keep him standing in her wagon while she polished her nails or sewed or wrote letters, utterly indifferent to his presence. After about ten minutes she would look up, glancing at some point above his head, and ask him, in her soft languid voice, if he liked circus life and whether he was happy with them. She would chat for some time, casually asking him searching questions about the other performers; then suddenly she would look direct at him, with a strange brooding stare, while she said:

"Better than tramp ships, isn't it, eh? You are more comfortable here than you were as a stoker, I suppose?"

Sometimes she would add: "Tell me something about a stoker's life, Anatole. What were your duties, and your hours?"

Always, when she dismissed him, his hair was damp with sweat.

The Circus Brandt wandered gradually northward toward the Basque country, until the French border was almost in sight. They were to cut across France into Holland and Belgium, then back again. The Brandts could never stay long anywhere. Just before the circus entered French territory Anatole gave his notice to the head keeper. He was a hard worker and so popular with his mates that the keeper went grumbling to Carl Brandt, who agreed to an increase of salary. Anatole refused to stay on.

Madam Brandt was in the wagon when this news was told to her husband. She said to Carl: "If you want the Alsatian to stay, I will arrange it. Leave it to me. I think I understand the trouble, and, as you say, he is a useful man."

The next day she sent for Anatole, and after ignoring him for about five minutes she asked him listlessly what he meant by leaving them.

Anatole, standing rigid near the door, stammered some awkward apology.

"Why is it?"

"I have—I have had offered me a job."

"Better than this?" she pursued, stitching at her work.

"Yes, Madam."

"Yet," she continued idly, "you were happy with us in Africa, happy in Spain. Why not then in France?"

"Madam—"

She snapped a thread with her teeth. "Why not in France, Anatole?"

There was no reply.

Suddenly she flung her sewing to the ground and fixed him with an unswerving glance. Something leaped into her eyes that startled him, an ugly, naked, hungry look that he had never before seen there. Her eyes burned him, like a devil's eyes. She said, speaking rapidly, scarcely moving her lips:

"I will tell you why you are afraid of France—shall I, Anatole? I have guessed your secret, my friend. . . . You are a deserter from the Foreign Legion and you are afraid of being recaptured. That is it, isn't it? Oh, don't trouble to lie; I have known ever since Africa. It's true, isn't it, what I have said?"

He shook his head, swallowing, unable to speak.

It was a hot day and he wore only a thin shirt. In a second, she sprang from her chair across the wagon and threw herself upon him, tearing at this garment with her fingers. Terrified, he struggled, but she was too quick, too violent, too relentless. The shirt ripped in two and she saw upon his white chest the seam of livid scars.

"Bullet wounds!" she laughed in his ear, "a stoker with bullet-wounds! I was right, wasn't I, Anatole?"

He was conscious, above his fear, of a strange shrinking sensation of repulsion at her proximity. God, he thought, she's after me. And he was sickened, as some people are sickened by the sight of a deadly snake. And then, surprisingly, he was saved.

She darted away from him, sank down in her chair, snatched up her sewing. Her quick ear had heard the footsteps of Carl Brandt. Anatole stood there dazed, clutching the great rent in his shirt. Carl Brandt entered the wagon softly, for he always wore rubber soles to his shoes. His wife addressed him in her low unflurried voice.

"You see Anatole there? He has just been telling me why he is afraid to come with us to France. He is a deserter from the Foreign Legion. Look at the wounds there, on his chest."

Anatole gazed helplessly at the long yellow face of Brandt, who stared at him for some moments in silence.

"A deserter?" Brandt said at length, and chuckled. "A deserter? You needn't be afraid, my lad, to come with us to France. They've something better to do than hunt for obscure escaped legionaries there. Oh, yes, you'll be safe enough. I'll protect you."

And he stood rubbing his hands and staring thoughtfully at Anatole with his gleaming black eyes. Anatole, to escape from them, promised to stay. He had the unpleasant sensation of having faced in the wagon that afternoon not one snake but two. He disliked reptiles.

He meant to bolt, but he had lied to Madam Brandt when he talked of a new job, and he was comfortable where he was. He was, too, an unimaginative creature and the horrors of the Legion now seemed very remote. Soon he was in France, utterly unable to believe that he was in any danger. To his delight his mistress ignored him after the scene in the wagon. She had obviously realized, he thought to himself, that he found her disgusting, almost obscene, in spite of her good looks. And he would have been completely happy had he not known that he had made a dangerous enemy.

3

The Circus Brandt employed as lion-tamer an ex-*matador*, a man named "Captain" da Silva. This individual was not best pleased with his situation. He had lost his nerve about a year before, but after working the same group of lions for ten months he had become more confident and consequently more content. Then, without any warning, Carl Brandt bought a mixed group of animals and told da Silva to start work at once. The tamer was furious. Lions, tigers, bears and leopards!

He shrugged his shoulders and obeyed sulkily. Soon the mixed group was ready for the ring, and appeared for a week with great success.

Then one morning da Silva went to the cages and found his animals in a wild abnormal state. Snarling, bristling, foaming at the mouth, they seemed unable even to recognise their tamer. He stared at them in cold dismay. A comrade, coming to watch, whispered in his ear.

"She walked last night."

Da Silva shuddered. There was a legend in the Circus Brandt that whenever the animals were nervous or upset Lya Brandt, the "she-devil," had walked in her sleep the night before, wandering into the menagerie and terrifying the beasts who presumably knew her for what she was.

The tiger roared, and was answered by the lioness. Da Silva listened for a minute, then turned to his companion.

"I'm off. I wouldn't work these cats tonight for a fortune. There are other circuses in the world. The Circus Brandt must find another tamer."

In twenty minutes' time, he was at the railway station.

Carl Brandt heard the news in silence. Then he raised his arm and struck his head keeper savagely on the mouth. Wrapping his black cloak about his tall thin figure he left the office and sought his own wagon. His wife was engaged in drinking a cup of coffee. They eyed each other in silence for a moment.

Then she said, calmly:

"It's da Silva, I suppose?"

"Da Silva, yes. Already he has gone. Now who will work the mixed group?"

She drained her cup and answered thoughtfully:

"I know of several tamers."

"Probably. And how long will they take to get here?"

"Exactly," she said, pouring out more coffee, "that, I agree, is the great objection. Is there no one on the lot who could work the cats for a week or two?"

"What nonsense are you talking?"

She put her hand over her eyes. "You seem to forget Anatole. An escaped Legionary in French territory. Would he disobey your orders, do you think?"

There was a pause.

"I'll send for him," said Brandt at length.

They were silent as they waited for the Alsatian. When he came in

Lya did not look at him, but began to polish her nails.

Carl Brandt turned his yellow wrinkled face toward Anatole. His eyes were dark and smouldering hollows. He said gently, pleasantly:

"You know that da Silva has left?"

"Yes, sir." Anatole was perplexed. He could not imagine why he had been sent for.

"There is no one, now, to work the animals until a new tamer is engaged."

"No, sir."

"It is not my custom to fail my patrons. I show always what I advertise. The new tamer should be here in a week. It is about this week that I wish to speak."

Another pause. Anatole's heart began to pump against his ribs. A monstrous suspicion was forming in his mind.

Brandt said placidly:

"I am about to promote you, my friend. For a week you shall be tamer and work the mixed group."

Anatole turned dusky red. He was furiously angry, so angry indeed that his fear of the silent woman sitting at the table vanished entirely. No longer conscious of her presence he blurted out violently:

"What, you wish me to go in the cage with those animals? Then you must find someone else; I'm not such a fool. I wouldn't do it for a fortune."

Brandt smiled, showing his black, broken teeth. His wife, utterly indifferent, continued to paint her nails bright red. Brandt said pleasantly:

"Are you perhaps in a position to dictate, my friend? I may be wrong, of course, but I am under the impression that we are now in French territory. *French territory*. Charming words, eh?"

Anatole was silent. He thought suddenly and with horror of the Legion—blistering sun, filth, and brutality. He thought, too, of the salt-mines, that ghastly living death to which he would inevitably be condemned in the event of capture. Then he remembered the animals as he had last seen them, ferocious, maddened, abnormal. He shook his head.

"That's bluff," he said shakily; "I'm no tamer. You can't force me into the cage."

Carl Brandt chuckled. The delicate yellow ivory of his skin seamed itself into a thousand crinkles. He pulled out his watch.

"Five minutes, Anatole, to come with me to the menagerie. Otherwise, I telephone the police. If I may be permitted to advise you, I suggest the menagerie. Even the belly of a lion is preferable, I should imagine, to the African salt-mines. But take your choice."

Madam Brandt, snapping an orange-stick in two, now obtruded herself quietly into the conversation.

"No, Anatole," she said musingly, "it will not be possible to run away in the night. The Herr Director will take trouble, great trouble, to have you traced. The Herr Director has no wish to shelter criminals."

Once again she looked directly at him, fixing him with the burning and threatening glance that was like a sword. Then she dropped her eyes, absorbed in her manicure.

A pause.

Brandt glanced at his watch.

"I must remind you, Anatole, that you have only two minutes left," he said with an air of great courtesy. "How many years did you serve in the Legion, I wonder? And is it eight years in the salt-mines for deserters or perhaps more?"

"I'll work the animals," said Anatole shortly. He knew that Lya Brandt had read his thoughts, and he wiped the sweat from his face as he went toward the menagerie. It was not possible for the mixed group to appear at the matinee, but it was announced to the circus in general that the cats would work that night without fail. Anatole was to spend the afternoon rehearsing them.

His face was grey as he shut himself in the cage armed only with a tamer's switch. Outside the bars stood two keepers with loaded revolvers. They, too, were nervous. The animals stood motionless to stare at the stranger, hackles raised, restless yellow eyes fixed upon him. Around the cage were painted wooden pedestals, upon which the animals were trained to sit at the word of command. The Alsatian now gave that command. They took no notice. He repeated it louder, slapping the bars with his switch, and they scattered, in a sudden panic, to take up their accustomed seats.

He pulled out the paper hoop through which the lions must jump. They snarled for several minutes, striking out with their savage paws; then, in the end, possibly deciding that obedience was less trouble, they bounded through the hoop with an ill grace. The two keepers, and Anatole as well, were soon streaming with perspiration as though they had been plunged into water. The Alsatian was now, however, more confident. He turned to the bears.

Twenty minutes later Carl Brandt rejoined his wife in the living-wagon. She was standing near the window with her back toward him.

"Better than I expected," said the director coolly. "I see no reason why things should not go well tonight. He has courage, this Legionary! And what good fortune that we are in France!"

Madam Brandt made no reply, nor did she turn her head. She seemed utterly indifferent to the affairs of Anatole.

That evening the Alsatian was supplied with a splendid sky-blue uniform and cherry-coloured breeches from the circus wardrobe. He dressed himself mechanically, taking no notice of the dresser's encouragements. Out on the lot his comrades glanced at him sympathetically. One or two, unconscious of his antecedents, warned him to defy Brandt and keep out of the cage. Anatole merely shook his head, incapable of giving an explanation.

"I must go; it is useless to warn me," he said at length.

And the circus folk were unanimous in their bitter abuse of the Brandts.

It was dusk. The bandsmen, splendid in their green and gold uniforms, played the overture inside the huge tent. A group of clowns, glittering in brilliant spangles, stood waiting to make their comic entry. Behind the clowns, six or seven grooms controlled twenty milk-white Arab stallions with fleecy white manes and tails. These horses were magnificent in scarlet trappings. The Chinese troupe, dark kimonos over gorgeous brocade robes, diligently practised near the bears' cage. Anatole sat on a bale of hay near the tigers, deaf to the advice muttered in his ear by various comrades. The circus proceeded.

Up in the dome of the tent two muscular young men in peach-coloured tights flung themselves from bar to bar with thrilling grace and swiftness. Down below the attendants rapidly constructed a vast cage, staggering beneath sections of heavy iron bars. Soon the cage was ready; the aerialists had swung themselves down from the dome. The band crashed out a chord, and Anatole, the Legionary, stepped into the cage, bowing modestly in response to the applause which greeted his spectacular entrance. Then an iron door was slid aside and down the narrow tunnel crept a file of tawny shapes.

Lions, tigers, leopards, bears. Gracefully they padded into the arena, stretching themselves, rubbing against the bars of the cage, yawning at the bright lights, showing their teeth, slinking with a catlike agility about the ring.

Gripping his switch, Anatole uttered the first command. One minute later the animals were seated with a certain docility upon their wooden pedestals. Anatole produced his hoop. At first the people of the circus held their breath; then, gradually, as five minutes passed, they relaxed. He was doing well. They sighed with relief. The climax of the art was a tableau during the course of which the animals grouped themselves, standing erect on their hind legs, about the trainer, who himself sprang upon a pedestal, arm upraised to give more effect to this subjugation of the beasts. The biggest tiger lay at his feet during the tableau, and while the other animals soon assumed their accustomed positions when ordered, the tiger was at first always unwilling to fling himself upon the sawdust.

Posing the lions and leopards, Anatole, one foot on the pedestal, spoke briskly, curtly, to the great beast, which stared at him sulkily, motionless save for the twitching of its tail. A second passed, seeming longer than a minute to the circus watchers. The tiger continued to stare, and Anatole, banging at the bars with his switch, pointed stubbornly at the ground at his feet.

His back was toward the ring entrance and he did not see the grooms and attendants draw back respectfully to allow someone to pass through the red velvet curtains. His comrades did, and nudged one another, for Madam Brandt seldom came near the arena during a performance. She stood for a moment near the curtains, tall and straight in her flowing white dress, her face pale against the dense blackness of her hair.

Then, suddenly, there was tumult in the peaceful cage as, snarling furiously, the animals leaped from their pedestals to dash themselves savagely against the bars. Caught by surprise, Anatole turned, slashing with his switch, shouting, oblivious of the sullen tiger behind him. A leopard, maddened with fright, collided against him and sent him stumbling to the ground. With the fierce swiftness of a mighty hawk the great tiger sprang. A thick choking growl that made the blood run cold, yells of terror from the crowd and then the crack of two revolver shots. Armed with hose-pipes the menagerie men drove the animals back. The tiger was wounded in the shoulder and clawed the ground, biting at itself in a frenzy of fear and pain.

Anatole lay doubled up on the sawdust looking like a rag-dummy, so limp and twisted was his body. On the bright blue of his uniform oozed a clotted stream of red. His face? Anatole had no longer a face; only a huge and raw and gaping wound. Opening a side door, they dragged his body from the cage and swiftly wrapped it in the gorgeous coat of a Chinese acrobat standing nearby. Screaming, weeping, cursing, the horrified audience fought, struggling and stampeding to leave the tent. In the noise and tumult Madam Brandt slipped through the red velvet curtains and vanished like a white shadow.

Pale-faced, haggard, the bandsmen were ordered to play their most cheerful march. Soon the tent was empty, save for a little group of brightly-clad people bending over the huddled shape that was Anatole and for a doctor, hastily summoned, who soon went away, for there was nothing for him to do.

That night the body was laid temporarily in a little canvas dressing-room belonging to the clowns. It was late before the show-people retired to bed, but by one o'clock in the morning all was still in the tent-town of Brandt's Circus. Only the night watchman, a stolid, un-imaginative fellow, paced slowly up and down swinging his lantern, but from time to time a lion would whimper and growl in the silence of the night, or a horse kick impatiently against the wooden partition of its stall.

It was the watchman, however, who afterward related to his com-rades what he saw during this lonely vigil. . . . It was about an hour before dawn, and the man was lolling on a heap of hay, relieved, no doubt, to think the night would soon be over, when all at once his quick ear caught the soft sound of approaching footsteps. He turned, hiding his lantern beneath his coat. It was Madam Brandt, of course, walking slowly, like a sleepwalker, across the deserted arena toward the dressing-rooms, seeming no more tangible than a shadow, a white shadow that gleamed for a moment in the darkness and then was gone, swallowed by the gloom of the night. Now the watchman was a brave fellow, and inclined to be inquisitive. He slipped off his shoes and crept after her.

Madam Brandt glided straight to the little dressing-room wherein lay the mangled body of the Legionary. The watchman had not dared to bring his lantern, and it was therefore difficult for him to see what was happening, but at the same time he managed to observe quite enough. He glimpsed her white figure kneeling down near the dark shape on the floor; as he watched she struggled with some drapery or other, and he saw that she was trying to drag away the sheet that cov-ered the corpse; having apparently achieved her purpose she remained still for a moment, staring at what she saw; this immobility, which lasted only for a second, was succeeded by a sudden revulsion of feel-ing more horrible than anything that had gone before, for with all the ferocity of a starving animal she flung herself upon the body, shaking it, gripping it tight to steady its leaden weight, while she thrust her face, her mouth, down upon that torn and bleeding throat . . . then in the distant menagerie the lions and tigers broke the silence of the night with sudden tumult.

★★★★★★★★★★★★★★★★★

"Yes," said the juggler after a long pause, "we liked Anatole. He was a good comrade, although, mind you, he had probably been a murderer and most certainly a thief. But in the Circus Brandt, you know, that means nothing at all."

"Where is the Circus Brandt now?" I asked, after another pause.

He shrugged his shoulders.

"Poland, I think; or possibly Peru. How can I tell? The Brandts are gipsies, nomads. Here today, gone tomorrow. Possibly they travel fast because there is always something to hush up. But who can say? The devil has an admirable habit of looking after his friends."

I was silent, for I was thinking both of Lya Brandt and Anatole. Suddenly I felt rather sick. "Look here," I said, "do you mind if we don't talk any more about the Brandt Circus for the moment?"

Let Loose

Mary Cholmondeley

The dead abide with us! Though stark and cold
Earth seems to grip them, they are with us still.

Some years ago, I took up architecture, and made a tour through
Holland, studying the buildings of that interesting country. I was not
then aware that it is not enough to take up art. Art must take you up,
too. I never doubted but that my passing enthusiasm for her would be
returned. When I discovered that she was a stern mistress, who did not
immediately respond to my attentions, I naturally transferred them to
another shrine. There are other things in the world besides art. I am
now a landscape gardener.

But at the time of which I write I was engaged in a violent flirtation with architecture. I had one companion on this expedition, who
has since become one of the leading architects of the day. He was
a thin, determined-looking man with a screwed-up face and heavy
jaw, slow of speech, and absorbed in his work to a degree which I
quickly found tiresome. He was possessed of a certain quiet power of
overcoming obstacles which I have rarely seen equalled. He has since
become my brother-in-law, so I ought to know; for my parents did
not like him much and opposed the marriage, and my sister did not
like him at all, and refused him over and over again; but, nevertheless,
he eventually married her.

I have thought since that one of his reasons for choosing me as his
travelling companion on this occasion was because he was getting up
steam for what he subsequently termed 'an alliance with my family',
but the idea never entered my head at the time. A more careless man
as to dress I have rarely met, and yet, in all the heat of July in Holland,
I noticed that he never appeared without a high, starched collar, which

had not even fashion to commend it at that time.

I often chaffed him about his splendid collars, and asked him why he wore them, but without eliciting any response. One evening, as we were walking back to our lodgings in Middeburg, I attacked him for about the thirtieth time on the subject.

'Why on earth do you wear them?' I said.

'You have, I believe, asked me that question many times,' he replied, in his slow, precise utterance; 'but always on occasions when I was occupied. I am now at leisure, and I will tell you.'

And he did.

I have put down what he said, as nearly in his own words as I can remember them.

Ten years ago, I was asked to read a paper on English Frescoes at the Institute of British Architects. I was determined to make the paper as good as I could, down to the slightest details, and I consulted many books on the subject, and studied every fresco I could find. My father, who had been an architect, had left me, at his death, all his papers and note-books on the subject of architecture. I searched them diligently, and found in one of them a slight unfinished sketch of nearly fifty years ago that specially interested me. Underneath was noted, in his clear, small hand—Frescoed east wall of crypt. Parish Church. Wet Waste-on-the-Wolds, Yorkshire (*via* Pickering).

The sketch had such a fascination for me that I decided to go there and see the fresco for myself. I had only a very vague idea as to where Wet Waste-on-the-Wolds was, but I was ambitious for the success of my paper; it was hot in London, and I set off on my long journey not without a certain degree of pleasure, with my dog Brian, a large non-descript brindled creature, as my only companion.

I reached Pickering, in Yorkshire, in the course of the afternoon, and then began a series of experiments on local lines which ended, after several hours, in my finding myself deposited at a little out-of-the-world station within nine or ten miles of Wet Waste. As no conveyance of any kind was to be had, I shouldered my portmanteau, and set out on a long white road that stretched away into the distance over the bare, treeless wold. I must have walked for several hours, over a waste of moorland patched with heather, when a doctor passed me, and gave me a lift to within a mile of my destination. The mile was a long one, and it was quite dark by the time I saw the feeble glimmer of lights in front of me, and found that I had reached Wet Waste. I had considerable difficulty in getting any one to take me in; but at last I persuaded the owner of the public-house to give me a bed, and, quite tired out, I got into it as soon as possible, for fear he should change his mind, and fell asleep to the sound of a little stream below my window.

I was up early next morning, and inquired directly after breakfast the way to the clergyman's house, which I found was close at hand. At Wet Waste everything was close at hand. The whole village seemed composed of a straggling row of one-storeyed grey stone houses, the same colour as the stone walls that separated the few fields enclosed from the surrounding waste, and as the little bridges over the beck that ran down one side of the grey wide street. Everything was grey.

The church, the low tower of which I could see at a little distance, seemed to have been built of the same stone; so was the parsonage when I came up to it, accompanied on my way by a mob of rough, uncouth children, who eyed me and Brian with half-defiant curiosity.

The clergyman was at home, and after a short delay I was admitted. Leaving Brian in charge of my drawing materials, I followed the serv-ant into a low panelled room, in which, at a latticed window, a very old man was sitting. The morning light fell on his white head bent low over a litter of papers and books.

'Mr er—?' he said, looking up slowly, with one finger keeping his place in a book.

'Blake.'

'Blake,' he repeated after me, and was silent.

I told him that I was an architect; that I had come to study a fresco in the crypt of his church, and asked for the keys.

'The crypt,' he said, pushing up his spectacles and peering hard at me. 'The crypt has been closed for thirty years. Ever since—' and he stopped short.

'I should be much obliged for the keys,' I said again.

He shook his head.

'No,' he said. 'No one goes in there now.'

'It is a pity,' I remarked, 'for I have come a long way with that one object'; and I told him about the paper I had been asked to read, and the trouble I was taking with it.

He became interested. 'Ah!' he said, laying down his pen, and re-moving his finger from the page before him, 'I can understand that. I also was young once, and fired with ambition. The lines have fallen to me in somewhat lonely places, and for forty years I have held the cure of souls in this place, where, truly, I have seen but little of the world, though I myself may be not unknown in the paths of literature. Possibly you may have read a pamphlet, written by myself, on the Syrian version of the Three Authentic Epistles of Ignatius?'

'Sir,' I said, 'I am ashamed to confess that I have not time to read even the most celebrated books. My one object in life is my art. *Ars longa, vita brevis*, you know.'

'You are right, my son,' said the old man, evidently disappointed, but looking at me kindly.

'There are diversities of gifts, and if the Lord has entrusted you with a talent, look to it. Lay it not up in a napkin.'

I said I would not do so if he would lend me the keys of the crypt. He seemed startled by my recurrence to the subject and looked undecided.

'Why not?' he murmured to himself. 'The youth appears a good youth. And superstition! What is it but distrust in God!'

He got up slowly, and taking a large bunch of keys out of his pocket, opened with one of them an oak cupboard in the corner of the room.

'They should be here,' he muttered, peering in; 'but the dust of many years deceives the eye.

See, my son, if among these parchments there be two keys; one of iron and very large, and the other steel, and of a long thin appearance.'

I went eagerly to help him, and presently found in a back drawer two keys tied together, which he recognised at once.

'Those are they,' he said. 'The long one opens the first door at the bottom of the steps which go down against the outside wall of the church hard by the sword graven in the wall. The second opens (but it is hard of opening and of shutting) the iron door within the passage leading to the crypt itself. My son, is it necessary to your treatise that you should enter this crypt?'

I replied that it was absolutely necessary.

'Then take them,' he said, 'and in the evening you will bring them to me again.'

I said I might want to go several days running, and asked if he would not allow me to keep them till I had finished my work; but on that point he was firm.

'Likewise,' he added, 'be careful that you lock the first door at the foot of the steps before you unlock the second, and lock the second also while you are within. Furthermore, when you come out lock the iron inner door as well as the wooden one.'

I promised I would do so, and, after thanking him, hurried away, delighted at my success in obtaining the keys. Finding Brian and my sketching materials waiting for me in the porch, I eluded the vigilance of my escort of children by taking the narrow private path between the parsonage and the church which was close at hand, standing in a quadrangle of ancient yews.

The church itself was interesting, and I noticed that it must have arisen out of the ruins of a previous building, judging from the number of fragments of stone caps and arches, bearing traces of very early carving, now built into the walls. There were incised crosses, too, in some places, and one especially caught my attention, being flanked by a large sword. It was in trying to get a nearer look at this that I stumbled, and, looking down, saw at my feet a flight of narrow stone steps green with moss and mildew. Evidently this was the entrance to the crypt. I at once descended the steps, taking care of my footing, for they were damp and slippery in the extreme.

Brian accompanied me, as nothing would induce him to remain behind. By the time I had reached the bottom of the stairs, I found myself almost in darkness, and I had to strike a light before I could find the keyhole and the proper key to fit into it. The door, which was of wood, opened inwards fairly easily, although an accumulation of mould and rubbish on the ground outside showed it had not been used for many years. Having got through it, which was not altogether an easy matter, as nothing would induce it to open more than about eighteen inches, I carefully locked it behind me, although I should have preferred to leave it open, as there is to some minds an unpleasant feeling in being locked in anywhere, in case of a sudden exit seeming advisable.

I kept my candle alight with some difficulty, and after groping my way down a low and of course exceedingly dank passage, came to another door. A toad was squatting against it, who looked as if he had been sitting there about a hundred years. As I lowered the candle to the floor, he gazed at the light with unblinking eyes, and then retreated slowly into a crevice in the wall, leaving against the door a small cavity in the dry mud which had gradually silted up round his person. I noticed that this door was of iron, and had a long bolt, which, however, was broken.

Without delay, I fitted the second key into the lock, and pushing the door open after considerable difficulty, I felt the cold breath of the crypt upon my face. I must own I experienced a momentary regret at locking the second door again as soon as I was well inside, but I felt it my duty to do so. Then, leaving the key in the lock, I seized my candle and looked round. I was standing in a low vaulted chamber with groined roof, cut out of the solid rock. It was difficult to see where the crypt ended, as further light thrown on any point only showed other rough archways or openings, cut in the rock, which had probably served at one time for family vaults.

A peculiarity of the Wet Waste crypt, which I had not noticed in other places of that description, was the tasteful arrangement of skulls and bones which were packed about four feet high on either side. The skulls were symmetrically built up to within a few inches of the top of the low archway on my left, and the shin bones were arranged in the same manner on my right. But the fresco! I looked round for it in vain. Perceiving at the further end of the crypt a very low and very massive archway, the entrance to which was not filled up with bones, I passed under it, and found myself in a second smaller chamber. Holding my candle above my head, the first object its light fell upon was— the fresco, and at a glance I saw that it was unique.

Setting down some of my things with a trembling hand on a rough stone shelf hard by, which had evidently been a credence table, I examined the work more closely. It was a reredos over what had probably been the altar at the time the priests were proscribed. The fresco belonged to the earliest part of the fifteenth century, and was so perfectly preserved that I could almost trace the limits of each day's work in the plaster, as the artist had dashed it on and smoothed it out with his trowel. The subject was the Ascension, gloriously treated. I can hardly describe my elation as I stood and looked at it, and reflected that this magnificent specimen of English fresco painting would be made known to the world by myself. Recollecting myself at last, I opened my sketching bag, and, lighting all the candles I had brought with me, set to work.

Brian walked about near me, and though I was not otherwise than glad of his company in my rather lonely position, I wished several times I had left him behind. He seemed restless, and even the sight of so many bones appeared to exercise no soothing effect upon him. At last, however, after repeated commands, he lay down, watchful but motionless, on the stone floor.

I must have worked for several hours, and I was pausing to rest my eyes and hands, when I noticed for the first time the intense stillness that surrounded me. No sound from me reached the outer world. The church clock which had clanged out so loud and ponderously as I went down the steps, had not since sent the faintest whisper of its iron tongue down to me below. All was silent as the grave. This was the grave. Those who had come here had indeed gone down into silence. I repeated the words to myself, or rather they repeated themselves to me.

Gone down into silence.

I was awakened from my reverie by a faint sound. I sat still and listened. Bats occasionally frequent vaults and underground places.

The sound continued, a faint, stealthy, rather unpleasant sound. I do not know what kinds of sounds bats make, whether pleasant or otherwise. Suddenly there was a noise as of something falling, a momentary pause—and then—an almost imperceptible but distant jangle as of a key.

I had left the key in the lock after I had turned it, and I now regretted having done so. I got up, took one of the candles, and went back into the larger crypt—for though I trust I am not so effeminate as to be rendered nervous by hearing a noise for which I cannot instantly account; still, on occasions of this kind, I must honestly say I should prefer that they did not occur. As I came towards the iron door, there was another distinct (I had almost said hurried) sound. The impression on my mind was one of great haste. When I reached the door, and held the candle near the lock to take out the key, I perceived that the other one, which hung by a short string to its fellow, was vibrating slightly. I should have preferred not to find it vibrating, as there seemed no occasion for such a course; but I put them both into my pocket, and turned to go back to my work.

As I turned, I saw on the ground what had occasioned the louder noise I had heard, namely, a skull which had evidently just slipped from its place on the top of one of the walls of bones, and had rolled almost to my feet. There, disclosing a few more inches of the top of an archway behind, was the place from which it had been dislodged. I stooped to pick it up, but fearing to displace any more skulls by meddling with the pile, and not liking to gather up its scattered teeth, I let it lie, and went back to my work, in which I was soon so completely absorbed that I was only roused at last by my candles beginning to burn low and go out one after another.

Then, with a sigh of regret, for I had not nearly finished, I turned to go. Poor Brian, who had never quite reconciled himself to the place, was beside himself with delight. As I opened the iron door he pushed past me, and a moment later I heard him whining and scratching, and I had almost added, beating, against the wooden one. I locked the iron door, and hurried down the passage as quickly as I could, and almost before I had got the other one ajar there seemed to be a rush past me into the open air, and Brian was bounding up the steps and out of sight. As I stopped to take out the key, I felt quite deserted and left behind. When I came out once more into the sunlight, there was a vague sensation all about me in the air of exultant freedom.

It was already late in the afternoon, and after I had sauntered back to the parsonage to give up the keys, I persuaded the people of the public-house to let me join in the family meal, which was spread out in the kitchen. The inhabitants of Wet Waste were primitive people, with the frank, unabashed manner that flourishes still in lonely places, especially in the wilds of Yorkshire; but I had no idea that in these days of penny posts and cheap newspapers such entire ignorance of the outer world could have existed in any corner, however remote, of Great Britain.

When I took one of the neighbour's children on my knee—a pretty little girl with the palest aureole of flaxen hair I had ever seen—and began to draw pictures for her of the birds and beasts of other countries, I was instantly surrounded by a crowd of children, and even grown-up people, while others came to their doorways and looked on from a distance, calling to each other in the strident unknown tongue which I have since discovered goes by the name of 'Broad Yorkshire'.

The following morning, as I came out of my room, I perceived that something was amiss in the village. A buzz of voices reached me as I passed the bar, and in the next house I could hear through the open window a high-pitched wail of lamentation.

The woman who brought me my breakfast was in tears, and in answer to my questions, told me that the neighbour's child, the little girl whom I had taken on my knee the evening before, had died in the night.

I felt sorry for the general grief that the little creature's death seemed to arouse, and the uncontrolled wailing of the poor mother took my appetite away.

I hurried off early to my work, calling on my way for the keys, and with Brian for my companion descended once more into the crypt, and drew and measured with an absorption that gave me no time that day to listen for sounds real or fancied. Brian, too, on this occasion seemed quite content, and slept peacefully beside me on the stone floor. When I had worked as long as I could, I put away my books with regret that even then I had not quite finished, as I had hoped to do. It would be necessary to come again for a short time on the morrow. When I returned the keys late that afternoon, the old clergyman met me at the door, and asked me to come in and have tea with him.

'And has the work prospered?' he asked, as we sat down in the long, low room, into which I had just been ushered, and where he seemed to live entirely.

I told him it had, and showed it to him.

'You have seen the original, of course?' I said.

'Once,' he replied, gazing fixedly at it. He evidently did not care to be communicative, so I turned the conversation to the age of the church.

'All here is old,' he said. 'When I was young, forty years ago, and came here because I had no means of mine own, and was much moved to marry at that time, I felt oppressed that all was so old; and that this place was so far removed from the world, for which I had at times longings grievous to be borne; but I had chosen my lot, and with it I was forced to be content. My son, marry not in youth, for love, which truly in that season is a mighty power, turns away the heart from study, and young children break the back of ambition. Neither marry in middle life, when a woman is seen to be but a woman and her talk a weariness, so you will not be burdened with a wife in your old age.

I had my own views on the subject of marriage, for I am of opinion that a well-chosen companion of domestic tastes and docile and devoted temperament may be of material assistance to a professional man. But my opinions once formulated, it is not of moment to me to discuss them with others, so I changed the subject, and asked if the neighbouring villages were as antiquated as Wet Waste 'Yes, all about here is old,' he repeated. 'The paved road leading to Dyke Fens is an ancient pack road, made even in the time of the Romans. Dyke Fens, which is very near here, a matter of but four or five miles, is likewise old, and forgotten by the world.

'The Reformation never reached it. It stopped here. And at Dyke Fens they still have a priest and a bell, and bow down before the saints. It is a damnable heresy, and weekly I expound it as such to my people, showing them true doctrines; and I have heard that this same priest has so far yielded himself to the Evil One that he has preached against me as withholding gospel truths from my flock; but I take no heed of it, neither of his pamphlet touching the Clementine Homilies, in which he vainly contradicts that which I have plainly set forth and proven beyond doubt, concerning the word Asaph.'

The old man was fairly off on his favourite subject, and it was some time before I could get away. As it was, he followed me to the door, and I only escaped because the old clerk hobbled up at that moment, and claimed his attention.

The following morning, I went for the keys for the third and last time. I had decided to leave early the next day. I was tired of Wet Waste, and a certain gloom seemed to my fancy to be gathering over the place. There was a sensation of trouble in the air, as if, although the day was bright and clear, a storm were coming.

This morning, to my astonishment, the keys were refused to me when I asked for them. I did not, however, take the refusal as, final—I make it a rule never to take a refusal as final—and after a short delay I was shown into the room where, as usual, the clergyman was sitting, or rather, on this occasion, was walking up and down.

'My son,' he said with vehemence, 'I know wherefore you have come, but it is of no avail. I cannot lend the keys again.'

I replied that, on the contrary, I hoped he would give them to me at once.

'It is impossible,' he repeated. 'I did wrong, exceeding wrong. I will never part with them again.'

'Why not?'

He hesitated, and then said slowly:

'The old clerk, Abraham Kelly, died last night.' He paused, and then went on: 'The doctor has just been here to tell me of that which is a mystery to him. I do not wish the people of the place to know it, and only to me he has mentioned it, but he has discovered plainly on the throat of the old man, and also, but more faintly on the child's, marks as of strangulation. None but he has observed it, and he is at a loss how to account for it. I, alas! can account for it but in one way, but in one way!'

I did not see what all this had to do with the crypt, but to humour the old man, I asked what that way was.

'It is a long story, and, haply, to a stranger it may appear but foolishness, but I will even tell it; for I perceive that unless I furnish a reason for withholding the keys, you will not cease to entreat me for them.

'I told you at first when you inquired of me concerning the crypt, that it had been closed these thirty years, and so it was. Thirty years ago, a certain Sir Roger Despard departed this life, even the Lord of the manor of Wet Waste and Dyke Fens, the last of his family, which is now, thank the Lord, extinct. He was a man of a vile life, neither fearing God nor regarding man, nor having compassion on innocence, and the Lord appeared to have given him over to the tormentors even in this world, for he suffered many things of his vices, more especially from drunkenness, in which seasons, and they were many, he was as one possessed by seven devils, being an abomination to his household and a root of bitterness to all, both high and low.

'And, at last, the cup of his iniquity being full to the brim, he came to die, and I went to exhort him on his deathbed; for I heard that terror had come upon him, and that evil imaginations encompassed him so thick on every side, that few of them that were with him could abide in his presence. But when I saw him, I perceived that there was no place of repentance left for him, and he scoffed at me and my superstition, even as he lay dying, and swore there was no God and no angel, and all were damned even as he was. And the next day, towards evening, the pains of death came upon him, and he raved the more exceedingly, inasmuch as he said he was being strangled by the Evil One.

'Now on his table was his hunting knife, and with his last strength he crept and laid hold upon it, no man withstanding him, and swore a great oath that if he went down to burn in hell, he would leave one of his hands behind on earth, and that it would never rest until it had drawn blood from the throat of another and strangled him, even as he himself was being strangled. And he cut off his own right hand at the wrist, and no man dared go near him to stop him, and the blood went through the floor, even down to the ceiling of the room below, and thereupon he died.

'And they called me in the night, and told me of his oath, and I for I thought it better he should take it with him, so that he might have it, I counselled that no man should speak of it, and I took the dead hand, which none had ventured to touch, and I laid it beside him in his coffin; if haply some day after much tribulation he should perchance be moved to stretch forth his hands towards God. But the story got spread about, and the people were affrighted, so, when he came to be buried in the place of his fathers, he being the last of his family, and the crypt likewise full, I had it closed, and kept the keys myself, and suffered no man to enter therein anymore; for truly he was a man of an evil life, and the devil is not yet wholly overcome, nor cast chained into the lake of fire.

'So, in time the story died out, for in thirty years much is forgotten. And when you came and asked me for the keys, I was at the first minded to withhold them; but I thought it was a vain superstition, and I perceived that you do but ask a second time for what is first refused;

so I let you have them, seeing it was not an idle curiosity, but a desire to improve the talent committed to you, that led you to require them.'

The old man stopped, and I remained silent, wondering what would be the best way to get them just once more.

'Surely, sir,' I said at last, 'one so cultivated and deeply read as yourself cannot be biased by an idle superstition.'

'I trust not,' he replied, 'and yet—it is a strange thing that since the crypt was opened two people have died, and the mark is plain upon the throat of the old man and visible on the young child. No blood was drawn, but the second time the grip was stronger than the first. The third time, perchance—'

'Superstition such as that,' I said with authority, 'is an entire want of faith in God. You once said so yourself.'

I took a high moral tone which is often efficacious with conscientious, humble-minded people.

He agreed, and accused himself of not having faith as a grain of mustard seed; but even when I had got him so far as that, I had a severe struggle for the keys. It was only when I finally explained to him that if any malign influence had been let loose the first day, at any rate, it was out now for good or evil, and no further going or coming of mine could make any difference, that I finally gained my point. I was young, and he was old; and, being much shaken by what had occurred, he gave way at last, and I wrested the keys from him.

I will not deny that I went down the steps that day with a vague, indefinable repugnance, which was only accentuated by the closing of the two doors behind me. I remembered then, for the first time, the faint jangling of the key and other sounds which I had noticed the first day, and how one of the skulls had fallen. I went to the place where it still lay. I have already said these walls of skulls were built up so high as to be within a few inches of the top of the low archways that led into more distant portions of the vault. The displacement of the skull in question had left a small hole just large enough for me to put my hand through.

I noticed for the first time, over the archway above it, a carved coat-of-arms, and the name, now almost obliterated, of Despard. This, no doubt, was the Despard vault. I could not resist moving a few more skulls and looking in, holding my candle as near the aperture as I could. The vault was full. Piled high, one upon another, were old coffins, and remnants of coffins, and strewn bones. I attribute my present determination to be cremated to the painful impression produced on me by this spectacle. The coffin nearest the archway alone was intact, save for a large crack across the lid. I could not get a ray from my candle to fall on the brass plates, but I felt no doubt this was the coffin of the wicked Sir Roger. I put back the skulls, including the one which had rolled down, and carefully finished my work. I was not there much more than an hour, but I was glad to get away.

If I could have left Wet Waste at once I should have done so, for I had a totally unreasonable longing to leave the place; but I found that only one train stopped during the day at the station from which I had come, and that it would not be possible to be in time for it that day.

Accordingly, I submitted to the inevitable, and wandered about with Brian for the remainder of the afternoon and until late in the evening, sketching and smoking. The day was oppressively hot, and even after the sun had set across the burnt stretches of the Wolds, it seemed to grow very little cooler. Not a breath stirred. In the evening, when I was tired of loitering in the lanes, I went up to my own room, and after contemplating afresh my finished study of the fresco, I suddenly set to work to write the part of my paper bearing upon it. As a rule, I write with difficulty, but that evening words came to me with winged speed, and with them a hovering impression that I must make haste, that I was much pressed for time. I wrote and wrote, until my candles guttered out and left me trying to finish by the moonlight, which, until I endeavoured to write by it, seemed as clear as day.

I had to put away my MS., and, feeling it was too early to go to bed, for the church clock was just counting out ten, I sat down by the open window and leaned out to try and catch a breath of air. It was a night of exceptional beauty; and as I looked out my nervous haste and hurry of mind were allayed. The moon, a perfect circle, was—if so poetic an expression be permissible—as it were, sailing across a calm sky. Every detail of the little village was as clearly illuminated by its beams as if it were broad day; so, also, was the adjacent church with its primeval yews, while even the Wolds beyond were dimly indicated, as if through tracing paper.

I sat a long time leaning against the window-sill. The heat was still intense. I am not, as a rule, easily elated or readily cast down; but as I sat that light in the lonely village on the moors, with Brian's head against my knee, how, or why, I know not, a great depression gradually came upon me.

My mind went back to the crypt and the countless dead who had been laid there. The sight of the goal to which all human life, and strength, and beauty, travel in the end, had not affected me at the time, but now the very air about me seemed heavy with death.

What was the good, I asked myself, of working and toiling, and grinding down my heart and youth in the mill of long and strenuous effort, seeing that in the grave folly and talent, idleness and labour lie together, and are alike forgotten? Labour seemed to stretch before me till my heart ached to think of it, to stretch before me even to the end of life, and then came, as the recompense of my labour—the grave. Even if I succeeded, if, after wearing my life threadbare with toil, I succeeded, what remained to me in the end? The grave. A little sooner, while the hands and eyes were still strong to labour, or a little later, when all power and vision had been taken from them; sooner or later only—the grave.

I do not apologise for the excessively morbid tenor of these reflections, as I hold that they were caused by the lunar effects which I have endeavoured to transcribe. The moon in its various quarterings has always exerted a marked influence on what I may call the subdominant, namely, the poetic side of my nature.

I roused myself at last, when the moon came to look in upon me where I sat, and, leaving the window open, I pulled myself together and went to bed.

I fell asleep almost immediately, but I do not fancy I could have been asleep very long when I was wakened by Brian. He was growling in a low, muffled tone, as he sometimes did in his sleep, when his nose was buried in his rug. I called out to him to shut up; and as he did not do so, turned in bed to find my match box or something to throw at him. The moonlight was still in the room, and as I looked at him, I saw him raise his head and evidently wake up. I admonished him, and was just on the point of falling asleep when he began to growl again in a low, savage manner that waked me most effectually.

Presently he shook himself and got up, and began prowling about the room. I sat up in bed and called to him, but he paid no attention. Suddenly I saw him stop short in the moonlight; he showed his teeth, and crouched down, his eyes following something in the air. I looked at him in horror. Was he going mad? His eyes were glaring, and his head moved slightly as if he were following the rapid movements of an enemy.

Then, with a furious snarl, he suddenly sprang from the ground, and rushed in great leaps across the room towards me, dashing himself against the furniture, his eyes rolling, snatching and tearing wildly in the air with his teeth. I saw he had gone mad. I leaped out of bed, and rushing at him, caught him by the throat. The moon had gone behind a cloud; but in the darkness I felt him turn upon me, felt him rise up, and his teeth close in my throat. I was being strangled. With all the strength of despair, I kept my grip of his neck, and, dragging him across the room, tried to crush in his head against the iron rail of my bedstead. It was my only chance. I felt the blood running down my neck. I was suffocating. After one moment of frightful struggle, I beat his head against the bar and heard his skull give way. I felt him give one strong shudder, a groan, and then I fainted away.

When I came to myself, I was lying on the floor, surrounded by the people of the house, my reddened hands still clutching Brian's throat. Someone was holding a candle towards me, and the draught from the window made it flare and waver. I looked at Brian. He was stone dead. The blood from his battered head was trickling slowly over my hands. His great jaw was fixed in something that—in the uncertain light—I could not see.

They turned the light a little.

'Oh, God!' I shrieked. 'There! Look! Look!'

'He's off his head,' said someone, and I fainted again.

I was ill for about a fortnight without regaining consciousness, a waste of time of which even now I cannot think without poignant regret. When I did recover consciousness, I found I was being carefully nursed by the old clergyman and the people of the house. I have often heard the unkindness of the world in general inveighed against, but for my part I can honestly say that I have received many more kindnesses than I have time to repay. Country people especially are remarkably attentive to strangers in illness.

I could not rest until I had seen the doctor who attended me, and had received his assurance that I should be equal to reading my paper on the appointed day. This pressing anxiety removed, I told him of what I had seen before I fainted the second time. He listened attentively, and then assured me, in a manner that was intended to be soothing, that I was suffering from an hallucination, due, no doubt, to the shock of my dog's sudden madness.

'Did you see the dog after it was dead?' I asked.

He said he did. The whole jaw was covered with blood and foam; the teeth certainly seemed convulsively fixed, but the case being evidently one of extraordinarily virulent hydrophobia, owing to the intense heat, he had had the body buried immediately.

My companion stopped speaking as we reached our lodgings, and went upstairs. Then, lighting a candle, he slowly turned down his collar.

'You see I have the marks still,' he said, 'but I have no fear of dying of hydrophobia. I am told such peculiar scars could not have been made by the teeth of a dog. If you look closely you see the pressure of the five fingers. That is the reason why I wear high collars.'

Luella Miller

Mary Wilkins Freeman

Close to the village street stood the one-storey house in which Luella Miller, who had an evil name in the village, had dwelt. She had been dead for years, yet there were those in the village who, in spite of the clearer light which comes on a vantage-point from a long-past danger, half believed in the tale which they had heard from their childhood. In their hearts, although they scarcely would have owned it, was a survival of the wild horror and frenzied fear of their ancestors who had dwelt in the same age with Luella Miller. Young people even would stare with a shudder at the old house as they passed, and children never played around it as was their wont around an untenanted building. Not a window in the old Miller house was broken: the panes reflected the morning sunlight in patches of emerald and blue, and the latch of the sagging front door was never lifted, although no bolt secured it.

Since Luella Miller had been carried out of it, the house had had no tenant except one friendless old soul who had no choice between that and the far-off shelter of the open sky. This old woman, who had survived her kindred and friends, lived in the house one week, then one morning no smoke came out of the chimney, and a body of neighbours, a score strong, entered and found her dead in her bed. There were dark whispers as to the cause of her death, and there were those who testified to an expression of fear so exalted that it showed forth the state of the departing soul upon the dead face. The old woman had been hale and hearty when she entered the house, and in seven days she was dead; it seemed that she had fallen a victim to some uncanny power. The minister talked in the pulpit with covert severity against the sin of superstition; still the belief prevailed. Not a soul in the village but would have chosen the almshouse rather than that dwelling. No vagrant, if he heard the tale, would seek shelter beneath that old roof, unhallowed by nearly half a century of superstitious fear.

There was only one person in the village who had actually known Luella Miller. That person was a woman well over eighty, but a marvel of vitality and unextinct youth. Straight as an arrow, with the spring of one recently let loose from the bow of life, she moved about the streets, and she always went to church, rain or shine. She had never married, and had lived alone for years in a house across the road from Luella Miller's.

This woman had none of the garrulousness of age, but never in all her life had she ever held her tongue for any will save her own, and she never spared the truth when she essayed to present it. She it was who bore testimony to the life, evil, though possibly wittingly or designedly so, of Luella Miller, and to her personal appearance. When this old woman spoke—and she had the gift of description, although her thoughts were clothed in the rude vernacular of her native vil-lage—one could seem to see Luella Miller as she had really looked. According to this woman, Lydia Anderson by name, Luella Miller had been a beauty of a type rather unusual in New England. She had been a slight, pliant sort of creature, as ready with a strong yielding to fate and as unbreakable as a willow. She had glimmering lengths of straight, fair hair, which she wore softly looped round a long, lovely face. She had blue eyes full of soft pleading, little slender, clinging hands, and a wonderful grace of motion and attitude.

"Luella Miller used to sit in a way nobody else could if they sat up and studied a week of Sundays," said Lydia Anderson, "and it was a sight to see her walk. If one of them willows over there on the edge of the brook could start up and get its roots free of the ground, and move off, it would go just the way Luella Miller used to. She had a green shot silk she used to wear, too, and a hat with green ribbon streamers, and a lace veil blowing across her face and out sideways, and a green ribbon flyin' from her waist. That was what she came out bride in when she married Erastus Miller. Her name before she was married was Hill. There was always a sight of "l's" in her name, mar-ried or single. Erastus Miller was good lookin', too, better lookin' than Luella. Sometimes I used to think that Luella wa'n't so handsome after all. Erastus just about worshiped her. I used to know him pretty well. He lived next door to me, and we went to school together. Folks used to say he was waitin' on me, but he wa'n't. I never thought he was except once or twice when he said things that some girls might have suspected meant somethin'. That was before Luella came here to teach the district school. It was funny how she came to get it, for folks said she hadn't any education, and that one of the big girls, Lottie Henderson, used to do all the teachin' for her, while she sat back and did embroidery work on a cambric pocket-handkerchief.

"Lottie Henderson was a real smart girl, a splendid scholar, and she just set her eyes by Luella, as all the girls did. Lottie would have made a real smart woman, but she died when Luella had been here about a year—just faded away and died: nobody knew what ailed her. She dragged herself to that schoolhouse and helped Luella teach till the very last minute. The committee all knew how Luella didn't do much of the work herself, but they winked at it. It wa'n't long after Lottie died that Erastus married her. I always thought he hurried it up because she wa'n't fit to teach. One of the big boys used to help her after Lottie died, but he hadn't much government, and the school didn't do very well, and Luella might have had to give it up, for the committee couldn't have shut their eyes to things much longer.

"The boy that helped her was a real honest, innocent sort of fellow, and he was a good scholar, too. Folks said he overstudied, and that was the reason he was took crazy the year after Luella married, but I don't know. And I don't know what made Erastus Miller go into consumption of the blood the year after he was married: consumption wa'n't in his family. He just grew weaker and weaker, and went almost bent double when he tried to wait on Luella, and he spoke feeble, like an old man. He worked terrible hard till the last trying to save up a little to leave Luella. I've seen him out in the worst storms on a wood-sled—he used to cut and sell wood—and he was hunched up on top lookin' more dead than alive. Once I couldn't stand it: I went over and helped him pitch some wood on the cart—I was always strong in my arms. I wouldn't stop for all he told me to, and I guess he was glad enough for the help. That was only a week before he died. He fell on the kitchen floor while he was gettin' breakfast. He always got the breakfast and let Luella lay abed. He did all the sweepin' and the washin' and the ironin' and most of the cookin'.

"He couldn't bear to have Luella lift her finger, and she let him do for her. She lived like a queen for all the work she did. She didn't even do her sewin'. She said it made her shoulder ache to sew, and poor Erastus's sister Lily used to do all her sewin'. She wa'n't able to, either; she was never strong in her back, but she did it beautifully. She had to, to suit Luella, she was so dreadful particular. I never saw anythin' like

91

the fagottin' and hemstitchin' that Lily Miller did for Luella. She made all Luella's weddin' outfit, and that green silk dress, after Maria Babbit cut it. Maria she cut it for nothin', and she did a lot more cuttin' and fittin' for nothin' for Luella, too. Lily Miller went to live with Luella after Erastus died. She gave up her home, though she was real attached to it and wa'n't a mite afraid to stay alone. She rented it and she went to live with Luella right away after the funeral."

Then this old woman, Lydia Anderson, who remembered Luella Miller, would go on to relate the story of Lily Miller. It seemed that on the removal of Lily Miller to the house of her dead brother, to live with his widow, the village people first began to talk. This Lily Miller had been hardly past her first youth, and a most robust and blooming woman, rosy-cheeked, with curls of strong, black hair overshadowing round, candid temples and bright dark eyes. It was not six months after she had taken up her residence with her sister-in-law that her rosy colour faded and her pretty curves became wan hollows. White shadows began to show in the black rings of her hair, and the light died out of her eyes, her features sharpened, and there were pathetic lines at her mouth, which yet wore always an expression of utter sweetness and even happiness. She was devoted to her sister; there was no doubt that she loved her with her whole heart, and was perfectly content in her service. It was her sole anxiety lest she should die and leave her alone.

"The way Lily Miller used to talk about Luella was enough to make you mad and enough to make you cry," said Lydia Anderson. "I've been in there sometimes toward the last when she was too feeble to cook and carried her some blancmange or custard—somethin' I thought she might relish, and she'd thank me, and when I asked her how she was, say she felt better than she did yesterday, and asked me if I didn't think she looked better, dreadful pitiful, and say poor Luella had an awful time takin' care of her and doin' the work—she wa'n't strong enough to do anythin'—when all the time Luella wa'n't liftin' her finger and poor Lily didn't get any care except what the neighbours gave her, and Luella eat up everythin' that was carried in for Lily. I had it real straight that she did. Luella used to just sit and cry and do nothin'.

"She did act real fond of Lily, and she pined away considerable, too. There was those that thought she'd go into a decline herself. But after Lily died, her Aunt Abby Mixter came, and then Luella picked up and grew as fat and rosy as ever. But poor Aunt Abby begun to droop just

92

the way Lily had, and I guess somebody wrote to her married daughter, Mrs. Sam Abbot, who lived in Barre, for she wrote her mother that she must leave right away and come and make her a visit, but Aunt Abby wouldn't go. I can see her now. She was a real good-lookin' woman, tall and large, with a big, square face and a high forehead that looked of itself kind of benevolent and good.

"She just tended out on Luella as if she had been a baby, and when her married daughter sent for her she wouldn't stir one inch. She'd always thought a lot of her daughter, too, but she said Luella needed her and her married daughter didn't. Her daughter kept writin' and writin', but it didn't do any good. Finally she came, and when she saw how bad her mother looked, she broke down and cried and all but went on her knees to have her come away. She spoke her mind out to Luella, too. She told her that she'd killed her husband and everybody that had anythin' to do with her, and she'd thank her to leave her mother alone.

"Luella went into hysterics, and Aunt Abby was so frightened that she called me after her daughter went. Mrs. Sam Abbot she went away fairly cryin' out loud in the buggy, the neighbours heard her, and well she might, for she never saw her mother again alive. I went in that night when Aunt Abby called for me, standin' in the door with her little green-checked shawl over her head. I can see her now. 'Do come over here, Miss Anderson,' she sung out, kind of gasping for breath. I didn't stop for anythin'. I put over as fast as I could, and when I got there, there was Luella laughin' and cryin' all together, and Aunt Abby trying to hush her, and all the time she herself was white as a sheet and shakin' so she could hardly stand. 'For the land sakes, Mrs. Mixter,' says I, 'you look worse than she does. You ain't fit to be up out of your bed.'

"'Oh, there ain't anythin' the matter with me,' says she. Then she went on talkin' to Luella. 'There, there, don't, don't, poor little lamb,' says she. 'Aunt Abby is here. She ain't goin' away and leave you. Don't, poor little lamb.'

"'Do leave her with me, Mrs. Mixter, and you get back to bed,' says I, for Aunt Abby had been layin' down considerable lately, though somehow she contrived to do the work.

"'I'm well enough,' says she. 'Don't you think she had better have the doctor, Miss Anderson?'

"'The doctor,' says I, 'I think *you* had better have the doctor. I think you need him much worse than some folks I could mention.' And I looked right straight at Luella Miller laughin' and cryin' and goin' on as if she was the centre of all creation. All the time she was actin' so—seemed as if she was too sick to sense anythin'—she was keepin' a sharp lookout as to how we took it out of the corner of one eye. I see her. You could never cheat me about Luella Miller. Finally I got real mad and I run home and I got a bottle of valerian I had, and I poured some boilin' hot water on a handful of catnip, and I mixed up that catnip tea with most half a wineglass of valerian, and I went with it over to Luella's. I marched right up to Luella, a-holdin' out of that cup, all smokin'. 'Now,' says I, 'Luella Miller, *'You swaller this!'*

"'What is—what is it, oh, what is it?' she sort of screeches out. Then she goes off a-laughin' enough to kill.

"'Poor lamb, poor little lamb,' says Aunt Abby, standin' over her, all kind of tottery, and tryin' to bathe her head with camphor.

"'*You swaller this right down,*' says I. And I didn't waste any ceremony. I just took hold of Luella Miller's chin and I tipped her head back, and I caught her mouth open with laughin', and I clapped that cup to her lips, and I fairly hollered at her: 'Swaller, swaller, swaller!' and she gulped it right down. She had to, and I guess it did her good. Anyhow, she stopped cryin' and laughin' and let me put her to bed, and she went to sleep like a baby inside of half an hour. That was more than poor Aunt Abby did. She lay awake all that night and I stayed with her, though she tried not to have me; said she wa'n't sick enough for watchers. But I stayed, and I made some good cornmeal gruel and I fed her a teaspoon every little while all night long. It seemed to me as if she was jest dyin' from bein' all wore out.

"In the mornin' as soon as it was light I run over to the Bisbees and sent Johnny Bisbee for the doctor. I told him to tell the doctor to hurry, and he come pretty quick. Poor Aunt Abby didn't seem to know much of anythin' when he got there. You couldn't hardly tell she breathed, she was so used up. When the doctor had gone, Luella came into the room lookin' like a baby in her ruffled nightgown. I can see her now. Her eyes were as blue and her face all pink and white like a blossom, and she looked at Aunt Abby in the bed sort of innocent and surprised. 'Why,' says she, 'Aunt Abby ain't got up yet?'

"'No, she ain't,' says I, pretty short.

"'I thought I didn't smell the coffee,' says Luella.

"'Coffee,' says I. 'I guess if you have coffee this mornin' you'll make it yourself.'

"'I never made the coffee in all my life,' says she, dreadful astonished. 'Erastus always made the coffee as long as he lived, and then Lily she made it, and then Aunt Abby made it. I don't believe I *can* make the coffee, Miss Anderson.'

"'You can make it or go without, jest as you please,' says I.

"'Ain't Aunt Abby goin' to get up?' says she.

"'I guess she won't get up,' says I, 'sick as she is.' I was gettin' madder and madder. There was somethin' about that little pink-and-white thing standin' there and talkin' about coffee, when she had killed so many better folks than she was, and had jest killed another, that made me feel 'most as if I wished somebody would up and kill her before she had a chance to do any more harm.

"'Is Aunt Abby sick?' says Luella, as if she was sort of aggrieved and injured.

"'Yes,' says I, 'she's sick, and she's goin' to die, and then you'll be left alone, and you'll have to do for yourself and wait on yourself, or do without things.' I don't know but I was sort of hard, but it was the truth, and if I was any harder than Luella Miller had been I'll give up. I ain't never been sorry that I said it. Well, Luella, she up and had hysterics again at that, and I jest let her have 'em. All I did was to bundle her into the room on the other side of the entry where Aunt Abby couldn't hear her, if she wa'n't past it—I don't know but she was—and set her down hard in a chair and told her not to come back into the other room, and she minded. She had her hysterics in there till she got tired. When she found out that nobody was comin' to coddle her and do for her she stopped.

"At least I suppose she did. I had all I could do with poor Aunt Abby tryin' to keep the breath of life in her. The doctor had told me that she was dreadful low, and give me some very strong medicine to give to her in drops real often, and told me real particular about the nourishment. Well, I did as he told me real faithful till she wa'n't able to swaller any longer. Then I had her daughter sent for. I had begun to realize that she wouldn't last any time at all. I hadn't realized it before, though I spoke to Luella the way I did. The doctor he came, and Mrs. Sam Abbot, but when she got there it was too late; her mother was dead. Aunt Abby's daughter just give one look at her mother layin' there, then she turned sort of sharp and sudden and looked at me.

"'Where is she?' says she, and I knew she meant Luella.

"'She's out in the kitchen,' says I. 'She's too nervous to see folks die. She's afraid it will make her sick.'

"The doctor he speaks up then. He was a young man. Old Doctor Park had died the year before, and this was a young fellow just out of college. 'Mrs. Miller is not strong,' says he, kind of severe, 'and she is quite right in not agitating herself.'

"'You are another, young man; she's got her pretty claw on you,' thinks I, but I didn't say anythin' to him. I just said over to Mrs. Sam Abbot that Luella was in the kitchen, and Mrs. Sam Abbot she went out there, and I went, too, and I never heard anythin' like the way she talked to Luella Miller. I felt pretty hard to Luella myself, but this was more than I ever would have dared to say. Luella she was too scared to go into hysterics. She jest flopped. She seemed to jest shrink away to nothin' in that kitchen chair, with Mrs. Sam Abbot standin' over her and talkin' and tellin' her the truth. I guess the truth was most too much for her and no mistake, because Luella presently actually did faint away, and there wa'n't any sham about it, the way I always suspected there was about them hysterics. She fainted dead away and we had to lay her flat on the floor, and the doctor he came runnin' out and he said somethin' about a weak heart dreadful fierce to Mrs. Sam Abbot, but she wa'n't a mite scared. She faced him jest as white as even Luella was layin' there lookin' like death and the doctor feelin' of her pulse.

"'Weak heart,' says she, 'weak heart; weak fiddlesticks! There ain't nothin' weak about that woman. She's got strength enough to hang onto other folks till she kills 'em. Weak? It was my poor mother that was weak: this woman killed her as sure as if she had taken a knife to her.'

"But the doctor he didn't pay much attention. He was bendin' over Luella layin' there with her yellow hair all streamin' and her pretty pink-and-white face all pale, and her blue eyes like stars gone out, and he was holdin' onto her hand and smoothin' her forehead, and tellin' me to get the brandy in Aunt Abby's room, and I was sure as I wanted to be that Luella had got somebody else to hang onto, now Aunt Abby was gone, and I thought of poor Erastus Miller, and I sort of pitied the poor young doctor, led away by a pretty face, and I made up my mind I'd see what I could do.

"I waited till Aunt Abby had been dead and buried about a month, and the doctor was goin' to see Luella steady and folks were beginnin' to talk; then one evenin', when I knew the doctor had been called out of town and wouldn't be round, I went over to Luella's. I found her all dressed up in a blue muslin with white polka dots on it, and her hair curled jest as pretty, and there wa'n't a young girl in the place could compare with her. There was somethin' about Luella Miller seemed to draw the heart right out of you, but she didn't draw it out of ME. She was settin' rocking in the chair by her sittin'-room window, and Maria Brown had gone home. Maria Brown had been in to help her, or rather to do the work, for Luella wa'n't helped when she didn't do anythin'.

"Maria Brown was real capable and she didn't have any ties; she wa'n't married, and lived alone, so she'd offered. I couldn't see why she should do the work any more than Luella; she wa'n't any too strong; but she seemed to think she could and Luella seemed to think so, too, so she went over and did all the work—washed, and ironed, and baked, while Luella sat and rocked. Maria didn't live long afterward. She began to fade away just the same fashion the others had. Well, she was warned, but she acted real mad when folks said anythin': said Luella was a poor, abused woman, too delicate to help herself, and they'd ought to be ashamed, and if she died helpin' them that couldn't help themselves she would—and she did.

"'I s'pose Maria has gone home,' says I to Luella, when I had gone in and sat down opposite her.

"'Yes, Maria went half an hour ago, after she had got supper and washed the dishes,' says Luella, in her pretty way.

"'I suppose she has got a lot of work to do in her own house tonight,' says I, kind of bitter, but that was all thrown away on Luella Miller. It seemed to her right that other folks that wa'n't any better able than she was herself should wait on her, and she couldn't get it through her head that anybody should think it *wa'n't* right.

"'Yes,' says Luella, real sweet and pretty, 'yes, she said she had to do her washin' tonight. She has let it go for a fortnight along of comin' over here.'

"'Why don't she stay home and do her washin' instead of comin' over here and doin' *your* work, when you are just as well able, and enough sight more so, than she is to do it?' says I.

"Then Luella she looked at me like a baby who has a rattle shook at it. She sort of laughed as innocent as you please. 'Oh, I can't do the work myself, Miss Anderson,' says she. 'I never did. Maria *has* to do it.'

"Then I spoke out: 'Has to do it I' says I. 'Has to do it!' She don't have to do it, either. Maria Brown has her own home and enough to live on. She ain't beholden to you to come over here and slave for you and kill herself.'

"Luella she jest set and stared at me for all the world like a doll-baby that was so abused that it was comin' to life.

"'Yes,' says I, 'she's killin' herself. She's goin' to die just the way Erastus did, and Lily, and your Aunt Abby. You're killin' her jest as you did them. I don't know what there is about you, but you seem to bring a curse,' says I. 'You kill everybody that is fool enough to care anythin' about you and do for you.'

"She stared at me and she was pretty pale.

"'And Maria ain't the only one you're goin' to kill,' says I. 'You're goin' to kill Doctor Malcom before you're done with him.'

"Then a red colour came flamin' all over her face. 'I ain't goin' to kill him, either,' says she, and she begun to cry.

"'Yes, you *be!*' says I. Then I spoke as I had never spoke before. You see, I felt it on account of Erastus. I told her that she hadn't any business to think of another man after she'd been married to one that had died for her: that she was a dreadful woman; and she was, that's true enough, but sometimes I have wondered lately if she knew it—if she wa'n't like a baby with scissors in its hand cuttin' everybody without knowin' what it was doin'.

"Luella she kept gettin' paler and paler, and she never took her eyes off my face. There was somethin' awful about the way she looked at me and never spoke one word. After awhile I quit talkin' and I went home. I watched that night, but her lamp went out before nine o'clock, and when Doctor Malcom came drivin' past and sort of slowed up he see there wa'n't any light and he drove along. I saw her sort of shy out of meetin' the next Sunday, too, so he shouldn't go home with her, and I begun to think mebbe she did have some conscience after all. It was only a week after that that Maria Brown died—sort of sudden at the last, though everybody had seen it was comin'. Well, then there was a good deal of feelin' and pretty dark whispers. Folks said the days of witchcraft had come again, and they were pretty shy of Luella.

"She acted sort of offish to the doctor and he didn't go there, and there wa'n't anybody to do anythin' for her. I don't know how she *did* get along. I wouldn't go in there and offer to help her—not because I was afraid of dyin' like the rest, but I thought she was just as well able to do her own work as I was to do it for her, and I thought it was about time that she did it and stopped killin' other folks. But it wa'n't very long before folks began to say that Luella herself was goin' into a decline jest the way her husband, and Lily, and Aunt Abby and the others had, and I saw myself that she looked pretty bad. I used to see her goin' past from the store with a bundle as if she could hardly crawl, but I remembered how Erastus used to wait and 'tend when he couldn't hardly put one foot before the other, and I didn't go out to help her.

"But at last one afternoon I saw the doctor come drivin' up like mad with his medicine chest, and Mrs. Babbit came in after supper and said that Luella was real sick.

"'I'd offer to go in and nurse her,' says she, 'but I've got my children to consider, and mebbe it ain't true what they say, but it's queer how many folks that have done for her have died.'

"I didn't say anythin', but I considered how she had been Erastus's wife and how he had set his eyes by her, and I made up my mind to go in the next mornin', unless she was better, and see what I could do; but the next mornin' I see her at the window, and pretty soon she came steppin' out as spry as you please, and a little while afterward Mrs. Babbit came in and told me that the doctor had got a girl from out of town, a Sarah Jones, to come there, and she said she was pretty sure that the doctor was goin' to marry Luella.

"I saw him kiss her in the door that night myself, and I knew it was true. The woman came that afternoon, and the way she flew around was a caution. I don't believe Luella had swept since Maria died. She swept and dusted, and washed and ironed; wet clothes and dusters and carpets were flyin' over there all day, and every time Luella set her foot out when the doctor wa'n't there there was that Sarah Jones helpin' of her up and down the steps, as if she hadn't learned to walk.

"Well, everybody knew that Luella and the doctor were goin' to be married, but it wa'n't long before they began to talk about his lookin' so poorly, jest as they had about the others; and they talked about Sarah Jones, too.

"Well, the doctor did die, and he wanted to be married first, so as to leave what little he had to Luella, but he died before the minister could get there, and Sarah Jones died a week afterward.

"Well, that wound up everything for Luella Miller. Not another soul in the whole town would lift a finger for her. There got to be a sort of panic. Then she began to droop in good earnest. She used to have to go to the store herself, for Mrs. Babbit was afraid to let Tommy go for her, and I've seen her goin' past and stoppin' every two or three steps to rest. Well, I stood it as long as I could, but one day I see her comin' with her arms full and stoppin' to lean against the Babbit fence, and I run out and took her bundles and carried them to her house. Then I went home and never spoke one word to her though she called after me dreadful kind of pitiful. Well, that night I was taken sick with a chill, and I was sick as I wanted to be for two weeks. Mrs. Babbit had seen me run out to help Luella and she came in and told me I was goin' to die on account of it. I didn't know whether I was or not, but I considered I had done right by Erastus's wife.

"That last two weeks Luella she had a dreadful hard time, I guess. She was pretty sick, and as near as I could make out nobody dared go near her. I don't know as she was really needin' anythin' very much, for there was enough to eat in her house and it was warm weather, and she made out to cook a little flour gruel every day, I know, but I guess she had a hard time, she that had been so petted and done for all her life.

"When I got so I could go out, I went over there one morning. Mrs. Babbit had just come in to say she hadn't seen any smoke and she didn't know but it was somebody's duty to go in, but she couldn't help thinkin' of her children, and I got right up, though I hadn't been out of the house for two weeks, and I went in there, and Luella she was layin' on the bed, and she was dyin'.

"She lasted all that day and into the night. But I sat there after the new doctor had gone away. Nobody else dared to go there. It was about midnight that I left her for a minute to run home and get some medicine I had been takin', for I begun to feel rather bad.

"It was a full moon that night, and just as I started out of my door to cross the street back to Luella's, I stopped short, for I saw something."

Lydia Anderson at this juncture always said with a certain defiance that she did not expect to be believed, and then proceeded in a hushed voice:

"I saw what I saw, and I know I saw it, and I will swear on my death bed that I saw it. I saw Luella Miller and Erastus Miller, and Lily, and Aunt Abby, and Maria, and the doctor, and Sarah, all goin' out of her door, and all but Luella shone white in the moonlight, and they were all helpin' her along till she seemed to fairly fly in the midst of them. Then it all disappeared. I stood a minute with my heart poundin', then I went over there. I thought of goin' for Mrs. Babbit, but I thought she'd be afraid. So I went alone, though I knew what had happened. Luella was layin' real peaceful, dead on her bed."

This was the story that the old woman, Lydia Anderson, told, but the sequel was told by the people who survived her, and this is the tale which has become folklore in the village.

Lydia Anderson died when she was eighty-seven. She had continued wonderfully hale and hearty for one of her years until about two weeks before her death.

One bright moonlight evening she was sitting beside a window in her parlour when she made a sudden exclamation, and was out of the house and across the street before the neighbour who was taking care of her could stop her. She followed as fast as possible and found Lydia Anderson stretched on the ground before the door of Luella Miller's deserted house, and she was quite dead.

The next night there was a red gleam of fire athwart the moonlight and the old house of Luella Miller was burned to the ground. Nothing is now left of it except a few old cellar stones and a lilac bush, and in summer a helpless trail of morning glories among the weeds, which might be considered emblematic of Luella herself.

Man-Size in Marble

Edith Nesbit

Although every word of this story is as true as despair, I do not expect people to believe it. Nowadays a "rational explanation" is required before belief is possible. Let me then, at once, offer the "rational explanation" which finds most favour among those who have heard the tale of my life's tragedy. It is held that we were "under a delusion," Laura and I, on that 31st of October; and that this supposition places the whole matter on a satisfactory and believable basis. The reader can judge, when he, too, has heard my story, how far this is an "explanation," and in what sense it is "rational." There were three who took part in this: Laura and I and another man. The other man still lives, and can speak to the truth of the least credible part of my story.

I never in my life knew what it was to have as much money as I required to supply the most ordinary needs—good colours, books, and cab-fares—and when we were married we knew quite well that we should only be able to live at all by "strict punctuality and attention to business." I used to paint in those days, and Laura used to write, and we felt sure we could keep the pot at least simmering. Living in town was out of the question, so we went to look for a cottage in the country, which should be at once sanitary and picturesque. So rarely do these two qualities meet in one cottage that our search was for some time quite fruitless. We tried advertisements, but most of the desirable rural residences which we did look at proved to be lacking in both essentials, and when a cottage chanced to have drains it always had stucco as well and was shaped like a tea-caddy. And if we found a vine or rose-covered porch, corruption invariably lurked within.

Our minds got so befogged by the eloquence of house-agents and the rival disadvantages of the fever-traps and outrages to beauty which we had seen and scorned, that I very much doubt whether either of us, on our wedding morning, knew the difference between a house and a haystack. But when we got away from friends and house-agents, on our honeymoon, our wits grew clear again, and we knew a pretty cottage when at last we saw one. It was at Brenzett—a little village set on a hill over against the southern marshes. We had gone there, from the seaside village where we were staying, to see the church, and two fields from the church we found this cottage. It stood quite by itself, about two miles from the village. It was a long, low building, with rooms sticking out in unexpected places. There was a bit of stone-work—ivy-covered and moss-grown, just two old rooms, all that was left of a big house that had once stood there—and round this stone-work the house had grown up. Stripped of its roses and jasmine it would have been hideous.

As it stood it was charming, and after a brief examination we took it. It was absurdly cheap. The rest of our honeymoon we spent in grubbing about in second-hand shops in the county town, picking up bits of old oak and Chippendale chairs for our furnishing. We wound up with a run up to town and a visit to Liberty's, and soon the low oak-beamed lattice-windowed rooms began to be home. There was a jolly old-fashioned garden, with grass paths, and no end of holly-hocks and sunflowers, and big lilies. From the window you could see the marsh-pastures, and beyond them the blue, thin line of the sea. We were as happy as the summer was glorious, and settled down into work sooner than we ourselves expected. I was never tired of sketching the view and the wonderful cloud effects from the open lattice, and Laura would sit at the table and write verses about them, in which I mostly played the part of foreground.

We got a tall old peasant woman to do for us. Her face and figure were good, though her cooking was of the homeliest; but she understood all about gardening, and told us all the old names of the coppices and cornfields, and the stories of the smugglers and highwaymen, and, better still, of the "things that walked," and of the "sights" which met one in lonely glens of a starlight night. She was a great comfort to us, because Laura hated housekeeping as much as I loved folklore, and we soon came to leave all the domestic business to Mrs. Dorman, and to use her legends in little magazine stories which brought in the jingling guinea.

We had three months of married happiness, and did not have a single quarrel. One October evening I had been down to smoke a pipe with the doctor—our only neighbour—a pleasant young Irishman. Laura had stayed at home to finish a comic sketch of a village episode for the Monthly Marplot. I left her laughing over her own jokes, and came in to find her a crumpled heap of pale muslin weeping on the window seat.

"Good heavens, my darling, what's the matter?" I cried, taking her in my arms. She leaned her little dark head against my shoulder and went on crying. I had never seen her cry before—we had always been so happy, you see—and I felt sure some frightful misfortune had happened.

"What is the matter? Do speak."

"It's Mrs. Dorman," she sobbed.

"What has she done?" I inquired, immensely relieved.

"She says she must go before the end of the month, and she says her niece is ill; she's gone down to see her now, but I don't believe that's the reason, because her niece is always ill. I believe someone has been setting her against us. Her manner was so queer—"

"Never mind, Pussy," I said; "whatever you do, don't cry, or I shall have to cry too, to keep you in countenance, and then you'll never respect your man again!"

She dried her eyes obediently on my handkerchief, and even smiled faintly.

"But you see," she went on, "it is really serious, because these village people are so sheepy, and if one won't do a thing you may be quite sure none of the others will. And I shall have to cook the dinners, and wash up the hateful greasy plates; and you'll have to carry cans of water about, and clean the boots and knives—and we shall never have any time for work, or earn any money, or anything. We shall have to work all day, and only be able to rest when we are waiting for the kettle to boil!"

I represented to her that even if we had to perform these duties, the day would still present some margin for other toils and recreations. But she refused to see the matter in any but the greyest light. She was very unreasonable, my Laura, but I could not have loved her any more if she had been as reasonable as Whately.

"I'll speak to Mrs. Dorman when she comes back, and see if I can't come to terms with her," I said. "Perhaps she wants a rise in her screw. It will be all right. Let's walk up to the church."

The church was a large and lonely one, and we loved to go there, especially upon bright nights. The path skirted a wood, cut through it once, and ran along the crest of the hill through two meadows, and round the churchyard wall, over which the old yews loomed in black masses of shadow. This path, which was partly paved, was called "the bier-balk," for it had long been the way by which the corpses had been carried to burial. The churchyard was richly treed, and was shaded by great elms which stood just outside and stretched their majestic arms in benediction over the happy dead. A large, low porch let one into the building by a Norman doorway and a heavy oak door studded with iron. Inside, the arches rose into darkness, and between them the reticulated windows, which stood out white in the moonlight. In the chancel, the windows were of rich glass, which showed in faint light their noble colouring, and made the black oak of the choir pews hardly more solid than the shadows.

But on each side of the altar lay a grey marble figure of a knight in full plate armour lying upon a low slab, with hands held up in everlasting prayer, and these figures, oddly enough, were always to be seen if there was any glimmer of light in the church. Their names were lost, but the peasants told of them that they had been fierce and wicked men, marauders by land and sea, who had been the scourge of their time, and had been guilty of deeds so foul that the house they had lived in—the big house, by the way, that had stood on the site of our cottage—had been stricken by lightning and the vengeance of Heaven. But for all that, the gold of their heirs had bought them a place in the church. Looking at the bad hard faces reproduced in the marble, this story was easily believed.

The church looked at its best and weirdest on that night, for the shadows of the yew trees fell through the windows upon the floor of the nave and touched the pillars with tattered shade. We sat down together without speaking, and watched the solemn beauty of the old church, with some of that awe which inspired its early builders. We walked to the chancel and looked at the sleeping warriors. Then we rested some time on the stone seat in the porch, looking out over the stretch of quiet moonlit meadows, feeling in every fibre of our being the peace of the night and of our happy love; and came away at last with a sense that even scrubbing and blackleading were but small troubles at their worst.

Mrs. Dorman had come back from the village, and I at once invited her to a *tête-à-tête*.

"Now, Mrs. Dorman," I said, when I had got her into my painting room, "what's all this about your not staying with us?"

"I should be glad to get away, sir, before the end of the month," she answered, with her usual placid dignity.

"Have you any fault to find, Mrs. Dorman?"

"None at all, sir; you and your lady have always been most kind, I'm sure—"

"Well, what is it? Are your wages not high enough?"

"No, sir, I gets quite enough."

"Then why not stay?"

"I'd rather not"—with some hesitation—"my niece is ill."

"But your niece has been ill ever since we came."

No answer. There was a long and awkward silence. I broke it.

"Can't you stay for another month?" I asked.

"No, sir. I'm bound to go by Thursday."

And this was Monday!

"Well, I must say, I think you might have let us know before. There's no time now to get anyone else, and your mistress is not fit to do heavy housework. Can't you stay till next week?"

"I might be able to come back next week."

I was now convinced that all she wanted was a brief holiday, which we should have been willing enough to let her have, as soon as we could get a substitute.

"But why must you go this week?" I persisted. "Come, out with it."

Mrs. Dorman drew the little shawl, which she always wore, tightly across her bosom, as though she were cold. Then she said, with a sort of effort—

"They say, sir, as this was a big house in Catholic times, and there was a many deeds done here."

The nature of the "deeds" might be vaguely inferred from the inflection of Mrs. Dorman's voice—which was enough to make one's blood run cold. I was glad that Laura was not in the room. She was always nervous, as highly-strung natures are, and I felt that these tales about our house, told by this old peasant woman, with her impressive manner and contagious credulity, might have made our home less dear to my wife.

"Tell me all about it, Mrs. Dorman," I said; "you needn't mind about telling me. I'm not like the young people who make fun of such things."

Which was partly true.

"Well, sir"—she sank her voice—"you may have seen in the church, beside the altar, two shapes."

"You mean the effigies of the knights in armour," I said cheerfully.

"I mean them two bodies, drawed out man-size in marble," she returned, and I had to admit that her description was a thousand times more graphic than mine, to say nothing of a certain weird force and uncanniness about the phrase "drawed out man-size in marble."

"They do say, as on All Saints' Eve them two bodies sits up on their slabs, and gets off of them, and then walks down the aisle, in their marble"—(another good phrase, Mrs. Dorman)—"and as the church clock strikes eleven they walks out of the church door, and over the graves, and along the bier-balk, and if it's a wet night there's the marks of their feet in the morning."

"And where do they go?" I asked, rather fascinated.

"They comes back here to their home, sir, and if anyone meets them—"

"Well, what then?" I asked.

But no—not another word could I get from her, save that her niece was ill and she must go. After what I had heard I scorned to discuss the niece, and tried to get from Mrs. Dorman more details of the legend. I could get nothing but warnings.

"Whatever you do, sir, lock the door early on All Saints' Eve, and make the cross-sign over the doorstep and on the windows."

"But has anyone ever seen these things?" I persisted.

"That's not for me to say. I know what I know, sir."

"Well, who was here last year?"

"No one, sir; the lady as owned the house only stayed here in summer, and she always went to London a full month afore the night. And I'm sorry to inconvenience you and your lady, but my niece is ill and I must go on Thursday."

I could have shaken her for her absurd reiteration of that obvious fiction, after she had told me her real reasons.

She was determined to go, nor could our united entreaties move her in the least.

I did not tell Laura the legend of the shapes that "walked in their marble," partly because a legend concerning our house might perhaps trouble my wife, and partly, I think, from some more occult reason. This was not quite the same to me as any other story, and I did not want to talk about it till the day was over. I had very soon ceased to think of the legend, however. I was painting a portrait of Laura, against the lattice window, and I could not think of much else. I had got a splendid background of yellow and grey sunset, and was working away with enthusiasm at her lace. On Thursday Mrs. Dorman went. She relented, at parting, so far as to say—

"Don't you put yourself about too much, ma'am, and if there's any little thing I can do next week, I'm sure I shan't mind."

From which I inferred that she wished to come back to us after Hallowe'en. Up to the last she adhered to the fiction of the niece with touching fidelity.

Thursday passed off pretty well. Laura showed marked ability in the matter of steak and potatoes, and I confess that my knives, and the plates, which I insisted upon washing, were better done than I had dared to expect.

Friday came. It is about what happened on that Friday that this is written. I wonder if I should have believed it, if anyone had told it to me. I will write the story of it as quickly and plainly as I can. Everything that happened on that day is burnt into my brain. I shall not forget anything, nor leave anything out.

I got up early, I remember, and lighted the kitchen fire, and had just achieved a smoky success, when my little wife came running down, as sunny and sweet as the clear October morning itself. We prepared breakfast together, and found it very good fun. The housework was soon done, and when brushes and brooms and pails were quiet again, the house was still indeed. It is wonderful what a difference one makes in a house. We really missed Mrs. Dorman, quite apart from considerations concerning pots and pans. We spent the day in dusting our books and putting them straight, and dined gaily on cold steak and coffee. Laura was, if possible, brighter and gayer and sweeter than usual, and I began to think that a little domestic toil was really good for her.

We had never been so merry since we were married, and the walk we had that afternoon was, I think, the happiest time of all my life. When we had watched the deep scarlet clouds slowly pale into leaden grey against a pale-green sky, and saw the white mists curl up along the hedgerows in the distant marsh, we came back to the house, silently, hand in hand.

"You are sad, my darling," I said, half-jestingly, as we sat down together in our little parlour. I expected a disclaimer, for my own silence had been the silence of complete happiness. To my surprise she said—

"Yes. I think I am sad, or rather I am uneasy. I don't think I'm very well. I have shivered three or four times since we came in, and it is not cold, is it?"

"No," I said, and hoped it was not a chill caught from the treacherous mists that roll up from the marshes in the dying light. No—she said, she did not think so. Then, after a silence, she spoke suddenly—

"Do you ever have presentiments of evil?"

"No," I said, smiling, "and I shouldn't believe in them if I had."

"I do," she went on; "the night my father died I knew it, though he was right away in the north of Scotland." I did not answer in words.

She sat looking at the fire for some time in silence, gently stroking my hand. At last she sprang up, came behind me, and, drawing my head back, kissed me.

"There, it's over now," she said. "What a baby I am! Come, light the candles, and we'll have some of these new Rubinstein duets."

And we spent a happy hour or two at the piano.

At about half-past ten I began to long for the goodnight pipe, but Laura looked so white that I felt it would be brutal of me to fill our sitting-room with the fumes of strong cavendish.

"I'll take my pipe outside," I said.

"Let me come, too."

"No, sweetheart, not tonight; you're much too tired. I shan't be long. Get to bed, or I shall have an invalid to nurse tomorrow as well as the boots to clean."

I kissed her and was turning to go, when she flung her arms round my neck, and held me as if she would never let me go again. I stroked her hair.

"Come, Pussy, you're over-tired. The housework has been too much for you."

She loosened her clasp a little and drew a deep breath.

"No. We've been very happy today, Jack, haven't we? Don't stay out too long."

"I won't, my dearie."

I strolled out of the front door, leaving it unlatched. What a night it was! The jagged masses of heavy dark cloud were rolling at intervals from horizon to horizon, and thin white wreaths covered the stars. Through all the rush of the cloud river, the moon swam, breasting the waves and disappearing again in the darkness. When now and again her light reached the woodlands they seemed to be slowly and noiselessly waving in time to the swing of the clouds above them. There was a strange grey light over all the earth; the fields had that shadowy bloom over them which only comes from the marriage of dew and moonshine, or frost and starlight.

I walked up and down, drinking in the beauty of the quiet earth and the changing sky. The night was absolutely silent. Nothing seemed to be abroad. There was no scurrying of rabbits, or twitter of the half-asleep birds. And though the clouds went sailing across the sky, the wind that drove them never came low enough to rustle the dead leaves in the woodland paths. Across the meadows I could see the church tower standing out black and grey against the sky. I walked there thinking over our three months of happiness—and of my wife, her dear eyes, her loving ways. Oh, my little girl! my own little girl; what a vision came then of a long, glad life for you and me together!

I heard a bell-beat from the church. Eleven already! I turned to go in, but the night held me. I could not go back into our little warm rooms yet. I would go up to the church. I felt vaguely that it would be good to carry my love and thankfulness to the sanctuary whither so many loads of sorrow and gladness had been borne by the men and women of the dead years.

I looked in at the low window as I went by. Laura was half lying on her chair in front of the fire. I could not see her face, only her little head showed dark against the pale blue wall. She was quite still. Asleep, no doubt. My heart reached out to her, as I went on. There must be a God, I thought, and a God who was good. How otherwise could anything so sweet and dear as she have ever been imagined?

I walked slowly along the edge of the wood. A sound broke the stillness of the night, it was a rustling in the wood. I stopped and listened. The sound stopped too. I went on, and now distinctly heard another step than mine answer mine like an echo. It was a poacher or a wood-stealer, most likely, for these were not unknown in our Arcadian neighbourhood. But whoever it was, he was a fool not to step more lightly. I turned into the wood, and now the footstep seemed to come from the path I had just left. It must be an echo, I thought. The wood looked perfect in the moonlight. The large dying ferns and the brushwood showed where through thinning foliage the pale light came down.

The tree trunks stood up like Gothic columns all around me. They reminded me of the church, and I turned into the bier-balk, and passed through the corpse-gate between the graves to the low porch. I paused for a moment on the stone seat where Laura and I had watched the fading landscape. Then I noticed that the door of the church was open, and I blamed myself for having left it unlatched the other night. We were the only people who ever cared to come to the church except on Sundays, and I was vexed to think that through our carelessness the damp autumn airs had had a chance of getting in and injuring the old fabric. I went in. It will seem strange, perhaps, that I should have gone half-way up the aisle before I remembered—with a sudden chill, followed by as sudden a rush of self-contempt—that this was the very day and hour when, according to tradition, the "shapes drawed out man-size in marble" began to walk.

Having thus remembered the legend, and remembered it with a shiver, of which I was ashamed, I could not do otherwise than walk up towards the altar, just to look at the figures—as I said to myself; really what I wanted was to assure myself, first, that I did not believe the legend, and, secondly, that it was not true. I was rather glad that I had come. I thought now I could tell Mrs. Dorman how vain her fancies were, and how peacefully the marble figures slept on through the ghastly hour. With my hands in my pockets I passed up the aisle. In the grey dim light, the eastern end of the church looked larger than usual, and the arches above the two tombs looked larger too. The moon came out and showed me the reason. I stopped short, my heart gave a leap that nearly choked me, and then sank sickeningly.

The "bodies drawn out man-size" were gone, and their marble slabs lay wide and bare in the vague moonlight that slanted through the east window.

Were they really gone? or was I mad? Clenching my nerves, I stooped and passed my hand over the smooth slabs, and felt their flat unbroken surface. Had someone taken the things away? Was it some vile practical joke? I would make sure, anyway. In an instant I had made a torch of a newspaper, which happened to be in my pocket, and lighting it held it high above my head. Its yellow glare illumined the dark arches and those slabs. The figures were gone. And I was alone in the church; or was I alone?

And then a horror seized me, a horror indefinable and indescribable—an overwhelming certainty of supreme and accomplished calamity. I flung down the torch and tore along the aisle and out through the porch, biting my lips as I ran to keep myself from shrieking aloud. Oh, was I mad—or what was this that possessed me? I leaped the churchyard wall and took the straight cut across the fields, led by the light from our windows. Just as I got over the first stile, a dark figure seemed to spring out of the ground. Mad still with that certainty of misfortune, I made for the thing that stood in my path, shouting, "Get out of the way, can't you!"

But my push met with a more vigorous resistance than I had expected. My arms were caught just above the elbow and held as in a vice, and the raw-boned Irish doctor actually shook me.

"Would ye?" he cried, in his own unmistakable accents—"would ye, then?"

"Let me go, you fool," I gasped. "The marble figures have gone from the church; I tell you they've gone."

He broke into a ringing laugh. "I'll have to give ye a draught tomorrow, I see. Ye've bin smoking too much and listening to old wives' tales."

"I tell you, I've seen the bare slabs."

"Well, come back with me. I'm going up to old Palmer's—his daughter's ill; we'll look in at the church and let me see the bare slabs."

"You go, if you like," I said, a little less frantic for his laughter; "I'm going home to my wife."

"Rubbish, man," said he; "d'ye think I'll permit of that? Are ye to go saying all yer life that ye've seen solid marble endowed with vitality, and me to go all me life saying ye were a coward? No, sir—ye shan't do ut."

The night air—a human voice—and I think also the physical contact with this six feet of solid common sense, brought me back a little to my ordinary self, and the word "coward" was a mental shower-bath.

"Come on, then," I said sullenly; "perhaps you're right."

He still held my arm tightly. We got over the stile and back to the church. All was still as death. The place smelt very damp and earthy. We walked up the aisle. I am not ashamed to confess that I shut my eyes: I knew the figures would not be there. I heard Kelly strike a match.

"Here they are, ye see, right enough; ye've been dreaming or drinking, asking yer pardon for the imputation."

I opened my eyes. By Kelly's expiring vesta I saw two shapes lying "in their marble" on their slabs. I drew a deep breath, and caught his hand.

"I'm awfully indebted to you," I said. "It must have been some trick of light, or I have been working rather hard, perhaps that's it. Do you know, I was quite convinced they were gone."

"I'm aware of that," he answered rather grimly; "ye'll have to be careful of that brain of yours, my friend, I assure ye."

He was leaning over and looking at the right-hand figure, whose stony face was the most villainous and deadly in expression.

"By Jove," he said, "something has been afoot here—this hand is broken."

And so, it was. I was certain that it had been perfect the last time Laura and I had been there.

"Perhaps someone has tried to remove them," said the young doctor.

"That won't account for my impression," I objected.

"Too much painting and tobacco will account for that, well enough."

"Come along," I said, "or my wife will be getting anxious. You'll come in and have a drop of whisky and drink confusion to ghosts and better sense to me."

"I ought to go up to Palmer's, but it's so late now I'd best leave it till the morning," he replied. "I was kept late at the Union, and I've had to see a lot of people since. All right, I'll come back with ye."

I think he fancied I needed him more than did Palmer's girl, so, discussing how such an illusion could have been possible, and deducing from this experience large generalities concerning ghostly apparitions, we walked up to our cottage. We saw, as we walked up the garden-path, that bright light streamed out of the front door, and presently saw that the parlour door was open too. Had she gone out?

"Come in," I said, and Dr. Kelly followed me into the parlour. It was all ablaze with candles, not only the wax ones, but at least a dozen guttering, glaring tallow dips, stuck in vases and ornaments in unlikely places. Light, I knew, was Laura's remedy for nervousness. Poor child! Why had I left her? Brute that I was.

We glanced round the room, and at first, we did not see her. The window was open, and the draught set all the candles flaring one way. Her chair was empty and her handkerchief and book lay on the floor. I turned to the window. There, in the recess of the window, I saw her. Oh, my child, my love, had she gone to that window to watch for me? And what had come into the room behind her? To what had she turned with that look of frantic fear and horror? Oh, my little one, had she thought that it was I whose step she heard, and turned to meet—what?

She had fallen back across a table in the window, and her body lay half on it and half on the window-seat, and her head hung down over the table, the brown hair loosened and fallen to the carpet. Her lips were drawn back, and her eyes wide, wide open. They saw nothing now. What had they seen last?

The doctor moved towards her, but I pushed him aside and sprang to her; caught her in my arms and cried—-

"It's all right, Laura! I've got you safe, wifie."

She fell into my arms in a heap. I clasped her and kissed her, and

114

called her by all her pet names, but I think I knew all the time that she was dead. Her hands were tightly clenched. In one of them she held something fast. When I was quite sure that she was dead, and that nothing mattered at all any more, I let him open her hand to see what she held.

It was a grey marble finger.

The Yellow Wallpaper

Charlotte Perkins Gilman

It is very seldom that mere ordinary people like John and myself secure ancestral halls for the summer.

A colonial mansion, a hereditary estate, I would say a haunted house, and reach the height of romantic felicity—but that would be asking too much of fate!

Still, I will proudly declare that there is something queer about it.

Else, why should it be let so cheaply? And why have stood so long untenanted?

John laughs at me, of course, but one expects that in marriage.

John is practical in the extreme. He has no patience with faith, an intense horror of superstition, and he scoffs openly at any talk of things not to be felt and seen and put down in figures.

John is a physician, and *perhaps*—(I would not say it to a living soul, of course, but this is dead paper and a great relief to my mind)—*perhaps* that is one reason I do not get well faster.

You see he does not believe I am sick!

And what can one do?

If a physician of high standing, and one's own husband, assures friends and relatives that there is really nothing the matter with one but temporary nervous depression—a slight hysterical tendency—what is one to do?

My brother is also a physician, and also of high standing, and he says the same thing.

So, I take phosphates or phosphites—whichever it is, and tonics, and journeys, and air, and exercise, and am absolutely forbidden to "work" until I am well again.

Personally, I disagree with their ideas.

Personally, I believe that congenial work, with excitement and change, would do me good.

But what is one to do?

I did write for a while in spite of them; but it *does* exhaust me a good deal—having to be so sly about it, or else meet with heavy opposition.

I sometimes fancy that in my condition if I had less opposition and more society and stimulus—but John says the very worst thing I can do is to think about my condition, and I confess it always makes me feel bad.

So, I will let it alone and talk about the house.

The most beautiful place! It is quite alone, standing well back from the road, quite three miles from the village. It makes me think of English places that you read about, for there are hedges and walls and gates that lock, and lots of separate little houses for the gardeners and people.

There is a *delicious* garden! I never saw such a garden—large and shady, full of box-bordered paths, and lined with long grape-covered arbours with seats under them.

There were greenhouses, too, but they are all broken now.

There was some legal trouble, I believe, something about the heirs and coheirs; anyhow, the place has been empty for years.

That spoils my ghostliness, I am afraid, but I don't care—there is something strange about the house—I can feel it.

I even said so to John one moonlight evening, but he said what I felt was a *draught*, and shut the window.

I get unreasonably angry with John sometimes. I'm sure I never used to be so sensitive. I think it is due to this nervous condition.

But John says if I feel so, I shall neglect proper self-control; so, I take pains to control myself—before him, at least, and that makes me very tired.

I don't like our room a bit. I wanted one downstairs that opened on the *piazza* and had roses all over the window, and such pretty old-fashioned chintz hangings! but John would not hear of it.

He said there was only one window and not room for two beds, and no near room for him if he took another.

He is very careful and loving, and hardly lets me stir without special direction.

I have a schedule prescription for each hour in the day; he takes all care from me, and so I feel basely ungrateful not to value it more.

He said we came here solely on my account, that I was to have perfect rest and all the air I could get. "Your exercise depends on your strength, my dear," said he, "and your food somewhat on your appetite; but air you can absorb all the time." So, we took the nursery at the top of the house.

It is a big, airy room, the whole floor nearly, with windows that look all ways, and air and sunshine galore. It was nursery first and then playroom and gymnasium, I should judge; for the windows are barred for little children, and there are rings and things in the walls.

The paint and paper look as if a boys' school had used it. It is stripped off—the paper—in great patches all around the head of my bed, about as far as I can reach, and in a great place on the other side of the room low down. I never saw a worse paper in my life.

One of those sprawling flamboyant patterns committing every artistic sin.

It is dull enough to confuse the eye in following, pronounced enough to constantly irritate and provoke study, and when you follow the lame uncertain curves for a little distance, they suddenly commit suicide—plunge off at outrageous angles, destroy themselves in unheard of contradictions.

The colour is repellent, almost revolting; a smouldering unclean yellow, strangely faded by the slow-turning sunlight.

It is a dull yet lurid orange in some places, a sickly sulphur tint in others.

No wonder the children hated it! I should hate it myself if I had to live in this room long.

There comes John, and I must put this away—he hates to have me write a word.

We have been here two weeks, and I haven't felt like writing before, since that first day.

I am sitting by the window now, up in this atrocious nursery, and there is nothing to hinder my writing as much as I please, save lack of strength.

John is away all day, and even some nights when his cases are serious.

I am glad my case is not serious!

But these nervous troubles are dreadfully depressing.

John does not know how much I really suffer. He knows there is no *reason* to suffer, and that satisfies him.

Of course, it is only nervousness. It does weigh on me so not to do my duty in any way!

I meant to be such a help to John, such a real rest and comfort, and here I am a comparative burden already!

Nobody would believe what an effort it is to do what little I am able—to dress and entertain, and order things.

It is fortunate Mary is so good with the baby. Such a dear baby!

And yet I *cannot* be with him, it makes me so nervous.

I suppose John never was nervous in his life. He laughs at me so about this wallpaper!

At first, he meant to repaper the room, but afterwards he said that I was letting it get the better of me, and that nothing was worse for a nervous patient than to give way to such fancies.

He said that after the wallpaper was changed it would be the heavy bedstead, and then the barred windows, and then that gate at the head of the stairs, and so on.

"You know the place is doing you good," he said, "and really, dear, I don't care to renovate the house just for a three months' rental."

"Then do let us go downstairs," I said, "there are such pretty rooms there."

Then he took me in his arms and called me a blessed little goose, and said he would go down to the cellar, if I wished, and have it whitewashed into the bargain.

But he is right enough about the beds and windows and things.

It is an airy and comfortable room as any one need wish, and, of course, I would not be so silly as to make him uncomfortable just for a whim.

I'm really getting quite fond of the big room, all but that horrid paper.

Out of one window I can see the garden, those mysterious deep-shaded arbours, the riotous old-fashioned flowers, and bushes and gnarly trees.

Out of another I get a lovely view of the bay and a little private wharf belonging to the estate. There is a beautiful shaded lane that runs down there from the house. I always fancy I see people walking in these numerous paths and arbours, but John has cautioned me not to give way to fancy in the least. He says that with my imaginative power and habit of story-making, a nervous weakness like mine is sure to lead to all manner of excited fancies, and that I ought to use my will and good sense to check the tendency. So, I try.

I think sometimes that if I were only well enough to write a little it would relieve the press of ideas and rest me.

But I find I get pretty tired when I try.

It is so discouraging not to have any advice and companionship about my work. When I get really well, John says we will ask Cousin Henry and Julia down for a long visit; but he says he would as soon put fireworks in my pillow-case as to let me have those stimulating people about now.

I wish I could get well faster.

But I must not think about that. This paper looks to me as if it *knew* what a vicious influence it had!

There is a recurrent spot where the pattern lolls like a broken neck and two bulbous eyes stare at you upside down.

I get positively angry with the impertinence of it and the everlastingness. Up and down and sideways they crawl, and those absurd, unblinking eyes are everywhere. There is one place where two breadths didn't match, and the eyes go all up and down the line, one a little higher than the other.

I never saw so much expression in an inanimate thing before, and we all know how much expression they have! I used to lie awake as a child and get more entertainment and terror out of blank walls and plain furniture than most children could find in a toy store.

I remember what a kindly wink the knobs of our big, old bureau used to have, and there was one chair that always seemed like a strong friend.

I used to feel that if any of the other things looked too fierce, I could always hop into that chair and be safe.

The furniture in this room is no worse than inharmonious, however, for we had to bring it all from downstairs. I suppose when this was used as a playroom, they had to take the nursery things out, and no wonder! I never saw such ravages as the children have made here.

The wallpaper, as I said before, is torn off in spots, and it sticketh closer than a brother—they must have had perseverance as well as hatred.

Then the floor is scratched and gouged and splintered, the plaster itself is dug out here and there, and this great heavy bed which is all we found in the room, looks as if it had been through the wars.

But I don't mind it a bit—only the paper.

There comes John's sister. Such a dear girl as she is, and so careful of me! I must not let her find me writing.

She is a perfect and enthusiastic housekeeper, and hopes for no better profession. I verily believe she thinks it is the writing which made me sick!

But I can write when she is out, and see her a long way off from these windows.

There is one that commands the road, a lovely shaded winding road, and one that just looks off over the country. A lovely country, too, full of great elms and velvet meadows.

This wallpaper has a kind of sub-pattern in a different shade, a particularly irritating one, for you can only see it in certain lights, and not clearly then.

But in the places where it isn't faded and where the sun is just so—I can see a strange, provoking, formless sort of figure, that seems to skulk about behind that silly and conspicuous front design.

There's sister on the stairs!

Well, the Fourth of July is over! The people are gone and I am tired out. John thought it might do me good to see a little company, so we just had mother and Nellie and the children down for a week.

Of course, I didn't do a thing. Jennie sees to everything now.

But it tired me all the same.

John says if I don't pick up faster, he shall send me to Weir Mitchell in the fall.

But I don't want to go there at all. I had a friend who was in his hands once, and she says he is just like John and my brother, only more so!

Besides, it is such an undertaking to go so far.

I don't feel as if it was worthwhile to turn my hand over for anything, and I'm getting dreadfully fretful and querulous.

I cry at nothing, and cry most of the time.

Of course, I don't when John is here, or anybody else, but when I am alone.

And I am alone a good deal just now. John is kept in town very often by serious cases, and Jennie is good and lets me alone when I want her to.

So, I walk a little in the garden or down that lovely lane, sit on the porch under the roses, and lie down up here a good deal.

I'm getting really fond of the room in spite of the wallpaper. Perhaps *because* of the wallpaper.

It dwells in my mind so!

I lie here on this great immovable bed—it is nailed down, I believe—and follow that pattern about by the hour. It is as good as gymnastics, I assure you. I start, we'll say, at the bottom, down in the corner over there where it has not been touched, and I determine for the thousandth time that I *will* follow that pointless pattern to some sort of a conclusion.

I know a little of the principle of design, and I know this thing was not arranged on any laws of radiation, or alternation, or repetition, or symmetry, or anything else that I ever heard of.

It is repeated, of course, by the breadths, but not otherwise.

Looked at in one way each breadth stands alone, the bloated curves and flourishes—a kind of "debased Romanesque" with *delirium tremens*—go waddling up and down in isolated columns of fatuity.

But, on the other hand, they connect diagonally, and the sprawling outlines run off in great slanting waves of optic horror, like a lot of wallowing seaweeds in full chase.

The whole thing goes horizontally, too, at least it seems so, and I exhaust myself in trying to distinguish the order of its going in that direction.

They have used a horizontal breadth for a frieze, and that adds wonderfully to the confusion.

There is one end of the room where it is almost intact, and there, when the cross-lights fade and the low sun shines directly upon it, I can almost fancy radiation after all—the interminable grotesques seem to form around a common centre and rush off in headlong plunges of equal distraction.

It makes me tired to follow it. I will take a nap, I guess.

I don't know why I should write this.

I don't want to.

I don't feel able.

And I know John would think it absurd. But I *must* say what I feel and think in some way—it is such a relief!

But the effort is getting to be greater than the relief.

Half the time now I am awfully lazy, and lie down ever so much.

John says I musn't lose my strength, and has me take cod liver oil and lots of tonics and things, to say nothing of ale and wine and rare meat.

Dear John! He loves me very dearly, and hates to have me sick. I tried to have a real earnest reasonable talk with him the other day, and tell him how I wish he would let me go and make a visit to Cousin Henry and Julia.

But he said I wasn't able to go, nor able to stand it after I got there; and I did not make out a very good case for myself, for I was crying before I had finished.

It is getting to be a great effort for me to think straight. Just this nervous weakness I suppose.

And dear John gathered me up in his arms, and just carried me upstairs and laid me on the bed, and sat by me and read to me till it tired my head.

He said I was his darling and his comfort and all he had, and that I must take care of myself for his sake, and keep well.

He says no one but myself can help me out of it, that I must use my will and self-control and not let any silly fancies run away with me.

There's one comfort, the baby is well and happy, and does not have to occupy this nursery with the horrid wallpaper.

If we had not used it, that blessed child would have! What a fortunate escape! Why, I wouldn't have a child of mine, an impressionable little thing, live in such a room for worlds.

I never thought of it before, but it is lucky that John kept me here after all, I can stand it so much easier than a baby, you see.

Of course, I never mention it to them any more—I am too wise—but I keep watch of it all the same.

There are things in that paper that nobody knows but me, or ever will.

Behind that outside pattern the dim shapes get clearer every day.

It is always the same shape, only very numerous.

And it is like a woman stooping down and creeping about behind that pattern. I don't like it a bit. I wonder—I begin to think—I wish John would take me away from here!

It is so hard to talk with John about my case, because he is so wise, and because he loves me so.

But I tried it last night.

It was moonlight. The moon shines in all around just as the sun does.

I hate to see it sometimes, it creeps so slowly, and always comes in by one window or another.

John was asleep and I hated to waken him, so I kept still and watched the moonlight on that undulating wallpaper till I felt creepy.

The faint figure behind seemed to shake the pattern, just as if she wanted to get out.

I got up softly and went to feel and see if the paper *did* move, and when I came back John was awake.

"What is it, little girl?" he said. "Don't go walking about like that—you'll get cold."

I thought it was a good time to talk, so I told him that I really was not gaining here, and that I wished he would take me away.

"Why darling!" said he, "our lease will be up in three weeks, and I can't see how to leave before.

"The repairs are not done at home, and I cannot possibly leave town just now. Of course, if you were in any danger, I could and would, but you really are better, dear, whether you can see it or not. I am a doctor, dear, and I know. You are gaining flesh and colour, your appetite is better, I feel really much easier about you."

"I don't weigh a bit more," said I, "nor as much; and my appetite may be better in the evening when you are here, but it is worse in the morning when you are away!"

"Bless her little heart!" said he with a big hug, "she shall be as sick as she pleases! But now let's improve the shining hours by going to sleep, and talk about it in the morning!"

"And you won't go away?" I asked gloomily.

"Why, how can I, dear? It is only three weeks more and then we will take a nice little trip of a few days while Jennie is getting the house ready. Really dear you are better!"

"Better in body perhaps—" I began, and stopped short, for he sat up straight and looked at me with such a stern, reproachful look that I could not say another word.

"My darling," said he, "I beg of you, for my sake and for our child's sake, as well as for your own, that you will never for one instant let that idea enter your mind! There is nothing so dangerous, so fascinating, to a temperament like yours. It is a false and foolish fancy. Can you not trust me as a physician when I tell you so?"

So of course, I said no more on that score, and we went to sleep before long. He thought I was asleep first, but I wasn't, and lay there for hours trying to decide whether that front pattern and the back pattern really did move together or separately.

On a pattern like this, by daylight, there is a lack of sequence, a defiance of law, that is a constant irritant to a normal mind.

The color is hideous enough, and unreliable enough, and infuriating enough, but the pattern is torturing.

You think you have mastered it, but just as you get well underway in following, it turns a back-somersault and there you are. It slaps you in the face, knocks you down, and tramples upon you. It is like a bad dream.

The outside pattern is a florid arabesque, reminding one of a fungus. If you can imagine a toadstool in joints, an interminable string of toadstools, budding and sprouting in endless convolutions—why, that is something like it.

That is, sometimes!

There is one marked peculiarity about this paper, a thing nobody seems to notice but myself, and that is that it changes as the light changes.

When the sun shoots in through the east window—I always watch for that first long, straight ray—it changes so quickly that I never can quite believe it.

That is why I watch it always.

By moonlight—the moon shines in all night when there is a moon—I wouldn't know it was the same paper.

At night in any kind of light, in twilight, candle light, lamplight, and worst of all by moonlight, it becomes bars! The outside pattern I mean, and the woman behind it is as plain as can be.

I didn't realise for a long time what the thing was that showed behind, that dim sub-pattern, but now I am quite sure it is a woman.

By daylight she is subdued, quiet. I fancy it is the pattern that keeps her so still. It is so puzzling. It keeps me quiet by the hour.

I lie down ever so much now. John says it is good for me, and to sleep all I can.

Indeed, he started the habit by making me lie down for an hour after each meal.

It is a very bad habit I am convinced, for you see I don't sleep.

And that cultivates deceit, for I don't tell them I'm awake—O no!

The fact is I am getting a little afraid of John.

He seems very queer sometimes, and even Jennie has an inexplicable look.

It strikes me occasionally, just as a scientific hypothesis—that perhaps it is the paper!

I have watched John when he did not know I was looking, and come into the room suddenly on the most innocent excuses, and I've caught him several times *looking at the paper*! And Jennie too. I caught Jennie with her hand on it once.

She didn't know I was in the room, and when I asked her in a quiet, a very quiet voice, with the most restrained manner possible, what she was doing with the paper—she turned around as if she had been caught stealing, and looked quite angry—asked me why I should frighten her so!

Then she said that the paper stained everything it touched, that she had found yellow smooches on all my clothes and John's, and she wished we would be more careful!

Did not that sound innocent? But I know she was studying that pattern, and I am determined that nobody shall find it out but myself!

Life is very much more exciting now than it used to be. You see I have something more to expect, to look forward to, to watch. I really do eat better, and am more quiet than I was.

John is so pleased to see me improve! He laughed a little the other day, and said I seemed to be flourishing in spite of my wallpaper.

I turned it off with a laugh. I had no intention of telling him it was *because* of the wallpaper—he would make fun of me. He might even want to take me away.

I don't want to leave now until I have found it out. There is a week more, and I think that will be enough.

I'm feeling ever so much better! I don't sleep much at night, for it is so interesting to watch developments; but I sleep a good deal in the daytime.

In the daytime it is tiresome and perplexing.

There are always new shoots on the fungus, and new shades of yellow all over it. I cannot keep count of them, though I have tried conscientiously.

It is the strangest yellow, that wallpaper! It makes me think of all the yellow things I ever saw—not beautiful ones like buttercups, but old foul, bad yellow things.

But there is something else about that paper—the smell! I noticed it the moment we came into the room, but with so much air and sun it was not bad. Now we have had a week of fog and rain, and whether the windows are open or not, the smell is here.

It creeps all over the house.

I find it hovering in the dining-room, skulking in the parlour, hiding in the hall, lying in wait for me on the stairs.

It gets into my hair.

Even when I go to ride, if I turn my head suddenly and surprise it—there is that smell!

Such a peculiar odour, too! I have spent hours in trying to analyse it, to find what it smelled like.

It is not bad—at first, and very gentle, but quite the subtlest, most enduring odour I ever met.

In this damp weather it is awful, I wake up in the night and find it hanging over me.

It used to disturb me at first. I thought seriously of burning the house—to reach the smell.

But now I am used to it. The only thing I can think of that it is like is the *colour* of the paper! A yellow smell.

There is a very funny mark on this wall, low down, near the mop-board. A streak that runs round the room. It goes behind every piece of furniture, except the bed, a long, straight, even *smooch*, as if it had been rubbed over and over.

I wonder how it was done and who did it, and what they did it for. Round and round and round—round and round and round—it makes me dizzy!

I really have discovered something at last.

Through watching so much at night, when it changes so, I have finally found out.

The front pattern *does* move—and no wonder! The woman behind shakes it!

Sometimes I think there are a great many women behind, and sometimes only one, and she crawls around fast, and her crawling shakes it all over.

Then in the very bright spots she keeps still, and in the very shady spots she just takes hold of the bars and shakes them hard.

And she is all the time trying to climb through. But nobody could climb through that pattern—it strangles so; I think that is why it has so many heads.

They get through, and then the pattern strangles them off and turns them upside down, and makes their eyes white!

If those heads were covered or taken off it would not be half so bad.

I think that woman gets out in the daytime!

And I'll tell you why—privately—I've seen her!

I can see her out of every one of my windows!

It is the same woman, I know, for she is always creeping, and most women do not creep by daylight.

I see her on that long road under the trees, creeping along, and when a carriage comes, she hides under the blackberry vines.

I don't blame her a bit. It must be very humiliating to be caught creeping by daylight!

I always lock the door when I creep by daylight. I can't do it at night, for I know John would suspect something at once.

And John is so queer now, that I don't want to irritate him. I wish he would take another room! Besides, I don't want anybody to get that woman out at night but myself.

I often wonder if I could see her out of all the windows at once.

But, turn as fast as I can, I can only see out of one at one time.

And though I always see her, she *may* be able to creep faster than I can turn!

I have watched her sometimes away off in the open country, creeping as fast as a cloud shadow in a high wind.

If only that top pattern could be gotten off from the under one! I mean to try it, little by little.

I have found out another funny thing, but I shan't tell it this time! It does not do to trust people too much.

There are only two more days to get this paper off, and I believe John is beginning to notice. I don't like the look in his eyes.

And I heard him ask Jennie a lot of professional questions about me. She had a very good report to give.

She said I slept a good deal in the daytime.

John knows I don't sleep very well at night, for all I'm so quiet!

He asked me all sorts of questions, too, and pretended to be very loving and kind.

As if I couldn't see through him!

Still, I don't wonder he acts so, sleeping under this paper for three months.

It only interests me, but I feel sure John and Jennie are secretly affected by it.

Hurrah! This is the last day, but it is enough. John is to stay in town overnight, and won't be out until this evening.

Jennie wanted to sleep with me—the sly thing! but I told her I should undoubtedly rest better for a night all alone.

That was clever, for really, I wasn't alone a bit! As soon as it was moonlight and that poor thing began to crawl and shake the pattern, I got up and ran to help her.

I pulled and she shook, I shook and she pulled, and before morning we had peeled off yards of that paper.

A strip about as high as my head and half around the room.

And then when the sun came and that awful pattern began to laugh at me, I declared I would finish it today!

We go away tomorrow, and they are moving all my furniture down again to leave things as they were before.

Jennie looked at the wall in amazement, but I told her merrily that I did it out of pure spite at the vicious thing.

She laughed and said she wouldn't mind doing it herself, but I must not get tired.

How she betrayed herself that time!

But I am here, and no person touches this paper but me—not *alive*!

She tried to get me out of the room—it was too patent! But I said it was so quiet and empty and clean now that I believed I would lie down again and sleep all I could; and not to wake me even for dinner—I would call when I woke.

So now she is gone, and the servants are gone, and the things are gone, and there is nothing left but that great bedstead nailed down, with the canvas mattress we found on it.

We shall sleep downstairs tonight, and take the boat home tomorrow.

I quite enjoy the room, now it is bare again.

How those children did tear about here!

This bedstead is fairly gnawed!

But I must get to work.

I have locked the door and thrown the key down into the front path.

I don't want to go out, and I don't want to have anybody come in, till John comes.

I want to astonish him.

I've got a rope up here that even Jennie did not find. If that woman does get out, and tries to get away, I can tie her!

But I forgot I could not reach far without anything to stand on!

This bed will *not* move!

I tried to lift and push it until I was lame, and then I got so angry I bit off a little piece at one corner—but it hurt my teeth.

Then I peeled off all the paper I could reach standing on the floor. It sticks horribly and the pattern just enjoys it! All those strangled heads and bulbous eyes and waddling fungus growths just shriek with derision!

I am getting angry enough to do something desperate. To jump out of the window would be admirable exercise, but the bars are too strong even to try.

Besides I wouldn't do it. Of course not. I know well enough that a step like that is improper and might be misconstrued.

I don't like to *look* out of the windows even—there are so many of

130

those creeping women, and they creep so fast.

I wonder if they all come out of that wallpaper as I did?

But I am securely fastened now by my well-hidden rope—you don't get *me* out in the road there!

I suppose I shall have to get back behind the pattern when it comes night, and that is hard!

It is so pleasant to be out in this great room and creep around as I please!

I don't want to go outside. I won't, even if Jennie asks me to.

For outside you have to creep on the ground, and everything is green instead of yellow.

But here I can creep smoothly on the floor, and my shoulder just fits in that long smooch around the wall, so I cannot lose my way.

Why there's John at the door!

It is no use, young man, you can't open it!

How he does call and pound!

Now he's crying for an axe.

It would be a shame to break down that beautiful door!

"John dear!" said I in the gentlest voice, "the key is down by the front steps, under a plantain leaf!"

That silenced him for a few moments.

Then he said—very quietly indeed, "Open the door, my darling!"

"I can't," said I. "The key is down by the front door under a plantain leaf!"

And then I said it again, several times, very gently and slowly, and said it so often that he had to go and see, and he got it of course, and came in. He stopped short by the door.

"What is the matter?" he cried. "For God's sake, what are you doing!"

I kept on creeping just the same, but I looked at him over my shoulder.

"I've got out at last," said I, "in spite of you and Jane. And I've pulled off most of the paper, so you can't put me back!"

Now why should that man have fainted? But he did, and right across my path by the wall, so that I had to creep over him every time!

Reality or Delusion?

Mrs Henry Wood

This is a ghost story. Every word of it is true. And I don't mind confessing that for ages afterwards some of us did not care to pass the spot alone at night. Some people do not care to pass it yet.

It was autumn, and we were at Crabb Cot. Lena had been ailing; and in October Mrs. Todhetley proposed to the squire that they should remove with her there, to see if the change would do her good.

We Worcestershire people call North Crabb a village; but one might count the houses in it, little and great, and not find four-and-twenty. South Crabb, half a mile off, is ever so much larger; but the church and school are at North Crabb.

John Ferrar had been employed by Squire Todhetley as a sort of overlooker on the estate, or working bailiff. He had died the previous winter; leaving nothing behind him except some debts; for he was not provident; and his handsome son Daniel. Daniel Ferrar, who was rather superior as far as education went, disliked work: he would make a show of helping his father, but it came to little. Old Ferrar had not put him to any particular trade or occupation, and Daniel, who was as proud as Lucifer, would not turn to it himself. He liked to be a gentleman. All he did now was to work in his garden, and feed his fowls, ducks, rabbits, and pigeons, of which he kept a great quantity, selling them to the houses around and sending them to market.

But, as everyone said, poultry would not maintain him. Mrs. Lease, in the pretty cottage hard by Ferrar's, grew tired of saying it. This Mrs. Lease and her daughter, Maria, must not be confounded with Lease the pointsman: they were in a better condition of life, and not related to him. Daniel Ferrar used to run in and out of their house at will when a boy, and he was now engaged to be married to Maria. She would have a little money, and the Leases were respected in North Crabb. People began to whisper a query as to how Ferrar got his corn for the poultry: he was not known to buy much: and he would have to go out of his house at Christmas, for its owner, Mr. Coney, had given him notice. Mrs. Lease, anxious about Maria's prospects, asked Daniel what he intended to do then, and he answered, 'Make his fortune: he should begin to do it as soon as he could turn himself round.' But the time was going on, and the turning round seemed to be as far off as ever.

After Midsummer, a niece of the schoolmistress's, Miss Timmens, had come to the school to stay: her name was Harriet Roe. The father, Humphrey Roe, was half-brother to Miss Timmens. He had married a Frenchwoman, and lived more in France than in England until his death. The girl had been christened Henriette; but North Crabb, not understanding much French, converted it into Harriet. She was a showy, free-mannered, good-looking girl, and made speedy acquaintance with Daniel Ferrar; or he with her. They improved upon it so rapidly that Maria Lease grew jealous, and North Crabb began to say he cared for Harriet more than for Maria.

When Tod and I got home the latter end of October, to spend the squire's birthday, things were in this state. James Hill, the bailiff who had been taken on by the squire in John Ferrar's place (but a far inferior man to Ferrar; not much better, in fact, than a common workman, and of whose doings you will hear soon in regard to his little stepson, David Garth) gave us an account of matters in general. Daniel Ferrar had been drinking lately, Hill added, and his head was not strong enough to stand it; and he was also beginning to look as if he had some care upon him.

'A nice lot, he, for them two women to be fighting for,' cried Hill, who was no friend to Ferrar. 'There'll be mischief between 'm if they don't draw in a bit. Maria Lease is next door to mad over it, I know; and t'other, finding herself the best liked, crows over her. It's something like the Bible story of Leah and Rachel, young gents, Dan Ferrar likes the one, and he's bound by promise to the t'other. As to the French jade,' concluded Hill, giving his head a toss, 'she'd make a show of liking any man that followed her, she would; a dozen of 'em on a string.'

It was all very well for surly Hill to call Daniel Ferrar a 'nice lot', but he was the best-looking fellow in the church on Sunday morning well-dressed too. But his colour seemed brighter; and his hands shook as they were raised, often, to push back his hair, that the sun shone upon through the south-window, turning it to gold. He scarcely looked up, not even at Harriet Roe, with her dark eyes roving everywhere, and her streaming pink ribbons. Maria Lease was pale, quiet, and nice, as usual; she had no beauty, but her face was sensible, and her deep grey eyes had a strange and curious earnestness. The new parson preached, a young man just appointed to the parish of Crabb. He went in for great observances of Saints' days, and told his congregation that he should expect to see them at church on the morrow, which would be the Feast of All Saints.

Daniel Ferrar walked home with Mrs. Lease and Maria after service, and was invited to dinner. I ran across to shake hands with the old dame, who had once nursed me through an illness, and promised to look in and see her later. We were going back to school on the morrow. As I turned away, Harriet Roe passed, her pink ribbons and her cheap gay silk dress gleaming in the sunlight. She stared at me, and I stared back again. And now, the explanation of matters being over, the real story begins. But I shall have to tell some of it as it was told by others.

The tea-things waited on Mrs. Lease's table in the afternoon; waited for Daniel Ferrar. He had left them shortly before to go and attend to his poultry. Nothing had been said about his coming back for tea: that he would do so had been looked upon as a matter of course. But he did not make his appearance, and the tea was taken without him. At half-past five the church-bell rang out for evening service, and Maria put her things on. Mrs. Lease did not go out at night.

'You are starting early, Maria. You'll be in church before other people.'

'That won't matter, mother.'

A jealous suspicion lay on Maria—that the secret of Daniel Ferrar's absence was his having fallen in with Harriet Roe: perhaps he had gone of his own accord to seek her. She walked slowly along. The gloom of dusk, and a deep dusk, had stolen over the evening, but the moon would be up later. As Maria passed the schoolhouse, she halted to glance in at the little sitting-room window: the shutters were not closed yet, and the room was lighted by the blazing fire. Harriet was not there. She only saw Miss Timmens, the mistress, who was putting on her bonnet before a hand-glass propped upright on the mantelpiece. Without warning, Miss Timmens turned and threw open the window. It was only for the purpose of pulling-to the shutters, but Maria thought she must have been observed, and spoke.

'Good evening, Miss Timmens.'

'Who is it?' cried out Miss Timmens, in answer, peering into the dusk. 'Oh, it's you, Maria Lease! Have you seen anything of Harriet? She went off somewhere this afternoon, and never came in to tea.'

'I have not seen her.'

'She's gone to the Batleys', I'll be bound. She knows I don't like her to be with the Batley girls: they make her ten times flightier than she would otherwise be.'

Miss Timmens drew in her shutters with a jerk, without which they would not close, and Maria Lease turned away.

'Not at the Batleys', not at the Batleys', but with *him*,' she cried, in bitter rebellion, as she turned away from the church. From the church, not to it. Was Maria to blame for wishing to see whether she was right or not?—for walking about a little in the thought of meeting them? At any rate it is what she did. And had her reward; such as it was.

As she was passing the top of the withy walk, their voices reached her ear. People often walked there, and it was one of the ways to South Crabb. Maria drew back amidst the trees, and they came on: Harriet Roe and Daniel Ferrar, walking arm-in-arm.

'I think I had better take it off,' Harriet was saying. 'No need to invoke a storm upon my head. And that would come in a shower of hail from stiff old Aunt Timmens.'

The answer seemed one of quick accent, but Ferrar spoke low. Maria Lease had hard work to control herself: anger, passion, jealousy, all blazed up. With her arms stretched out to a friendly tree on either side,—with her heart beating,—with her pulses coursing on to fever-heat, she watched them across the bit of common to the road. Harriet went one way then; he another, in the direction of Mrs. Lease's cottage. No doubt to fetch her Maria—to church, with a plausible excuse of having been detained. Until now she had had no proof of his falseness; had never perfectly believed in it.

She took her arms from the trees and went forward, a sharp faint cry of despair breaking forth on the night air. Maria Lease was one of those silent-natured girls who can never speak of a wrong like this. She had to bury it within her; down, down, out of sight and show; and she went into church with her usual quiet step. Harriet Roe with Miss Timmens came next, quite demure, as if she had been singing some of the infant scholars to sleep at their own homes. Daniel Ferrar did not go to church at all: he stayed, as was found afterwards, with Mrs. Lease.

Maria might as well have been at home as at church: better perhaps that she had been. Not a syllable of the service did she hear: her brain was a sea of confusion; the tumult within it rising higher and higher. She did not hear even the text, 'Peace, be still', or the sermon; both so singularly appropriate. The passions in men's minds, the preacher said, raged and foamed just like the angry waves of the sea in a storm, until Jesus came to still them.

I ran after Maria when church was over, and went in to pay the promised visit to old Mother Lease. Daniel Ferrar was sitting in the parlour. He got up and offered Maria a chair at the fire, but she turned her back and stood at the table under the window, taking off her gloves. An open Bible was before Mrs. Lease: I wondered whether she had been reading aloud to Daniel.

'What was the text, child?' asked the old lady.

No answer.

'Do you hear, Maria! What was the text?'

Maria turned at that, as if suddenly awakened. Her face was white; her eyes had in them an uncertain terror.

'The text?' she stammered. 'I—I forget it, mother. It was from Genesis, I think.'

'Was it, Master Johnny?'

'It was from the fourth chapter of St. Mark, 'Peace, be still."

Mrs. Lease stared at me. 'Why, that is the very chapter I've been reading. Well now, that's curious. But there's never a better in the Bible, and never a better text was taken from it than those three words. I have been telling Daniel here, Master Johnny, that when once that peace, Christ's peace, is got into the heart, storms can't hurt us much. And you are going away again tomorrow, sir?' she added, after a pause. 'It's a short stay?'

I was not going away on the morrow. Tod and I, taking the squire in a genial moment after dinner, had pressed to be let stay until Tuesday, Tod using the argument, and laughing while he did it, that it must be wrong to travel on All Saints' Day, when the parson had specially enjoined us to be at church. The squire told us we were a couple of encroaching rascals, and if he did let us stay it should be upon condition that we did go to church. This I said to them.

'He may send you all the same, sir, when the morning comes,' remarked Daniel Ferrar.

'Knowing Mr. Todhetley as you do Ferrar, you may remember that he never breaks his promises.'

Daniel laughed. 'He grumbles over them, though, Master Johnny.'

'Well, he may grumble tomorrow about our staying, say it is wasting time that ought to be spent in study, but he will not send us back until Tuesday.'

Until Tuesday! If I could have foreseen then what would have happened before Tuesday! If all of us could have foreseen! Seen the few hours between now and then depicted, as in a mirror, event by event! Would it have saved the calamity, the dreadful sin that could never be redeemed? Why, yes; surely it would. Daniel Ferrar turned and looked at Maria.

'Why don't you come to the fire?'

'I am very well here, thank you.'

She had sat down where she was, her bonnet touching the curtain. Mrs. Lease, not noticing that anything was wrong, had begun talking about Lena, whose illness was turning to low fever, when the house door opened and Harriet Roe came in.

'What a lovely night it is!' she said, taking of own accord the chair I had not cared to take, for I kept saying I must go. 'Maria, what went with you after church? I hunted for you everywhere.'

Maria gave no answer. She looked black and angry, and her bosom heaved as if a storm were brewing. Harriet Roe slightly laughed.

'Do you intend to take holiday tomorrow, Mrs. Lease?'

'Me take holiday! what is there in tomorrow to take holiday for?' returned Mrs. Lease.

'I shall,' continued Harriet, not answering the question: 'I have been used to it in France. All Saints' Day is a grand holiday there; we go to church in our best clothes, and pay visits afterwards. Following it, like a dark shadow, comes the gloomy *Jour des Morts*.'

'The what?' cried Mrs. Lease, bending her ear.

'The day of the dead. All Souls' Day. But you English don't go to the cemeteries to pray.'

Mrs. Lease put on her spectacles, which lay upon the open pages of the Bible, and stared at Harriet. Perhaps she thought they might help her to understand. The girl laughed.

'On All Souls' Day, whether it be wet or dry, the French cemeteries are full of kneeling women draped in black; all praying for the repose of their dead relatives, after the manner of the Roman Catholics.'

Daniel Ferrar, who had not spoken a word since she came in, but sat with his face to the fire, turned and looked at her. Upon which she tossed back her head and her pink ribbons, and smiled till all her teeth were seen. Good teeth they were. As to reverence in her tone, there was none.

'I have seen them kneeling when the slosh and wet have been ankle-deep. Did you ever see a ghost?' added she, with energy. 'The French believe that the spirits of the dead come abroad on the night of All Saints' Day. You'd scarcely get a French woman to go out of her house after dark. It is their chief superstition.'

'What *is* the superstition?' questioned Mrs. Lease.

'Why, *that*,' said Harriet. 'They believe that the dead are allowed to revisit the world after dark on the Eve of All Souls; that they hover in the air, waiting to appear to any of their living relatives, who may venture out, lest they should forget to pray on the morrow for the rest of their souls.' (A superstition obtaining amongst some of the lower orders in France.)

'Well, I never!' cried Mrs. Lease, staring excessively. 'Did you ever hear the like of that, sir?' turning to me.

'Yes; I have heard of it.'

Harriet Roe looked up at me; I was standing at the corner of the mantelpiece. She laughed a free laugh.

'I say, wouldn't it be fun to go out tomorrow night, and meet the ghosts? Only, perhaps they don't visit this country, as it is not under Rome.'

'Now just you behave yourself before your betters, Harriet Roe, put in Mrs. Lease, sharply. 'That gentleman is young Mr. Ludlow of Crabb Cot.'

'And very happy I am to make young Mr. Ludlow's acquaintance,' returned easy Harriet, flinging back her mantle from her shoulders. 'How hot your parlour is, Mrs. Lease.'

The hook of the cloak had caught in a thin chain of twisted gold that she wore round her neck, displaying it to view. She hurriedly folded her cloak together, as if wishing to conceal the chain. But Mrs. Lease's spectacles had seen it.

'What's that you've got on, Harriet? A gold chain?'

A moment's pause, and then Harriet Roe flung back her mantle again, defiance upon her face, and touched the chain with her hand.

'That's what it is, Mrs. Lease: a gold chain. And a very pretty one, too.'

'Was it your mother's?'

'It was never anybody's but mine. I had it made a present to me this afternoon; for a keepsake.'

Happening to look at Maria, I was startled at her face, it was so white and dark: white with emotion, dark with an angry despair that

I for one did not comprehend. Harriet Roe, throwing at her a look of saucy triumph, went out with as little ceremony as she had come in, just calling back a general good night; and we heard her footsteps outside getting gradually fainter in the distance. Daniel Ferrar rose.

'I'll take my departure too, I think. You are very unsociable tonight, Maria.'

'Perhaps I am. Perhaps I have cause to be.'

She flung his hand back when he held it out; and in another moment, as if a thought struck her, ran after him into the passage to speak. I, standing near the door in the small room, caught the words.

'I must have an explanation with you, Daniel Ferrar. Now. Tonight. We cannot go on thus for a single hour longer.'

'Not tonight, Maria; I have no time to spare. And I don't know what you mean.'

'You do know. Listen. I will not go to my rest, no, though it were for twenty nights to come, until we have had it out. I vow I will not. There. You are playing with me. Others have long said so, and I know it now.'

He seemed to speak some quieting words to her, for the tone was low and soothing; and then went out, closing the door behind him. Maria came back and stood with her face and its ghastliness turned from us. And still the old mother noticed nothing.

'Why don't you take your things off, Maria?' she asked.

'Presently,' was the answer.

I said goodnight in my turn, and went away. Halfway home I met Tod with the two young Lexoms. The Lexoms made us go in and stay to supper, and it was ten o'clock before we left them.

'We shall catch it,' said Tod, setting off at a run. They never let us stay out late on a Sunday evening, on account of the reading.

But, as it happened, we escaped scot-free this time, for the house was in a commotion about Lena. She had been better in the afternoon, but at nine o'clock the fever returned worse than ever. Her little cheeks and lips were scarlet as she lay on the bed, her wide-open eyes were bright and glistening. The squire had gone up to look at her, and was fuming and fretting in his usual fashion.

'The doctor has never sent the medicine,' said patient Mrs. Todhetley, who must have been worn out with nursing. 'She ought to take it; I am sure she ought.'

'These boys are good to run over to Cole's for that,' cried the squire. 'It won't hurt them; it's a fine night.'

Of course we were good for it. And we got our caps again; being charged to enjoin Mr. Cole to come over the first thing in the morning.

'Do you care much about my going with you, Johnny?' Tod asked as we were turning out at the door. 'I am awfully tired.'

'Not a bit. I'd as soon go alone as not. You'll see me back in half-an-hour.'

I took the nearest way; flying across the fields at a canter, and startling the hares. Mr. Cole lived near South Crabb, and I don't believe more than ten minutes had gone by when I knocked at his door. But to get back as quickly was another thing. The doctor was not at home. He had been called out to a patient at eight o'clock, and had not yet returned.

I went in to wait: the servant said he might be expected to come in from minute to minute. It was of no use to go away without the medicine; and I sat down in the surgery in front of the shelves, and fell asleep counting the white jars and physic bottles. The doctor's entrance awoke me.

'I am sorry you should have had to come over and to wait,' he said. 'When my other patient, with whom I was detained a considerable time, was done with, I went on to Crabb Cot with the child's medicine, which I had in my pocket.'

'They think her very ill tonight, sir.'

'I left her better, and going quietly to sleep. She will soon be well again, I hope.'

'Why! is that the time?' I exclaimed, happening to catch sight of the clock as I was crossing the hall. It was nearly twelve. Mr. Cole laughed, saying time passed quickly when folk were asleep.

I went back slowly. The sleep, or the canter before it, had made me feel as tired as Tod had said he was. It was a night to be abroad in and to enjoy; calm, warm, light. The moon, high in the sky, illumined every blade of grass; sparkled on the water of the little rivulet; brought out the moss on the grey walls of the old church; played on its round-faced clock, then striking twelve.

Twelve o'clock at night at North Crabb answers to about three in the morning in London, for country people are mostly in bed and asleep at ten. Therefore, when loud and angry voices struck up in dispute, just as the last stroke of the hour was dying away on the midnight air, I stood still and doubted my ears.

I was getting near home then. The sounds came from the back of a building standing alone in a solitary place on the left-hand side of the road. It belonged to the squire, and was called the yellow barn, its walls being covered with a yellow wash; but it was in fact used as a storehouse for corn. I was passing in front of it when the voices rose upon the air. Round the building I ran, and saw Maria Lease: and something else that I could not at first comprehend. In the pursuit of her vow, not to go to rest until she had 'had it out' with Daniel Ferrar, Maria had been abroad searching for him. What ill fate brought her looking for him up near our barn?—perhaps because she had fruitlessly searched in every other spot.

At the back of this barn, up some steps, was an unused door. Unused partly because it was not required, the principal entrance being in front; partly because the key of it had been for a long time missing. Stealing out at this door, a bag of corn upon his shoulders, had come Daniel Ferrar in a smock-frock. Maria saw him, and stood back in the shade. She watched him lock the door and put the key in his pocket; she watched him give the heavy bag a jerk as he turned to come down the steps. Then she burst out. Her loud reproaches petrified him, and he stood there as one suddenly turned to stone. It was at that moment that I appeared.

I understood it all soon; it needed not Maria's words to enlighten me. Daniel Ferrar possessed the lost key and could come in and out at will in the midnight hours when the world was sleeping, and help himself to the corn. No wonder his poultry throve; no wonder there had been grumblings at Crabb Cot at the mysterious disappearance of the good grain.

Maria Lease was decidedly mad in those few first moments. Stealing is looked upon in an honest village as an awful thing; a disgrace, a crime; and there was the night's earlier misery besides. Daniel Ferrar was a thief! Daniel Ferrar was false to her! A storm of words and reproaches poured forth from her in confusion, none of it very distinct. 'Living upon theft! Convicted felon! Transportation for life! Squire Todhetley's corn! Fattening poultry on stolen goods! Buying gold chains with the profits for that bold, flaunting French girl, Harriet Roe! Taking his stealthy walks with her!'

My going up to them stopped the charge. There was a pause; and then Maria, in her mad passion, denounced him to me, as representative (so she put it) of the squire—the breaker-in upon our premises! the robber of our stored corn!

Daniel Ferrar came down the steps; he had remained there still as

142

a statue, immovable; and turned his white face to me. Never a word in defence said he: the blow had crushed him; he was a proud man (if anyone can understand that), and to be discovered in this ill-doing was worse than death to him.

'Don't think of me more hardly than you can help, Master Johnny,' he said in a quiet tone. 'I have been almost tired of my life this long while.'

Putting down the bag of corn near the steps, he took the key from his pocket and handed it to me. The man's aspect had so changed; there was something so grievously subdued and sad about him altogether, that I felt as sorry for him as if he had not been guilty. Maria Lease went on in her fiery passion.

'You'll be more tired of it tomorrow when the police are taking you to Worcester gaol. Squire Todhetley will not spare you, though your father was his many-years bailiff. He could not, you know, if he wished; Master Ludlow has seen you in the act.'

'Let me have the key again for a minute, sir,' he said, as quietly as though he had not heard a word. And I gave it to him. I'm not sure but I should have given him my head had he asked for it.

He swung the bag on his shoulders, unlocked the granary door, and put the bag beside the other sacks. The bag was his own, as we found afterwards, but he left it there. Locking the door again, he gave me the key, and went away with a weary step.

'Goodbye, Master Johnny.'

I answered back goodnight civilly, though he had been stealing. When he was out of sight, Maria Lease, her passion full upon her still, dashed off towards her mother's cottage, a strange cry of despair breaking from her lips.

'Where have you been lingering, Johnny?' roared the squire, who was sitting up for me. 'You have been throwing at the owls, sir, that's what you've been at; you have been scudding after the hares.'

I said I had waited for Mr. Cole, and had come back slower than I went; but I said no more, and went up to my room at once. And the squire went to his.

I know I am only a muff; people tell me so, often: but I can't help it; I did not make myself. I lay awake till nearly daylight, first wishing Daniel Ferrar could be screened, and then thinking it might perhaps be done. If he would only take the lesson to heart and go straight for the future, what a capital thing it would be. We had liked old Ferrar; he had done me and Tod many a good turn: and, for the matter of that, we liked Daniel. So I never said a word when morning came of the past night's work.

'Is Daniel at home?' I asked, going to Ferrar's the first thing before breakfast. I meant to tell him that if he would keep right, I would keep counsel.

'He went out at dawn, sir,' answered the old woman who did for him, and sold his poultry at market. 'He'll be in presently: he have had no breakfast yet.'

'Then tell him when he comes, to wait in, and see me: tell him it's all right. Can you remember, Goody? 'It is all right."

'I'll remember, safe enough, Master Ludlow.'

Tod and I, being on our honour, went to church, and found about ten people in the pews. Harriet Roe was one, with her pink ribbons, the twisted gold chain showing outside a short-cut velvet jacket.

'No, sir; he has not been home yet; I can't think where he can have got to,' was the old Goody's reply when I went again to Ferrar's. And so I wrote a word in pencil, and told her to give it him when he came in, for I could not go dodging there every hour of the day.

After luncheon, strolling by the back of the barn: a certain reminiscence I suppose taking me there, for it was not a frequented spot: I saw Maria Lease coming along.

Well, it was a change! The passionate woman of the previous night had subsided into a poor, wild-looking, sorrow-stricken thing, ready to die of remorse. Excessive passion had wrought its usual consequences; a reaction: a reaction in favour of Daniel Ferrar. She came up to me, clasping her hands in agony—beseeching that I would spare him; that I would not tell of him; that I would give him a chance for the future: and her lips quivered and trembled, and there were dark circles round her hollow eyes.

I said that I had not told and did not intend to tell. Upon which she was going to fall down on her knees, but I rushed off.

'Do you know where he is?' I asked, when she came to her sober senses.

'Oh, I wish I did know! Master Johnny, he is just the man to go and do something desperate. He would never face shame; and I was a mad, hard-hearted, wicked girl to do what I did last night. He might run away to sea; he might go and enlist for a soldier.'

'I dare say he is at home by this time. I have left a word for him there, and promised to go in and see him tonight. If he will undertake not to be up to wrong things again, no one shall ever know of this from me.'

She went away easier, and I sauntered on towards South Crabb. Eager as Tod and I had been for the day's holiday, it did not seem to be turning out much of a boon. In going home again—there was nothing worth staying out for—I had come to the spot by the three-cornered grove where I saw Maria, when a galloping policeman overtook me. My heart stood still; for I thought he must have come after Daniel Ferrar.

'Can you tell me if I am near to Crabb Cot—Squire Todhetley's?' he asked, reining-in his horse.

'You will reach it in a minute or two. I live there. Squire Todhetley is not at home. What do you want with him?'

'It's only to give in an official paper, sir. I have to leave one personally upon all the county magistrates.'

He rode on. When I got in I saw the folded paper upon the hall-table; the man and horse had already gone onwards. It was worse indoors than out; less to be done. Tod had disappeared after church; the squire was abroad; Mrs. Todhetley sat upstairs with Lena: and I strolled out again. It was only three o'clock then.

An hour, or more, was got through somehow; meeting one, talking to another, throwing at the ducks and geese; anything. Mrs. Lease had her head, smothered in a yellow shawl, stretched out over the palings as I passed her cottage.

'Don't catch cold, mother.'

'I am looking for Maria, sir. I can't think what has come to her today, Master Johnny,' she added, dropping her voice to a confidential tone. 'The girl seems demented: she has been going in and out ever since daylight like a dog in a fair.'

'If I meet her I will send her home.'

And in another minute I did meet her. For she was coming out of Daniel Ferrar's yard. I supposed he was at home again.

'No,' she said looking more wild, worn, haggard than before; 'that's what I have been to ask. I am just out of my senses, sir. He has gone for certain. Gone!'

I did not think it. He would not be likely to go away without clothes.

'Well, I know he is, Master Johnny; something tells me. I've been all about everywhere. There's a great dread upon me, sir; I never felt anything like it.'

'Wait until night, Maria; I dare say he will go home then. Your

145

mother is looking out for you; I said if I met you I'd send you in.'

Mechanically she turned towards the cottage, and I went on. Presently, as I was sitting on a gate watching the sunset, Harriet Roe passed towards the withy walk, and gave me a nod in her free but good-natured way.

'Are you going there to look out for the ghosts this evening?' I asked: and I wished not long afterwards I had not said it. 'It will soon be dark.'

'So it will,' she said, turning to the red sky in the west. 'But I have no time to give to the ghosts tonight.'

'Have you seen Ferrar today?' I cried, an idea occurring to me.

'No. And I can't think where he has got to; unless he is off to Worcester. He told me he should have to go there someday this week.'

She evidently knew nothing about him, and went on her way with another free-and-easy nod. I sat on the gate till the sun had gone down, and then thought it was time to be getting homewards.

Close against the yellow barn, the scene of last night's trouble, whom should I come upon but Maria Lease. She was standing still, and turned quickly at the sound of my footsteps. Her face was bright again, but had a puzzled look upon it.

'I have just seen him: he has not gone,' she said in a happy whisper. 'You were right, Master Johnny, and I was wrong.'

'Where did you see him?'

'Here; not a minute ago. I saw him twice. He is angry, very, and will not let me speak to him; both times he got away before I could reach him. He is close by somewhere.'

I looked round, naturally; but Ferrar was nowhere to be seen. There was nothing to conceal him except the barn, and that was locked up. The account she gave was this and her face grew puzzled again as she related it.

Unable to rest indoors, she had wandered up here again, and saw Ferrar standing at the corner of the barn, looking very hard at her. She thought he was waiting for her to come up, but before she got close to him he had disappeared, and she did not see which way. She hastened past the front of the barn, ran round to the back, and there he was. He stood near the steps looking out for her; waiting for her, as it again seemed; and was gazing at her with the same fixed stare. But again she missed him before she could get quite up; and it was at that moment that I arrived on the scene.

I went all round the barn, but could see nothing of Ferrar. It was an extraordinary thing where he could have got to. Inside the barn he could not be: it was securely locked; and there was no appearance of him in the open country. It was, so to say, broad daylight yet, or at least not far short of it; the red light was still in the west. Beyond the field at the back of the barn, was a grove of trees in the form of a triangle; and this grove was flanked by Crabb Ravine, which ran right and left. Crabb Ravine had the reputation of being haunted; for a light was sometimes seen dodging about its deep descending banks at night that no one could account for. A lively spot altogether for those who liked gloom.

'Are you sure it was Ferrar, Maria?'

'Sure!' she returned in surprise. 'You don't think I could mistake him Master Johnny, do you? He wore that ugly seal-skin winter-cap of his tied over his ears, and his thick grey coat. The coat was buttoned closely round him. I have not seen him wear either since last winter.'

That Ferrar must have gone into hiding somewhere seemed quite evident; and yet there was nothing but the ground to receive him. Maria said she lost sight of him the last time in a moment; both times in fact; and it was absolutely impossible that he could have made off to the triangle or elsewhere, as she must have seen him cross the open land. For that matter I must have seen him also.

On the whole, not two minutes had elapsed since I came up, though it seems to have been longer in telling it: when, before we could look further, voices were heard approaching from the direction of Crabb Cot; and Maria, not caring to be seen, went away quickly. I was still puzzling about Ferrar's hiding-place, when they reached me—the squire, Tod, and two or three men. Tod came slowly up, his face dark and grave.

'I say, Johnny, what a shocking thing this is!'

'What is a shocking thing?'

'You have not heard of it?—But I don't see how you could hear it.'

I had heard nothing. I did not know what there was to hear. Tod told me in a whisper.

'Daniel Ferrar's dead, lad.'

'*What?*'

'He has destroyed himself Not more than half-an-hour ago. Hung himself in the grove.'

I turned sick, taking one thing with another, comparing this recollection with that; which I dare say you will think no one but a muff would do.

147

Ferrar was indeed dead. He had been hiding all day in the three-cornered grove: perhaps waiting for night to get away—perhaps only waiting for night to go home again. Who can tell? About half-past two, Luke Macintosh, a man who sometimes worked for us, sometimes for old Coney happening to go through the grove, saw him there, and talked with him. The same man, passing back a little before sunset, found him hanging from a tree, dead. Macintosh ran with the news to Crabb Cot, and they were now flocking to the scene. When facts came to be examined there appeared only too much reason to think that the unfortunate appearance of the galloping policeman had terrified Ferrar into the act; perhaps—we all hoped it!—had scared his senses quite away. Look at it as we would, it was very dreadful.

But what of the appearance Maria Lease saw? At that time, Ferrar had been dead at least half-an-hour. Was it reality or delusion? That is (as the squire put it), did her eyes see a real, spectral Daniel Ferrar; or were they deceived by some imagination of the brain? Opinions were divided. Nothing can shake her own steadfast belief in its reality; to her it remains an awful certainty, true and sure as heaven.

If I say that I believe in it too, I shall be called a muff and a double muff. But there is no stumbling-block difficult to be got over. Ferrar, when found, was wearing the seal-skin cap tied over the ears and the thick grey coat buttoned up round him, just as Maria Lease had described to me; and he had never worn them since the previous winter, or taken them out of the chest where they were kept. The old woman at his home did not know he had done it then. When told that he had died in these things, she protested that they were in the chest, and ran up to look for them. But the things were gone.

The Open Door

Mrs Oliphant

I took the house of Brentwood on my return from India in 18—,
for the temporary accommodation of my family, until I could find a
permanent home for them. It had many advantages which made it
peculiarly appropriate. It was within reach of Edinburgh; and my boy
Roland, whose education had been considerably neglected, could go
in and out to school; which was thought to be better for him than
either leaving home altogether or staying there always with a tutor.
The first of these expedients would have seemed preferable to me; the
second commended itself to his mother. The doctor, like a judicious
man, took the midway between. "Put him on his pony, and let him
ride into the High School every morning; it will do him all the good
in the world," Dr. Simson said; "and when it is bad weather, there is
the train."

His mother accepted this solution of the difficulty more easily than
I could have hoped; and our pale-faced boy, who had never known
anything more invigorating than Simla, began to encounter the brisk
breezes of the North in the subdued severity of the month of May.
Before the time of the vacation in July we had the satisfaction of seeing him begin to acquire something of the brown and ruddy complexion of his schoolfellows. The English system did not commend
itself to Scotland in these days. There was no little Eton at Fettes; nor
do I think, if there had been, that a genteel exotic of that class would
have tempted either my wife or me. The lad was doubly precious to
us, being the only one left us of many; and he was fragile in body, we
believed, and deeply sensitive in mind. To keep him at home, and yet
to send him to school,—to combine the advantages of the two systems,—seemed to be everything that could be desired.

The two girls also found at Brentwood everything they wanted.
They were near enough to Edinburgh to have masters and lessons

as many as they required for completing that never-ending education which the young people seem to require nowadays. Their mother
married me when she was younger than Agatha; and I should like to
see them improve upon their mother! I myself was then no more than
twenty-five,—an age at which I see the young fellows now groping
about them, with no notion what they are going to do with their lives.
However; I suppose every generation has a conceit of itself which el-
evates it, in its own opinion, above that which comes after it.

Brentwood stands on that fine and wealthy slope of country—one
of the richest in Scotland—which lies between the Pentland Hills and
the Firth. In clear weather you could see the blue gleam—like a bent
bow, embracing the wealthy fields and scattered houses—of the great
estuary on one side of you, and on the other the blue heights, not
gigantic like those we had been used to, but just high enough for all
the glories of the atmosphere, the play of clouds, and sweet reflections,
which give to a hilly country an interest and a charm which nothing
else can emulate. Edinburgh—with its two lesser heights, the Castle
and the Calton Hill, its spires and towers piercing through the smoke,
and Arthur's Seat lying crouched behind, like a guardian no longer
very needful, taking his repose beside the well-beloved charge, which
is now, so to speak, able to take care of itself without him—lay at our
right hand. From the lawn and drawing-room windows we could see
all these varieties of landscape. The colour was sometimes a little chilly,
but sometimes, also, as animated and full of vicissitude as a drama. I
was never tired of it. Its colour and freshness revived the eyes which
had grown weary of arid plains and blazing skies. It was always cheery,
and fresh, and full of repose.

The village of Brentwood lay almost under the house, on the other
side of the deep little ravine, down which a stream—which ought to
have been a lovely, wild, and frolicsome little river—flowed between
its rocks and trees. The river, like so many in that district, had, however, in its earlier life been sacrificed to trade, and was grimy with
paper-making. But this did not affect our pleasure in it so much as
I have known it to affect other streams. Perhaps our water was more
rapid; perhaps less clogged with dirt and refuse. Our side of the dell
was charmingly *accidenté*, and clothed with fine trees, through which
various paths wound down to the river-side and to the village bridge
which crossed the stream. The village lay in the hollow, and climbed,
with very prosaic houses, the other side.

Village architecture does not flourish in Scotland. The blue slates and the gray stone are sworn foes to the picturesque; and though I do not, for my own part, dislike the interior of an old-fashioned hewed and galleried church, with its little family settlements on all sides, the square box outside, with its bit of a spire like a handle to lift it by, is not an improvement to the landscape. Still a cluster of houses on differing elevations, with scraps of garden coming in between, a hedgerow with clothes laid out to dry, the opening of a street with its rural sociability, the women at their doors, the slow wagon lumbering along, gives a centre to the landscape. It was cheerful to look at, and convenient in a hundred ways. Within ourselves we had walks in plenty, the glen being always beautiful in all its phases, whether the woods were green in the spring or ruddy in the autumn.

In the park which surrounded the house were the ruins of the former mansion of Brentwood,—a much smaller and less important house than the solid Georgian edifice which we inhabited. The ruins were picturesque, however, and gave importance to the place. Even we, who were but temporary tenants, felt a vague pride in them, as if they somehow reflected a certain consequence upon ourselves. The old building had the remains of a tower,—an indistinguishable mass of mason-work, over-grown with ivy; and the shells of walls attached to this were half filled up with soil. I had never examined it closely, I am ashamed to say. There was a large room, or what had been a large room, with the lower part of the windows still existing, on the principal floor, and underneath other windows, which were perfect, though half filled up with fallen soil, and waving with a wild growth of brambles and chance growths of all kinds. This was the oldest part of all. At a little distance were some very commonplace and disjointed fragments of building, one of them suggesting a certain *pathos* by its very commonness and the complete wreck which it showed. This was the end of a low gable, a bit of gray wall, all incrusted with lichens, in which was a common doorway. Probably it had been a servants' entrance, a backdoor, or opening into what are called "the offices" in Scotland.

No offices remained to be entered,—pantry and kitchen had all been swept out of being; but there stood the doorway open and vacant, free to all the winds, to the rabbits, and every wild creature. It struck my eye, the first time I went to Brentwood, like a melancholy comment upon a life that was over. A door that led to nothing,—closed once, perhaps, with anxious care, bolted and guarded, now void of any meaning. It impressed me, I remember, from the first; so perhaps it may be said that my mind was prepared to attach to it an importance which nothing justified.

The summer was a very happy period of repose for us all. The warmth of Indian suns was still in our veins. It seemed to us that we could never have enough of the greenness, the dewiness, the freshness of the northern landscape. Even its mists were pleasant to us, taking all the fever out of us, and pouring in vigour and refreshment. In autumn we followed the fashion of the time, and went away for change which we did not in the least require. It was when the family had settled down for the winter, when the days were short and dark, and the rigorous reign of frost upon us, that the incidents occurred which alone could justify me in intruding upon the world my private affairs. These incidents were, however, of so curious a character, that I hope my inevitable references to my own family and pressing personal interests will meet with a general pardon.

I was absent in London when these events began. In London an old Indian plunges back into the interests with which all his previous life has been associated, and meets old friends at every step. I had been circulating among some half-dozen of these,—enjoying the return to my former life in shadow, though I had been so thankful in substance to throw it aside,—and had missed some of my home letters, what with going down from Friday to Monday to old Benbow's place in the country, and stopping on the way back to dine and sleep at Sellar's and to take a look into Cross's stables, which occupied another day.

It is never safe to miss one's letters. In this transitory life, as the Prayer-book says, how can one ever be certain what is going to happen? All was well at home. I knew exactly (I thought) what they would have to say to me: "The weather has been so fine, that Roland has not once gone by train, and he enjoys the ride beyond anything." "Dear papa, be sure that you don't forget anything, but bring us so-and-so, and so-and-so,"—a list as long as my arm. Dear girls and dearer mother! I would not for the world have forgotten their commissions, or lost their little letters, for all the Benbows and Crosses in the world.

But I was confident in my home-comfort and peacefulness. When I got back to my club, however, three or four letters were lying for one, upon some of which I noticed the "immediate," "urgent," which old-fashioned people and anxious people still believe will influence the post-office and quicken the speed of the mails. I was about to open one of these, when the club porter brought me two telegrams, one of which, he said, had arrived the night before. I opened, as was to be expected, the last first, and this was what I read:

Why don't you come or answer? For God's sake, come. He is much worse.

This was a thunderbolt to fall upon a man's head who had one only son, and he the light of his eyes! The other telegram, which I opened with hands trembling so much that I lost time by my haste, was to much the same purport:

No better; doctor afraid of brain-fever. Calls for you day and night. Let nothing detain you.

The first thing I did was to look up the timetables to see if there was any way of getting off sooner than by the night-train, though I knew well enough there was not; and then I read the letters, which furnished, alas! too clearly, all the details. They told me that the boy had been pale for some time, with a scared look. His mother had noticed it before I left home, but would not say anything to alarm me. This look had increased day by day: and soon it was observed that Roland came home at a wild gallop through the park, his pony panting and in foam, himself "as white as a sheet," but with the perspiration streaming from his forehead.

For a long time he had resisted all questioning, but at length had developed such strange changes of mood, showing a reluctance to go to school, a desire to be fetched in the carriage at night,—which was a ridiculous piece of luxury,—an unwillingness to go out into the grounds, and nervous start at every sound, that his mother had insisted upon an explanation. When the boy—our boy Roland, who had never known what fear was—began to talk to her of voices he had heard in the park, and shadows that had appeared to him among the ruins, my wife promptly put him to bed and sent for Dr. Simson, which, of course, was the only thing to do.

I hurried off that evening, as may be supposed, with an anxious heart. How I got through the hours before the starting of the train, I cannot tell. We must all be thankful for the quickness of the railway when in anxiety; but to have thrown myself into a postchaise as soon as horses could be put to, would have been a relief. I got to Edinburgh very early in the blackness of the winter morning, and scarcely dared look the man in the face, at whom I gasped, "What news?" My wife had sent the brougham for me, which I concluded, before the man spoke, was a bad sign. His answer was that stereotyped answer which leaves the imagination so wildly free,—"Just the same."

Just the same! What might that mean? The horses seemed to me to creep along the long dark country road. As we dashed through the park, I thought I heard someone moaning among the trees, and clenched my fist at him (whoever he might be) with fury. Why had the fool of a woman at the gate allowed anyone to come in to disturb the quiet of the place? If I had not been in such hot haste to get home, I think I should have stopped the carriage and got out to see what tramp it was that had made an entrance, and chosen my grounds, of all places in the world,—when my boy was ill!—to grumble and groan in. But I had no reason to complain of our slow pace here. The horses flew like lightning along the intervening path, and drew up at the door all panting, as if they had run a race.

My wife stood waiting to receive me, with a pale face, and a candle in her hand, which made her look paler still as the wind blew the flame about. "He is sleeping," she said in a whisper, as if her voice might wake him. And I replied, when I could find my voice, also in a whisper, as though the jingling of the horses' furniture and the sound of their hoofs must not have been more dangerous. I stood on the steps with her a moment, almost afraid to go in, now that I was here; and it seemed to me that I saw without observing, if I may say so, that the horses were unwilling to turn round, though their stables lay that way, or that the men were unwilling. These things occurred to me afterwards, though at the moment I was not capable of anything but to ask questions and to hear of the condition of the boy.

I looked at him from the door of his room, for we were afraid to go near, lest we should disturb that blessed sleep. It looked like actual sleep, not the lethargy into which my wife told me he would sometimes fall. She told me everything in the next room, which communicated with his, rising now and then and going to the door of communication; and in this there was much that was very startling and confusing to the mind. It appeared that ever since the winter began—since it was early dark, and night had fallen before his return from school—he had been hearing voices among the ruins: at first only a groaning, he said, at which his pony was as much alarmed as he was, but by degrees a voice. The tears ran down my wife's cheeks as she described to me how he would start up in the night and cry out, "Oh, mother, let me in! oh, mother, let me in!" with a *pathos* which rent her heart. And she sitting there all the time, only longing to do everything his heart could desire!

But though she would try to soothe him, crying, "You are at home, my darling. I am here. Don't you know me? Your mother is here!" he would only stare at her, and after a while spring up again with the same cry. At other times he would be quite reasonable, she said, asking eagerly when I was coming, but declaring that he must go with me as soon as I did so, "to let them in."

"The doctor thinks his nervous system must have received a shock," my wife said. "Oh, Henry, can it be that we have pushed him on too much with his work—a delicate boy like Roland? And what is his work in comparison with his health? Even you would think little of honours or prizes if it hurt the boy's health."

Even I!—as if I were an inhuman father sacrificing my child to my ambition. But I would not increase her trouble by taking any notice. After awhile they persuaded me to lie down, to rest, and to eat, none of which things had been possible since I received their letters. The mere fact of being on the spot, of course, in itself was a great thing; and when I knew that I could be called in a moment, as soon as he was awake and wanted me, I felt capable, even in the dark, chill morning twilight, to snatch an hour or two's sleep. As it happened, I was so worn out with the strain of anxiety, and he so quieted and consoled by knowing I had come, that I was not disturbed till the afternoon, when the twilight had again settled down.

There was just daylight enough to see his face when I went to him; and what a change in a fortnight! He was paler and more worn, I thought, than even in those dreadful days in the plains before we left India. His hair seemed to me to have grown long and lank; his eyes were like blazing lights projecting out of his white face. He got hold of my hand in a cold and tremulous clutch, and waved to everybody to go away. "Go away—even mother," he said; "go away." This went to her heart; for she did not like that even I should have more of the boy's confidence than herself; but my wife has never been a woman to think of herself, and she left us alone.

"Are they all gone?" he said eagerly. "They would not let me speak. The doctor treated me as if I were a fool. You know I am not a fool, papa."

"Yes, yes, my boy, I know. But you are ill, and quiet is so necessary. You are not only not a fool, Roland, but you are reasonable and understand. When you are ill you must deny yourself; you must not do everything that you might do being well."

He waved his thin hand with a sort of indignation. "Then, father, I am not ill," he cried. "Oh, I thought when you came you would not stop me,—you would see the sense of it! What do you think is the matter with me, all of you? Simson is well enough; but he is only a doctor. What do you think is the matter with me? I am no more ill than you are. A doctor, of course, he thinks you are ill the moment he looks at you—that's what he's there for—and claps you into bed."

"Which is the best place for you at present, my dear boy."

"I made up my mind," cried the little fellow, "that I would stand it till you came home. I said to myself, I won't frighten mother and the girls. But now, father," he cried, half jumping out of bed, "it's not illness: it's a secret."

His eyes shone so wildly, his face was so swept with strong feeling, that my heart sank within me. It could be nothing but fever that did it, and fever had been so fatal. I got him into my arms to put him back into bed. "Roland," I said, humouring the poor child, which I knew was the only way, "if you are going to tell me this secret to do any good, you know you must be quite quiet, and not excite yourself. If you excite yourself, I must not let you speak."

"Yes, father," said the boy. He was quiet directly, like a man, as if he quite understood. When I had laid him back on his pillow, he looked up at me with that grateful, sweet look with which children, when they are ill, break one's heart, the water coming into his eyes in his weakness. "I was sure as soon as you were here you would know what to do," he said.

"To be sure, my boy. Now keep quiet, and tell it all out like a man." To think I was telling lies to my own child! for I did it only to humour him, thinking, poor little fellow, his brain was wrong.

"Yes, father. Father, there is someone in the park—someone that has been badly used."

"Hush, my dear; you remember there is to be no excitement. Well, who is this somebody, and who has been ill-using him? We will soon put a stop to that."

"All," cried Roland, "but it is not so easy as you think. I don't know who it is. It is just a cry. Oh, if you could hear it! It gets into my head in my sleep. I heard it as clear—as clear; and they think that I am dreaming, or raving perhaps," the boy said, with a sort of disdainful smile.

This look of his perplexed me; it was less like fever than I thought. "Are you quite sure you have not dreamed it, Roland?" I said.

"Dreamed?—that!" He was springing up again when he suddenly

bethought himself, and lay down flat, with the same sort of smile on his face. "The pony heard it, too," he said. "She jumped as if she had been shot. If I had not grasped at the reins—for I was frightened, father—"

"No shame to you, my boy," said I, though I scarcely knew why.

"If I hadn't held to her like a leech, she'd have pitched me over her head, and never drew breath till we were at the door. Did the pony dream it?" he said, with a soft disdain, yet indulgence for my foolishness. Then he added slowly, "It was only a cry the first time, and all the time before you went away. I wouldn't tell you, for it was so wretched to be frightened. I thought it might be a hare or a rabbit snared, and I went in the morning and looked; but there was nothing. It was after you went I heard it really first; and this is what he says." He raised himself on his elbow close to me, and looked me in the face: "'Oh, mother, let me in! oh, mother, let me in!'" As he said the words a mist came over his face, the mouth quivered, the soft features all melted and changed, and when he had ended these pitiful words, dissolved in a shower of heavy tears.

Was it a hallucination? Was it the fever of the brain? Was it the disordered fancy caused by great bodily weakness? How could I tell? I thought it wisest to accept it as if it were all true.

"This is very touching, Roland," I said.

"Oh, if you had just heard it, father! I said to myself, if father heard it he would do something; but mamma, you know, she's given over to Simson, and that fellow's a doctor, and never thinks of anything but clapping you into bed."

"We must not blame Simson for being a doctor, Roland."

"No, no," said my boy, with delightful toleration and indulgence; "oh, no; that's the good of him; that's what he's for; I know that. But you—you are different; you are just father; and you'll do something—directly, papa, directly; this very night."

"Surely," I said. "No doubt it is some little lost child."

He gave me a sudden, swift look, investigating my face as though to see whether, after all, this was everything my eminence as "father" came to,—no more than that. Then he got hold of my shoulder, clutching it with his thin hand. "Look here," he said, with a quiver in his voice; "suppose it wasn't—living at all!"

"My dear boy, how then could you have heard it?" I said.

He turned away from me with a pettish exclamation,—"As if you didn't know better than that!"

"Do you want to tell me it is a ghost?" I said.

Roland withdrew his hand; his countenance assumed an aspect of great dignity and gravity; a slight quiver remained about his lips. "Whatever it was—you always said we were not to call names. It was something—in trouble. Oh, father, in terrible trouble!"

"But, my boy," I said (I was at my wits' end), "if it was a child that was lost, or any poor human creature—but, Roland, what do you want me to do?"

"I should know if I was you," said the child eagerly. "That is what I always said to myself,—Father will know. Oh, papa, papa, to have to face it night after night, in such terrible, terrible trouble, and never to be able to do it any good! I don't want to cry; it's like a baby, I know; but what can I do else? Out there all by itself in the ruin, and nobody to help it! I can't bear it! I can't bear it!" cried my generous boy. And in his weakness he burst out, after many attempts to restrain it, into a great childish fit of sobbing and tears.

I do not know that I ever was in a greater perplexity, in my life; and afterwards, when I thought of it, there was something comic in it too. It is bad enough to find your child's mind possessed with the conviction that he has seen, or heard, a ghost; but that he should require you to go instantly and help that ghost was the most bewildering experience that had ever come my way. I am a sober man myself, and not superstitious—at least any more than everybody is superstitious. Of course I do not believe in ghosts; but I don't deny, any more than other people, that there are stories which I cannot pretend to understand.

My blood got a sort of chill in my veins at the idea that Roland should be a ghost-seer; for that generally means a hysterical temperament and weak health, and all that men most hate and fear for their children. But that I should take up his ghost and right its wrongs, and save it from its trouble, was such a mission as was enough to confuse any man. I did my best to console my boy without giving any promise of this astonishing kind; but he was too sharp for me: he would have none of my caresses. With sobs breaking in at intervals upon his voice, and the raindrops hanging on his eyelids, he yet returned to the charge.

"It will be there now!—it will be there all the night! Oh, think, papa,—think if it was me! I can't rest for thinking of it. Don't!" he cried, putting away my hand,—"don't! You go and help it, and mother can take care of me."

"But, Roland, what can I do?"

My boy opened his eyes, which were large with weakness and fever, and gave me a smile such, I think, as sick children only know the secret of. "I was sure you would know as soon as you came. I always said, Father will know. And mother," he cried, with a softening of repose upon his face, his limbs relaxing, his form sinking with a luxurious ease in his bed,—"mother can come and take care of me."

I called her, and saw him turn to her with the complete dependence of a child; and then I went away and left them, as perplexed a man as any in Scotland. I must say, however, I had this consolation, that my mind was greatly eased about Roland. He might be under a hallucination; but his head was clear enough, and I did not think him so ill as everybody else did. The girls were astonished even at the ease with which I took it. "How do you think he is?" they said in a breath, coming round me, laying hold of me.

"Not half so ill as I expected," I said; "not very bad at all."

"Oh, papa, you are a darling!" cried Agatha, kissing me, and crying upon my shoulder; while little Jeanie, who was as pale as Roland, clasped both her arms round mine, and could not speak at all. I knew nothing about it, not half so much as Simson; but they believed in me: they had a feeling that all would go right now. God is very good to you when your children look to you like that. It makes one humble, not proud. I was not worthy of it; and then I recollected that I had to act the part of a father to Roland's ghost,—which made me almost laugh, though I might just as well have cried. It was the strangest mission that ever was intrusted to mortal man.

It was then I remembered suddenly the looks of the men when they turned to take the brougham to the stables in the dark that morning. They had not liked it, and the horses had not liked it. I remembered that even in my anxiety about Roland I had heard them tearing along the avenue back to the stables, and had made a memorandum mentally that I must speak of it. It seemed to me that the best thing I could do was to go to the stables now and make a few inquiries. It is impossible to fathom the minds of rustics; there might be some devilry of practical joking, for anything I knew; or they might have some interest in getting up a bad reputation for the Brentwood avenue. It was getting dark by the time I went out, and nobody who knows the country will need to be told how black is the darkness of a November night under high laurel-bushes and yew-trees.

I walked into the heart of the shrubberies two or three times, not seeing a step before me, till I came out upon the broader carriage-road, where the trees opened a little, and there was a faint gray glimmer of sky visible, under which the great limes and elms stood darkling like ghosts; but it grew black again as I approached the corner where the ruins lay. Both eyes and ears were on the alert, as may be supposed; but I could see nothing in the absolute gloom, and, so far as I can recollect, I heard nothing. Nevertheless there came a strong impression upon me that somebody was there. It is a sensation which most people have felt. I have seen when it has been strong enough to awake me out of sleep, the sense of someone looking at me. I suppose my imagination had been affected by Roland's story; and the mystery of the darkness is always full of suggestions.

I stamped my feet violently on the gravel to rouse myself, and called out sharply, "Who's there?" Nobody answered, nor did I expect anyone to answer, but the impression had been made. I was so foolish that I did not like to look back, but went sideways, keeping an eye on the gloom behind. It was with great relief that I spied the light in the stables, making a sort of oasis in the darkness. I walked very quickly into the midst of that lighted and cheerful place, and thought the clank of the groom's pail one of the pleasantest sounds I had ever heard. The coachman was the head of this little colony, and it was to his house I went to pursue my investigations. He was a native of the district, and had taken care of the place in the absence of the family for years; it was impossible but that he must know everything that was going on, and all the traditions of the place. The men, I could see, eyed me anxiously when I thus appeared at such an hour among them, and followed me with their eyes to Jarvis's house, where he lived alone with his old wife, their children being all married and out in the world. Mrs. Jarvis met me with anxious questions. How was the poor young gentleman? But the others knew, I could see by their faces, that not even this was the foremost thing in my mind.

★★★★★★

"Noises?—ou ay, there'll be noises,—the wind in the trees, and the water soughing down the glen. As for tramps, Cornel, no, there's little o' that kind o' cattle about here; and Merran at the gate's a careful body." Jarvis moved about with some embarrassment from one leg to another as he spoke. He kept in the shade, and did not look at me more than he could help. Evidently his mind was perturbed, and he had reasons for keeping his own counsel. His wife sat by, giving him a quick look now and then, but saying nothing. The kitchen was very snug and warm and bright,—as different as could be from the chill and mystery of the night outside.

"I think you are trifling with me, Jarvis," I said.

"Triflin', cornel? No me. What would I trifle for? If the deevil himsel was in the auld hoose, I have no interest in 't one way or another—"

"Sandy, hold your peace!" cried his wife imperatively.

"And what am I to hold my peace for, wi' the Cornel standing there asking a' thae questions? I'm saying, if the deevil himsel—"

"And I'm telling ye hold your peace!" cried the woman, in great excitement. "Dark November weather and lang nichts, and us that ken a' we ken. How daur ye name—a name that shouldna be spoken?" She threw down her stocking and got up, also in great agitation. "I tellt ye you never could keep it. It's no a thing that will hide, and the haill toun kens as weel as you or me. Tell the cornel straight out—or see, I'll do it. I dinna hold wi' your secrets, and a secret that the haill toun kens!" She snapped her fingers with an air of large disdain. As for Jarvis, ruddy and big as he was, he shrank to nothing before this decided woman.

He repeated to her two or three times her own adjuration, "Hold your peace!" then, suddenly changing his tone, cried out, "Tell him then, confound ye! I'll wash my hands o't. If a' the ghosts in Scotland were in the auld hoose, is that ony concern o' mine?"

After this I elicited without much difficulty the whole story. In the opinion of the Jarvises, and of everybody about, the certainty that the place was haunted was beyond all doubt. As Sandy and his wife warmed to the tale, one tripping up another in their eagerness to tell everything, it gradually developed as distinct a superstition as I ever heard, and not without poetry and pathos. How long it was since the voice had been heard first, nobody could tell with certainty. Jarvis's opinion was that his father, who had been coachman at Brentwood before him, had never heard anything about it, and that the whole thing had arisen within the last ten years, since the complete dismantling of the old house; which was a wonderfully modern date for a tale so well authenticated.

According to these witnesses, and to several whom I questioned afterwards, and who were all in perfect agreement, it was only in the months of November and December that "the visitation" occurred. During these months, the darkest of the year, scarcely a night passed without the recurrence of these inexplicable cries. Nothing, it was said, had ever been seen,—at least, nothing that could be identified. Some people, bolder or more imaginative than the others, had seen the darkness moving, Mrs. Jarvis said, with unconscious poetry. It began when night fell, and continued, at intervals, till day broke. Very often it was only all inarticulate cry and moaning, but sometimes the words which had taken possession of my poor boy's fancy had been distinctly audible,—"Oh, mother, let me in!"

The Jarvises were not aware that there had ever been any investigation into it. The estate of Brentwood had lapsed into the hands of a distant branch of the family, who had lived but little there; and of the many people who had taken it, as I had done, few had remained through two Decembers. And nobody had taken the trouble to make a very close examination into the facts.

"No, no," Jarvis said, shaking his head, "No, no, Cornel. Wha wad set themsels up for a laughin'-stock to a' the countryside, making a wark about a ghost? Naebody believes in ghosts. It bid to be the wind in the trees, the last gentleman said, or some effec' o' the water wrastlin' among the rocks. He said it was a' quite easy explained; but he gave up the hoose. And when you cam, cornel, we were awfu' anxious you should never hear. What for should I have spoiled the bargain and hairmed the property for nothing?"

"Do you call my child's life nothing?" I said in the trouble of the moment, unable to restrain myself. "And instead of telling this all to me, you have told it to him,—to a delicate boy, a child unable to sift evidence or judge for himself, a tender-hearted young creature—"

I was walking about the room with an anger all the hotter that I felt it to be most likely quite unjust. My heart was full of bitterness against the stolid retainers of a family who were content to risk other people's children and comfort rather than let a house be empty. If I had been warned I might have taken precautions, or left the place, or sent Roland away, a hundred things which now I could not do; and here I was with my boy in a brain-fever, and his life, the most precious life on earth, hanging in the balance, dependent on whether or not I could get to the reason of a commonplace ghost-story! I paced about in high wrath, not seeing what I was to do; for to take Roland away, even if he were able to travel, would not settle his agitated mind; and I feared even that a scientific explanation of refracted sound or reverberation, or any other of the easy certainties with which we elder men are silenced, would have very little effect upon the boy.

"Cornel," said Jarvis solemnly, "and *she'll* bear me witness,—the young gentleman never heard a word from me—no, nor from either groom or gardener; I'll gie ye my word for that. In the first place, he's no a lad that invites ye to talk. There are some that are, and some that arena. Some will draw ye on, till ye've tellt them a' the clatter of the toun, and a' ye ken, and whiles mair. But Maister Roland, his mind's fu' of his books. He's aye civil and kind, and a fine lad; but no that sort. And ye see it's for a' our interest, cornel, that you should stay at Brentwood. I took it upon me mysel to pass the word,—'No a syllable to Maister Roland, nor to the young leddies—no a syllable.' The women-servants, that have little reason to be out at night, ken little or nothing about it. And some think it grand to have a ghost so long as they're no in the way of coming across it. If you had been tellt the story to begin with, maybe ye would have thought so yourself."

This was true enough, though it did not throw any light upon my perplexity. If we had heard of it to start with, it is possible that all the family would have considered the possession of a ghost a distinct advantage. It is the fashion of the times. We never think what a risk it is to play with young imaginations, but cry out, in the fashionable jargon, "A ghost!—nothing else was wanted to make it perfect." I should not have been above this myself. I should have smiled, of course, at the idea of the ghost at all, but then to feel that it was mine would have pleased my vanity. Oh, yes, I claim no exemption. The girls would have been delighted. I could fancy their eagerness, their interest, and excitement. No; if we had been told, it would have done no good,— we should have made the bargain all the more eagerly, the fools that we are. "And there has been no attempt to investigate it," I said, "to see what it really is?"

"Eh, cornel," said the coachman's wife, "wha would investigate, as ye call it, a thing that nobody believes in? Ye would be the laughin'-stock of a' the countryside, as my man says."

"But you believe in it," I said, turning upon her hastily. The woman was taken by surprise. She made a step backward out of my way.

"Lord, cornel, how ye frichten a body! Me!—there's awfu' strange things in this world. An unlearned person doesna ken what to think. But the minister and the gentry they just laugh in your face. Inquire into the thing that is not! Na, na, we just let it be."

"Come with me, Jarvis," I said hastily, "and we'll make an attempt at least. Say nothing to the men or to anybody. I'll come back after dinner, and we'll make a serious attempt to see what it is, if it is anything. If I hear it,—which I doubt,—you may be sure I shall never rest till I make it out. Be ready for me about ten o'clock."

"Me, cornel!" Jarvis said, in a faint voice. I had not been look-ing at him in my own preoccupation, but when I did so, I found that the greatest change had come over the fat and ruddy coachman. "Me, cornel!" he repeated, wiping the perspiration from his brow. His ruddy face hung in flabby folds, his knees knocked together, his voice seemed half extinguished in his throat. Then he began to rub his hands and smile upon me in a deprecating, imbecile way. "There's nothing I wouldna do to pleasure ye, cornel," taking a step further back. "I'm sure *she* kens I've aye said I never had to do with a mair fair, weel-spoken gentleman—" Here Jarvis came to a pause, again looking at me, rubbing his hands.

"Well?" I said.

"But eh, sir!" he went on, with the same imbecile yet insinuating smile, "if ye'll reflect that I am no used to my feet. With a horse atween my legs, or the reins in my hand, I'm maybe nae worse than other men; but on fit, cornel—It's no the—bogles—but I've been cavalry, ye see," with a little hoarse laugh, "a' my life. To face a thing ye dinna understan'—on your feet, cornel."

"Well, sir, if *I* do it," said I tartly, "why shouldn't you?"

"Eh, cornel, there's an awfu' difference. In the first place, ye tramp about the haill countryside, and think naething of it; but a walk tires me mair than a hunard miles' drive; and then ye're a gentleman, and do your ain pleasure; and you're no so auld as me; and it's for your ain bairn, ye see, cornel; and then—"

"He believes in it, cornel, and you dinna believe in it," the woman said.

"Will you come with me?" I said, turning to her.

She jumped back, upsetting her chair in her bewilderment. "Me!" with a scream, and then fell into a sort of hysterical laugh. "I wouldna say but what I would go; but what would the folk say to hear of Cor-nel Mortimer with an auld silly woman at his heels?"

The suggestion made me laugh too, though I had little inclination for it. "I'm sorry you have so little spirit, Jarvis," I said. "I must find someone else, I suppose."

Jarvis, touched by this, began to remonstrate, but I cut him short. My butler was a soldier who had been with me in India, and was not supposed to fear anything,—man or devil,—certainly not the former; and I felt that I was losing time. The Jarvises were too thankful to get rid of me. They attended me to the door with the most anxious cour-

164

tesies. Outside, the two grooms stood close by, a little confused by my sudden exit. I don't know if perhaps they had been listening,—as least standing as near as possible, to catch any scrap of the conversation. I waved my hand to them as I went past, in answer to their salutations, and it was very apparent to me that they also were glad to see me go.

And it will be thought very strange, but it would be weak not to add, that I myself, though bent on the investigation I have spoken of, pledged to Roland to carry it out, and feeling that my boy's health, perhaps his life, depended on the result of my inquiry,—I felt the most unaccountable reluctance to pass these ruins on my way home. My curiosity was intense; and yet it was all my mind could do to pull my body along. I daresay the scientific people would describe it the other way, and attribute my cowardice to the state of my stomach. I went on; but if I had followed my impulse, I should have turned and bolted. Everything in me seemed to cry out against it: my heart thumped, my pulses all began, like sledge-hammers, beating against my ears and every sensitive part.

It was very dark, as I have said; the old house, with its shapeless tower, loomed a heavy mass through the darkness, which was only not entirely so solid as itself. On the other hand, the great dark cedars of which we were so proud seemed to fill up the night. My foot strayed out of the path in my confusion and the gloom together, and I brought myself up with a cry as I felt myself knock against something solid. What was it? The contact with hard stone and lime and prickly bramble-bushes restored me a little to myself. "Oh, it's only the old gable," I said aloud, with a little laugh to reassure myself. The rough feeling of the stones reconciled me. As I groped about thus, I shook off my visionary folly. What so easily explained as that I should have strayed from the path in the darkness?

This brought me back to common existence, as if I had been shaken by a wise hand out of all the silliness of superstition. How silly it was, after all! What did it matter which path I took? I laughed again, this time with better heart, when suddenly, in a moment, the blood was chilled in my veins, a shiver stole along my spine, my faculties seemed to forsake me. Close by me, at my side, at my feet, there was a sigh. No, not a groan, not a moaning, not anything so tangible,—a perfectly soft, faint, inarticulate sigh. I sprang back, and my heart stopped beating. Mistaken! no, mistake was impossible. I heard it as clearly as I hear myself speak; a long, soft, weary sigh, as if drawn to the utmost, and emptying out a load of sadness that filled the breast.

To hear this in the solitude, in the dark, in the night (though it was still early), had an effect which I cannot describe. I feel it now,—something cold creeping over me, up into my hair, and down to my feet, which refused to move. I cried out, with a trembling voice, "Who is there?" as I had done before; but there was no reply.

I got home I don't quite know how; but in my mind there was no longer any indifference as to the thing, whatever it was, that haunted these ruins. My scepticism disappeared like a mist. I was as firmly determined that there was something as Roland was. I did not for a moment pretend to myself that it was possible I could be deceived; there were movements and noises which I understood all about,— cracklings of small branches in the frost, and little rolls of gravel on the path, such as have a very eerie sound sometimes, and perplex you with wonder as to who has done it, *when there is no real mystery*; but I assure you all these little movements of nature don't affect you one bit *when there is something*. I understood *them*. I did not understand the sigh. That was not simple nature; there was meaning in it, feeling, the soul of a creature invisible. This is the thing that human nature trembles at,—a creature invisible, yet with sensations, feelings, a power somehow of expressing itself. I had not the same sense of unwillingness to turn my back upon the scene of the mystery which I had experienced in going to the stables; but I almost ran home, impelled by eagerness to get everything done that had to be done, in order to apply myself to finding it out.

Bagley was in the hall as usual when I went in. He was always there in the afternoon, always with the appearance of perfect occupation, yet, so far as I know, never doing anything. The door was open, so that I hurried in without any pause, breathless; but the sight of his calm regard, as he came to help me off with my overcoat, subdued me in a moment. Anything out of the way, anything incomprehensible, faded to nothing in the presence of Bagley. You saw and wondered how *he* was made: the parting of his hair, the tie of his white neckcloth, the fit of his trousers, all perfect as works of art; but you could see how they were done, which makes all the difference. I flung myself upon him, so to speak, without waiting to note the extreme unlikeness of the man to anything of the kind I meant. "Bagley," I said, "I want you to come out with me tonight to watch for—"

"Poachers, colonel?" he said, a gleam of pleasure running all over him.

"No, Bagley; a great deal worse," I cried.

"Yes, colonel; at what hour, sir?" the man said; but then I had not told him what it was.

It was ten o'clock when we set out. All was perfectly quiet indoors. My wife was with Roland, who had been quite calm, she said, and who (though, no doubt, the fever must run its course) had been better ever since I came. I told Bagley to put on a thick greatcoat over his evening coat, and did the same myself, with strong boots; for the soil was like a sponge, or worse. Talking to him, I almost forgot what we were going to do. It was darker even than it had been before, and Bagley kept very close to me as we went along. I had a small lantern in my hand, which gave us a partial guidance. We had come to the corner where the path turns. On one side was the bowling-green, which the girls had taken possession of for their croquet-ground,—a wonderful enclosure surrounded by high hedges of holly, three hundred years old and more; on the other, the ruins. Both were black as night; but before we got so far, there was a little opening in which we could just discern the trees and the lighter line of the road. I thought it best to pause there and take breath.

"Bagley," I said, "there is something about these ruins I don't understand. It is there I am going. Keep your eyes open and your wits about you. Be ready to pounce upon any stranger you see,—anything, man or woman. Don't hurt, but seize anything you see."

"Colonel," said Bagley, with a little tremor in his breath, "they do say there's things there—as is neither man nor woman."

There was no time for words.

"Are you game to follow me, my man? that's the question," I said. Bagley fell in without a word, and saluted. I knew then I had nothing to fear.

We went, so far as I could guess, exactly as I had come; when I heard that sigh. The darkness, however, was so complete that all marks, as of trees or paths, disappeared. One moment we felt our feet on the gravel, another sinking noiselessly into the slippery grass, that was all. I had shut up my lantern, not wishing to scare anyone, whoever it might be. Bagley followed, it seemed to me, exactly in my footsteps as I made my way, as I supposed, towards the mass of the ruined house. We seemed to take a long time groping along seeking this; the squash of the wet soil under our feet was the only thing that marked our progress.

After a while I stood still to see, or rather feel, where we were. The darkness was very still, but no stiller than is usual in a winter's

167

night. The sounds I have mentioned—the crackling of twigs, the roll
of a pebble, the sound of some rustle in the dead leaves, or creeping
creature on the grass—were audible when you listened, all mysterious enough when your mind is disengaged, but to me cheering now
as signs of the livingness of nature, even in the death of the frost. As
we stood still there came up from the trees in the glen the prolonged
hoot of an owl. Bagley started with alarm, being in a state of general
nervousness, and not knowing what he was afraid of. But to me the
sound was encouraging and pleasant, being so comprehensible.

"An owl," I said, under my breath.

"Y—es, colonel," said Bagley, his teeth chattering. We stood still
about five minutes, while it broke into the still brooding of the air, the
sound widening out in circles, dying upon the darkness. This sound,
which is not a cheerful one, made me almost gay. It was natural, and
relieved the tension of the mind. I moved on with new courage, my
nervous excitement calming down.

When all at once, quite suddenly, close to us, at our feet, there
broke out a cry. I made a spring backwards in the first moment of surprise and horror, and in doing so came sharply against the same rough
masonry and brambles that had struck me before. This new sound
came upwards from the ground,—a low, moaning, wailing voice, full
of suffering and pain. The contrast between it and the hoot of the owl
was indescribable,—the one with a wholesome wildness and natural-
ness that hurt nobody; the other, a sound that made one's blood cur-
dle, full of human misery.

With a great deal of fumbling,—for in spite of everything I could
do to keep up my courage my hands shook,—I managed to remove
the slide of my lantern. The light leaped out like something living,
and made the place visible in a moment. We were what would have
been inside the ruined building had anything remained but the gable-
wall which I have described. It was close to us, the vacant doorway
in it going out straight into the blackness outside. The light showed
the bit of wall, the ivy glistening upon it in clouds of dark green, the
bramble-branches waving, and below, the open door,—a door that led
to nothing. It was from this the voice came which died out just as the
light flashed upon this strange scene. There was a moment's silence,
and then it broke forth again. The sound was so near, so penetrating,
so pitiful, that, in the nervous start I gave, the light fell out of my hand.

As I groped for it in the dark my hand was clutched by Bagley,
who, I think, must have dropped upon his knees; but I was too much

perturbed myself to think much of this. He clutched at me in the confusion of his terror, forgetting all his usual decorum. "For God's sake, what is it, sir?" he gasped. If I yielded, there was evidently an end of both of us.

"I can't tell," I said, "any more than you; that's what we've got to find out. Up, man, up!" I pulled him to his feet. "Will you go round and examine the other side, or will you stay here with the lantern?" Bagley gasped at me with a face of horror.

"Can't we stay together, colonel?" he said; his knees were trembling under him. I pushed him against the corner of the wall, and put the light into his hands.

"Stand fast till I come back; shake yourself together, man; let nothing pass you," I said. The voice was within two or three feet of us; of that there could be no doubt.

I went myself to the other side of the wall, keeping close to it. The light shook in Bagley's hand, but, tremulous though it was, shone out through the vacant door, one oblong block of light marking all the crumbling corners and hanging masses of foliage. Was that something dark huddled in a heap by the side of it? I pushed forward across the light in the doorway, and fell upon it with my hands; but it was only a juniper-bush growing close against the wall. Meanwhile, the sight of my figure crossing the doorway had brought Bagley's nervous excitement to a height: he flew at me, gripping my shoulder.

"I've got him, Colonel! I've got him!" he cried, with a voice of sudden exultation. He thought it was a man, and was at once relieved. But at that moment the voice burst forth again between us, at our feet,—more close to us than any separate being could be. He dropped off from me, and fell against the wall, his jaw dropping as if he were dying. I suppose, at the same moment, he saw that it was me whom he had clutched. I, for my part, had scarcely more command of myself. I snatched the light out of his hand, and flashed it all about me wildly. Nothing,—the juniper-bush which I thought I had never seen before, the heavy growth of the glistening ivy, the brambles waving. It was close to my ears now, crying, crying, pleading as if for life.

Either I heard the same words Roland had heard, or else, in my excitement, his imagination got possession of mine. The voice went on, growing into distinct articulation, but wavering about, now from one point, now from another, as if the owner of it were moving slowly back and forward. "Mother! mother!" and then an outburst of wailing. As my mind steadied, getting accustomed (as one's mind gets accustomed

169

to anything), it seemed to me as if some uneasy, miserable creature was pacing up and down before a closed door. Sometimes—but that must have been excitement—I thought I heard a sound like knocking, and then another burst, "Oh, mother! mother!" All this close, close to the space where I was standing with my lantern, now before me, now behind me: a creature restless, unhappy, moaning, crying, before the vacant doorway, which no one could either shut or open more.

"Do you hear it, Bagley? do you hear what it is saying?" I cried, stepping in through the doorway. He was lying against the wall, his eyes glazed, half dead with terror. He made a motion of his lips as if to answer me, but no sounds came; then lifted his hand with a curious imperative movement as if ordering me to be silent and listen. And how long I did so I cannot tell. It began to have an interest, an exciting hold upon me, which I could not describe. It seemed to call up visibly a scene any one could understand,—a something shut out, restlessly wandering to and fro; sometimes the voice dropped, as if throwing itself down, sometimes wandered off a few paces, growing sharp and clear. "Oh, mother, let me in! oh, mother, mother, let me in! oh, let me in!" Every word was clear to me. No wonder the boy had gone wild with pity. I tried to steady my mind upon Roland, upon his conviction that I could do something, but my head swam with the excitement, even when I partially overcame the terror. At last the words died away, and there was a sound of sobs and moaning.

I cried out, "In the name of God, who are you?" with a kind of feeling in my mind that to use the name of God was profane, seeing that I did not believe in ghosts or anything supernatural; but I did it all the same, and waited, my heart giving a leap of terror lest there should be a reply. Why this should have been I cannot tell, but I had a feeling that if there was an answer it would be more than I could bear. But there was no answer; the moaning went on, and then, as if it had been real, the voice rose a little higher again, the words recommenced, "Oh, mother, let me in! oh, mother, let me in!" with an expression that was heart-breaking to hear.

As if it had been real! What do I mean by that? I suppose I got less alarmed as the thing went on. I began to recover the use of my senses,—I seemed to explain it all to myself by saying that this had once happened, that it was a recollection of a real scene. Why there should have seemed something quite satisfactory and composing in this explanation I cannot tell, but so it was. I began to listen almost as if it had been a play, forgetting Bagley, who, I almost think, had fainted, leaning against the wall. I was startled out of this strange spectator-ship that had fallen upon me by the sudden rush of something which made my heart jump once more, a large black figure in the doorway waving its arms.

"Come in! come in! come in!" it shouted out hoarsely at the top of a deep bass voice, and then poor Bagley fell down senseless across the threshold. He was less sophisticated than I,—he had not been able to bear it any longer. I took him for something supernatural, as he took me, and it was some time before I awoke to the necessities of the moment. I remembered only after, that from the time I began to give my attention to the man, I heard the other voice no more. It was some time before I brought him to. It must have been a strange scene: the lantern making a luminous spot in the darkness, the man's white face lying on the black earth, I over him, doing what I could for him, probably I should have been thought to be murdering him had any one seen us.

When at last I succeeded in pouring a little brandy down his throat, he sat up and looked about him wildly. "What's up?" he said; then recognizing me, tried to struggle to his feet with a faint "Beg your pardon, colonel." I got him home as best I could, making him lean upon my arm. The great fellow was as weak as a child. Fortunately he did not for some time remember what had happened. From the time Bagley fell the voice had stopped, and all was still.

★★★★★★

"You've got an epidemic in your house, colonel," Simson said to me next morning. "What's the meaning of it all? Here's your butler raving about a voice. This will never do, you know; and so far as I can make out, you are in it too."

"Yes, I am in it, doctor. I thought I had better speak to you. Of course you are treating Roland all right, but the boy is not raving, he is as sane as you or me. It's all true."

"As sane as—I—or you. I never thought the boy insane. He's got cerebral excitement, fever. I don't know what you've got. There's something very queer about the look of your eyes."

"Come," said I, "you can't put us all to bed, you know. You had better listen and hear the symptoms in full."

The doctor shrugged his shoulders, but he listened to me patiently. He did not believe a word of the story, that was clear; but he heard it all from beginning to end. "My dear fellow," he said, "the boy told me just the same. It's an epidemic. When one person falls a victim to this sort of thing, it's as safe as can be,—there's always two or three."

"Then how do you account for it?" I said.

"Oh, account for it!—that's a different matter; there's no accounting for the freaks our brains are subject to. If it's delusion, if it's some trick of the echoes or the winds,—some phonetic disturbance or other—"

"Come with me tonight, and judge for yourself," I said.

Upon this he laughed aloud, then said, "That's not such a bad idea; but it would ruin me forever if it were known that John Simson was ghost-hunting."

"There it is," said I; "you dart down on us who are unlearned with your phonetic disturbances, but you daren't examine what the thing really is for fear of being laughed at. That's science!"

"It's not science,—it's common-sense," said the doctor. "The thing has delusion on the front of it. It is encouraging an unwholesome tendency even to examine. What good could come of it? Even if I am convinced, I shouldn't believe."

"I should have said so yesterday; and I don't want you to be convinced or to believe," said I. "If you prove it to be a delusion, I shall be very much obliged to you for one. Come; somebody must go with me."

"You are cool," said the doctor. "You've disabled this poor fellow of yours, and made him—on that point—a lunatic for life; and now you want to disable me. But, for once, I'll do it. To save appearance, if you'll give me a bed, I'll come over after my last rounds."

It was agreed that I should meet him at the gate, and that we should visit the scene of last night's occurrences before we came to the house, so that nobody might be the wiser. It was scarcely possible to hope that the cause of Bagley's sudden illness should not somehow steal into the knowledge of the servants at least, and it was better that all should be done as quietly as possible. The day seemed to me a very long one. I had to spend a certain part of it with Roland, which was a terrible ordeal for me, for what could I say to the boy? The improvement continued, but he was still in a very precarious state, and the trembling vehemence with which he turned to me when his mother left the room filled me with alarm. "Father?" he said quietly.

"Yes, my boy, I am giving my best attention to it; all is being done that I can do. I have not come to any conclusion—yet. I am neglecting nothing you said," I cried. What I could not do was to give his active

172

mind any encouragement to dwell upon the mystery. It was a hard predicament, for some satisfaction had to be given him. He looked at me very wistfully, with the great blue eyes which shone so large and brilliant out of his white and worn face. "You must trust me," I said.

"Yes, father. Father understands," he said to himself, as if to soothe some inward doubt. I left him as soon as I could. He was about the most precious thing I had on earth, and his health my first thought; but yet somehow, in the excitement of this other subject, I put that aside, and preferred not to dwell upon Roland, which was the most curious part of it all.

That night at eleven I met Simson at the gate. He had come by train, and I let him in gently myself. I had been so much absorbed in the coming experiment that I passed the ruins in going to meet him, almost without thought, if you can understand that. I had my lantern; and he showed me a coil of taper which he had ready for use. "There is nothing like light," he said, in his scoffing tone. It was a very still night, scarcely a sound, but not so dark. We could keep the path without difficulty as we went along.

As we approached the spot we could hear a low moaning, broken occasionally by a bitter cry. "Perhaps that is your voice," said the doctor; "I thought it must be something of the kind. That's a poor brute caught in some of these infernal traps of yours; you'll find it among the bushes somewhere." I said nothing. I felt no particular fear, but a triumphant satisfaction in what was to follow. I led him to the spot where Bagley and I had stood on the previous night. All was silent as a winter night could be,—so silent that we heard far off the sound of the horses in the stables, the shutting of a window at the house. Simson lighted his taper and went peering about, poking into all the corners.

We looked like two conspirators lying in wait for some unfortunate traveller; but not a sound broke the quiet. The moaning had stopped before we came up; a star or two shone over us in the sky, looking down as if surprised at our strange proceedings. Dr. Simson did nothing but utter subdued laughs under his breath. "I thought as much," he said. "It is just the same with tables and all other kinds of ghostly apparatus; a sceptic's presence stops everything. When I am present nothing ever comes off. How long do you think it will be necessary to stay here? Oh, I don't complain; only when *you* are satisfied, *I* am—quite."

I will not deny that I was disappointed beyond measure by this result. It made me look like a credulous fool. It gave the Doctor such a pull over me as nothing else could. I should point all his morals for years to come; and his materialism, his scepticism, would be increased beyond endurance. "It seems, indeed," I said, "that there is to be no—"

"Manifestation," he said, laughing; "that is what all the mediums say. No manifestations, in consequence of the presence of an unbeliever."

His laugh sounded very uncomfortable to me in the silence; and it was now near midnight. But that laugh seemed the signal; before it died away the moaning we had heard before was resumed. It started from some distance off, and came towards us, nearer and nearer, like someone walking along and moaning to himself. There could be no idea now that it was a hare caught in a trap. The approach was slow, like that of a weak person, with little halts and pauses. We heard it coming along the grass straight towards the vacant doorway. Simson had been a little startled by the first sound. He said hastily, "That child has no business to be out so late."

But he felt, as well as I, that this was no child's voice. As it came nearer, he grew silent, and, going to the doorway with his taper, stood looking out towards the sound. The taper being unprotected blew about in the night air, though there was scarcely any wind. I threw the light of my lantern steady and white across the same space. It was in a blaze of light in the midst of the blackness. A little icy thrill had gone over me at the first sound, but as it came close, I confess that my only feeling was satisfaction. The scoffer could scoff no more. The light touched his own face, and showed a very perplexed countenance. If he was afraid, he concealed it with great success, but he was perplexed. And then all that had happened on the previous night was enacted once more.

It fell strangely upon me with a sense of repetition. Every cry, every sob seemed the same as before. I listened almost without any emotion at all in my own person, thinking of its effect upon Simson. He maintained a very bold front, on the whole. All that coming and going of the voice was, if our ears could be trusted, exactly in front of the vacant, blank doorway, blazing full of light, which caught and shone in the glistening leaves of the great hollies at a little distance. Not a rabbit could have crossed the turf without being seen; but there was nothing. After a time, Simson, with a certain caution and bodily reluctance, as it seemed to me, went out with his roll of taper into this space. His figure showed against the holly in full outline. Just at this moment the voice sank, as was its custom, and seemed to fling itself down at the door. Simson recoiled violently, as if someone had come up against him, then turned, and held his taper low, as if examining something.

"Do you see anybody?" I cried in a whisper, feeling the chill of nervous panic steal over me at this action.

"It's nothing but a—confounded juniper-bush," he said. This I knew very well to be nonsense, for the juniper-bush was on the other side. He went about after this round and round, poking his taper everywhere, then returned to me on the inner side of the wall. He scoffed no longer; his face was contracted and pale. "How long does this go on?" he whispered to me, like a man who does not wish to interrupt someone who is speaking. I had become too much perturbed myself to remark whether the successions and changes of the voice were the same as last night. It suddenly went out in the air almost as he was speaking, with a soft reiterated sob dying away. If there had been anything to be seen, I should have said that the person was at that moment crouching on the ground close to the door.

We walked home very silent afterwards. It was only when we were in sight of the house that I said, "What do you think of it?"

"I can't tell what to think of it," he said quickly. He took—though he was a very temperate man—not the claret I was going to offer him, but some brandy from the tray, and swallowed it almost undiluted. "Mind you, I don't believe a word of it," he said, when he had lighted his candle; "but I can't tell what to think," he turned round to add, when he was half-way upstairs.

All of this, however, did me no good with the solution of my problem. I was to help this weeping, sobbing thing, which was already to me as distinct a personality as anything I knew; or what should I say to Roland? It was on my heart that my boy would die if I could not find some way of helping this creature. You may be surprised that I should speak of it in this way. I did not know if it was man or woman; but I no more doubted that it was a soul in pain than I doubted my own being; and it was my business to soothe this pain,—to deliver it, if that was possible. Was ever such a task given to an anxious father trembling for his only boy? I felt in my heart, fantastic as it may appear, that I must fulfil this somehow, or part with my child; and you may conceive that rather than do that I was ready to die. But even my dying would not have advanced me, unless by bringing me into the same world with that seeker at the door.

Next morning Simson was out before breakfast, and came in with evident signs of the damp grass on his boots, and a look of worry and weariness, which did not say much for the night he had passed. He improved a little after breakfast, and visited his two patients,—for Bagley was still an invalid. I went out with him on his way to the train, to hear what he had to say about the boy. "He is going on very well," he said; "there are no complications as yet. But mind you, that's not a boy to be trifled with, Mortimer. Not a word to him about last night." I had to tell him then of my last interview with Roland, and of the impossible demand he had made upon me, by which, though he tried to laugh, he was much discomposed, as I could see.

"We must just perjure ourselves all round," he said, "and swear you exorcised it;" but the man was too kind-hearted to be satisfied with that. "It's frightfully serious for you, Mortimer. I can't laugh as I should like to. I wish I saw a way out of it, for your sake. By the way," he added shortly, "didn't you notice that juniper-bush on the left-hand side?"

"There was one on the right hand of the door. I noticed you made that mistake last night."

"Mistake!" he cried, with a curious low laugh, pulling up the collar of his coat as though he felt the cold,—"there's no juniper there this morning, left or right. Just go and see." As he stepped into the train a few minutes after, he looked back upon me and beckoned me for a parting word. "I'm coming back tonight," he said.

I don't think I had any feeling about this as I turned away from that common bustle of the railway which made my private preoccupations feel so strangely out of date. There had been a distinct satisfaction in my mind before, that his scepticism had been so entirely defeated. But the more serious part of the matter pressed upon me now. I went straight from the railway to the manse, which stood on a little *plateau* on the side of the river opposite to the woods of Brentwood. The minister was one of a class which is not so common in Scotland as it used to be. He was a man of good family, well educated in the Scotch way, strong in philosophy, not so strong in Greek, strongest of all in experience,—a man who had "come across," in the course of his life, most people of note that had ever been in Scotland, and who was said to be very sound in doctrine, without infringing the toleration with which old men, who are good men, are generally endowed. He was old-fashioned; perhaps he did not think so much about the troublous problems of theology as many of the young men, nor ask himself any hard questions about the Confession of Faith; but he understood human nature, which is perhaps better. He received me with a cordial welcome.

"Come away, Colonel Mortimer," he said; "I'm all the more glad to see you, that I feel it's a good sign for the boy. He's doing well?—God be praised,—and the Lord bless him and keep him. He has many a poor body's prayers, and that can do nobody harm."

"He will need them all, Dr. Moncrieff," I said, "and your counsel too." And I told him the story,—more than I had told Simson. The old clergyman listened to me with many suppressed exclamations, and at the end the water stood in his eyes.

"That's just beautiful," he said. "I do not mind to have heard anything like it; it's as fine as Burns when he wished deliverance to one—that is prayed for in no kirk. Ay, ay! so he would have you console the poor lost spirit? God bless the boy! There's something more than common in that, Colonel Mortimer. And also the faith of him in his father!—I would like to put that into a sermon." Then the old gentleman gave me an alarmed look, and said, "No, no; I was not meaning a sermon; but I must write it down for the 'Children's Record.'" I saw the thought that passed through his mind. Either he thought, or he feared I would think, of a funeral sermon. You may believe this did not make me more cheerful.

I can scarcely say that Dr. Moncrieff gave me any advice. How could anyone advise on such a subject? But he said, "I think I'll come too. I'm an old man; I'm less liable to be frightened than those that are further off the world unseen. It behooves me to think of my own journey there. I've no cut-and-dry beliefs on the subject. I'll come too; and maybe at the moment the Lord will put into our heads what to do."

This gave me a little comfort,—more than Simson had given me. To be clear about the cause of it was not my grand desire. It was another thing that was in my mind,—my boy. As for the poor soul at the open door, I had no more doubt, as I have said, of its existence than I had of my own. It was no ghost to me. I knew the creature, and it was in trouble. That was my feeling about it, as it was Roland's. To hear it first was a great shock to my nerves, but not now; a man will get accustomed to anything. But to do something for it was the great problem; how was I to be serviceable to a being that was invisible, that was mortal no longer? "Maybe at the moment the Lord will put it into our heads." This is very old-fashioned phraseology, and a week before,

177

most likely, I should have smiled (though always with kindness) at Dr. Moncrieff's credulity; but there was a great comfort, whether rational or otherwise I cannot say, in the mere sound of the words.

The road to the station and the village lay through the glen, not by the ruins; but though the sunshine and the fresh air, and the beauty of the trees, and the sound of the water were all very soothing to the spirits, my mind was so full of my own subject that I could not refrain from turning to the right hand as I got to the top of the glen, and going straight to the place which I may call the scene of all my thoughts. It was lying full in the sunshine, like all the rest of the world. The ruined gable looked due east, and in the present aspect of the sun the light streamed down through the doorway as our lantern had done, throwing a flood of light upon the damp grass beyond. There was a strange suggestion in the open door,—so futile, a kind of emblem of vanity: all free around, so that you could go where you pleased, and yet that semblance of an enclosure,—that way of entrance, unnecessary, leading to nothing.

And why any creature should pray and weep to get in—to nothing, or be kept out—by nothing, you could not dwell upon it, or it made your brain go round. I remembered, however, what Simson said about the juniper, with a little smile on my own mind as to the inaccuracy of recollection which even a scientific man will be guilty of. I could see now the light of my lantern gleaming upon the wet glistening surface of the spiky leaves at the right hand,—and he ready to go to the stake for it that it was the left! I went round to make sure. And then I saw what he had said. Right or left there was no juniper at all! I was confounded by this, though it was entirely a matter of detail nothing at all,—a bush of brambles waving, the grass growing up to the very walls.

But after all, though it gave me a shock for a moment, what did that matter? There were marks as if a number of footsteps had been up and down in front of the door, but these might have been our steps; and all was bright and peaceful and still. I poked about the other ruin—the larger ruins of the old house—for some time, as I had done before. There were marks upon the grass here and there—I could not call them footsteps—all about; but that told for nothing one way or another. I had examined the ruined rooms closely the first day. They were half filled up with soil and *debris*, withered brackens and bramble,—no refuge for any one there. It vexed me that Jarvis should see me coming from that spot when he came up to me for his orders. I don't know whether my nocturnal expeditions had got wind among the servants, but there was a significant look in his face. Something in it I felt was like my own sensation when Simson in the midst of his scepticism was struck dumb. Jarvis felt satisfied that his veracity had been put beyond question. I never spoke to a servant of mine in such a peremptory tone before. I sent him away "with a flea in his lug," as the man described it afterwards. Interference of any kind was intolerable to me at such a moment.

But what was strangest of all was, that I could not face Roland. I did not go up to his room, as I would have naturally done, at once. This the girls could not understand. They saw there was some mystery in it. "Mother has gone to lie down," Agatha said; "he has had such a good night."

"But he wants you so, papa!" cried little Jeanie, always with her two arms embracing mine in a pretty way she had. I was obliged to go at last, but what could I say? I could only kiss him, and tell him to keep still,—that I was doing all I could. There is something mystical about the patience of a child.

"It will come all right, won't it, father?" he said.

"God grant it may! I hope so, Roland."

"Oh, yes, it will come all right." Perhaps he understood that in the midst of my anxiety I could not stay with him as I should have done otherwise. But the girls were more surprised than it is possible to describe. They looked at me with wondering eyes.

"If I were ill, papa, and you only stayed with me a moment, I should break my heart," said Agatha. But the boy had a sympathetic feeling. He knew that of my own will I would not have done it. I shut myself up in the library, where I could not rest, but kept pacing up and down like a caged beast. What could I do? and if I could do nothing, what would become of my boy? These were the questions that, without ceasing, pursued each other through my mind.

Simson came out to dinner, and when the house was all still, and most of the servants in bed, we went out and met Dr. Moncrieff, as we had appointed, at the head of the glen. Simson, for his part, was disposed to scoff at the Doctor. "If there are to be any spells, you know, I'll cut the whole concern," he said. I did not make him any reply. I had not invited him; he could go or come as he pleased. He was very talkative, far more so than suited my humour, as we went on. "One thing is certain, you know; there must be some human agency," he said. "It is all bosh about apparitions. I never have investigated the laws of sound to any great extent, and there's a great deal in ventriloquism that we don't know much about."

"If it's the same to you," I said, "I wish you'd keep all that to yourself, Simson. It doesn't suit my state of mind."

"Oh, I hope I know how to respect idiosyncrasy," he said. The very tone of his voice irritated me beyond measure. These scientific fellows, I wonder people put up with them as they do, when you have no mind for their cold-blooded confidence. Dr. Moncrieff met us about eleven o'clock, the same time as on the previous night. He was a large man, with a venerable countenance and white hair,—old, but in full vigour, and thinking less of a cold night walk than many a younger man. He had his lantern, as I had. We were fully provided with means of lighting the place, and we were all of us resolute men. We had a rapid consultation as we went up, and the result was that we divided to different posts.

Dr. Moncrieff remained inside the wall—if you can call that inside where there was no wall but one. Simson placed himself on the side next the ruins, so as to intercept any communication with the old house, which was what his mind was fixed upon. I was posted on the other side. To say that nothing could come near without being seen was self-evident. It had been so also on the previous night. Now, with our three lights in the midst of the darkness, the whole place seemed illuminated. Dr. Moncrieff's lantern, which was a large one, without any means of shutting up,—an old-fashioned lantern with a pierced and ornamental top,—shone steadily, the rays shooting out of it upward into the gloom. He placed it on the grass, where the middle of the room, if this had been a room, would have been. The usual effect of the light streaming out of the doorway was prevented by the illumination which Simson and I on either side supplied. With these differences, everything seemed as on the previous night.

And what occurred was exactly the same, with the same air of repetition, point for point, as I had formerly remarked. I declare that it seemed to me as if I were pushed against, put aside, by the owner of the voice as he paced up and down in his trouble,—though these are perfectly futile words, seeing that the stream of light from my lantern, and that from Simson's taper, lay broad and clear, without a shadow, without the smallest break, across the entire breadth of the grass. I had ceased even to be alarmed, for my part. My heart was rent with pity and trouble,—pity for the poor suffering human creature that moaned and pleaded so, and trouble for myself and my boy. God! if I could not find any help,—and what help could I find?—Roland would die.

We were all perfectly still till the first outburst was exhausted, as I knew, by experience, it would be. Dr. Moncrieff, to whom it was new, was quite motionless on the other side of the wall, as we were in our places. My heart had remained almost at its usual beating during the voice. I was used to it; it did not rouse all my pulses as it did at first. But just as it threw itself sobbing at the door (I cannot use other words), there suddenly came something which sent the blood coursing through my veins, and my heart into my mouth. It was a voice inside the wall,—the minister's well-known voice. I would have been prepared for it in any kind of adjuration, but I was not prepared for what I heard. It came out with a sort of stammering, as if too much moved for utterance. "Willie, Willie! Oh, God preserve us! is it you?"

These simple words had an effect upon me that the voice of the invisible creature had ceased to have. I thought the old man, whom I had brought into this danger, had gone mad with terror. I made a dash round to the other side of the wall, half crazed myself with the thought. He was standing where I had left him, his shadow thrown vague and large upon the grass by the lantern which stood at his feet. I lifted my own light to see his face as I rushed forward. He was very pale, his eyes wet and glistening, his mouth quivering with parted lips. He neither saw nor heard me. We that had gone through this experience before, had crouched towards each other to get a little strength to bear it. But he was not even aware that I was there. His whole being seemed absorbed in anxiety and tenderness. He held out his hands, which trembled, but it seemed to me with eagerness, not fear. He went on speaking all the time. "Willie, if it is you,—and it's you, if it is not a delusion of Satan,—Willie, lad! why come ye here frighting them that know you not? Why came ye not to me?"

He seemed to wait for an answer. When his voice ceased, his countenance, every line moving, continued to speak. Simson gave me another terrible shock, stealing into the open doorway with his light, as much awe-stricken, as wildly curious, as I. But the minister resumed, without seeing Simson, speaking to someone else. His voice took a tone of expostulation:—

"Is this right to come here? Your mother's gone with your name on her lips. Do you think she would ever close her door on her own lad? Do ye think the Lord will close the door, ye faint-hearted creature? No!—I forbid ye! I forbid ye!" cried the old man. The sobbing voice had begun to resume its cries. He made a step forward, calling out the last words in a voice of command.

"I forbid ye! Cry out no more to man. Go home, ye wandering spirit! go home! Do you hear me?—me that christened ye, that have struggled with ye, that have wrestled for ye with the Lord!" Here the loud tones of his voice sank into tenderness. "And her too, poor woman! poor woman! her you are calling upon. She's not here. You'll find her with the Lord. Go there and seek her, not here. Do you hear me, lad? go after her there. He'll let you in, though it's late. Man, take heart! if you will lie and sob and greet, let it be at heaven's gate, and not your poor mother's ruined door."

He stopped to get his breath; and the voice had stopped, not as it had done before, when its time was exhausted and all its repetitions said, but with a sobbing catch in the breath as if overruled. Then the minister spoke again, "Are you hearing me, Will? Oh, laddie, you've liked the beggarly elements all your days. Be done with them now. Go home to the Father—the Father! Are you hearing me?" Here the old man sank down upon his knees, his face raised upwards, his hands held up with a tremble in them, all white in the light in the midst of the darkness. I resisted as long as I could, though I cannot tell why; then I, too, dropped upon my knees. Simson all the time stood in the doorway, with an expression in his face such as words could not tell, his under lip dropped, his eyes wild, staring. It seemed to be to him, that image of blank ignorance and wonder, that we were praying. All the time the voice, with a low arrested sobbing, lay just where he was standing, as I thought.

"Lord," the minister said,—"Lord, take him into Thy everlasting habitations. The mother he cries to is with Thee. Who can open to him but Thee? Lord, when is it too late for Thee, or what is too hard for Thee? Lord, let that woman there draw him inower! Let her draw him inower!"

I sprang forward to catch something in my arms that flung itself wildly within the door. The illusion was so strong, that I never paused till I felt my forehead graze against the wall and my hands clutch the ground,—for there was nobody there to save from falling, as in my foolishness I thought. Simson held out his hand to me to help me up. He was trembling and cold, his lower lip hanging, his speech almost inarticulate. "It's gone," he said, stammering,—"it's gone!"

We leaned upon each other for a moment, trembling so much, both of us, that the whole scene trembled as if it were going to dissolve and disappear; and yet as long as I live I will never forget it,—the shining of the strange lights, the blackness all round, the kneeling figure with all the whiteness of the light concentrated on its white venerable head and uplifted hands. A strange solemn stillness seemed to close all round us. By intervals a single syllable, "Lord! Lord!" came from the old minister's lips. He saw none of us, nor thought of us. I never knew how long we stood, like sentinels guarding him at his prayers, holding our lights in a confused dazed way, not knowing what we did. But at last he rose from his knees, and standing up at his full height, raised his arms, as the Scotch manner is at the end of a religious service, and solemnly gave the apostolical benediction,—to what? to the silent earth, the dark woods, the wide breathing atmosphere; for we were but spectators gasping an Amen!

It seemed to me that it must be the middle of the night, as we all walked back. It was in reality very late. Dr. Moncrieff put his arm into mine. He walked slowly, with an air of exhaustion. It was as if we were coming from a death-bed. Something hushed and solemnized the very air. There was that sense of relief in it which there always is at the end of a death-struggle. And nature, persistent, never daunted, came back in all of us, as we returned into the ways of life. We said nothing to each other, indeed, for a time; but when we got clear of the trees and reached the opening near the house, where we could see the sky, Dr. Moncrieff himself was the first to speak. "I must be going," he said; "it's very late, I'm afraid. I will go down the glen, as I came."

"But not alone. I am going with you, doctor."

"Well, I will not oppose it. I am an old man, and agitation wearies more than work. Yes; I'll be thankful of your arm. Tonight, Colonel, you've done me more good turns than one."

I pressed his hand on my arm, not feeling able to speak. But Simson, who turned with us, and who had gone along all this time with his taper flaring, in entire unconsciousness, came to himself, apparently at the sound of our voices, and put out that wild little torch with a quick movement, as if of shame. "Let me carry your lantern," he said; "it is heavy." He recovered with a spring; and in a moment, from the awe-stricken spectator he had been, became himself, sceptical and cynical. "I should like to ask you a question," he said. "Do you believe in Purgatory, Doctor? It's not in the tenets of the Church, so far as I know."

"Sir," said Dr. Moncrieff, "an old man like me is sometimes not very sure what he believes. There is just one thing I am certain of— and that is the loving-kindness of God."

"But I thought that was in this life. I am no theologian—"

"Sir," said the old man again, with a tremor in him which I could feel going over all his frame, "if I saw a friend of mine within the gates of hell, I would not despair but his Father would take him by the hand still, if he cried like *you*."

"I allow it is very strange, very strange. I cannot see through it. That there must be human agency, I feel sure. Doctor, what made you decide upon the person and the name?"

The minister put out his hand with the impatience which a man might show if he were asked how he recognized his brother. "Tuts!" he said, in familiar speech; then more solemnly, "How should I not recognize a person that I know better—far better—than I know you?"

"Then you saw the man?"

Dr. Moncrieff made no reply. He moved his hand again with a little impatient movement, and walked on, leaning heavily on my arm. And we went on for a long time without another word, threading the dark paths, which were steep and slippery with the damp of the winter. The air was very still,—not more than enough to make a faint sighing in the branches, which mingled with the sound of the water to which we were descending. When we spoke again, it was about indifferent matters,—about the height of the river, and the recent rains. We parted with the minister at his own door, where his old housekeeper appeared in great perturbation, waiting for him. "Eh, me, minister! the young gentleman will be worse?" she cried.

"Far from that—better. God bless him!" Dr. Moncrieff said.

I think if Simson had begun again to me with his questions, I should have pitched him over the rocks as we returned up the glen; but he was silent, by a good inspiration. And the sky was clearer than it had been for many nights, shining high over the trees, with here and there a star faintly gleaming through the wilderness of dark and bare branches. The air, as I have said, was very soft in them, with a subdued and peaceful cadence. It was real, like every natural sound, and came to us like a hush of peace and relief. I thought there was a sound in it as of the breath of a sleeper, and it seemed clear to me that Roland must be sleeping, satisfied and calm. We went up to his room when we went in. There we found the complete hush of rest. My wife looked up out of a doze, and gave me a smile:

"I think he is a great deal better; but you are very late," she said in a whisper, shading the light with her hand that the Doctor might see his patient. The boy had got back something like his own colour.

184

He woke as we stood all round his bed. His eyes had the happy, half-awakened look of childhood, glad to shut again, yet pleased with the interruption and glimmer of the light. I stooped over him and kissed his forehead, which was moist and cool.

"All is well, Roland," I said. He looked up at me with a glance of pleasure, and took my hand and laid his cheek upon it, and so went to sleep.

★★★★★★

For some nights after, I watched among the ruins, spending all the dark hours up to midnight patrolling about the bit of wall which was associated with so many emotions; but I heard nothing, and saw nothing beyond the quiet course of nature; nor, so far as I am aware, has anything been heard again. Dr. Moncrieff gave me the history of the youth, whom he never hesitated to name. I did not ask, as Simson did, how he recognized him. He had been a prodigal,—weak, foolish, easily imposed upon, and "led away," as people say. All that we had heard had passed actually in life, the doctor said. The young man had come home thus a day or two after his mother died,—who was no more than the housekeeper in the old house,—and distracted with the news, had thrown himself down at the door and called upon her to let him in. The old man could scarcely speak of it for tears.

To me it seemed as if—Heaven help us, how little do we know about anything!—a scene like that might impress itself somehow upon the hidden heart of nature. I do not pretend to know how, but the repetition had struck me at the time as, in its terrible strangeness and incomprehensibility, almost mechanical,—as if the unseen actor could not exceed or vary, but was bound to re-enact the whole. One thing that struck me, however, greatly, was the likeness between the old minister and my boy in the manner of regarding these strange phenomena. Dr. Moncrieff was not terrified, as I had been myself, and all the rest of us. It was no "ghost," as I fear we all vulgarly considered it, to him,—but a poor creature whom he knew under these conditions, just as he had known him in the flesh, having no doubt of his identity.

And to Roland it was the same. This spirit in pain,—if it was a spirit,—this voice out of the unseen,—was a poor fellow-creature in misery, to be succoured and helped out of his trouble, to my boy. He spoke to me quite frankly about it when he got better. "I knew father would find out some way," he said. And this was when he was strong and well, and all idea that he would turn hysterical or become a seer of visions had happily passed away.

I must add one curious fact, which does not seem to me to have any relation to the above, but which Simson made great use of, as the human agency which he was determined to find somehow. We had examined the ruins very closely at the time of these occurrences; but afterwards, when all was over, as we went casually about them one Sunday afternoon in the idleness of that unemployed day, Simson with his stick penetrated an old window which had been entirely blocked up with fallen soil. He jumped down into it in great excitement, and called me to follow. There we found a little hole,—for it was more a hole than a room,—entirely hidden under the ivy and ruins, in which there was a quantity of straw laid in a corner, as if someone had made a bed there, and some remains of crusts about the floor. Someone had lodged there, and not very long before, he made out; and that this unknown being was the author of all the mysterious sounds we heard he is convinced.

"I told you it was human agency," he said triumphantly. He forgets, I suppose, how he and I stood with our lights, seeing nothing, while the space between us was audibly traversed by something that could speak, and sob, and suffer. There is no argument with men of this kind. He is ready to get up a laugh against me on this slender ground. "I was puzzled myself,—I could not make it out,—but I always felt convinced human agency was at the bottom of it. And here it is,—and a clever fellow he must have been," the doctor says.

Bagley left my service as soon as he got well. He assured me it was no want of respect, but he could not stand "them kind of things;" and the man was so shaken and ghastly that I was glad to give him a present and let him go. For my own part, I made a point of staying out the time—two years—for which I had taken Brentwood; but I did not renew my tenancy. By that time we had settled, and found for ourselves a pleasant home of our own.

I must add, that when the doctor defies me, I can always bring back gravity to his countenance, and a pause in his railing, when I remind him of the juniper-bush. To me that was a matter of little importance. I could believe I was mistaken. I did not care about it one way or other; but on his mind the effect was different. The miserable voice, the spirit in pain, he could think of as the result of ventriloquism, or reverberation, or—anything you please: an elaborate prolonged hoax, executed somehow by the tramp that had found a lodging in the old tower; but the juniper-bush staggered him. Things have effects so different on the minds of different men.

The Vengeance of a Tree

Eleanor F. Lewis

Through the windows of Jim Daly's saloon, in the little town of C——, the setting sun streamed in yellow patches, lighting up the glasses scattered on the tables and the faces of several men who were gathered near the bar. Farmers mostly they were, with a sprinkling of shopkeepers, while prominent among them was the village editor, and all were discussing a startling piece of news that had spread through the town and its surroundings. The tidings that Walter Stedman, a labourer on Albert Kelsey's ranch, had assaulted and murdered his employer's daughter, had reached them, and had spread universal horror among the people.

A farmer declared that he had seen the deed committed as he walked through a neighbouring lane, and, having always been noted for his cowardice, instead of running to the girl's aid, had hailed a party of miners who were returning from their mid-day meal through a field nearby. When they reached the spot, however, where Stedman (as they supposed) had done his black deed, only the girl lay there, in the stillness of death. Her murderer had taken the opportunity to fly. The party had searched the woods of the Kelsey estate, and just as they were nearing the house itself the appearance of Walter Stedman, walking in a strangely unsteady manner toward it, made them quicken their pace.

He was soon in custody, although he had protested his innocence of the crime. He said that he had just seen the body himself on his way to the station, and that when they had found him, he was going to the house for help. But they had laughed at his story and had flung him into the tiny, stifling calaboose of the town.

What were their proofs? Walter Stedman, a young fellow of about twenty-six, had come from the city to their quiet town, just when times were at their hardest, in search of work. The most of the men living in the town were honest fellows, doing their work faithfully, when they could get it, and when they had socially asked Stedman to have a drink with them, he had refused in rather a scornful manner. "That infernal city chap," he was called, and their hate and envy increased in strength when Albert Kelsey had employed him in preference to any of themselves. As time went on, the story of Stedman's admiration for Margaret Kelsey had gone afloat, with the added information that his employer's daughter had repulsed him, saying that she would not marry a common labourer. So, Stedman, when this news reached his employer's ears, was discharged, and this, then, was his revenge! For them, these proofs were sufficient to pronounce him guilty.

Yet that afternoon, as Stedman, crouched on the floor of the calaboose, grew hopeless in the knowledge that no one would believe his story, and that his undeserved punishment would be swift and sure, a tramp, boarding a freight car several miles from the town, sped away from the spot where his crime had been committed, and knew that forever its shadow would follow him.

From the tiny window of his prison Walter Stedman could see the red glow of the heavens that betokened the setting of the sun. So, the red sun of his life was soon to set, a life that had been innocent of all crime, and that now was to be ended for a deed that he had never committed. Most prominent of all the visions that swept through his mind was that of Margaret Kelsey, lying as he had first found her, fresh from the hands of her murderer. But there was another of a more tender nature. How long he and Margaret had tried to keep their secret, until Walter could be promoted to a higher position, so that he could ask for her hand with no fear of the father's antagonism!

Then came the remembrance of an afternoon meeting between the two in the woods of the Kelsey estate—how, just as they were parting, Walter had heard footsteps near them, and, glancing sharply around, saw an evil, scowling, murderous face peering through the brush. He had started toward it, but the owner of the countenance had taken himself hurriedly off.

The gossiping townspeople had misconstrued this romance, and when Albert Kelsey had heard of this clandestine meeting from the man who was later on to appear as a leader of the mob, and that he had discharged Stedman, they had believed that the young man had formally proposed and had been rejected. But justice had gone wrong, as it had done innumerable times before, and will again. An innocent man was to be hanged, even without the comfort of a trial, while the man who was guilty was free to wander where he would.

That autumn night the darkness came quickly, and only the stars did their best to light the scene. A body of men, all masked, and having as a leader one who had ever since Stedman's arrival in town, cherished a secret hatred of the young man, dragged Stedman from the calaboose and tramped through the town, defying all, defying even God himself. Along the highway, and into Farmer Brown's "cross cut," they went, vigilantly guarding their prisoner, who, with the lanterns lighting up his haggard face, walked among them with the lagging step of utter hopelessness.

"That's a good tree," their leader said, presently, stopping and pointing out a spreading oak; when the slipknot was adjusted and Stedman had stepped on the box, he added: "If you've got anything to say, you'd better say it now."

"I am innocent, I swear before God," the doomed man answered; "I never took the life of Margaret Kelsey."

"Give us your proof," jeered the leader, and when Stedman kept a despairing silence, he laughed shortly.

"Ready, men!" he gave the order. The box was kicked aside, and then—only a writhing body swung to and fro in the gloom.

In front of the men stood their leader, watching the contortions of the body with silent glee. "I'll tell you a secret, boys," he said suddenly. "I was after that poor murdered girl myself. A d—— little chance I had; but, by ——, he had just as little!"

A pause—then: "He's shunted this earth. Cut him down, you fellows!"

★★★★★★★★★★★★★★★★

"It's no use, son. I'll give up the blasted thing as a bad job. There's something queer about that there tree. Do you see how its branches balance it? We have cut the trunk nearly in two, but it won't come down. There's plenty of others around; we'll take one of them. If I'd a long rope with me I'd get that tree down, and yet the way the thing stands it would be risking a fellow's life to climb it. It's got the devil in it, sure."

So old Farmer Brown shouldered his axe and made for another tree, his son following. They had sawed and chopped and chopped and sawed, and yet the tall white oak, with its branches jutting out almost as regularly as if done by the work of a machine, stood straight and firm.

Farmer Brown, well known for his weak, cowardly spirit, who in beholding the murder of Albert Kelsey's daughter, had in his fright mistaken the criminal, now in his superstition let the oak stand, because its well-balanced position saved it from falling, when other trees would have been down. And so, this tree, the same one to which an innocent man had been hanged, was left—for other work.

It was a bleak, rainy night—such a night as can be found only in central California. The wind howled like a thousand demons, and lashed the trees together in wild embraces. Now and then the weird "hoot, hoot!" of an owl came softly from the distance in the lulls of the storm, while the barking of coyotes woke the echoes of the hills into sounds like fiendish laughter.

In the wind and rain a man fought his path through the bush and into Farmer Brown's "cross cut," as the shortest way home. Suddenly he stopped, trembling, as if held by some unseen impulse. Before him rose the white oak, wavering and swaying in the storm.

"Good God! it's the tree I swung Stedman from!" he cried, and a strange fear thrilled him.

His eyes were fixed on it, held by some undefinable fascination. Yes, there on one of the longest branches a small piece of rope still dangled. And then, to the murderer's excited vision, this rope seemed to lengthen, to form at the end into a slipknot, a knot that encircled a purple neck, while below it writhed and swayed the body of a man!

"Damn him!" he muttered, starting toward the hanging form, as if about to help the rope in its work of strangulation; "will he forever follow me? And yet he deserved it, the black-hearted villain! He took her life——"

He never finished the sentence. The white oak, towering above him in its strength, seemed to grow like a frenzied, living creature. There was a sudden splitting sound, then came a crash, and under the fallen tree lay Stedman's murderer, crushed and mangled.

From between the broken trunk and the stump that was left, a grey, dim shape sprang out, and sped past the man's still form, away into the wild blackness of the night.

The Devil's Motor

Marie Corelli

A Fantasy

In the dead midnight, at that supreme moment when the hours that are past slip away from the grasp of the hours yet to be, there came rushing between Earth and Heaven the sound of giant wheels—the glare of great lights—the stench and the muffled roar of a huge car, tearing at full speed along the pale line dividing the darkness from the dawn. And he who stood within the car, steering it straight onward, was clothed in black and crowned with fire; large bat-like wings flared out on either side of him in woven webs of smoke and flame, and his face was white as bleached bone. Like glowing embers his eyes burned in their cavernous sockets, shedding terrific glances through the star-strewn space—and on his thin lips there was a frozen shadow of a smile more cruel than hate—more deadly than despair.

"On!" he cried—"Still on! On with an endless rush and roar! Over the plains of the world that is gone—over the heights. of the world to come—on, still on! Without pause, without pity, without love, without regret! Follow me, all ye forces which are destined to work the ruin of mankind—follow! On, on, over all beauty, all tenderness, all truth I ride—I, the Avenger, the Destroyer, the Torturer of souls, the Arch-Enemy of God! The Kingdom of Hell grows wide and deep—praise be to man who makes it! I count up my growing possessions in the ever-breeding spawn of human lust and avarice—I breathe and live and rejoice in the fat poison-vapours of human selfishness!

"The men of these latter days are my food and sustenance—the women my choice morsels, my dainty delicates! Brute beasts and blind, they snatch at every lie I offer them;—rejecting Eternal Life, they choose Eternal Death—verily they shall have their reward! Like a blight my spirit shall encompass them!—and whosoever would scour the air and scorch the earth must run on the straight road of his desire with Me!"

The great car flashed along with grinding, thunderous wheels, and as it flew, vast phantom-forms followed it, like rolling clouds jagged with the lightning—the fairness of the world grew black, and sulphureous fumes quenched all sweetness from the air. The forests dropped like broken reeds—the mountains crumbled into pits and quarries, the seas and rivers, the lakes and waterfalls dried up into black and muddy waters, and all the land was bereft of beauty. In the place of wholesome green fields and leafy woods, there rose up gigantic cities, built in on every side, and bristling with thousands upon thousands of chimneys belching forth sickening smoke into the overhanging gloom which hid the skies; and the cities were full of a deafening noise and crashing confusion as of ten million million hammers beating incessantly—beating away all peace, all solitude, all health, all rest. On—on, and into these countless prisons of stone and mortar the Demon of the car swept vast and ever-hurrying crowds of human beings, with the furious force of a mighty whirlwind sweeping dead leaves into the sea.

"No room to breathe—no time to think—no good to serve!" he cried—"Now shall you forget that God exists! Now shall you all have your own wild way, for Your way is My way! Now shall you resolve yourselves back to an embryo of worms and apes, and none shall rescue you, no, not one! For the Seven Angels of the Judgment Day are sounding their—trumpets of terror, and who shall silence the voices, or stay the thunderings and lightnings, or the great earthquake? Hail and fire!—and the trees, and the green grass burnt up and destroyed!—the sun and the moon, the day and the night smitten into one blackness! We will have no more virtues!—no more hopes of Heaven!

"Honour shall be as a rag on a fool's back, and Gold shall be the pulse of Life! Gold, gold, gold! Fight for it, steal it, pile it up, hoard it, count it, hug it, eat it, sleep with it, die with it! Lo, I give it to you in millions, packed down and pressed together in full and overflowing measure—I scatter it on you even as a destroying rain! Build with it, buy with it, gamble with it, sell your souls and bodies for it—there are devils enough in hell to drive all your bargains! Sneer at truth, defeat justice, snatch virtue's mask to cover vice, drug conscience, feed and fatten yourselves with the lusts of animalism till the cancer of sin makes of you a putrefaction and an open sore in the sight of the sun! Come, learn from me such wisdom as shall compass your own destruction!

"Unto you shall be unlocked the under-mysteries of Nature, and the secrets of the upper air—you shall bend the lightning to your service, and the lightning shall slay!—you shall hollow out the ground, and delve a swift road through it for yourselves in fancied proud security, and the earth shall crumble in upon you as a grave, and the cities you have built shall crush you in their falling!—you shall seek to bind the winds in and sail the skies, and Death shall wait for you in the clouds, and exult in your downfall. Come, tie your pigmy chariots to the sun, and so be drawn into its flaming vortex of perdition! All Creation shall rejoice to be cleansed from the pollution of your presence, for God hath sworn to give unto Me all who reject Him, and the Hour of the Gift has come!"

Still faster and more furiously flew the car—red meteors flashed in its course—and the phantom shapes which followed its flight crowded together in an ever-thickening, ever-darkening multitude, while bright stars were shaken down from heaven like snowflakes whirling in a winter blast. And mingling with the grinding roar of its wheels came other sounds—sounds of fierce laughter and loud cursing—yells and shrieks and groans of torture—the screams of the suffering, the sobs of the dying—and as the fiend drove on with swiftly quickening speed, men and women and little children were trampled down one upon another and killed in their thousands, and the car was splashed thick with human blood. And He who was clothed in black and crowned with fire, shouted exultingly as He dashed along over massacred heaps of dead nations and the broken remnants of thrones.

"Progress and Speed!" he yelled—"Rush on, world, with me!—rush on! There is but one end—hasten we to reach it! No halt by the way to gather the flowers of thought—the fruits of feeling;—no pause for a lifting of the eyes to the wide firmament, where millions of spheres, more beautiful than this which men make wretched, sail on their courses like fair ships bound for God's golden harbours! No time to listen to the singing of the birds of hope, the ripple of the sweet waters of refreshment, the murmur of cool grasses waving in the fields of peace;—no time, no stop—no lull for quiet breathing—on!—forever on!

"Up and ride with me all ye who would reach the goal! Come, ye fools of avarice! Come, ye blown and bursting windbags of world's conceit and vain pretension! Come, ye greedy maws of gluttony—ye human pottles of drink—ye wolves of vice! Come, ye shameless women of lusts and lies and vanities! Come, false hearts and treacherous tongues and painted faces!—come, dear demons all, and ride with me! Come, ye pretenders to holiness—ye thieves of virtue, who give 'charity' to the poor with the right hand, and cheat your neighbour with the left! Come, ye gamblers with a Nation's honour, stake your last throw! Come, all ye morphia-fed vampires and slaves to poison!—grasp at my wheels and cling!

"On—on—over the fragments of mighty Empires—over the hearts of kings and queens,—over the lives of the brave, the good, and the wise!—trample them all down and crush them into dust and ashes! What shall we do with wisdom, we who have done with God? What with purity?—what with courage? Naught are these but reproach and bitterness—mere obstacles in the broad way which leadeth to destruction;— ride them down! On—on! to the destined end!—on with rush and hurry and panting eagerness to reach the only goal—the last of winning-posts—the close of certainties—the Grave!"

Like a flashing blur of fiery wheels, the car now spun along in the blackness of the night, and the drifting phantoms round about it were as great grey sails swelling with the angry blast, and sweeping it onward through the dark.

"Pray no more—hope no more—love no more!" cried the fiend. "Be as the shifting sands, or as the trembling quicksilver—inconstant capricious—ever in motion, never at rest! Change—change and re-volt! All ye who weary of old things, behold I give you new! Bodies shall be pampered and souls killed for your pleasure;—foulest vices shall be called merely 'sensations,'—each to be tried, excused, and condemned in turn—and virtues shall have no more place at all in the scale of feeling! The music of life shall clash into wild discord—the love of home shall be a lost glory—tenderness for the young, and reverence for the old, shall be the faded sentiments of the past, only fit fora mummer's jest! Change—Change and Sensation!

"Roll out your columns of vaporous notoriety, ye printing-presses of the world!—spread wide the fame of the anarchist and the courte-san—mock and revile the spirits of the wise and true—noise abroad the name of the murderer, and treat the poet with derision—give flat-tery to the rich, and scorn to the humble—teach nothing but the art of lying—add venom to the tongue of scandal—dig up the graves of the great, and kill the reputations of the brave and pure! Help nothing on that is noble—nothing that is honest—nothing that is of God, or for God—print every lie, grudge every truth, and let your trumpet-note be that of blatant atheism and devilry to the end!

"Set trade against trade—community against community—nation against nation—till with your windy bombast and senseless twaddle you fill your witches' cauldron of mischief and contention to the full! Up and ride with me, ye plotters against peace!—ye whose hands are against every man!—there is no time to be lost—up and away with a rush and a roar!—for the Great Star has fallen from heaven to earth, and to Him is given the key of the bottomless pit! The pit is open—the gate stands wide—up, and speed on with Me!"

Like lightning now, the great car tore through space—its flaring lamps flashing, its wheels grinding with the sullen noise of a bursting volcano—and amidst cries and shrieks indescribable, it leaped, as it were, from peak to peak of toppling clouds that towered above and around it like mighty mountains. And presently it seemed as if a thin, pale line of purple fire glimmered afar off, and by this light was seen a monstrous ridge of dense blackness jutting sharply over some vast incalculable depth of horror. On—still on—the car rushed; and He of the sable robes and flaming crown urged apace its reckless speed with wild shouts of wilder laughter.

"All the world in such haste to die!" he cried. "All the world gone mad with the craze of movement! Up in the air, down on the earth—all turned to whirling, flying, tossing atoms of dust in a storm, and lo, the End! Be patient now, for ye shall never wander again!—be silent now, for prayer and cursing, laughter and tears are done!—let the hoarded gold drop from your grasp—it can purchase nothing yonder! Was it worthwhile, think you—this rush headlong, to be cast into silence? Was it worthwhile to leave the sunshine for this dark?—beauty for this decay?—sweet sounds of love and tenderness for this still glow of the eternal flame which is not quenched—We this gnawing of the eternal worm whose appetite is never satisfied? Lo, ye have burnt up a Day world to light Hell with its flame!—but the world shall blossom again like a flower springing from the dust, and ye whose soulless lives have been a curse and an outrage on its fairness, shall pace its pleasant paths no more!

"Rejoice, O earth!—rejoice, O sea!—to be freed of the burden of mankind! Rejoice, O birds, that the hand of the spoiler shall no longer wound or slay!—rejoice O trees, that the axe of the destroyer shall no more cast ye down!—rejoice, O all ye living creatures of the field and forest, that Treachery no longer stalks the world in man's disguise! Take back thy planet, O great God, cleansed of a pigmy race! Create a new Humanity!—for This is past!"

On—on—along the black ridge jutting darkly over silent immensity, with a whirl of fire and roar of thunder the car flew—and then—as if for one brief breathing part of a second it paused! Like a vast shadow between Earth and Heaven the Demon stood—his bony hand on the steering-wheel—and every point in his flaming crown scintillating with the sparkle of a million stars. Round about him soared and stooped countless terrific phantom-shapes—some like wrecked ships—some like torn flags of honour—some like mounted warriors—some like throned kings—some like fair women veiled in a mist of tears—and beneath his batlike pinions, outstretched to north and south, there glimmered a pale crowd of white faces, upturned wild eyes and imploring hands—all crushed together in a writhing mass of agony!

But no sound came from those dumb mouths agape with terror—all were silent as Death itself, and only the thunderous roar of the car echoed through space, as, after that infinitely brief pause, it dashed furiously onward and down!—down—down sheer over the edge of that mystic precipice into the fathomless abyss of the Unseen and Unknown!

A thousand lightnings leaped after it—a thousand crashing echoes vibrated through the Universe with its fall—one frightful human cry shuddered up to Heaven—and then—silence! Gradually, gently, and by faint degrees, a purpling fire crimsoned the wavering rise of dawn—a cool wind parted the air into sweet breadths of fragrance—and in the centre of the awful stillness a scarlet sun rose slowly in a clear sky, fixing the red seal of God on the closed history of a World!

The Hidden Door

Vernon Lee

It seemed to Decimus Little that there could be no doubt left. His only wonder was whether anyone else had been near making that discovery. As he sat in a deep window of the big drawing-room, the light of the candles falling yellow upon the shining white arms and shoulders, the shining white expanses of shirt-front, the lustrous silks and lustrous black cloth within doors; the great wave of moor and fell unfurling greyish-green in the pale-blue twilight without; as he sat there alone in the window, he wondered how it would be if any of these creatures assembled for the coming of age of the heir of Hotspur Hall could guess that he knew. His eyes mechanically followed the tall figure of his host, as his broad shoulders and grey beard appeared and reappeared in the crowd; they sought out the yellow ridge of curls of the son and heir, as his head rose and fell while talking to the ladies in the corner.

What if either of them could guess? If old Kir Hugh Hotspur could guess that there was in the world another creature beside himself who knew the position of that secret door; if young Hotspur could guess that there existed close by another man who might, any day, penetrate into that secret chamber to which, at the close of these merry-making days, the youth must be solemnly admitted, to lose, during that fatal hour among unspeakable mysteries, all lightness of heart forever?

Mr. Little was not at all surprised at the fact of having made this extraordinary discovery. Although in no way a conceited man, he was accustomed to think of himself as connected with extraordinary matters, and in some way destined for an extraordinary end. He was one of those men who, without ever having done, or even said, or perhaps even thought, anything especially remarkable, are yet remarkable men. Whenever he came into a room, he felt people's eyes upon him, and knew that they were asking, "Who is that young man?" And still Mr.

Decimus Little did not consider himself handsome, nor did anyone else consider him so, to his knowledge. From the matter-of-fact point of view, all one could say was that he was of middle height, more inclined to be fat than thin, with small not irregular features, hair varying between yellow and grey, a slight stoop, a somewhat defective sight, and a preference for clothes of ample cut and of neutral tints.

But then the matter-of-fact eye just missed that something indefinable which constituted the remarkable character of Mr. Little's appearance. As it was with, his person, so likewise was it with his history; there was more significance therein than could easily be defined. A distant relative, on the female side, of the illustrious border house of Hotspur, Mr. Little possessed a modest income and the education of a gentleman. He had never been to school, and had left college without taking his degree. He had begun reading for the law, and left off. He had tried writing for the magazines, but without success. He had at one time inclined to High-Church asceticism and the moralizing of Whitechapel; he had also been addicted to socialism, and spent six months learning to make a chest of drawers in a Birmingham co-operative workshop.

He had begun writing a biography of Ninon de Lenclos, studying singing, and forming a collection of rare medals; and he was now considerably interested in Esoteric Buddhism and the Society for Psychical Research, although he felt by no means prepared to accept the new theosophy, nor to indorse the conclusions concerning thought transference. And finally, and quite lately, Mr. Decimus Little had also been in love, and had become engaged to a cousin of his, a young lady studying at Girton College; but he was not quite sure whether the engagement was absolutely binding on either side, or whether marriage would be certainly conducive to the happiness of both parties.

For Mr. Decimus Little was gradually maturing a theory to the effect of his being a person with a double nature, reflective and idealistic on the one hand, and capable, on the other, of extraordinary impulses of lawlessness; and it is notorious that such persons, and indeed, perhaps, all very complex and out-of-the-common personalities are not very fit for the marriage state. It was consonant with what Mr. Little often lamented as the excessive scepticism of his temper, that he should not have made up his mind about the hidden chamber at Hotspur Hall, and the strange stories concerning it. He had often discussed the matter, which, as he remarked, was a crucial one in all questions of the supernatural He had triumphantly argued with a physiologist at his club that mere delusion could not be a sufficient explanation for so old and diffused a belief, as, indeed, mere delusion could not account for any belief of any kind.

He had argued equally triumphantly with a clergyman in the train against the notion that the occupant of the secret chamber was the Evil One, and had added that the existence of evil spirits offered serious, very serious, difficulties to a thoughtful mind. And Mr. Little, being, as he often remarked, open to arguments and evidence on all points, had elaborated various explanations of the mystery of the hidden chamber, and had even attempted to sound the inhabitants of Hotspur Hall on the subject. But the servants had not understood his polished but rather shadowy Oxford English, or he had not understood their thick Northumbrian, and the members of the family had dropped the subject with a somewhat disconcerting sharpness of manner; and Mr. Little was the last man in the world to rudely invade the secrets of others, by experiments of towels hung out of windows, and such like; indeed, the person capable of such courses would have inspired him with horror.

And by an irony of fate—Mr. Little believed in the irony of fate, and was occasionally ironical himself—it had been given to him, to this sceptical and unobtrusive man, to discover that room hidden in the thickness of the Norman wall, and whose position had baffled so much ingenious, pertinacious, and impertinent inquiry.

There could no longer be any doubt about it; this door, revealed only by its hollow sound and its rusty iron bolt, against which Mr. Little had accidentally leaned that day when the shame of having intruded upon a flirtation (and a flirtation, too, between the heir of Hotspur and the heiress of his hereditary foes the Blenkinsops) had made him rush, like a mad creature, along unknown passages and up the winding staircase of the peel tower—this door, whitewashed to look like stone and hidden just under the highest battlements of Hotspur, could only be that of the mysterious chamber. It had flashed across Mr. Little's mind when first he had leaned, confused and panting, against the wall of the staircase, and the wall had yielded to his pressure and creaked perceptibly; and the certainty had grown with every subsequent examination of the spot, and of the exterior of the castle.

People had hitherto wasted their ingenuity upon seeking a window in Hotspur Hall which should correspond with no ostensible room; accident had revealed to Mr. Little a room which corresponded with no window visible from without. It now seemed so simple that it was impossible to conceive how the secret could so long have been kept. The secret chamber was, could be, only in the oldest portion of the castle, in the peel tower, built for the protection of stock and goods from the Scottish raids; and it was, it could be, only under the very roof of the tower, taking air and light through some chimney or trap-door from the battlements above.

There could be no doubt about it; and as Mr. Decimus Little sat in the window-seat of the great drawing-room at Hotspur, with on the one side the crowd of guests brilliant in the yellow candle-light, and the great dark wave of fell and moor rising into the blue twilight on the other, he thought how strange it was that of all these people there was only one, besides the master of Hotspur, who knew the position of the fatal room: only one besides the heir of Hotspur who might—who knows!—penetrate into its secrets, and that one person should be himself. Strange; and yet, somehow, it did not take him by surprise.

And, after all, what was the secret of that chamber? A monstrous creature, or race of creatures, hidden away by the unrightful heirs? An ancient ancestor, living on by diabolic arts throughout the centuries? A demon, a spectre, some horror nameless because inconceivable to those who had not seen it, or perhaps some almost immaterial evil, some curse lurking in the very atmosphere of the place? It was notorious that the something, whatever it was, made it impossible for a Hotspur ever to marry a Blenkinsop; that the heir of Hotspur was introduced to this mystery on coming of age; and that no Hotspur, after coming of age, had ever been known to smile: those were well authenticated facts; but what mystery or horror upon earth or in hell could be sufficient cause for these well ascertained results, no one had ever discovered. Every explanation was futile and insufficient.

These were the thoughts which went on in Mr. Little's mind throughout that week of coming of age at Hotspur Hall. All day and all night—at least, as much of the night as he could account for—these questions kept going round and round in his mind, presenting now one surface, now another, but ever present and ever active. He walked about, ate his dinner, talked, danced automatically, knowing that he did it all, but as one knows what another person is doing, or what one is reading in a book, without any sense of its being one's self or its being real; nay, with a sense of being removed miles and miles from it all, living in a different time and place, to which this present is as the past and the distant.

The secret chamber—its mystery; the door, the colour of the wall, the shape of the iron bolt, the slant of the corkscrew steps—these were reality in the midst of all this unreality. And withal a strange longing: to stand again before that door, to handle once more that rusty bolt; a wish like that for some song, or some beloved presence, the desire for that ineffable consciousness, that overwhelming sense of concentrated life and feeling, of being there, of realising the thing. No one, reflected Mr. Little, can know what strange joys are reserved for strange natures; how certain creatures, too delicate and unreal for the everyday interests and pleasures of existence to penetrate through the soul-atmosphere in which they wander, will vibrate, with almost agonized joy, live their full life on contact with certain mysteries. Every day Mr. Little would seek that winding staircase in the peel tower; at first with hesitation and shyness, stealing up almost ashamed of himself; then secretly and stealthily, but excited, resolute, like a man seeking the woman he loves, bent upon the joy of his life.

Once a day at first, then twice, then thrice, counting the hours between the visits, longing to go back as soon as he had left, as a drunkard longs to drink again when he has just drunk. He would watch for the moment when the way was clear, steal along the corridors and up the winding stairs. Then, having reached close to the top of the staircase, near a trapdoor in the ceiling which led on to the battlements of the tower, he would stop, and lean against the shelving turning wall opposite the door, or sit down on the steps, his eyes fixed on the tower wall, where a faint line and the rusty little bolt revealed the presence of the hidden chamber.

What he did it would be hard to say; indeed, he did nothing, he merely felt. There was nothing at all to see, in the material sense; and this piece of winding staircase was just like any other piece of winding staircase in the world: it was not anything external that he wanted, it was that ineffable something within himself. So at least Mr. Little imagined at first, frequently persuading himself that, to a nature like his, all baser satisfaction of curiosity was as nothing; telling himself that he did not care what was inside the room, that he did not even wish to know. Why, if by the pulling of that bolt he might see and know all, he would not pull it. And, saying this to himself, by way of proving it, he laid his fingers gently on the bolt.

And in so doing he discovered the depth of his self-delusion. How different was this emotion when he felt—he actually felt—the bolt begin to slide in his hand, from what he had experienced before, while merely contemplating it! The blood seemed to rush through his veins, he felt almost faint. This was reality, this was possession. The mystery lay there, with the bolt, in the hollow of his hand; at any instant he might .. Mr. Little had no intention of drawing the bolt. He never reasoned about it, but he knew that that bolt never must, never should, be drawn by him. But in proportion to this knowledge was the entrancing excitement of feeling that the bolt might be drawn, that he grasped it in his fingers, that a little electric current through some of his nerves, a little twitch in some of his muscles, and the mystery would be disclosed.

It was the last of the seven days' revelry of the coming of age. All the other neighbouring properties of the Hotspurs had been visited in turn; tenants had been made to dine and dance on one lawn after another; innumerable grouse had been massacred on the moors; endless sets of Venetian lanterns had been lighted, had caught fire, and tumbled on to people's heads; Sir Hugh's old port and Johannisberg, and the strange honey-beer, called Morocco, brewed for centuries at Hotspur, had flowed like water, or rather like the rain, which freely fell, but did not quench that northern ardour. There was to be a grand ball that night, and a grand display of fireworks. But Mr. Little's soul was not attuned to merriment, nor were the souls, as he suspected, of Sir Hugh Hotspur and his son. For, according to popular tradition, it was on this last night of the seven days' merry-making that the heir of Hotspur must be introduced into the hidden chamber.

Throughout lunch Mr. Little kept his eyes on the face of his host and his host's son. What might be passing in their mind? Was it hidden terror or a dare-devil desperation at the thought of what the night must bring? But neither Sir Hugh nor young Harry showed the slightest emotion; their faces, it seemed to Mr. Little, were imperturbable like stone.

Mr. Little waited till the family and guests were safely assembled on the tennis-lawn, then hastened along the corridor and up the steps of the peel tower. The afternoon, after all the rain, was hot and steamy, clearly foreboding a storm; and as Mr. Little groped his way up the tower steps, he felt his heart moving slackly and irregularly, and a clamminess spread over his face and hands; he had to stop several times in order to take breath. As usual, he seated himself on the topmost step, holding his knees with his arms, and looking at the piece of wall opposite, which concealed the mysterious door.

Mr. Little sat there a long time, while the tower stairs grew darker and darker, the faint line betraying the door grew invisible, and even the bolt was lost in the general darkness. Tonight—the thought, nay, almost the sentence in which it was framed, went on like a bell in Mr. Little's mind—tonight they would creep up those stairs, they would stand before that door. Sir Hugh's hand would be upon that bolt: he saw it all so plainly, he felt every tingle and shudder that would pass through their bodies.

Mr. Little rose and gently grasped the bolt; how easily it would move! Sir Hugh would not require the smallest effort. Or would it be young Harry Hotspur? No; it would doubtless be Sir Hugh. He would pause like that a moment, his hand on the bolt, whispering a few words of encouragement, perhaps a prayer. No; he would be silent. He would hold the bolt, little guessing how recently another hand had been upon it, little dreaming that, but a few hours before another member of the family of Hotspur (for Mr. Little always regarded himself in that light) had had it in his power to . . .

The thought remained unfinished in Mr. Little's mind. With a cry he fell all of a heap upon the steps, a blinding light in his eyes, a deafening roar in his ears. He had opened the secret door.

He came slowly to his senses, and with life there returned an overwhelming, vague sense of horror. What he had done he did not know; but he knew he had done something terrible. He slid, it seemed to him that he almost trickled—for his limbs had turned to water—down the stairs. He ran, and yet seemed to be dragging himself, along the corridors and out of one of the many ivy-grown doorways of the old border castle. To the left hand of the gate, at a little distance, was the tennis-court; a long beam of sun, yellow among the storm-clouds, fell upon the grass, burnishing it into metallic green, and making the white, red, yellow, and blue of the players' dresses stand out like coloured enamel.

Some of them shouted to him, among others young Harry Hotspur; but Mr. Little rushed on, heedless of their shouts, scaling the banks of grass, breaking through the hedges, scrambling up hillside after hillside, until he had got to the top of the fells, where the short greyish-green grass began to be variegated with brown patches of bog and lilac and black patches of heather, and cut in all directions by the low walls of loose black stones. He stopped and looked back. But he started off again, as he saw in the distance below, among the ashes and poplars of the narrow valley which furrowed those treeless undulations of moorland, the chimney-stacks of Hotspur Hall, the battlements of the square, black peel tower, reddened by the low light.

On he went, slower, indeed, but still onward, until every vestige of Hotspur and of every other human habitation was out of sight, and the chain of fells had closed round him, billow upon billow, under the fading light. On he went, looking neither to the right nor to the left, save when he was startled by the bubbling of a brook, spurting from the brown moor bog on to the stony road; or by the bleating of the sheep who wandered, vague white specks, upon the greyish grass of the hillside. The clouds accumulated in grey masses, with an ominous yellow clearing in their midst, and across the fells there came the sound of distant thunder. Presently a few heavy drops began to fall; but Mr. Little did not heed them, but went quickly on, among the bleating of the sheep and the cry of the curlews, along the desolate road across the fells; rain-drop succeeding rain-drop, till the hill-tops were enveloped in a sheet of rain.

But Mr. Little did not turn back. He was dazed, vacant, quite unconscious of all save one thing: he had opened the hidden door at Hotspur Hall.

At length the road made a turn, began to descend, and in a dip of the fells some light shone forth in the darkness and the mist. Mr. Little started, and very nearly ran back: he had thought for a moment that these must be the lights of Hotspur: but a second's reflection told him that Hotspur must lie far behind, and presently, among the blinding rain which fell in cold sheets, he found himself among some low black cottages. In the window of one of them was a light, and over the door, in the darkness, swung an inn sign. He knocked, and entered the inn kitchen, a trickle of water following him wherever he went, and, in the tone and with the look of a sleep-walker, said something about having been overtaken by a storm during a walk on the moors, and wanting a night's shelter.

The innkeeper and his wife were evidently too pastoral-minded to reflect that gentlemen do not usually walk on the fells without a hat, and in blue silk socks and patent-leather shoes; and they heaped up the fire, by the side of which Mr. Little collapsed into an armchair, indifferent to the charms of bacon and beer and hot griddle-cakes.

He tried to settle his ideas. Of what had passed he knew but this much for certain, that he had opened the secret door.

The following morning Mr. Little summoned up his courage, and, after a great argument with himself, turned his steps toward Hotspur Hall. The day was fresh and blowy; a delicate blue haze hung over the hills, out of which, larger and larger, emerged a brilliant blue sky. In the valley the towers of Hotspur and its tall chimneys rose among the trees. Soon Mr. Little could see the bright patches of geranium on the lawn. All this, he argued with himself, must have been a delusion, a result of over-psychological study and a thunder-storm upon a nervous and poetical temperament. He tried to remember what he had read about delusions in Carpenter's *Mental Physiology*, and about that supposed robbery, or burglary, which Shelley believed himself to have witnessed.

Mr. Little couldn't remember the details, but he was pleased it should have been Shelley. He felt quite foolish and almost happy as he passed through the rose garden, among the strawberry nets, and in at the by-entrance of Hotspur. He walked straight into the dining-room, where he knew the family was assembled at breakfast, jauntily, and one hand in his pocket. "Why, Little, where the deuce have you spent the night?" cried Sir Hugh Hotspur; and the question was echoed in various forms by the rest of the company.

"Why, Little, have you been in the horse-pond?" cried young Harry, pointing to his guest's clothes, which, drenched the previous night, did indeed suggest some such immersion. Mr. Little did not answer; he felt himself grow cold and pale, and grasped a chair-back. In making this rude remark, the heir of Hotspur had burst into a peal of laughter.

Mr. Little understood; they had found the mysterious chamber empty, its horror fled; he had really opened that door; the heir of Hotspur could still laugh. He explained automatically how he had been caught by a storm on the fells, and been obliged to pass the night at a wayside inn; but the whole time, while he pretended to be eating his breakfast, his brain was on fire with a thought—

"Where had it gone—it, the something which he had let loose?"

That night Mr. Little slept, or rather, as our ancestors more correctly expressed it, lay, at Hotspur. For the word sleep was but a mockery. There was a second storm, and all night the wind howled in the trees, the drops fell from the eaves, and the room was illumined by fitful gleams of lightning. It seemed to Mr. Little that the evil spirit, or whatever else it might be, which had once been safely locked up in the hidden chamber, was now loose in the house. On reflection he could not doubt it: when he had fallen senseless on the stairs, something had passed out of the door; he had heard and felt the wind of its passage. It had issued from the room; it must now be somewhere else, at loose, free to wreak its will with every flash of lightning. Mr. Little expected that the solid masonry of Hotspur would catch fire and burn like a match; with every crash of thunder, he expected that the great peel tower would come rattling on to the roof.

He realised for the first time the tales of the companions of Ulysses opening the bag of the winds; of the Arabian fisherman breaking Solomon's seal on the flask which held the *djinn*; they no longer struck him as in the least ridiculous, these stories. He too had done alike. For, after all, was it not possible that there existed in Nature forces, beings, unknown to our ordinary every-day life? Did not all modern investigations point in that direction, and was it not possible, then, that by the mercy of Providence such a force or being, fatal to our weak humanity, might have been permitted to be enclosed within four walls— one family, or rather, one unhappy member of one family, being sacrificed for the good of mankind, and facing this terror alone, that the rest of his kind might not look upon that ineffable mystery?

And now he, in the lawlessness of his scepticism, had stepped in and opened that sacred door. . . . He understood now why he had often felt that he was destined to commit some terrible crime. Mr. Little sat up in bed, and as the lightning fitfully lit up the antique furniture of his room, he began mechanically to mutter some prayers of his childhood, and some Latin *formulae* of exorcism which he had learned at the time of his offering to do the article *Incubus* for the *Encyclopaedia Britannica*. What should he do? Confess to Sir Hugh Hotspur? or to Sir Hugh's son? He felt terrified at the mere notion; but he understood that his terror was no mere vulgar fear of being reprimanded for a gross breach of hospitality and honour—that it was due to the sense that, having this terrible secret, he had no right to ruin therewith the lives of innocent men. The Hotspurs would know but too soon!

Meanwhile Mr. Little felt an imperative need to confess what he had done, to ask advice and assistance. He wished for once that he had been able to go over to Rome that time that Monsignor Tassel had tried to convert him, instead of being deterred by the oleographs in Monsignor Tassel's chapel. What would he not give to kneel down in a confessional, and pour out the horrible secret through the perforated brass plate!

All of a sudden, he jumped out of bed, struck a light, and dragged his portmanteau into the middle of the room. He had remembered Esmé St. John, and the fact that Esmé St. John, his former chum at Oxford, was working in the slums of Newcastle, not three hours hence. How could he ever, in the lawless hardness of his heart, have thought Esmé ridiculous, have actually tried to reason him out of his High

Church asceticism? This was indeed the just retribution, the fall of the proud, that he should now seek shelter and peace in Earners spiritual arms, and bring to the man, nay, rather to the saint, at whom he had once scoffed, a story which, he would himself have once ridiculed as the most childish piece of superstition.

The mere thought of that act of humiliation did him good; and the terrors of the night seemed to diminish as Mr. Little stooped over his portmanteau and folded his clothes with neat but feverish hands. As soon as it was light, he stole out of the house, walked to the neighbouring village, knocked up the half-idiotic girl who had charge of the post-office, and sent off a sixpenny telegram telling the Reverend Esmé St. John that he would join him at Newcastle that afternoon.

Mr. Little was rather surprised, and in truth rather dashed, when he met his old friend. He had spent the hours in the train framing his confession: a terrible tale to tell, yet which he felt a sudden disappointment at being prevented from telling. Prevented he did feel. He found the Reverend Esmé St. John making a round among his parishioners; they had told him so at Mr. St. John's chapel, and he had realised vividly the whole scene; Esmé, emaciated, hollow-voiced, fresh from some death-bed, leaving the rest of his flock to follow the call of this pale creature, in whom he would scarcely recognize an old friend, and the very touch of whose hand would tell him that things more terrible than death were at stake. But it was otherwise.

After wandering about various black and grimy slums under the thick black Newcastle sky, and up various precipitous alleys and flights of steps strewed with egg-shells and herring-heads, Mr. Little found his old friend in a back yard sheltered by the crumbling red roof of "The Musician's Rest" inn (where the first bars of *Auld Lang Syne* swung over the door). By his side was a fat, tattered, but extremely jovial red-haired woman washing in a tub, and opposite, an unkempt ragamuffin with his hands in his pockets, singing at the top of his little voice a comic song in Northumbrian dialect Mr. Esmé St John was leaning against the doorway, laughing with all his might; he was fat, bald, had a red face, and a very humorous eye—in fact, did not resemble in the least the hollow-cheeked, flashing-eyed young fanatic of ten years before.

He stretched out his broad hand to Mr. Little, and said: "Do listen to this song, it's about the Board School man—it's really too delicious, and the little chap sings it quite nicely!" Mr. Little listened, not understanding a word, and thinking how little this man, laughing over a foolish song sung by a street-boy, guessed the terrible confession he was about to receive.

When the song was finished, the Reverend Esmé St John took Little's arm, and began to overwhelm him with futile questions while leading him down the steep streets of Old Newcastle, until they got to the door of a large and gorgeous eating-house.

"You must be hungry," said Mr. St. John. "I've ordered dinner here for a treat, because my old housekeeper, although an excellent creature, does not rise above mutton chops and boiled potatoes, and one should do honour to an old friend."

Mr. Little shook his head. "I am not hungry," he answered, while his friend unfolded his napkin opposite him. He felt inclined to say, grimly, "When a man has let loose a mysterious unknown terror that has been locked up in Hotspur Hall for centuries, he doesn't feel inclined for roast mutton and Bass's beer."

But the place, the tables, plates, napkins, the smell of cooking, stopped him, and he felt stopped also by the face—the jovial, red face—of his old friend. This was not the Esmé to whom he had longed to unbosom himself. And he felt very irritated.

Mr. Little's irritation began to subside when he followed his friend to his lodgings.

"You asked for a bed, in your telegram," said the Reverend Esmé St. John, as they left the eating-rooms, "and I have had a bed put in a spare room of mine, just to show my hospitable intentions. But I shan't be the least bit offended if you prefer to go to the hotel, my dear fellow. You see, I think a clergyman, trying to reclaim the people of these slums, ought to live among his flock, and no better than they. But there is no reason why anyone also should live in this crazy old barrack."

They walked, in the twilight, along some precipitous streets, lined with tinkers' dens and old-clothes shops, under the high-level bridge, over whose colossal span the square old castle stood out black against the sky.

Mr. Little crept through a battered wooden gateway, and picked his way among the puddles, the fallen beams, and the refuse heaps of a court-yard. A light appeared at a window.

"Here we are," said Esmé, and they followed an old, witch-like woman, herself following a thin, black cat, up some crazy, wooden stairs, and into a suite of low, large rooms. Mr. St. John held up a lantern. The room in which they stood was utterly dismantled, the very wainscoting torn out, the ceiling gaping in rent lath and plaster. In a corner stood a bed, a crazy chest of drawers, and washing apparatus, a table, and chair; and in the next room, where the old woman's light had preceded them, was a similar bed, a shelf of books, a large black cross nailed to the wall, and a wooden step for kneeling.

"That's my room," said the clergyman. "You may have it if you prefer. But here's a fireplace in this one, so you'd better keep it."

So saying, Mr. St. John applied a match to the fagots, and the gaunt apartment was flooded with a red light

"I must make some arrowroot for an old woman of mine," said the clergyman, producing a tin can and saucepan. "May I make it on your fire?"

Mr. Little watched him in silence, then suddenly said: "Esmé, I thought at first you were changed from old days, but I see you are still a saint. Alas! I fear it is I who have changed but too sadly;" and he sighed.

"You are growing too fat," answered Mr. St. John good-humoured-ly, but quite missing the fact that this was the exordium of a confession. Then, to Mr. Little's annoyance, he asked him leave to carry the arrowroot to his old woman, who lived in a lane hard by. Mr. Little remained seated by the fire, while the housekeeper (since she must be dignified by such a title) unpacked his portmanteau. Yes, indeed, this was the man to whom he could make his confession, and this was the place—this dismantled, tumble-down old mansion, tenanted now only by a few poor bargees' families and by countless generations of rats. And Mr. Little put another piece of coal on, in preparation of the nightly conference he was about to have.

Presently Mr. St. John returned.

"Esmé," said Mr. Little, putting his hand on his friend's sleeve, "I wish to speak to you."

"About what?" asked Mr. St. John. "It's very late to begin talking."

"About myself," answered Mr. Little, gravely.

"Do you want anything else? Would you like some brandy and water, or another pillow? You may have mine—or an additional blanket?" asked his friend.

Mr. Little shook his head. "I have all I want in the way of material comforts."

"In that case," replied the clergyman, "I shall leave you at once. If, as you imply, you want spiritual comforts, you must wait till tomorrow, for I am perfectly worn out, and have to be up tomorrow at half-past four. I've been nursing a man from the chemical works these five nights. Goodnight!" and, taking his candle, Mr. St. John walked into his room, leaving his friend greatly disconcerted by this want of sympathy.

The following day Mr. Little accompanied his friend on one of his rounds. After visiting a number of squalid places, where Mr. Little would certainly have thought about measles and smallpox had he not been thinking about the mystery of Hotspur Hall, they returned to the row of houses, once fashionable mansions, with their fronts on the river, among which loomed, next to the black and crumbling former Town Hall, the shell of a family mansion in which they were lodged.

"This was once the fashionable part of Newcastle," said Mr. St. John. "An old lady of ninety once told me she could remember the time when this street used to be crowded with coaches and footmen and link boys of a winter's night. I want to show you my mission-room; I'm very proud of it."

They entered a black passage, close to an inexpressibly shabby public-house, and ascended a wide stone staircase, unswept for ages, as was attested by the cabbage-stalks and herring-heads which lay about in various stages of decomposition. On the first landing a rope was stretched, and a line of clothes, or rather rags, drying after the wash-tub, formed a picturesque screen before several open doors, whence issued squealing of babies, grind of sewing machines, and various un-savoury odours. Mr. St. John unlocked a door and admitted his friend into a large hall, gracefully decorated with pastoral *stucco* mouldings, but filled with church seats, and whose raised extremity, suggestive of the dais for an orchestra, was occupied by an altar duly appointed according to ritualistic notions. The place smelt considerably of stale tobacco and damp straw.

"These were the former assembly rooms," explained Mr. St. John; "and this, which is now my little chapel for the lowest scum of New-castle slums, was once the ballroom. What would those ladies in hoops and powder think of the change, I wonder?"

Mr. Little saw his opportunity.

"This place must be haunted," he said. "By-the-way, Esmé, what are your views on the subject of ghosts and the supernatural? I should be very interested to know."

Mr. St. John had locked the door behind them.

"Never mention the word ghost before me," he exclaimed; it drives me perfectly wild to see all the tomfooling that has been going on of late about apparitions, haunted houses, secret chambers, and all that blasphemous rubbish. It is really a retribution of Heaven to see you agnostic wiseacres taking up such contemptible twaddle. I'm very sorry to hear that you have been in correspondence with those people, Little."

"But—" objected Mr. Little.

"No buts for me!" cried the Reverend Esmé St. John, hotly; "I cannot conceive how any man of education and character can fiddle-faddle about idiotic superstitions which it is the duty of every Christian and every gentleman to pluck out of the minds of the vulgar."

It was clear that this was not the moment to begin a confession about the mysterious room at Hotspur.

"How surprised he will be," thought Mr. Little (and a vague sense of satisfaction mingled with the horror of the thought), "when he hears that I, even I, the sceptical, antinomian Little, have come in contact with mysteries more strange and awful than any ever examined into by any society for psychical research."

Despite his old friend's want of sympathy, Mr. Decimus Little continued to lodge with the Reverend Esmé St. John, in the grimy and crumbling old mansion by the Tyneside, following him about on his various errands of mercy. "A man situated like me," Mr. Little had said to himself, "a great sinner (if you like the pious formula of former ages), a character predestined to evil (if you prefer the more modern phraseology of determinism), does well to live in the shadow of a truly good man: his saintliness is a bulwark against evil spirits; or, at all events, the sight of perfect serenity and purity of mind must calm a deeply troubled spirit." Indeed, he more than once began to make this remark, in terms even more subtle, to his friend; but Mr. St. John, whether from fear of Mr. Little's dialectic power, which might shake some of his most cherished beliefs, or from some other reason, invariably turned a deaf ear to all such beginnings of confession.

But either the serenity of the ritualistic philanthropist was inadequate to calm a brain so over-excited or the evil spirits let loose by Mr. Little made short work of the bulwarks of Esmé's saintliness. The thought of that opened door began to haunt him like a nightmare: the effort at guessing what had been liberated when that door was opened wore out his energies. Was it a monster—a poor, loathsome, half-human thing, hiding, perhaps lying starving at this moment, in some corner of the castle: a thing without mind, or speech, or shape, but endowed with monstrous strength, starting forth in the night and throttling the unrightful owner or his young children with stupid glee?

Or, more horrible almost, forcing by its presence that honourable and kindly old man into crime; tempting him, with the fear lest this hideousness should become known to the world, into spilling the blood of what seemed but a loathly reptile, but might be his third cousin, or his great-uncle? Mr. Little buried his face in his pillow at the thought. But it might be worse still—in that room might have been enclosed some ghastly mediaeval plague, some crumbling long-dead corpse, whose every particle was ready to take wing and spread forgotten diseases over the country. Or was it something less tangible, less conceivable—a ghost, a demon, some fearful supernatural evil?

Every morning, when his tea was set down by the housekeeper upon the rickety table in his dismantled bedroom, Mr. Little would unfold, with trembling fingers, the local newspaper, half expecting that his eye would fall upon a notice headed "Hotspur Hall." And there were moments when he could scarce resist the impulse of rushing to the station, and buying a ticket for the village nearest Hotspur.

But a stop was put to such fears about a week after his arrival at Newcastle; alas! only to be succeeded by fears much more terrible. Returning home one day he saw a letter on his table; a presentiment told him it was about *that*. Yet he shook all over when he saw the address on the back of the envelope, "Hotspur Hall, Northumberland." He sank on to a chair, and was for some time unable to open the letter. It was from Sir Hugh—Sir Hugh writing to the guest, the cousin who had betrayed all the sacred laws of hospitality, to inform him of all the horrors in which his act had involved an innocent, honourable, and happy household. Mr. Little groaned, and held the letter unopened. Then suddenly he opened it, tore it open madly. It ran as follows:

My dear Little:—I have been too busy of late to let you know that Edwardes discovered in your room here, two days after your sudden departure from Hotspur, a whole outfit which you had apparently forgotten. It consists of a shirt, a pair of check breeches, two white ties, a coloured silk handkerchief, a sponge, and a razor-strap. Let us know where you wish all this to be sent. I write to relieve your mind on the subject, as you have doubtless missed these valuables. Lady Hotspur and Harry unite in hoping that you are enjoying yourself, and that we may see you soon again.

Yours, sincerely,

Hugh North Hotspur.

P. S.—I may tell you—but in strict confidence—a piece of news that will doubtless give you pleasure. Our Hal is engaged since the day before yesterday to the Honourable Cynthia Blenkinsop, whom you admired the evening of the Yeomanry ball. The wedding is for next May.

What did this mean? They did not suspect him, that was clear; and nothing terrible had occurred, that was clear also. What then? Was it possible that   But Mr. Little's eyes rested on the postscript. Harry Hotspur engaged to the Honourable Cynthia Blenkinsop: a marriage between the two hereditary enemies, whose enmity dated from the time of Chevy Chase! And there returned to his mind the ancient Northumbrian prophecy (he could not quite pronounce it in the original), that as long as the fell is green and the moor is purple, as long as deer haunt the woods (they don't, thought Mr. Little) and the seamew the rocks, as long as the secret door at the Hall remains closed, so long will never a Hotspur wed a Blenkinsop.

The secret door had been opened, they knew it, and with its opening the curse had been removed from the family. The heir might laugh, though he had come of age (he had laughed at Mr. Little's wet clothes, if you remember); he might marry a Miss Blenkinsop; the door had been opened, and he had opened it!

Mr. Little jumped up from his chair and rushed to his friend's door.

"Esmé," he cried, "we'll dine at the *Kafé*" (that being the local pronunciation of the word *Café*) "tonight; and here's a sovereign for the poor woman who broke her leg. Harry Hotspur is going—" But he stopped himself, and when the clergyman opened the door, astounded at these high spirits, and asking why this sudden launching into festivities and lavish charities, he could only answer, "Only a letter I've had from Sir Hugh Hotspur. It seems—it seems I left quite a lot of things behind; a pair of check trowsers among others. Quite valuable, you know—quite valuable!"

But Mr. Little's happiness—nay, self-congratulation—came to a speedy end. That night, as he lay awake, owing, to the unwonted luxury of coffee after dinner, a thought struck him. If the—the thing, the mystery, the whatever it was, had been liberated from the secret chamber, as was proved beyond doubt, not only by his consciousness of having opened the door, but by the news in Sir Hugh's letter; and if, at the same time, it had not manifested itself to the inhabitants of the Hall, as was likewise clearly the case from the cheerful tone in which the master of Hotspur wrote, why, then what had become of it? Mr. Little, who believed in the indestructibility of force, could not have imagined it to have come to an end; and, if still existing, it must be somewhere.

At this moment a sound—a moan, which made his blood run cold—issued from the darkness of the room. Mr. Little struck a light. The bare, dismantled room, with its unwainscoted walls and torn lath ceiling, was empty, and its bareness admitted of no hiding-place anywhere.

"It is the wind in the chimney!" he said to himself, and extinguished his candle.

But the ghastly moan, this time ending in a sort of gurgling laugh, was repeated, and with it a horrible thought flashed across Mr. Little's mind: What if that mysterious something should attach itself to the man who had disturbed its long seclusion—if the Terror of Hotspur Hall should have fastened upon the rash creature who had let it loose!

And again, there issued from the darkness of that dismantled room the moan, the gurgling laugh. In what shape would it reveal itself? Mr. Little, in the course of his studies, had read M. Maury's *Magie au Moyen Age*; a similar work by the Rev. Baring Gould; the valuable *Essay on Superstition in the Middle Ages*, by Dr. Schindler, Royal Prussian Sanitary Councillor and Manmidwife at Greiffenberg; he had also once bought the works of Theophrastus Bombastes of Hohenheim, called *Paracelsus*, but found them too boring to read. So that his mind was well stocked with alternatives among which a mediaeval mystery could select. His suspicions were one day aroused by a strange-looking man, dark and grimy, who got on to the Tyne steamer one evening at Wallsend, kept his hat over his face and his eyes fixed upon Mr. Little, and then dodged him up and down Newcastle to the very door of his house.

"Who are you?" suddenly exclaimed Mr. Little, stopping short and facing him. He half expected the man to unmask—that is, to take off his hat, and, displaying the face of a corpse, to answer, like the mysterious stranger in Calderon's play, "I am thyself." But the man muttered something about its being very hard on a fellow; that since Mr. St. John had been good to the wife, he ought also to be good to the husband; that he had never touched a drop of liquor till after his marriage with that woman—he hadn't, etc. Mr. Little turned away in disgust. On another occasion, his suspicions were awakened by a large black dog, which insisted upon following him, and oven walked into his room, but he proved to have his master's address on his collar, and was consequently sent home next morning.

One day, again, as Mr. Little was leaning out of the lattice window, looking at the red roofs of Gateshead, the solitary black church on the green mound, surrounded by cinder-heaps and chemical refuse, above the Tyne, his eyes fell upon the grey mass of water which rolled slowly below him; and it seemed to him as if, suddenly, in the curl of a heavy-laden wave, he had seen—a face, upturned eyes staring at him. "Pooh!" said Esmé St. John, whom slumming had made slightly cynical, "it's only some wretched creature who's drowned himself. They'll take him up at the next dead-house."

But Mr. Little shook his head: those eyes had looked at him. Mr. Little had wondered whether he would be haunted: he soon began to be so, or very nearly. He scarcely ventured to enter his room alone, lest he should find waiting for him, he knew not what; or to approach his own bed, lest, on raising the sheet, he should find it already horribly occupied. Every knock made him start; and it was only by an effort that he could induce himself to cry "Come in!" to the old woman who brought him his hot water.

But the day was serene compared with the night. He would lie awake for hours listening to the sullen lapping of the Tyne under the windows, to the scurrying of the rats round the walls, the creaking of broken woodwork in the wind, the rattling of the incessant trains over the high-level bridge close by: lie awake breathless, feeling a presence in the room, but never daring to open his eyes; feeling it coming nearer and nearer, and at the same time expanding, filling the place, choking him, yet never daring to look; until the horrible consciousness would die away as it had come, and there remain only the sickening terror it had brought, and the speculations, while listening to the strokes of the Gateshead clock, as to what the terror might be. Yet, was it something visible, definable, or was it merely a vague curse?

"Esmé," said Mr. Little one day, "do you consider—do you consider—that a man who knows his life to be under a curse; well, suppose something like insanity, you know: but not that— nothing really hereditary, merely a personal thing, a curse, a something making life quite unbearable to him and everyone else—do you think that such a man would have a right to marry?"

Mr. St. John looked at him long and fixedly. "Such a man, in my humble opinion, ought to have a good course of iron, or phosphorus, or, best of all, of whipping, to take down his conceit; and he certainly oughtn't to get married, unless he knew for certain that the lady would administer some such treatment to him."

"You have grown very coarse, Esmé!" exclaimed Mr. Little, "I admit that you do a great deal of good to others, but I sometimes question whether a man of refinement by associating wholesale with laundresses and bargees does much good to himself."

"Very likely not," replied the clergyman, dryly. "Happily, some men aren't always thinking all day long whether they are doing good to themselves or not"

"He is right, all the same, he is right," said Mr. Little to himself.

Whatever the coarseness of fibre of Mr. St John, and his lack of all power of sympathy and intuition, there was no denying that he had given expression to a very sound ethical view.

No; a man in the position of Decimus Little must not marry. He must not drag another life into the atmosphere of horror with which, in one second of lawlessness, he had surrounded himself. It was impossible to conceive a happy home with the mysterious horror of Hotspur Hall constantly in the' background. No; he must never marry. But had he not foreseen this answer before putting the question to his friend? Nay, had he not always felt, long before setting his foot in Hotspur Hall, that some dark fate would come between him and happiness; that the joys of wife and children were not for a creature like him, unreal and lawless, marked for some strange and horrible destiny? All this had not been mere silly despondency, or, as his friend Esmé would have thought, morbid self-importance.

He determined to write to his cousin and break off at once. But how convey to this charming, buoyant, and decidedly positivistic and positive young student of Girton a fact so contrary to all her beliefs and tendencies, as that an unknown terror, enclosed for centuries in the secret chamber of a border castle, had suddenly, through his fault, shunted itself upon him? Mr. Little revolved the matter in his mind, and found a melancholy little pleasure in so doing. He determined at last upon merely telling the young lady that this marriage had become impossible, and hinting dimly to her that this was due to no diminution of affection, no want of duty on his part, but to a terrible and mysterious curse *(not insanity, nor consumption*—he would underline that) under which he was labouring, and which forbade his ever sharing a life which meant unspeakable horror.

Mr. Little sat for a long time before his writing-case, resting his chin on his hand, and jotting down half sentences at intervals.

Yes, he could see it all: the surprise and mystification of the dear girl, her tears of rage (he knew she would rage), her feeling of faintness and sickness, her sadden calling upon her bosom friend, Miss Hopper (the student of political economy, with the cropped hair and divided skirts)—he had always disliked Miss Hopper, an unwomanly young person—to shed light upon it. And even Miss Hopper, who, he knew, had once said she was surprised her Gwendolen could love any man, and least of all a little, grey-haired muff—even Miss Hopper would have to admit that her friend's unhappy lover was marvellously magnanimous. And then Gwendolen would write imploringly to know what had happened; nay, rather (he knew her well), she would come herself, arrive at Newcastle, drive to his house, and then there would be a grand explanation.

Esmé St. John would be present, that would make everything proper, and Esmé would be so astounded; and Gwendolen would go on her knees to him and he on his knees to Gwendolen, and finally they would bid each other farewell, and Esmé would take her hand, and bid her kiss Decimus, and then lead her away to the nearest sister-hood, where she would immediately proceed to turn hospital nurse for the rest of her days, and wear a lock of Decimus's hair round her neck under a scapular.

Mr. Little covered his eyes with his hands, and began to cry. For the first time since opening that door he felt quite peaceable and pleased with himself.

He was startled by the entrance of Martha, Mr. St. John's old housekeeper.

"I beg your pardon, sir," she said, making a violent effort over a strong northern accent, "but would you mind my dusting a little?"

"Dust away," answered Mr. Little, sadly, implying that he, too, was dust and ashes.

In a room as scantily furnished as was Mr. Little's, the operation of dusting would, one might imagine, be necessarily a brief one; but Martha contrived to prolong it singularly. She was passing the duster for the fourth or fifth time over the lid of Mr. Little's portmanteau, when she suddenly turned round, and said—

"I beg your pardon, sir."

"I did not say anything," answered Mr. Little, gloomily. "No, sir, no more you did, sir. But I was a-saying, sir, if as I might take the liberty, sir, as I see—but there was no prying, sir, I assure you, for I'm greatly averse to prying into folks' concerns, especially the gentry's, and it was all casual like, as we say. I was a-saying, sir, seeing how you received a letter from Sir Hugh Hotspur the other day; if you would just put in a word for me now as they've got a new butler, for it would indeed be a charity, let alone all the injustice, to get a body back into her rights, and a widow, too, as I've been these fifteen years, and with only a third cousin in the world."

"My good woman," interrupted Mr. Little, "explain yourself. I fail to comprehend a word."

"Well, then, sir," proceeded Martha, resuming the violent efforts to get the better of her Northumbrian accent, "you should know that I was once in a better place than this, as good a place as any of them have, . . . for I was laundress at Hotspur Hall, and a better laundress you never seed, sir, nor linen better kept than mine was. And then, as Heaven would have it, on account of the wickedness of men, I lost my place through no fault of mine, but merely all along of that room in the peel tower, the room as is lit from the top and as has no windows, as perhaps, sir, you know."

"Hush!" cried Mr. Little, with a gesture like that of a man fainting, "for mercy's sake, woman . . . explain . . . that room . . . the room on the topmost landing of the peel tower . ."

"Yes, sir, with a door as is hidden in the wall—secret like."

"You opened that door? You were sent away for opening that door? Answer me—for Heaven's sake, Martha, answer me!" and Mr. Little clutched the old lady's arm.

"Lor, sir! there was no harm meant. I did not mean to be prying into other folks' concerns, as I always says is best left alone. Although there is such as is always a-prying into everything—"

"You opened that door? Yes, or no?"

"Well, yes, sir, I did, as I was a-going to tell you, sir," cried Martha, terrified at Mr. Little's face, and trying to extricate her arm from his hand. "I beg your pardon, sir, as you're a-tearing of my sleeve."

Mr. Little let her go.

"That door—the last door in the peel tower, on the left; a door hidden in the wall; the door of a room without a window; a room lit from the battlements above?"

"Yes, sir," answered Martha, beginning to quake all over; "exactly as you says, sir. The topmost door in the peel tower, on the left; a door hidden in the wall. It was all along of opening that, as you says, sir."

"Then, Martha," said Mr. Little, solemnly, sitting upright, and fixing his eyes on the old woman's, "you were sent away from Hotspur Hall for opening that door—the door of the secret chamber!"

"Well, sir, it may be called the secret chamber, for all as I know now, and the butler would have had *me* keep it a secret what I saw there, sure enough—all them bottles of wine as he had hidden away to sell to the 'Blue Bull' at Blenkinsop; but of my time there was no one 'as had a right to call it a secret room, seeing as it was the room as we used to put the drying lines in o' winter, when it was too damp to dry the clothes out of doors, as maybe it still is, on account of that draught from the skylight in the roof."

"Enough!" cried Mr. Little. "Woman, not one word more!"

Visitors at Hotspur Hall still continue to look for the secret room, to hang out towels from the windows, and pump the servants, all in vain. Young Harry Hotspur was never known to laugh quite as much as that time that Mr. Little appeared at breakfast in the clothes which he had worn that night on the fell; at least, he rarely laughed except when he chanced to see Mr. Little. As to the marriage question, and the difficulty of reconciling it to the prophecy that so long as the fell was green and the moor purple, and the deer haunted the woods and the seamew the rocks, as long as the secret chamber at Hotspur Hall remained undiscovered, so long would never a Hotspur wed a Blenkinsop, it might be interesting to examine into this incongruity in a serious psychological spirit.

Such persons as are destitute of any taste for serious psychology merely answer to any objection of the kind, that the Honourable Cynthia Blenkinsop was possessed not merely of a charming person but of sixty thousand a year; and that a secret chamber inhabited by an unspecified horror, although a very delightful heirloom in an ancient family, is not sufficient capital in these days of ostentatious living and riotous luxury. As regards Mr. Decimus Little, he is at present in Turkey, on a trial trip with his cousin Gwendolen and her mother, which will decide whether or not he shall be married to her next January by the Reverend Esmé St John.

Where Their Fire is Not Quenched

May Sinclair

There was nobody in the orchard. Harriott Leigh went out, carefully, through the iron gate into the field. She had made the latch slip into its notch without a sound.

The path slanted widely up the field from the orchard gate to the stile under the elder tree. George Waring waited for her there.

Years afterwards, when she thought of George Waring, she smelt the sweet, hot, wine-scent of the elder flowers. Years afterwards, when she smelt elder flowers, she saw George Waring, with his beautiful, gentle face, like a poet's or a musician's, his black-blue eyes, and sleek, olive-brown hair. He was a naval lieutenant.

Yesterday he had asked her to marry him and she had consented. But her father hadn't, and she had come to tell him that and say goodbye before he left her. His ship was to sail the next day.

He was eager and excited. He couldn't believe that anything could stop their happiness, that anything he didn't want to happen could happen.

"Well?" he said.

"He's a perfect beast, George. He won't let us. He says we're too young."

"I was twenty last August," he said, aggrieved.

"And I shall be seventeen in September."

"And this is June. We're quite old, really. How long does he mean us to wait?"

"Three years."

"Three years before we can be engaged even—Why, we might be dead."

She put her arms round him to make him feel safe. They kissed; and the sweet, hot, wine-scent of the elder flowers mixed with their kisses. They stood, pressed close together, under the elder tree.

Across the yellow fields of charlock, they heard the village clock strike seven. Up in the house a gong clanged.

"Darling, I must go," she said.

"Oh stay—Stay *five* minutes."

He pressed her close. It lasted five minutes, and five more. Then he was running fast down the road to the station, while Harriott went along the field-path, slowly, struggling with her tears.

"He'll be back in three months," she said. "I can live through three months."

But he never came back. There was something wrong with the engines of his ship, the *Alexandra*. Three weeks later she went down in the Mediterranean, and George with her.

Harriott said she didn't care how soon she died now. She was quite sure it would be soon, because she couldn't live without him.

The two lines of beech trees stretched on and on, the whole length of the park, a broad green drive between. When you came to the middle, they branched off right and left in the form of a cross, and at the end of the right arm there was a white *stucco* pavilion with pillars and a three-cornered pediment like a Greek temple. At the end of the left arm, the west entrance to the park, double gates and a side door.

Harriott, on her stone seat at the back of the pavilion, could see Stephen Philpotts the very minute he came through the side door.

He had asked her to wait for him there. It was the place he always chose to read his poems aloud in. The poems were a pretext. She knew what he was going to say. And she knew what she would answer.

There were elder bushes in flower at the back of the pavilion, and Harriott thought of George Waring. She told herself that George was nearer to her now than he could ever have been, living. If she married Stephen, she would not be unfaithful, because she loved him with another part of herself. It was not as though Stephen were taking George's place. She loved Stephen with her soul, in an unearthly way.

But her body quivered like a stretched wire when the door opened and the young man came towards her down the drive under the beech trees.

She loved him; she loved his slenderness, his darkness and sallow whiteness, his black eyes lighting up with the intellectual flame, the way his black hair swept back from his forehead, the way he walked, tiptoe, as if his feet were lifted with wings.

He sat down beside her. She could see his hands tremble. She felt that her moment was coming; it had come.

"I wanted to see you alone because there's something I must say to you. I don't quite know how to begin. . . ."

Her lips parted. She panted lightly.

"You've heard me speak of Sybill Foster?"

Her voice came stammering, "N-no, Stephen. Did you?"

"Well, I didn't mean to, till I knew it was all right. I only heard yesterday."

"Heard what?"

"Why, that she'll have me. Oh, Harriott—do you know what it's like to be terribly happy?"

She knew. She had known just now, the moment before he told her. She sat there, stone-cold and stiff, listening to his raptures; listening to her own voice saying she was glad.

Ten years passed.

Harriott Leigh sat waiting in the drawing-room of a small house in Maida Vale. She had lived there ever since her father's death two years before.

She was restless. She kept on looking at the clock to see if it was four, the hour that Oscar Wade had appointed. She was not sure that he would come, after she had sent him away yesterday.

She now asked herself, why, when she had sent him away yesterday, she had let him come today. Her motives were not altogether clear. If she really meant what she had said then, she oughtn't to let him come to her again. Never again.

She had shown him plainly what she meant. She could see herself, sitting very straight in her chair, uplifted by a passionate integrity, while he stood before her, hanging his head, ashamed and beaten; she could feel again the throb in her voice as she kept on saying that she couldn't, she couldn't; he must see that she couldn't; that no, nothing would make her change her mind; she couldn't forget he had a wife; that he must think of Muriel.

To which he had answered savagely: "I needn't. That's all over. We only live together for the look of the thing."

And she, serenely, with great dignity: "And for the look of the thing, Oscar, we must leave off seeing each other. Please go."

"Do you mean it?"

"Yes. We must never see each other again."

And he had gone then, ashamed and beaten.

She could see him, squaring his broad shoulders to meet the blow. And she was sorry for him. She told herself she had been unnecessarily hard. Why shouldn't they see each other again, now he understood where they must draw the line? Until yesterday the line had never been very clearly drawn. Today she meant to ask him to forget what he had said to her. Once it was forgotten, they could go on being friends as if nothing had happened.

It was four o'clock. Half-past. Five. She had finished tea and given him up when, between the half-hour and six o'clock, he came.

He came as he had come a dozen times, with his measured, deliberate, thoughtful tread, carrying himself well braced, with a sort of held-in arrogance, his great shoulders heaving. He was a man of about forty, broad and tall, lean-flanked and short-necked, his straight, handsome features showing small and even in the big square face and in the flush that swamped it. The close-clipped, reddish-brown moustache bristled forwards from the pushed-out upper lip. His small, flat eyes shone, reddish-brown, eager and animal.

She liked to think of him when he was not there, but always at the first sight of him she felt a slight shock. Physically, he was very far from her admired ideal. So different from George Waring and Stephen Philpotts.

He sat down, facing her.

There was an embarrassed silence, broken by Oscar Wade.

"Well, Harriott, you said I could come. He seemed to be throwing the responsibility on her.

"So, I suppose you've forgiven me," he said.

"Oh, yes, Oscar, I've forgiven you."

He said she'd better show it by coming to dine with him somewhere that evening.

She could give no reason to herself for going. She simply went.

He took her to a restaurant in Soho. Oscar Wade dined well, even extravagantly, giving each dish its importance. She liked his extravagance. He had none of the mean virtues.

It was over. His flushed, embarrassed silence told her what he was thinking. But when he had seen her home, he left her at her garden gate. He had thought better of it.

She was not sure whether she were glad or sorry. She had had her moment of righteous exaltation and she had enjoyed it. But there was no joy in the weeks that followed it. She had given up Oscar Wade because she didn't want him very much; and now she wanted him furiously, perversely, because she had given him up. Though he had no resemblance to her ideal, she couldn't live without him.

She dined with him again and again, till she knew Schnebler's Restaurant by heart, the white panelled walls picked out with gold; the white pillars, and the curling gold fronds of their capitals; the Turkey carpets, blue and crimson, soft under her feet; the thick crimson velvet cushions, that clung to her skirts; the glitter of silver and glass on the innumerable white circles of the tables. And the faces of the diners, red, white, pink, brown, grey and sallow, distorted and excited; the curled mouths that twisted as they ate; the convoluted electric bulbs pointing, pointing down at them, under the red, crinkled shades. All shimmering in a thick air that the red light stained as wine stains water.

And Oscar's face, flushed with his dinner. Always, when he leaned back from the table and brooded in silence, she knew what he was thinking. His heavy eyelids would lift; she would find his eyes fixed on hers, wondering, considering.

She knew now what the end would be. She thought of George Waring, and Stephen Philpotts, and of her life, cheated. She hadn't chosen Oscar, she hadn't really wanted him; but now he had forced himself on her she couldn't afford to let him go. Since George died no man had loved her, no other man ever would. And she was sorry for him when she thought of him going from her, beaten and ashamed.

She was certain, before he was, of the end. Only she didn't know when and where and how it would come. That was what Oscar knew.

It came at the close of one of their evenings when they had dined in a private sitting-room. He said he couldn't stand the heat and noise of the public restaurant.

She went before him, up a steep, red-carpeted stair to a white door on the second landing.

From time to time, they repeated the furtive, hidden adventure. Sometimes she met him in the room above Schnebler's. Sometimes, when her maid was out, she received him at her house in Maida Vale. But that was dangerous, not to be risked too often.

Oscar declared himself unspeakably happy. Harriott was not quite sure. This was love, the thing she had never had, that she had dreamed of, hungered and thirsted for; but now she had it she was not satisfied. Always she looked for something just beyond it, some mystic, heavenly rapture, always beginning to come, that never came. There was something about Oscar that repelled her. But because she had taken him for her lover, she couldn't bring herself to admit that it was a certain coarseness. She looked another way and pretended it wasn't there. To justify herself, she fixed her mind on his good qualities, his generosity, his strength, the way he had built up his engineering business. She made him take her over his works and show her his great dynamos. She made him lend her the books he read. But always, when she tried to talk to him, he let her see that, *that* wasn't what she was there for.

"My dear girl, we haven't time," he said. "It's waste of our priceless moments."

She persisted. "There's something wrong about it all if we can't talk to each other."

He was irritated. "Women never seem to consider that a man can get all the talk he wants from other men. What's wrong is our meeting in this unsatisfactory way. We ought to live together. It's the only sane thing. I would, only I don't want to break up Muriel's home and make her miserable."

"I thought you said she wouldn't care."

"My dear, she cares for her home and her position and the children. You forget the children."

Yes. She had forgotten the children. She had forgotten Muriel. She had left off thinking of Oscar as a man with a wife and children and a home.

He had a plan. His mother-in-law was coming to stay with Muriel in October and he would get away. He would go to Paris, and Harriott should come to him there. He could say he went on business. No need to lie about it; he *had* business in Paris.

He engaged rooms in an hotel in the rue de Rivoli. They spent two weeks there.

For three days Oscar was madly in love with Harriott and Harriott with him. As she lay awake, she would turn on the light and look at him as he slept at her side. Sleep made him beautiful and innocent; it laid a fine, smooth tissue over his coarseness; it made his mouth gentle; it entirely hid his eyes.

In six days, reaction had set in. At the end of the tenth day, Harriott, returning with Oscar from Montmartre, burst into a fit of crying. When questioned, she answered wildly that the Hotel Saint Pierre was too hideously ugly; it was getting on her nerves. Mercifully Oscar explained her state as fatigue following excitement. She tried hard to believe that she was miserable because her love was purer and more spiritual than Oscar's; but all the time she knew perfectly well she had cried from pure boredom. She was in love with Oscar, and Oscar bored her. Oscar was in love with her, and she bored him. At close quarters, day in and day out, each was revealed to the other as an incredible bore.

At the end of the second week, she began to doubt whether she had ever been really in love with him.

★★★★★★★★★★

Her passion returned for a little while after they got back to London. Freed from the unnatural strain which Paris had put on them, they persuaded themselves that their romantic temperaments were better fitted to the old life of casual adventure.

Then, gradually, the sense of danger began to wake in them. They lived in perpetual fear, face to face with all the chances of discovery. They tormented themselves and each other by imagining possibilities that they would never have considered in their first fine moments. It was as though they were beginning to ask themselves if it were, after all, worthwhile running such awful risks, for all they got out of it. Oscar still swore that if he had been free, he would have married her. He pointed out that his intentions at any rate were regular. But she asked herself: Would I marry *him?* Marriage would be the Hotel Saint Pierre all over again, without any possibility of escape. But, if she wouldn't marry him, was she in love with him? That was the test. Perhaps it was a good thing he wasn't free. Then she told herself that these doubts were morbid, and that the question wouldn't arise.

One evening Oscar called to see her. He had come to tell her that Muriel was ill.

"Seriously ill?"

"I'm afraid so. It's pleurisy. May turn to pneumonia. We shall know one way or another in the next few days."

A terrible fear seized upon Harriott. Muriel might die of her pleurisy; and if Muriel died, she would have to marry Oscar. He was looking at her queerly, as if he knew what she was thinking, and she could see that the same thought had occurred to him and that he was frightened too.

Muriel got well again; but their danger had enlightened them. Muriel's life was now inconceivably precious to them both; she stood between them and that permanent union, which they dreaded and yet would not have the courage to refuse.

After enlightenment the rupture.

It came from Oscar, one evening when he sat with her in her drawing-room.

"Harriott," he said, "do you know I'm thinking seriously of settling down?"

"How do you mean, settling down?"

"Patching it up with Muriel, poor girl.... Has it never occurred to you that this little affair of ours can't go on for ever?"

"You don't want it to go on?"

"I don't want to have any humbug about it. For God's sake, let's be straight. If it's done, it's done. Let's end it decently."

"I see. You want to get rid of me."

"That's a beastly way of putting it."

"Is there any way that isn't beastly? The whole thing's beastly. I should have thought you'd have stuck to it now you've made it what you wanted. When I haven't an ideal, I haven't a single illusion, when you've destroyed everything you didn't want."

"What didn't I want?"

"The clean, beautiful part of it. The part *I* wanted."

"My part at least was real. It was cleaner and more beautiful than all that putrid stuff you wrapped it up in. You were a hypocrite, Harriott, and I wasn't. You're a hypocrite now if you say you weren't happy with me."

"I was never really happy. Never for one moment. There was always something I missed. Something you didn't give me. Perhaps you couldn't."

"No. I wasn't spiritual enough," he sneered.

"You were not. And you made me what you were."

"Oh, I noticed that you were always very spiritual *after* you'd got what you wanted."

"What I wanted?" she cried. "Oh, my God—"

"If you ever knew what you wanted."

"What—I—wanted," she repeated, drawing out her bitterness.

"Come," he said, "why not be honest? Face facts. I was awfully gone on you. You were awfully gone on me—once. We got tired of each other and it's over. But at least you might own we had a good time while it lasted."

"A good time?"

"Good enough for me."

"For you, because for you love only means one thing. Everything that's high and noble in it you dragged down to that, till there's nothing left for us but that. That's what you made of love."

Twenty years passed.

★★★★★★★★★★

230

It was Oscar who died first, three years after the rupture. He did it suddenly one evening, falling down in a fit of apoplexy.

His death was an immense relief to Harriott. Perfect security had been impossible as long as he was alive. But now there wasn't a living soul who knew her secret.

Still, in the first moment of shock Harriott told herself that Oscar dead would be nearer to her than ever. She forgot how little she had wanted him to be near her, alive. And long before the twenty years had passed, she had contrived to persuade herself that he had never been near to her at all. It was incredible that she had ever known such a person as Oscar Wade. As for their affair, she couldn't think of Harriott Leigh as the sort of woman to whom such a thing could happen. Schnebler's and the Hotel Saint Pierre ceased to figure among prominent images of her past. Her memories, if she had allowed herself to remember, would have clashed disagreeably with the reputation for sanctity which she had now acquired.

For Harriott at fifty-two was the friend and helper of the Reverend Clement Farmer, Vicar of St. Mary the Virgin's, Maida Vale. She worked as a deaconess in his parish, wearing the uniform of a deaconess, the semireligious gown, the cloak, the bonnet and veil, the cross and rosary, the holy smile. She was also secretary to the Maida Vale and Kilburn Home for Fallen Girls.

Her moments of excitement came when Clement Farmer, the lean, austere likeness of Stephen Philpotts, in his cassock and lace-bordered surplice, issued from the vestry, when he mounted the pulpit, when he stood before the altar rails and lifted up his arms in the Benediction; her moments of ecstasy when she received the Sacrament from his hands. And she had moments of calm happiness when his study door closed on their communion. All these moments were saturated with a solemn holiness.

And they were insignificant compared with the moment of her dying.

She lay dozing in her white bed under the black crucifix with the ivory Christ. The basins and medicine bottles had been cleared from the table by her pillow; it was spread for the last rites. The priest moved quietly about the room, arranging the candles, the *Prayer Book* and the *Holy Sacrament*. Then he drew a chair to her bedside and watched with her, waiting for her to come up out of her doze.

She woke suddenly. Her eyes were fixed upon him. She had a flash of lucidity. She was dying, and her dying made her supremely important to Clement Farmer.

"Are you ready?" he asked.

"Not yet. I think I'm afraid. Make me not afraid."

He rose and lit the two candles on the altar. He took down the crucifix from the wall and stood it against the foot-rail of the bed.

She sighed. That was not what she had wanted.

"You will not be afraid now," he said.

"I'm not afraid of the hereafter. I suppose you get used to it. Only it may be terrible just at first."

"Our first state will depend very much on what we are thinking of at our last hour."

"There'll be my—confession," she said.

"And after it you will receive the Sacrament. Then you will have your mind fixed firmly upon God and your Redeemer. . . . . Do you feel able to make your confession now, Sister? Everything is ready."

Her mind went back over her past and found Oscar Wade there. She wondered: Should she confess to him about Oscar Wade? One moment she thought it was possible; the next she knew that she couldn't. She could not. It wasn't necessary. For twenty years he had not been part of her life. No. She wouldn't confess about Oscar Wade. She had been guilty of other sins.

She made a careful selection.

"I have cared too much for the beauty of this world. . . . I have failed in charity to my poor girls. Because of my intense repugnance to their sin. . . . I have thought, often, about—people I love, when I should have been thinking about God."

After that she received the Sacrament.

"Now," he said, "there is nothing to be afraid of."

"I won't be afraid if—if you would hold my hand."

He held it. And she lay still a long time, with her eyes shut. Then he heard her murmuring something. He stooped close.

"This—is—dying. I thought it would be horrible. And it's bliss. . . . . . .Bliss."

The priest's hand slackened, as if at the bidding of some wonder. She gave a weak cry.

"Oh—don't let me go."

His grasp tightened.

"Try," he said, "to think about God. Keep on looking at the crucifix."

"If I look," she whispered, "you won't let go my hand?"

"I will not let you go."

He held it till it was wrenched from him in the last agony.

****

She lingered for some hours in the room where these things had happened.

Its aspect was familiar and yet unfamiliar, and slightly repugnant to her. The altar, the crucifix, the lighted candles, suggested some tremendous and awful experience the details of which she was not able to recall. She seemed to remember that they had been connected in some way with the sheeted body on the bed; but the nature of the connection was not clear; and she did not associate the dead body with herself. When the nurse came in and laid it out, she saw that it was the body of a middle-aged woman. Her own living body was that of a young woman of about thirty-two.

Her mind had no past and no future, no sharp-edged, coherent memories, and no idea of anything to be done next.

Then, suddenly, the room began to come apart before her eyes, to split into shafts of floor and furniture and ceiling that shifted and were thrown by their commotion into different planes. They leaned slanting at every possible angle; they crossed and overlaid each other with a transparent mingling of dislocated perspectives, like reflections fallen on an interior seen behind glass.

The bed and the sheeted body slid away somewhere out of sight. She was standing by the door that still remained in position.

She opened it and found herself in the street, outside a building of yellowish-grey brick and freestone, with a tall slated spire. Her mind came together with a palpable click of recognition. This object was the Church of St. Mary the Virgin, Maida Vale. She could hear the droning of the organ. She opened the door and slipped in.

She had gone back into a definite space and time, and recovered a certain limited section of coherent memory. She remembered the rows of pitch-pine benches, with their Gothic peaks and mouldings; the stone-coloured walls and pillars with their chocolate stencilling; the hanging rings of lights along the aisles of the nave; the high altar with its lighted candles, and the polished brass cross, twinkling. These things were somehow permanent and real, adjusted to the image that now took possession of her.

She knew what she had come there for. The service was over. The choir had gone from the chancel; the sacristan moved before the altar, putting out the candles. She walked up the middle aisle to a seat that she knew under the pulpit. She knelt down and covered her face with her hands. Peeping sideways through her fingers, she could see the door of the vestry on her left at the end of the north aisle. She watched it steadily.

Up in the organ loft the organist drew out the Recessional, slowly and softly, to its end in the two solemn, vibrating chords.

The vestry door opened and Clement Farmer came out, dressed in his black cassock. He passed before her, close, close outside the bench where she knelt. He paused at the opening. He was waiting for her. There was something he had to say.

She stood up and went towards him. He still waited. He didn't move to make way for her. She came close, closer than she had ever come to him, so close that his features grew indistinct. She bent her head back, peering, short-sightedly, and found herself looking into Oscar Wade's face.

He stood still, horribly still, and close, barring her passage.

She drew back; his heaving shoulders followed her. He leaned forward, covering her with his eyes. She opened her mouth to scream and no sound came.

She was afraid to move lest he should move with her. The heaving of his shoulders terrified her.

One by one the lights in the side aisles were going out. The lights in the middle aisle would go next. They had gone. If she didn't get away, she would be shut up with him there, in the appalling darkness.

She turned and moved towards the north aisle, groping, steadying herself by the book ledge.

When she looked back, Oscar Wade was not there.

Then she remembered that Oscar Wade was dead. Therefore, what she had seen was not Oscar; it was his ghost. He was dead; dead seventeen years ago. She was safe from him for ever.

★★★★★★★★★★

When she came out on to the steps of the church, she saw that the road it stood in had changed. It was not the road she remembered. The pavement on this side was raised slightly and covered in. It ran under a succession of arches. It was a long gallery walled with glittering shop windows on one side; on the other a line of tall grey columns divided it from the street.

She was going along the arcades of the rue de Rivoli. Ahead of her she could see the edge of an immense grey pillar jutting out. That was the porch of the Hotel Saint Pierre. The revolving glass doors swung forward to receive her; she crossed the grey, sultry vestibule under the pillared arches. She knew it. She knew the porter's shining, wine-coloured mahogany pen on her left, and the shining wine-coloured mahogany barrier of the clerk's bureau on her right; she made straight for the great grey carpeted staircase; she climbed the endless flights that turned round and round the caged-in shaft of the well, past the latticed doors of the lift, and came up on to a landing that she knew, and into the long, ash-grey, foreign corridor lit by a dull window at one end.

It was there that the horror of the place came on her. She had no longer any memory of St. Mary's Church, so that she was unaware of her backward course through time. All space and time were here.

She remembered she had to go to the left, the left. But there was something there; where the corridor turned by the window; at the end of all the corridors. If she went the other way, she would escape it.

The corridor stopped there. A blank wall. She was driven back past the stairhead to the left.

At the corner, by the window, she turned down another long ash-grey corridor on her right, and to the right again where the night-light sputtered on the table-flap at the turn.

This third corridor was dark and secret and depraved. She knew the soiled walls and the warped door at the end. There was a sharp-pointed streak of light at the top. She could see the number on it now, 107.

Something had happened there. If she went in it would happen again.

Oscar Wade was in the room waiting for her behind the closed door. She felt him moving about in there. She leaned forward, her ear to the key-hole, and listened. She could hear the measured, deliberate, thoughtful footsteps. They were coming from the bed to the door.

She turned and ran; her knees gave way under her she sank and ran on, down the long grey corridors and the stairs, quick and blind, a hunted beast seeking for cover, hearing his feet coming after her.

The revolving doors caught her and pushed her out into the street.

****

The strange quality of her state was this, that it had no time. She remembered dimly that there had once been a thing called time; but she had forgotten altogether what it was like. She was aware of things happening and about to happen; she fixed them by the place they oc-cupied, and measured their duration by the space she went through.

So now she thought: If I could only go back and get to the place

235

where it hadn't happened.

To get back farther—

She was walking now on a white road that went between broad grass borders. To the right and left were the long raking lines of the hills, curve after curve, shimmering in a thin mist.

The road dropped to the green valley. It mounted the humped bridge over the river. Beyond it she saw the twin gables of the grey house pricked up over the high, grey garden wall. The tall iron gate stood in front of it between the ball-topped stone pillars.

And now she was in a large, low-ceilinged room with drawn blinds. She was standing before the wide double bed. It was her father's bed. The dead body, stretched out in the middle under the drawn white sheet, was her father's body.

The outline of the sheet sank from the peak of the upturned toes to the shin bone, and from the high bridge of the nose to the chin.

She lifted the sheet and folded it back across the breast of the dead man. The face she saw then was Oscar Wade's face, stilled and smoothed in the innocence of sleep, the supreme innocence of death. She stared at it, fascinated, in a cold, pitiless joy.

Oscar was dead.

She remembered how he used to lie like that beside her in the room in the Hotel Saint Pierre, on his back with his hands folded on his waist, his mouth half open, his big chest rising and falling. If he was dead, it would never happen again. She would be safe.

The dead face frightened her, and she was about to cover it up again when she was aware of a light heaving, a rhythmical rise and fall. As she drew the sheet up tighter, the hands under it began to struggle convulsively, the broad ends of the fingers appeared above the edge, clutching it to keep it down. The mouth opened; the eyes opened; the whole face stared back at her in a look of agony and horror.

Then the body drew itself forwards from the hips and sat up, its eyes peering into her eyes; he and she remained for an instant motionless, each held there by the other's fear.

Suddenly she broke away, turned and ran, out of the room, out of the house.

She stood at the gate, looking up and down the road, not knowing by which way she must go to escape Oscar. To the right, over the bridge and up the hill and across the downs she would come to the arcades of the rue de Rivoli and the dreadful grey corridors of the hotel. To the left the road went through the village.

236

If she could get further back, she would be safe, out of Oscar's reach. Standing by her father's death-bed she had been young, but not young enough. She must get back to the place where she was younger still, to the Park and the green drive under the beech trees and the white pavilion at the cross. She knew how to find it. At the end of the village the high road ran right and left, east and west, under the Park walls; the south gate stood there at the top, looking down the narrow street.

She ran towards it through the village, past the long grey barns of Goodyer's farm, past the grocer's shop, past the yellow front and blue sign of the "Queen's Head," past the post office, with its one black window blinking under its vine, past the church and the yew-trees in the churchyard, to where the south gate made a delicate black pattern on the green grass.

These things appeared insubstantial, drawn back behind a sheet of air that shimmered over them like thin glass. They opened out, floated past and away from her; and instead of the high road and park walls she saw a London street of dingy white *façades*, and instead of the south gate the swinging glass doors of Schnebler's Restaurant.

★★★★★★★★★★

The glass doors swung open and she passed into the restaurant. The scene beat on her with the hard impact of reality: the white and gold panels, the white pillars and their curling gold capitals, the white circles of the tables, glittering, the flushed faces of the diners, moving mechanically.

She was driven forward by some irresistible compulsion to a table in the corner, where a man sat alone. The table napkin he was using hid his mouth, and jaw, and chest; and she was not sure of the upper part of the face above the straight, drawn edge. It dropped; and she saw Oscar Wade's face. She came to him, dragged, without power to resist; she sat down beside him, and he leaned to her over the table; she could feel the warmth of his red, congested face; the smell of wine floated towards her on his thick whisper.

"I knew you would come."

She ate and drank with him in silence, nibbling and sipping slowly, staving off the abominable moment it would end in.

At last, they got up and faced each other. His long bulk stood before her, above her; she could almost feel the vibration of its power.

"Come," he said. "Come."

And she went before him, slowly, slipping out through the maze of the tables, hearing behind her Oscar's measured, deliberate, thoughtful tread. The steep, red-carpeted staircase rose up before her.

She swerved from it, but he turned her back.

"You know the way," he said.

At the top of the flight, she found the white door of the room she knew. She knew the long windows guarded by drawn muslin blinds; the gilt looking-glass over the chimney-piece that reflected Oscar's head and shoulders grotesquely between two white porcelain babies with bulbous limbs and garlanded loins, she knew the sprawling stain on the drab carpet by the table, the shabby, infamous couch behind the screen.

They moved about the room, turning and turning in it like beasts in a cage, uneasy, inimical, avoiding each other.

At last, they stood still, he at the window, she at the door, the length of the room between.

"It's no good your getting away like that," he said. "There couldn't be any other end to it—to what we did."

"But that *was* ended."

"Ended there, but not here."

"Ended forever. We've done with it forever."

"We haven't. We've got to begin again. And go on. And go on."

"Oh, no. No. Anything but that."

"There isn't anything else."

"We can't. We can't. Don't you remember how it bored us?"

"Remember? Do you suppose I'd touch you if I could help it?... That's what we're here for. We must. We must."

"No. No. I shall get away—now."

She turned to the door to open it.

"You can't," he said. "The door's locked,"

"Oscar—what did you do that for?"

"We always did it. Don't you remember?"

She turned to the door again and shook it; she beat on it with her hands.

"It's no use, Harriott. If you got out now, you'd only have to come back again. You might stave it off for an hour or so, but what's that in an immortality?"

"Immortality?"

"That's what we're in for."

"Time enough to talk about immortality when we're dead....
Ah—"

238

They were being drawn towards each other across the room, moving slowly, like figures in some monstrous and appalling dance, their heads thrown back over their shoulders, their faces turned from the horrible approach. Their arms rose slowly, heavy with intolerable reluctance; they stretched them out towards each other, aching, as if they held up an overpowering weight. Their feet dragged and were drawn.

Suddenly her knees sank under her; she shut her eyes; all her being went down before him in darkness and terror.

★★★★★★★★★★

It was over. She had got away, she was going back, back, to the green drive of the Park, between the beech trees, where Oscar had never been, where he would never find her. When she passed through the south gate her memory became suddenly young and clean. She forgot the rue de Rivoli and the Hotel Saint Pierre; she forgot Schnebler's Restaurant and the room at the top of the stairs. She was back in her youth. She was Harriott Leigh going to wait for Stephen Philpotts in the pavilion opposite the west gate. She could feel herself, a slender figure moving fast over the grass between the lines of the great beech trees. The freshness of her youth was upon her.

She came to the heart of the drive where it branched right and left in the form of a cross. At the end of the right arm the white Greek temple, with its pediment and pillars, gleamed against the wood.

She was sitting on their seat at the back of the pavilion, watching the side door that Stephen would come in by.

The door was pushed open; he came towards her, light and young, skimming between the beech trees with his eager, tiptoeing stride. She rose up to meet him. She gave a cry.

"Stephen!"

It had been Stephen. She had seen him coming. But the man who stood before her between the pillars of the pavilion was Oscar Wade.

And now she was walking along the field-path that slanted from the orchard door to the stile; further and further back, to where young George Waring waited for her under the elder tree. The smell of the elder flowers came to her over the field. She could feel on her lips and in all her body the sweet, innocent excitement of her youth.

"George, oh, George!"

As she went along the field-path she had seen him. But the man who stood waiting for her under the elder tree was Oscar Wade.

"I told you it's no use getting away, Harriott. Every path brings you back to me. You'll find me at every turn."

"But how did you get *here?*"

"As I got into the pavilion. As I got into your father's room, on to his death bed. Because I *was* there. I am in all your memories."

"My memories are innocent. How could you take my father's place, and Stephen's, and George Waring's? You?"

"Because I did take them."

"Never. My love for *them* was innocent."

"Your love for me was part of it. You think the past affects the future. Has it never struck you that the future may affect the past? In your innocence there was the beginning of your sin. You *were* what you *were to be.*"

"I shall get away," she said.

"And, this time, I shall go with you."

The stile, the elder tree, and the field floated away from her. She was going under the beech trees down the Park drive towards the south gate and the village, slinking close to the right-hand row of trees. She was aware that Oscar Wade was going with her under the left-hand row, keeping even with her, step by step, and tree by tree. And presently there was grey pavement under her feet and a row of grey pillars on her right hand. They were walking side by side down the rue de Rivoli towards the hotel.

They were sitting together now on the edge of the dingy white bed. Their arms hung by their sides, heavy and limp, their heads drooped, averted. Their passion weighed on them with the unbearable, unescapable boredom of immortality.

"Oscar—how long will it last?"

"I can't tell you. I don't know whether this is one moment of eternity, or the eternity of one moment."

"It must end some time," she said. "Life doesn't go on for ever. We shall die."

"Die? We *have* died. Don't you know what this is? Don't you know where you are? This is death. We're dead, Harriott. We're in hell."

"Yes. There can't be anything worse than this."

"This isn't the worst. We're not quite dead yet, as long as we've life in us to turn and run and get away from each other; as long as we can escape into our memories. But when you've got back to the farthest memory of all and there's nothing beyond it—When there's no memory but this—

"In the last hell we shall not run away any longer; we shall find no more roads, no more passages, no more open doors. We shall have no

240

need to look for each other.

"In the last death we shall be shut up in this room, behind that locked door, together. We shall lie here together, for ever and ever, joined so fast that even God can't put us asunder. We shall be one flesh and one spirit, one sin repeated for ever, and ever; spirit loathing flesh, flesh loathing spirit; you and I loathing each other."

"Why? Why?" she cried.

"Because that's all that's left us. That's what you made of love."

****

The darkness came down swamping, it blotted out the room. She was walking along a garden path between high borders of phlox and larkspur and lupin. They were taller than she was, their flowers swayed and nodded above her head. She tugged at the tall stems and had no strength to break them. She was a little thing.

She said to herself then that she was safe. She had gone back so far that she was a child again; she had the blank innocence of childhood. To be a child, to go small under the heads of the lupins, to be blank and innocent, without memory, was to be safe.

The walk led her out through a yew hedge on to a bright green lawn. In the middle of the lawn there was a shallow round pond in a ring of rockery cushioned with small flowers, yellow and white and purple. Goldfish swam in the olive brown water. She would be safe when she saw the goldfish swimming towards her. The old one with the white scales would come up first, pushing up his nose, making bubbles in the water.

At the bottom of the lawn there was a privet hedge cut by a broad path that went through the orchard. She knew what she would find there; her mother was in the orchard. She would lift her up in her arms to play with the hard red balls of the apples that hung from the tree. She had got back to the farthest memory of all; there was nothing beyond it.

There would be an iron gate in the wall of the orchard. It would lead into a field.

Something was different here, something that frightened her. An ash-grey door instead of an iron gate.

She pushed it open and came into the last corridor of the Hotel Saint Pierre.

The Affair at Grover Station

Willa Cather

I heard this story sitting on the rear platform of an accommodation freight that crawled along through the brown, sun-dried wilderness between Grover Station and Cheyenne. The narrator was "Terrapin" Rodgers, who had been a classmate of mine at Princeton, and who was then cashier in the B— railroad office at Cheyenne. Rodgers was an Albany boy, but after his father failed in business, his uncle got "Terrapin" a position on a Western railroad, and he left college and disappeared completely from our little world, and it was not until I was sent West, by the University with a party of geologists who were digging for fossils in the region about Sterling, Colorado, that I saw him again. On this particular occasion Rodgers had been down at Sterling to spend Sunday with me, and I accompanied him when he returned to Cheyenne.

When the train pulled out of Grover Station, we were sitting smoking on the rear platform, watching the pale-yellow disk of the moon that was just rising and that drenched the naked, grey plains in a soft lemon-coloured light. The telegraph poles scored the sky like a musical staff as they flashed by, and the stars, seen between the wires, looked like the notes of some erratic symphony. The stillness of the night and the loneliness and bareness of the plains were conducive to an uncanny train of thought. We had just left Grover Station behind us, and the murder of the station agent at Grover, which had occurred the previous winter, was still the subject of much conjecturing and theorising all along that line of railroad.

Rodgers had been an intimate friend of the murdered agent, and it was said that he knew more about the affair than any other living man, but with that peculiar reticence which at college had won him the soubriquet "Terrapin," he had kept what he knew to himself, and even the most accomplished reporter on the *New York Journal*, who had travelled halfway across the continent for the express purpose of pumping Rodgers, had given him up as impossible. But I had known Rodgers a long time, and since I had been grubbing in the chalk about Sterling, we had fallen into a habit of exchanging confidences, for it is good to see an old face in a strange land. So, as the little red station house at Grover faded into the distance, I asked him point blank what he knew about the murder of Lawrence O'Toole. Rodgers took a long pull at his black-briar pipe as he answered me.

"Well, yes, I could tell you something about it, but the question is how much you'd believe, and whether you could restrain yourself from reporting it to the Society for Psychical Research. I never told the story but once, and then it was to the Division Superintendent, and when I finished the old gentleman asked if I were a drinking man, and remarking that a fertile imagination was not a desirable quality in a railroad employee, said it would be just as well if the story went no further. You see it's a grewsome tale, and some way we don't like to be reminded that there are more things in heaven and earth than our systems of philosophy can grapple with. However, I should rather like to tell the story to a man who would look at it objectively and leave it in the domain of pure incident where it belongs. It would unburden my mind, and I'd like to get a scientific man's opinion on the yarn. But I suppose I'd better begin at the beginning, with the dance which preceded the tragedy, just as such things follow each other in a play. I notice that Destiny, who is a good deal of an artist in her way, frequently falls back upon that elementary principle of contrast to make things interesting for us.

"It was the thirty-first of December, the morning of the incoming Governor's inaugural ball, and I got down to the office early, for I had a heavy day's work ahead of me, and I was going to the dance and wanted to close up by six o'clock. I had scarcely unlocked the door when I heard someone calling Cheyenne on the wire, and hurried over to the instrument to see what was wanted. It was Lawrence O'Toole, at Grover, and he said he was coming up for the ball on the extra, due in Cheyenne at nine o'clock that night. He wanted me to go up to see Miss Masterson and ask her if she could go with him. He had had some trouble in getting leave of absence, as the last regular train for Cheyenne then left Grover at 5:45 in the afternoon, and as there was an east-bound going through Grover at 7:30. The dispatcher didn't want him away, in case there should be orders for the 7:30 train. So, Larry had made no arrangement with Miss Masterson, as he was uncertain about getting up until he was notified about the extra.

"I telephoned Miss Masterson and delivered Larry's message. She replied that she had made an arrangement to go to the dance with Mr. Freymark, but added laughingly that no other arrangement held when Larry could come.

"About noon Freymark dropped in at the office, and I suspected he'd got his time from Miss Masterson. While he was hanging around, Larry called me up to tell me that Helen's flowers would be up from Denver on the Union Pacific passenger at five, and he asked me to have them sent up to her promptly and to call for her that evening in case the extra should be late. Freymark, of course, listened to the message, and when the sounder stopped, he smiled in a slow, disagreeable way, and saying, 'Thank you. That's all I wanted to know,' left the office.

"Lawrence O'Toole had been my predecessor in the cashier's office at Cheyenne, and he needs a little explanation now that he is under ground, though when he was in the world of living men, he explained himself better than any man I have ever met, East or West. I've knocked about a good deal since I cut loose from Princeton, and I've found that there are a great many good fellows in the world, but I've not found many better than Larry. I think I can say, without stretching a point, that he was the most popular man on the Division. He had a faculty of making everyone like him that amounted to a sort of genius. When he first went to working on the road, he was the agent's assistant down at Sterling, a mere kid fresh from Ireland, without a dollar in his pocket, and no sort of backing in the world but his quick wit and handsome face. It was a face that served him as a sight draft, good in all banks.

"Freymark was cashier at the Cheyenne office then, but he had been up to some dirty work with the company, and when it fell in the line of Larry's duty to expose him, he did so without hesitating. Eventually Freymark was discharged, and Larry was made cashier in his place. There was, after that, naturally, little love lost between them, and to make matters worse, Helen Masterson took a fancy to Larry, and Freymark had begun to consider himself pretty solid in that direction. I doubt whether Miss Masterson ever really liked the blackguard, but he was a queer fish, and she was a queer girl and she found him interesting.

"Old John J. Masterson, her father, had been United States Senator from Wyoming, and Helen had been educated at Wellesley and had lived in Washington a good deal. She found Cheyenne dull and had got into the Washington way of tolerating anything but stupidity, and Freymark certainly was not stupid. He passed as an Alsatian Jew, but he had lived a good deal in Paris and had been pretty much all over the world, and spoke the more general European languages fluently. He was a wiry, sallow, unwholesome looking man, slight and meagrely built, and he looked as though he had been dried through and through by the blistering heat of the tropics.

"His movements were as lithe and agile as those of a cat, and invested with a certain unusual, stealthy grace. His eyes were small and black as bright jet beads; his hair very thick and coarse and straight, black with a sort of purple lustre to it, and he always wore it correctly parted in the middle and brushed smoothly about his ears. He had a pair of the most impudent red lips that closed over white, regular teeth. His hands, of which he took the greatest care, were the yellow, wrinkled hands of an old man, and shrivelled at the finger tips, though I don't think he could have been much over thirty. The long and short of it is that the fellow was uncanny. You somehow felt that there was that in his present, or in his past, or in his destiny which isolated him from other men. He dressed in excellent taste, was always accommodating, with the most polished manners and an address extravagantly deferential. He went into cattle after he lost his job with the company, and had an interest in a ranch ten miles out, though he spent most of his time in Cheyenne at the Capitol card rooms. He had an insatiable passion for gambling, and he was one of the few men who make it pay.

"About a week before the dance, Larry's cousin, Harry Burns, who was a reporter on the *London Times*, stopped in Cheyenne on his way to 'Frisco, and Larry came up to meet him. We took Burns up to the club, and I noticed that he acted rather queerly when Freymark came in. Burns went down to Grover to spend a day with Larry, and on Saturday Larry wired me to come down and spend Sunday with him, as he had important news for me.

"I went, and the gist of his information was that Freymark, then going by another name, had figured in a particularly ugly London scandal that happened to be in Burns' beat, and his record had been exposed. He was, indeed, from Paris, but there was not a drop of Jewish blood in his veins, and he dated from farther back than Israel. His father was a French soldier who, during his service in the East, had bought a Chinese slave girl, had become attached to her, and married her, and after her death had brought her child back to Europe with him. He had entered the civil service and held several subordinate offices in the capital, where his son was educated.

"The boy, socially ambitious and extremely sensitive about his Asiatic blood, after having been blackballed at a club, had left and lived by an exceedingly questionable traffic in London, assuming a Jewish patronymic to account for his oriental complexion and traits of feature. That explained everything. That explained why Freymark's hands were those of a centenarian. In his veins crept the sluggish amphibious blood of a race that was already old when Jacob tended the flocks of Laban upon the hills of Padan-Aram, a race that was in its mort cloth before Europe's swaddling clothes were made.

"Of course, the question at once came up as to what ought to be done with Burns's information. Cheyenne clubs are not exclusive, but a Chinaman who had been engaged in Freymark's peculiarly unsavoury traffic would be disbarred in almost any region outside of Whitechapel. One thing was sure; Miss Masterson must be informed of the matter at once.

"'On second thought,' said Larry, 'I guess I'd better tell her myself. It will have to be done easy like, not to hurt her self-respect too much. Like as not I'll go off my head the first time, I see him and call him rat-eater to his face.'

"Well, to get back to the day of the dance, I was wondering whether Larry would stay over to tell Miss Masterson about it the next day, for of course he couldn't spring such a thing on a girl at a party.

"That evening I dressed early and went down to the station at nine to meet Larry. The extra came in, but no Larry. I saw Connelly, the conductor, and asked him if he had seen anything of O'Toole, but he said he hadn't, that the station at Grover was open when he came through, but that he found no train orders and couldn't raise anyone, so supposed O'Toole had come up on 153. I went back to the office and called Grover, but got no answer. Then I sat down at the instrument and called for fifteen minutes straight. I wanted to go then and hunt up the conductor on 153, the passenger that went through Grover at 5.30 in the afternoon, and ask him what he knew about Larry, but it was then 9.45 and I knew Miss Masterson would be waiting, so I jumped into the carriage and told the driver to make up time.

"On my way to the Mastersons', I did some tall thinking. I could find no explanation for O'Toole's non-appearance, but the business of the moment was to invent one for Miss Masterson that would neither alarm nor offend her. I couldn't exactly tell her he wasn't coming, for he might show up yet, so I decided to say the extra was late, and I didn't know when it would be in.

"Miss Masterson had been an exceptionally beautiful girl to begin with, and life had done a great deal for her. Fond as I was of Larry, I used to wonder whether a girl who had led such a full and independent existence would ever find the courage to face life with a railroad man who was so near the bottom of a ladder that is so long and steep.

"She came down the stairs in one of her Paris gowns that are as meat and drink to Cheyenne society reporters, with her arms full of American Beauty roses and her eyes and cheeks glowing. I noticed the roses then, though I didn't know that they were the boy's last message to the woman he loved. She paused half way down the stairs and looked at me, and then over my head into the drawing room, and then her eyes questioned mine. I bungled at my explanation and she thanked me for coming, but she couldn't hide her disappointment, and scarcely glanced at herself in the mirror as I put her wrap about her shoulders.

"It was not a cheerful ride down to the Capitol. Miss Masterson did her duty by me bravely, but I found it difficult to be even decently attentive to what she was saying. Once arrived at Representative Hall, where the dance was held, the strain was relieved, for the fellows all pounced down on her for dances, and there were friends of hers there from Helena and Laramie, and my responsibility was practically at an end. Don't expect me to tell you what a Wyoming inaugural ball is like. I'm not good at that sort of thing, and this dance is merely incidental to my story.

"Dance followed dance, and still no Larry. The dances I had with Miss Masterson were torture. She began to question and cross-question me, and when I got tangled up in my lies, she became indignant. Freymark was late in arriving. It must have been after midnight when he appeared, correct and smiling, having driven in from his ranch. He was effusively gay and insisted upon shaking hands with me, though I never willingly touched those clammy hands of his. He was constantly dangling about Miss Masterson, who made rather a point of being gracious to him. I couldn't much blame her under the circumstances, but it irritated me, and I'm not ashamed to say that I rather spied on them, when they were on the balcony, I heard him say:

"'You see I've forgiven this morning entirely.'

"She answered him rather coolly:

"'Ah, but you are constitutionally forgiving. However, I'll be fair and forgive too. It's more comfortable.'

"Then he said in a slow insinuating tone, and I could fairly see him thrust out those impudent red lips of his as he said it: "If I can teach you to forgive, I wonder whether I could not also teach you to forget? I almost think I could. At any rate I shall make you remember this night. *Rappelles-toi lorsque les destinees*

M'auront de toi pour jamais separe.'

"As they came in, I saw him slip one of Larry's red roses into his pocket.

"It was not until near the end of the dance that the clock of destiny sounded the first stroke of the tragedy. I remember how gay the scene was, so gay that I had almost forgotten my anxiety in the music, flowers and laughter. The orchestra was playing a waltz, drawing the strains out long and sweet like the notes of a flute, and Freymark was dancing with Helen. I was not dancing myself then, and suddenly I noticed some confusion among the waiters who stood watching by one of the doors, and Larry's black dog, Duke, all foam at the mouth, shot in the side and bleeding, dashed in through the door, and eluding the caterer's men, ran half the length of the hall and threw himself at Freymark's feet, uttering a howl piteous enough to herald any sort of calamity.

"Freymark, who had not seen him before, turned with an exclamation of rage and a face absolutely livid and kicked the wounded brute half-way across the slippery floor. There was something fiendishly brutal and horrible in the episode, it was the breaking out of the barbarian blood through his mask of European civilization, a jet of black mud that spurted up from some nameless pest hole of filthy heathen cities. The music stopped, people began moving about in a confused mass, and I saw Helen's eyes seeking mine appealingly. I hurried to her, and by the time I reached her Freymark had disappeared.

"'Get the carriage and take care of Duke,' she said, and her voice trembled like that of one shivering with cold.

"When we were in the carriage, she spread one of the robes on her knee, and I lifted the dog up to her, and she took him in her arms, comforting him.

"'Where is Larry, and what does all this mean?' she asked. 'You can't put me off any longer, for I danced with a man who came up on the extra.'

"Then I made a clean breast of it, and told her what I knew, which was little enough.

"'Do you think he is ill?' she asked.

"I replied, 'I don't know what to think. I'm all at sea.'—For since the appearance of the dog, I was genuinely alarmed.

"She was silent for a long time, but when the rays of the electric street lights flashed at intervals into the carriage, I could see that she was leaning back with her eyes closed and the dog's nose against her throat. At last, she said with a note of entreaty in her voice, 'Can't you think of anything?' I saw that she was thoroughly frightened and told her that it would probably all end in a joke, and that I would telephone her as soon as I heard from Larry, and would more than likely have something amusing to tell her.

"It was snowing hard when we reached the Senator's, and when we got out of the carriage, she gave Duke tenderly over to me and I remember how she dragged on my arm and how played out and exhausted she seemed.

"'You really must not worry at all,' I said. 'You know how uncertain railroad men are. It's sure to be better at the next inaugural ball; we'll all be dancing together then.'

"'The next inaugural ball,' she said as we went up the steps, putting out her hand to catch the snowflakes.—'That seems a long way off.'

"I got down to the office late next morning, and before I had time to try Grover, the dispatcher at Holyoke called me up to ask whether Larry were still in Cheyenne. He couldn't raise Grover, he said, and he wanted to give Larry train orders for 151, the east bound passenger. When he heard what I had to say, he told me I had better go down to Grover on 151 myself, as the storm threatened to tie up all the trains and we might look for trouble.

"I had the veterinary surgeon fix up Duke's side, and I put him in the express car, and boarded 151 with a mighty cold, uncomfortable sensation in the region of my diaphragm.

"It had snowed all night long, and the storm had developed into a blizzard, and the passenger had difficulty in making any headway at all.

"When we got into Grover, I thought it was the most desolate spot I had ever looked on, and as the train pulled out, leaving me there, I felt like sending a message of farewell to the world. You know what Grover is, a red box of a station, section house barricaded by coal sheds and a little group of dwellings at the end of everything, with the desert running out on every side to the sky line. The houses and station were covered with a coating of snow that clung to them like wet plaster, and the siding was one deep snow drift, banked against the station door. The plain was a wide, white ocean of swirling, drifting snow, that beat and broke like the thrash of the waves in the merciless wind that swept, with nothing to break it, from the Rockies to the Missouri.

"When I opened the station door, the snow fell in upon the floor, and Duke sat down by the empty, fireless stove and began to howl and whine in a heart-breaking fashion. Larry's sleeping room upstairs was empty. Downstairs, everything was in order, and all the station work had been done up. Apparently, the last thing Larry had done was to bill out a car of wool from the Oasis sheep ranch for Dewey, Gould & Co., Boston. The car had gone out on 153, the east bound that left Grover at seven o'clock the night before, so he must have been there at that time. I copied the bill in the copy book, and went over to the section house to make inquiries.

"The section boss was getting ready to go out to look after his track. He said he had seen O'Toole at 5.30, when the west bound passenger went through, and, not having seen him since, supposed he was still in Cheyenne. I went over to Larry's boarding house, and the woman said he must be in Cheyenne, as he had eaten his supper at five o'clock the night before, so that he would have time to get his station work done and dress. The little girl, she said, had gone over at five to tell him that supper was ready. I questioned the child carefully. She said there was another man, a stranger, in the station with Larry when she went in and that though she didn't hear anything they said, and Larry was sitting with his chair tilted back and his feet on the stove, she somehow had thought they were quarrelling.

"The stranger, she said, was standing; he had a fur coat on and his eyes snapped like he was mad, and she was afraid of him. I asked her if she could recall anything else about him, and she said, 'Yes, he had very red lips.' When I heard that, my heart grew cold as a snow lump, and when I went out the wind seemed to go clear through me. It was evident enough that Freymark had gone down there to make trouble, had quarrelled with Larry and had boarded either the 5.30 passenger or the extra, and got the conductor to let him off at his ranch, and accounted for his late appearance at the dance.

"It was five o'clock then, but the 5.30 train was two hours late, so there was nothing to do but sit down and wait for the conductor, who had gone out on the seven o'clock east bound the night before, and who must have seen Larry when he picked up the car of wool. It was growing dark by that time. The sky was a dull lead colour, and the snow had drifted about the little town until it was almost buried, and was still coming down so fast that you could scarcely see your hand before you.

"I was never so glad to hear anything as that whistle, when old 153 came lumbering and groaning in through the snow. I ran out on the platform to meet her, and her headlight looked like the face of an old friend. I caught the conductor's arm the minute he stepped off the train, but he wouldn't talk until he got in by the fire. He said he hadn't seen O'Toole at all the night before, but he had found the bill for the wool car on the table, with a note from Larry asking him to take the car out on the Q.T., and he had concluded that Larry had gone up to Cheyenne on the 5.30. I wired the Cheyenne office and managed to catch the express clerk who had gone through on the extra the night before. He wired me saying that he had not seen Larry board the extra, but that his dog had crept into his usual place in the express car, and he had supposed Larry was in the coach. He had seen Freymark get on at Grover, and the train had slowed up a trifle at his ranch to let him off, for Freymark stood in with some of the boys and sent his cattle shipments our way.

"When the night fairly closed down on me, I began to wonder how a gay, expansive fellow like O'Toole had ever stood six months at Grover. The snow had let up by that time, and the stars were beginning to glitter cold and bright through the hurrying clouds. I put on my ulster and went outside. I began a minute tour of inspection, I went through empty freight cars run down by the siding, searched the coal houses and primitive cellar, examining them carefully, and calling O'Toole's name. Duke at my heels dragged himself painfully about, but seemed as much at sea as I, and betrayed the nervous suspense and alertness of a bird dog that has lost his game.

"I went back to the office and took the big station lamp upstairs to make a more careful examination of Larry's sleeping room. The suit of clothes that he usually wore at his work was hanging on the wall. His shaving things were lying about, and I recognized the silver-backed military hair brushes that Miss Masterson had given him at Christmas time, lying on his chiffonier. The upper drawer was open and a pair of white kid gloves was lying on the corner. A white string tie hung across his pipe rack, it was crumpled and had evidently proved unsatisfactory when he tied it. On the chiffonier lay several clean handkerchiefs with holes in them, where he had unfolded them and thrown them by in a hasty search for a whole one. A black silk muffler hung on the chair back, and a top hat was set awry on the head of a plaster cast of Parnell, Larry's hero.

"His dress suit was missing, so there was no doubt that he had dressed for the party. His overcoat lay on his trunk and his dancing shoes were on the floor, at the foot of the bed beside his everyday ones. I knew that his pumps were a little tight, he had joked about them when I was down the Sunday before the dance, but he had only one pair, and he couldn't have got another in Grover if he had tried himself. That set me to thinking. He was a dainty fellow about his shoes and I knew his collection pretty well. I went to his closet and found them all there. Even granting him a prejudice against overcoats, I couldn't conceive of his going out in that stinging weather without shoes. I noticed that a surgeon's case, such as are carried on passenger trains, and which Larry had once appropriated in Cheyenne, was open, and that the roll of medicated cotton had been pulled out and recently used. Each discovery I made served only to add to my perplexity. Granted that Freymark had been there, and granted that he had played the boy an ugly trick, he could not have spirited him away without the knowledge of the train crew.

"'Duke, old doggy,' I said to the poor spaniel who was sniffing and whining about the bed, 'you haven't done your duty. You must have seen what went on between your master and that clam-blooded Asiatic, and you ought to be able to give me a tip of some sort.'

"I decided to go to bed and make a fresh start on the ugly business in the morning. The bed looked as though someone had been lying on it, so I started to beat it up a little before I got in. I took off the pillow and as I pulled up the mattress, on the edge of the ticking at the head of the bed, I saw a dark red stain about the size of my hand. I felt the cold sweat come out on me, and my hands were dangerously unsteady, as I carried the lamp over and set it down on the chair by the bed. But Duke was too quick for me, he had seen that stain and leaping on the bed began sniffling it, and whining like a dog that is being whipped to death.

"I bent down and felt it with my fingers. It was dry but the colour and stiffness were unmistakably those of coagulated blood. I caught up my coat and vest and ran down stairs with Duke yelping at my heels. My first impulse was to go and call someone, but from the platform not a single light was visible, and I knew the section men had been in bed for hours. I remembered then, that Larry was often annoyed by haemorrhages at the nose in that high altitude, but even that did not altogether quiet my nerves, and I realized that sleeping in that bed was quite out of the question.

253

"Larry always kept a supply of brandy and soda on hand, so I made myself a stiff drink and filled the stove and locked the door, turned down the lamp and lay down on the operator's table. I had often slept there when I was night operator. At first it was impossible to sleep, for Duke kept starting up and limping to the door and scratching at it, yelping nervously. He kept this up until I was thoroughly unstrung, and though I'm ordinarily cool enough, there wasn't money enough in Wyoming to have bribed me to open that door. I felt cold all over every time I went near it, and I even drew the big rusty bolt that was never used, and it seemed to me that it groaned heavily as I drew it, or perhaps it was the wind outside that groaned. As for Duke, I threatened to put him out, and boxed his ears until I hurt his feelings, and he lay down in front of the door with his muzzle between his paws and his eyes shining like live coals and riveted on the crack under the door. The situation was grewsome enough, but the liquor had made me drowsy and at last I fell asleep.

"It must have been about three o'clock in the morning that I was awakened by the crying of the dog, a whimper low, continuous and pitiful, and indescribably human. While I was blinking my eyes in an effort to get thoroughly awake, I heard another sound, the grating sound of chalk on a wooden black board, or of a soft pencil on a slate. I turned my head to the right, and saw a man standing with his back to me, chalking something on the bulletin board. "At a glance I recognised the broad, high shoulders and the handsome head of my friend. Yet there was that about the figure which kept me from calling his name or from moving a muscle where I lay. He finished his writing and dropped the chalk, and I distinctly heard its click as it fell. He made a gesture as though he were dusting his fingers, and then turned facing me, holding his left hand in front of his mouth. I saw him clearly in the soft light of the station lamp. He wore his dress clothes, and began moving toward the door silently as a shadow in his black stocking feet.

"There was about his movements an indescribable stiffness, as though his limbs had been frozen. His face was chalky white, his hair seemed damp and was plastered down close about his temples. His eyes were colourless jellies, dull as lead, and staring straight before him. When he reached the door, he lowered the hand he held before his mouth to lift the latch. His face was turned squarely toward me, and the lower jaw had fallen and was set rigidly upon his collar, the mouth was wide open and was *stuffed full of white cotton*! Then I knew it was a dead man's face I looked upon.

"The door opened, and that stiff black figure in stockings walked as noiselessly as a cat out into the night. I think I went quite mad then. I dimly remember that I rushed out upon the siding and ran up and down screaming, 'Larry, Larry!' until the wind seemed to echo my call. The stars were out in myriads, and the snow glistened in their light, but I could see nothing but the wide, white plain, not even a dark shadow anywhere. When at last I found myself back in the station, I saw Duke lying before the door and dropped on my knees beside him, calling him by name. But Duke was past calling back. Master and dog had gone together, and I dragged him into the corner and covered his face, for his eyes were colorless and soft, like the eyes of that horrible face, once so beloved.

"The black board? O, I didn't forget that. I had chalked the time of the accommodation on it the night before, from sheer force of habit, for it isn't customary to mark the time of trains in unimportant stations like Grover. My writing had been rubbed out by a moist hand, for I could see the finger marks clearly, and in place of it was written in blue chalk simply, C. B. & Q. 26387.

"I sat there drinking brandy and muttering to myself before that black board until those blue letters danced up and down, like magic lantern pictures when you jiggle the slides. I drank until the sweat poured off me like rain and my teeth chattered, and I turned sick at the stomach. At last, an idea flashed upon me. I snatched the way bill off the hook. The car of wool that had left Grover for Boston the night before was numbered 26387.

"I must have got through the rest of the night somehow, for when the sun came up red and angry over the white plains, the section boss found me sitting by the stove, the lamp burning full blaze, the brandy bottle empty beside me, and with but one idea in my head, that box car 26387 must be stopped and opened as soon as possible, and that somehow it would explain.

"I figured that we could easily catch it in Omaha, and wired the freight agent there to go through it carefully and report anything unusual. That night I got a wire from the agent stating that the body of a man had been found under a woolsack at one end of the car with a fan and an invitation to the inaugural ball at Cheyenne in the pocket of his dress coat. I wired him not to disturb the body until I arrived, and started for Omaha. Before I left Grover the Cheyenne office wired me that Freymark had left the town, going west over the Union

Pacific. The company detectives never found him.

"The matter was clear enough then. Being a railroad man, he had hidden the body and sealed up the car and billed it out, leaving a note for the conductor. Since he was of a race without conscience or sensibilities, and since his past was more infamous than his birth, he had boarded the extra and had gone to the ball and danced with Miss Masterson with blood undried upon his hands.

"When I saw Larry O'Toole again, he was lying stiff and stark in the undertakers' rooms in Omaha. He was clad in his dress clothes, with black stockings on his feet, as I had seen him forty-eight hours before. Helen Masterson's fan was in his pocket. His mouth was wide open and stuffed full of white cotton.

"He had been shot in the mouth, the bullet lodging between the third and fourth vertebrae. The haemorrhage had been very slight and had been checked by the cotton. The quarrel had taken place about five in the afternoon. After supper Larry had dressed, all but his shoes, and had lain down to snatch a wink of sleep, trusting to the whistle of the extra to waken him. Freymark had gone back and shot him while he was asleep, afterward placing his body in the wool car, which, but for my telegram, would not have been opened for weeks.

"That's the whole story. There is nothing more to tell except one detail that I did not mention to the superintendent. When I said good-bye to the boy before the undertaker and coroner took charge of the body, I lifted his right hand to take off a ring that Miss Masterson had given him and the ends of the fingers were covered with blue chalk."

LEONAUR

ALSO FROM LEONAUR

AVAILABLE IN SOFTCOVER OR HARDCOVER WITH DUST JACKET

MR MUKERJI'S GHOSTS *by S. Mukerji*—Supernatural tales from the British Raj period by India's Ghost story collector.

KIPLINGS GHOSTS *by Rudyard Kipling*—Twelve stories of Ghosts, Hauntings, Curses, Werewolves & Magic.

THE COLLECTED SUPERNATURAL AND WEIRD FICTION OF WASHINGTON IRVING: VOLUME 1 *by Washington Irving*—Including one novel 'A History of New York', and nine short stories of the Strange and Unusual.

THE COLLECTED SUPERNATURAL AND WEIRD FICTION OF WASHINGTON IRVING: VOLUME 2 *by Washington Irving*—Including three novelettes 'The Legend of the Sleepy Hollow', 'Dolph Heyliger', 'The Adventure of the Black Fisherman' and thirty-two short stories of the Strange and Unusual.

THE COLLECTED SUPERNATURAL AND WEIRD FICTION OF JOHN KENDRICK BANGS: VOLUME 1 *by John Kendrick Bangs*—Including one novel 'Toppleton's Client or A Spirit in Exile', and ten short stories of the Strange and Unusual.

THE COLLECTED SUPERNATURAL AND WEIRD FICTION OF JOHN KENDRICK BANGS: VOLUME 2 *by John Kendrick Bangs*—Including four novellas 'A House-Boat on the Styx', 'The Pursuit of the House-Boat', 'The Enchanted Typewriter' and 'Mr. Munchausen' of the Strange and Unusual.

THE COLLECTED SUPERNATURAL AND WEIRD FICTION OF JOHN KENDRICK BANGS: VOLUME 3 *by John Kendrick Bangs*—Including twor novellas 'Olympian Nights', 'Roger Camerden: A Strange Story', and ten short stories of the Strange and Unusual.

THE COLLECTED SUPERNATURAL AND WEIRD FICTION OF MARY SHELLEY: VOLUME 1 *by Mary Shelley*—Including one novel 'Frankenstein or the Modern Prometheus', and fourteen short stories of the Strange and Unusual.

THE COLLECTED SUPERNATURAL AND WEIRD FICTION OF MARY SHELLEY: VOLUME 2 *by Mary Shelley*—Including one novel 'The Last Man', and three short stories of the Strange and Unusual.

THE COLLECTED SUPERNATURAL AND WEIRD FICTION OF AMELIA B. EDWARDS *by Amelia B. Edwards*—Contains two novelettes 'Monsieur Maurice', and 'The Discovery of the Treasure Isles', one ballad 'A Legend of Boisguilbert' and seventeen short stories to cill the blood.

LEONAUR

ALSO FROM LEONAUR

AVAILABLE IN SOFTCOVER OR HARDCOVER WITH DUST JACKET

THE COMPLETE FOUR JUST MEN: VOLUME 2 *by Edgar Wallace*—*The Law of the Four Just Men & The Three Just Men*—disillusioned with a world where the wicked and the abusers of power perpetually go unpunished, the Just Men set about to rectify matters according to their own standards, and retribution is dispensed on swift and deadly wings.

THE COMPLETE RAFFLES: 1 *by E. W. Hornung*—*The Amateur Cracksman & The Black Mask*—By turns urbane gentleman about town and accomplished cricketer, life is just too ordinary for Raffles and that sets him on a series of adventures that have long been treasured as a real antidote to the 'white knights' who are the usual heroes of the crime fiction of this period.

THE COMPLETE RAFFLES: 2 *by E. W. Hornung*—*A Thief in the Night & Mr Justice Raffles*—By turns urbane gentleman about town and accomplished cricketer, life is just too ordinary for Raffles and that sets him on a series of adventures that have long been treasured as a real antidote to the 'white knights' who are the usual heroes of the crime fiction of this period.

THE COLLECTED SUPERNATURAL AND WEIRD FICTION OF WILKIE COLLINS: VOLUME 1 *by Wilkie Collins*—Contains one novel 'The Haunted Hotel', one novella 'Mad Monkton', three novelettes 'Mr Percy and the Prophet', 'The Biter Bit' and 'The Dead Alive' and eight short stories to chill the blood.

THE COLLECTED SUPERNATURAL AND WEIRD FICTION OF WILKIE COLLINS: VOLUME 2 *by Wilkie Collins*—Contains one novel 'The Two Destinies', three novellas 'The Frozen deep', 'Sister Rose' and 'The Yellow Mask' and two short stories to chill the blood.

THE COLLECTED SUPERNATURAL AND WEIRD FICTION OF WILKIE COLLINS: VOLUME 3 *by Wilkie Collins*—Contains one novel 'Dead Secret,' two novelettes 'Mrs Zant and the Ghost' and 'The Nun's Story of Gabriel's Marriage' and five short stories to chill the blood.

FUNNY BONES *selected by Dorothy Scarborough*—An Anthology of Humorous Ghost Stories.

MONTEZUMA'S CASTLE AND OTHER WEIRD TALES *by Charles B. Cory*—Cory has written a superb collection of eighteen ghostly and weird stories to chill and thrill the avid enthusiast of supernatural fiction.

SUPERNATURAL BUCHAN *by John Buchan*—Stories of Ancient Spirits, Uncanny Places & Strange Creatures.